Invisible Branches

Diana McDaniel Hampo

AmErica House
Baltimore

© 2001 by Diana McDaniel Hampo.

All rights reserved. No part of this book may be reproduced in any form without written permission from the publishers, except by a reviewer who may quote brief passages in a review to be printed in a newspaper or magazine.

First printing

ISBN: 1-58851-394-7
PUBLISHED BY AMERICA HOUSE BOOK PUBLISHERS
www.publishamerica.com
Baltimore

Printed in the United States of America

Dedication:

I wrote this book all alone while my family stood
outside the door, yelling "Please, hurry up."
So, Invisible Branches is dedicated to Mary, Lexie and Jack.
It never occurred to you to stop believing
because you were born with shining and faithful hearts.
And then there's Alex, who is proof that good men do exist, and can
change the world with their steadfast love.

Acknowledgments

Thank you to:

Granger..it's good to know we're in this universe together.

Lisa Hopper, for her hours of hard work, artistic wizardry and proof reading.

Keith and Donna Bush, who showed me it's never too late to learn to jump.

My friends in Hot Springs, especially the Aldridges, the Crawfords-Capels and the Hot Springs Jazz Society.

John Keeble and Peter Baily, who liked my stories and

Artie, who taught me that bookies don't cry.

Chapter 1

Friday

Something is being dragged through the bedroom. Bare feet shuffle on the hardwood floor. I do not open my eyes. I don't really want to know what it is.

The air in the room is not moving. There is a soft grunt. Someone is hoisting and heaving, trying to lift something heavy.

I wonder if God is watching. Does He know what's going on in my bedroom? I hope so. He's supposed to take care of me right now, even though we're not getting along, because I am so pregnant. Last night, I couldn't pull off my panty hose. Defending myself against a dragging, grunting intruder might be tough. Maybe God has delegated and there's a saint who's supposed to watch over me.

But the air in the room feels reasonably safe; there's no immediate threat. I know this. I relax, despite the odd noises.

The sun coming through the window is warm on my right cheek and ear. The strange sounds continue but there are others mixed in, the soft humming of the fish tank and the television in the living room.

If I open my eyes the day will officially begin, so I play possum.

Finally, because I hear the unmistakable sound of someone breathing heavily, in frustration, I peek.

My son, Michael Justice, is hanging in the door frame. There is a three legged milking stool eight or nine inches below his dangling feet. That must be what he was snatching from my bedroom.

My contact lenses are dry so, I have to blink quickly and squint a little in order to focus.

Mike's skinny arms quiver. He squeezes his eyes closed, wrinkles his nose and bares his teeth as he tries to pull himself up. It's no use. He still can't do a chin-up. He's only ten. Maybe he'll get it in a couple of months. There are boys in his class who can do ten, even fifteen, chin-ups. Everyday, I remind him they are all short kids with rat bodies. He's very tall for his age, rangy with broad shoulders and bony arms. He'll fill out in a few years. Calling his friends 'rat bodied boys' usually makes him feel much better.

"Hi there," I whisper. Michael continues dangling from the silver bar.

Because I'm sleeping on my left side with a pillow between my knees, I don't have to move to see Mike. I've been sleeping like this for months. According to my OBGYN this position allows maximum blood flow to my placenta. I used to sleep on my back, but that doesn't work well for the very pregnant. When I'm on my back, seven pounds of baby and uterus squish your spine and intestines.

The smell of a sleeping man, warm brown skin, matted hair and heavy breathing, pulls me deeper into the mattress. Zoltan feels that I am awake. He wraps me all up like we are spoons, in a silverware drawer.

Closing my eyes again, I try to transmit a thought into his head. 'Do not ask me to get married. Don't bring the topic of marriage up today. Please, please, please.'

Zoltan's chest is pressed against my back. His heart pumps heat into my skin. The front of his thighs are warm and furry and his knee caps are nestled gently into the back of mine. One of his arms is draped over my body, pinning me to the bed. Under the covers, his big hand rests on my huge belly. It's a perfect fit. When I move just a little, shifting my weight so I can breath, he takes my hand and nestles it, along with his own, between my huge, engorged breasts.

I'm parallel parked in heaven.

But it's getting late. I have to get out of bed. Gently, I free my hand. Mike drops to the stool. "I already did ten pushups this morning."

"That's probably why you can't do a chin up. Your arms are tired," I whisper. He shrugs. "Yeah, right. Admit it Mom, I suck at chin-ups." It's 6:15 a.m.. Mike is too perky.

I whisper, "Don't use that word around women."

The word 'suck' is everywhere now, even in cartoons and on the radio. It can't mean what it used to mean. When I was a kid 'suck' was literal. If we said "Ginger sucks," we were actually saying she sucked on a particular part of a man's anatomy. All these people using the word today cannot be talking about oral sex.

Closing my eyes, I might fall asleep again. Zoltan's deep tissue heat leaks into me, like a baked potato. His warmth is internal and ancient. He tells me his blood is so rich and hot because he is a Magyar. This is typical hyperbole for a Hungarian. They place themselves several rungs above the rest of Europe.

I will admit his cuts, scratches and burns have always heeled at an accelerated rate, as though his body makes new cells and fresh blood a little faster than mine. And his temperature does hang around 99°, but the entire nation of Hungary can't be running a fever.

I want to wake Z up and ask him what he thinks about the word suck, but he lacks conversational skills in the morning. As though sensing my need, he groans softly, then we both listen to Mike, who is in the bathroom peeing. It's a big splashy sound. Our bathroom door is only a couple of feet from the bed. I bury my head in a pillow, then turn to look at Z's face.

"That boy has got to learn how to close a bathroom door," he says in a raspy voice.

Slowly, I start to sit up, but I stop. My necklace, a tiny gold elephant on a delicate chain, is snagged on the pillow case. Mom gave me this elephant and chain two days before she committed suicide, seven years ago. Gently, I appraise the situation with my right hand. His trunk is caught on three or four threads. I'm pinned, like a wrestler. Tied in place by my mother and her delicate strand of gold.

"Z, I'm stuck, my necklace is caught and I don't want to break the chain." I haven't taken my elephant off since the funeral.

Zolton pushes himself up on one elbow, leans over me and frees the elephant. Cautiously, I lift my head, then sit up as Z crashes back into the mattress and quilts.

Mike walks past our bed grinning. His long brown hair needs to be brushed and his sweat pants are wrong side out, but his big, toothy smile makes the sun rise. "Hi again," he says.

"Hi Sweetie." I say.

"Hi, Zoltan." Mike calls as he walks out of our bedroom and heads to the kitchen for food.

"Hey, boy " Zoltan mumbles, but Mike is long gone.

I stare stupidly, at one spot on the wall, next to the light switch. There is something yellow. My heart skips a single beat, then catches up, giving me an odd and almost prickly rush.

But they are still there, three post-it notes on the wall, on my wall. Yellow post-it notes Jesus Christ, I touch Zolton's arm. "What day is it? Did you put that there?"

He's gone back to asleep. "Put what, where?"

"There are post-it notes on the wall. What day is it Z?"

"October something," he mumbles.

"My God Z. Look, there's three of them. Somebody is dead, if they are doing this as a joke," I nudge him, he's the only one in the house who knows about the post-it notes my mother left for me. "You didn't stick those bastards on the wall, did you?"

Z sits up a little. Runs his hand through the dark hairs on his chest and looks at the wall. "It's ok." He slides off the bed and grabs all three post it notes then crawls back into bed."

"Is there anything written on them?" I ask. "You've got to read them for me."

He takes a breath and examines both sides of each piece of paper. "They're blank Liz, it's just paper, they don't mean anything. It's all ok."

But it's not ok, I already know that.

I want to be asleep again, dreaming about being skinny and having sweaty sex.

But in my world, before Z and our life, just a few years ago, my mother, B.Wallace, left me a trail of fourteen yellow post-it notes leading from her condominium parking spot, through her kitchen, past the dining room and living room. The yellow notes led me through her apartment and out to the well tended porch, where her dead, sixty five year old body lay in a expensive chaise lounge. The last post-it note in Mom's cryptic trail was stuck to the handle of the pistol she'd put in her mouth. It said, as they all did, that she loved me and then went on to explain that the gun was borrowed and I should return it to a bank guard she'd somehow befriended.

We don't keep post it notes in the house.

But here they are.

Somebody is fucking with me.

"I'll never ignore another square, yellow note again. I swear to you Mom. I'll give you all my attention next time you leave me a note," I whisper.

"You're mother didn't put post-it-notes on our wall, Liz. I promise," Z says without opening his eyes.

I loved my mother and I miss her all the time, but I sure as hell don't want her here. I can't fix breakfast for the kids all worked up like this, as though my dead mother is in the closet. Either one of the kids could have stuck it on the wall. They don't know about my post-it note fear. I walk around the bed room, trying to regain my composure. I will myself to do something normal.

Two pairs of Zolton's work jeans are on the floor along with t-shirts, a chef's coat and a red Arkansas Razorback t-shirt. I kick the pile "Ok, Honey, is all this stuff dirty?" I take a deep breath and rub my hard stomach counter-clock-wise. The skin doesn't have any more hairs on it because I rub so much.

Z mumbles, "I can get them dirtier. The coat's ok, shirts are probably pretty rank."

I make a face at him then kick all the clothes in front of his dresser. "I don't think I can bend down and get back up this early in the morning. Bring them in the kitchen, ok?"

"Ok," he says to his pillow.

I'm still clutching the stupid post-it notes.

Mike is already sitting on our worn orange couch. In 1965 it was an expensive piece of modern furniture, now it's dated, tired and really ugly.

The smell hits me first. Mike is eating a blueberry muffin and two pieces of left over fried chicken. The grease is nauseating, my stomach rolls like a carnival ride. I breathe through my mouth and walk past, quickly.

"Is Felicity up yet?' I ask.

A piece of chicken falls on his toast colored skin. He picks it up and shakes his head no. Mike's long brown hair is out of style right now. The Fountain Lake 5th grade class is full of little boys with very short hair. But Mike is determined to keep his long. He lets the barber cut the front reasonably short, but the hair in back rolls down his spine like a beautiful shiny snake. He doesn't care that his buddies tease him and that he's sometimes mistaken for a girl.

He likes it long.

I haven't figured out if he's copying Zoltan or somebody he listens to on the radio. Most likely, Mike is trying to flex a little attitude, trying to take the high gloss shine off his nice guy image. Image is everything, even in 5th grade. But Mike is my sweet boy, I'd never say that to him, but he's so good, responsible and warm hearted and that's something of a liability. There are days I worry he's too much of an old man for his own good.

Lightly, as though I'm talking about shoelaces or corn on the cob I say, "Hey, Kiddo, did you stick this piece of paper on the my wall."

Mike doesn't even look up from his breakfast and that means he's innocent. "What paper?"

When he's guilty he over reacts.

"These post-it notes." I hold them up, as though he's looking.

He glances over his shoulder and shakes his head. "Not mine," he says and buries his face in the blueberry muffin. The paper feels kind of warm. I look at them again. There's nothing strange but my fingers tips are almost burning. I put the paper in the other hand, then fold it into a tiny tight square.

The baby kicks just as I hear a sound I don't quite recognize. It's just running water. The kitchen faucet is running. Both knobs are turned completely on. "Michael, why are both faucets on full blast? You're gonna burn up the pump and dry out the well."

"I didn't turn them on. I haven't gotten any water this morning" he says with his mouth full.

I think about what he's eating. No water would be involved. "Well somebody turned it on and you're the only one up."

He looks at me, concerned and innocent. "I swear, I didn't use any water. I haven't even brushed my teeth yet. Man, Mom, I promise, I haven't done anything but pee and eat this morning."

"That's good to know. So the faucets turned themselves on?" I shut them off.

"Guess so," he grins. After a second of silence he realizes he's being harsh with me.

Zolton has instructed him to be overly loving and supportive as long as I'm pregnant. "Why don't you come sit down for a minute Mom. I'll get you some juice or something."

"I don't have time to sit down right now, but thanks for the offer." I pour cold coffee into a purple cup from the Little Rock Zoo. There are pictures of elephants, armadillos, orangutans and anteaters walking across the ceramic surface. The inside is clean but coffee stained. I need to bleach everything. But not today. I stick the cup in the microwave for 50 seconds then stare stupidly at the red digital numbers.

"Want some chicken?" Mike asks, his face shiny with grease. He picks methodically at the skin, pulls it away from the meat, then begins to gnaw.

"Please don't come near me with that dead bird."

He shrugs. "How's our baby this morning?"

"Just fine." My heart does a warm cartwheel every time he says 'our baby.' And I am able to smile, despite the early morning nausea, stray post-it notes and running water. Mike asks this question every morning, then actually listens, intently, to my response.

Everybody asks how I'm feeling, 'How's the baby, When are you due?" It's obligatory, but they don't want to hear the truth. Nobody wants to hear about a pregnant woman's bloating ankles and bleeding gums.

Mike studies my face. "Do you feel bad? You look kind of pukey." He pulls another strip of meat from the bone with his front teeth.

I have to turn away and swallow hard. "I only feel pukey when I smell fried chicken before my coffee."

"You shouldn't drink so much coffee anyway. It's not good."

"I know, but the stress of not having any coffee would probably be just as bad for me and the baby." We go around this caffeine tree all the time.

Mike looks doubtful, but drops the subject in order to concentrate on his blueberry muffin. Suddenly, he jumps up and runs into the kitchen.

He comes back with half a kiwi fruit and a spoon. "Eat this," he says and puts the hairy, golf ball sized fruit in my palm. "It's got more vitamin c than an orange, did you know that?"

I shake my head and stare at the beautiful bright green meat and tiny black seeds. There is a pattern in the fruit, but I can not understand it.

"And it's got more potassium than a banana. That's good for leg cramps."

"No kidding?" I take a couple of bites. The cool slick kiwi meat brings my mouth to life. It's so good, much better than the coffee, which I'll drink when he's not looking. As I stare at my kiwi, the refrigerator door swings open. Why is my kitchen acting up this morning? I bump it closed with my hip.

I yank the microwave door open with 1 second left. No beeping. The sound makes me want to scream. My intolerance for beepers and buzzers has something to do with pregnancy. One beep would be perfect, two acceptable. Four is rude. Maybe pregnancy is making me a little edgy.

And of course, there's the date and the post its.

Today is October 6th. "The day." It is the day my world ended, found a new shape and was reborn. I shouldn't be surprised by anything that happens today. Maybe Mom left me the note so I wouldn't forget what today is.

On the sixth day of the tenth month, twenty years ago, when I was 14, my father died. He was 50. Michael Justice McDade. Everybody called him Justice. He was my god, brilliant, inspiring and kind. A month after Daddy died, my 20-year-old brother, Daniel, was killed in a water skiing accident. I've been screwed up ever since. My mother should have dragged me into counseling, but she stopped functioning as a mother shortly after Daniel's funeral.

Opening my hand, I look at the folded yellow paper, unfold it, then wad it up in my fist, proving to myself, it's nothing but a piece of paper. But it has changed significantly since I found it this morning. That's my life as of October 6th. It changed with the crumpling, but it is still the same. After October 6th it wasn't plain anymore, there was a more intricate format, a beautiful crumpled pattern.

Chapter 2

Daniel
Even though it was early November and cold, beautiful, golden-haired Daniel took me out on the lake, with his friends, to cheer me up. He wanted to teach me to drop one ski. We decided Daniel should go first, just to show off his hot-dog technique. Grinning, (he had a wonderful gap between his two front teeth) he yelled "Nothin' to it," as he pulled on his ski. Then the driver of the boat put the engine in reverse while Daniel was still wrestling with his ski and rope. The propeller sucked up the rope, then dragged Daniel into the 175 Horse powered Johnson outboard motor.

He screamed as he was sucked underwater. We all heard him. The lake turned red and the driver tried to cut the ignition. Jason Que, Daniel's best friend, dove into the water and pulled him to the surface. Then everybody on board, except me, used beach towels to get him back into the boat. But Daniel bleed to death before we ever docked.

I was in the boat.

I was fourteen and in the boat.

I dropped from my seat to the floor, so I could hold Daniel's big hand. As the boat bounced across the lake, I tightened my grip, then put my head next to his because I didn't want to be alone. Daniel had always been that kind of brother. When I was afraid he never left me alone.

Daniel, with his wavy blond hair, heart breaking grin and honey colored skin was my mother's Golden Boy. He was dead before we reached the shore, but I never let go of his hand.

I was still only 14, though it seemed I aged decades after those two funerals.

Daddy died on October 6th. One month and two days later, Daniel was buried next to his dad. The dirt on my father's grave was still raw and lumpy. We all tried desperately not to step on Daddy's grave as we watched them lower Daniel into the ground. That's when all this started. When my life changed and began.

Now, B. Wallace, my mom, doesn't want me to forget. Jesus Christ, Mom, how could you think I'd ever forget? Just because I've got a family doesn't mean ours never existed. It's not an either/or situation.

Mike walks past with his empty plate. He puts it on the counter next to the sink. Why doesn't he go on and put it in the sink? Maybe even run some water on it so the food doesn't stick. "Mom," he says earnestly. "Coffee takes everything good out of your body and gives you bad breath."

"I know. Just one cup. That's all I'll drink." I try to take a sip but it's still about two hundred degrees too hot. "Hey, Doctor Mike, if you want to discuss health issues, how about that fried chicken and your cholesterol level? You'll probably have one artery completely clogged before first recess."

With grease still on his face, he changes the subject. "So are you gonna do it?"

I shake my head and smile at him over the cup. "I'm not discussing this with you."

"Come on, Mom. It's important. You should just do it real quick "

"I'll take that into consideration. But I don't want to talk about it. Besides, it's not really any of your business." Pregnancy and marriage, that's the topic of choice for my family and friends. Everybody assumes it is their right to ask me why Z and I haven't gotten married. I'm supposed to marry him, the man I love, who is now sleeping in our bed, before the baby is born. Or else.

Or else what? That's what I want to know. Or else the child will be a bastard. Or else her birth certificate will say, Father...unknown. I don't think so. Everybody will know who the daddy is. And the baby won't care for five or six years if we're married or not. As long as Z and I stand over his crib smiling, as long as we both hold her hand when we search for clean bottles in the middle of the night, as long as we both help him tie his shoes and brush his teeth. I really don't think she'll care whether or not we got married before or after her birth.

I sneeze. It is a monster, that shuts Mike up for a moment. I don't want a shot gun marriage. I don't want to get married wearing a maternity gown and I'm afraid to change my perfect and beautiful life.

Change has always stripped my universe and left me bleeding, alone and afraid. Zolton and I have a relationship that is built on all the right stuff. We love one another and are devoted to our family. Zoltan and I take care of each other. We laugh, pay our bills, have great sex and eat well. We get mad, but we're almost never mean. It's taken me so long to find happiness, why would I want to change any thing?

I guess, since it's me against the rest of the world, it's possible that I am the problem. I've always been able to see both sides of most issues.

But why should I back down on such an important issue. Just because I feel differently than the rest of the world, does that make me wrong?

With the boiling cup of coffee, which I won't be able to drink for half an hour, I walk into Felicity's room. It's so horrible I almost laugh.

This room feels like a carnival, all color and movement, a hippie crash pad with a twin bed and Little Mermaid bedspread. The walls are covered, every flat surface is covered with posters. Dolphins jumping into pools of moonlight, peace signs, horses, puppies and sunsets. There are even posters stapled to the ceiling. Clothes, some dirty, some clean, and toys (stuffed animals, action figures and a few decapitated Barbies), books and markers, a plate, a couple of clean paper towels and a very small black sleeping dog with an extreme overbite are all on the floor.

The room smells like little girls, a warm combination of cheap perfume, hidden candy, sweat and crayons. I walk with care and realize, as I try to make it from the door to the bed, that I can not see my feet. That's how far my belly sticks out. I try to pull my bath robe closed, but it won't quite reach. Leaning over a little, I see my toes. They are a mess. Funny how you can forget about things like toenails when they are out of sight.

"Felicity," I whisper, looking at the Garfield clock on the wall." It's 6:28."

She doesn't move.

I put my coffee cup on her desk, then sit down next to my sleeping child. I stare for a moment then touch her cheek with the back of my fingers. She is so smooth and, in the right light, seems to glow just a little.

Softly, I make a chimpanzee noise in her ear.

I have known, since my children were old enough to hold my hand with their chubby and soft baby fingers, that they were not simply my children. They are not patches or additions to my life. God has embroidered my children into the fabric of my soul. They are the color and the texture and the story. Together, we are a bright and poetic tapestry. "Felicity, Felicity, Felicity, it's almost 6:30, you have to get up."

After a moment Felicity, who is seven, says, "I hate waking up."

"No kidding? I hate waking up too, what a coincidence. But you're going to have a good day."

Felicity is beautiful. Like Mike, she is very tall for her age. A lot of people think they are twins. Both are dark with great big almond shaped eyes. Their personalities and temperaments however, are galaxies apart. Michael is the optimistic peacemaker and Felicity is my warrior.

She opens her foggy blue eyes. "Did Zoltan bring me a snake?"

"A snake? What do you want a snake for?"

"For a pet. He forgot, didn't he?"

Bear, the dog, stands up and stretches, then waits for attention.

Felicity smiles and I lie down next to her, slowly resting my head on her pillow. Though I barely fit in her tiny bed, I could stay here all day, hiding under the Little Mermaid. The fate of my universe will be decided in the next few days. I have to decide if I'm going to marry Z and I'll be giving birth, but my back hurts and all I want to do is go back to sleep.

I hold up my post-it-notes. "Are these yours?"

Felicity looks to see if anything is written on either side of the post it notes. "What is it?" I watch as she smooths the wrinkles out of the paper then presses them to the wall over her bed.

The notes stays in place and Felicity looks at me and smiles. Her first victory of the day. "So, what is it?"

"Nothing, just a piece of paper I found. Come on, you've got to get up."

Felicity sits up then bounds out of bed like a kangaroo. "So are you gonna say yes to Z. today?"

The post it note falls of the wall and lands on Felicity's bed.

She snatches it up and hands it back to me.

"That's none of your business, my precious angel."

Felicity rolls her eyes. "Mom, it's none of my business? but it's my life. There's a conundrum for you."

"Where did she get that word? You shouldn't use words you don't understand."

"A conundrum is like a puzzle or problem, " she states. "And your turning everything into a big stupid conundrum."

'Felicity," she looks at me. "Watch your mouth, you're about to get into trouble before you even get out of bed Ok?" She nods.

If we get married there will not be a photographer. No woman, who is nine months pregnant, wants to have her picture taken. All she really wants to do is take a warm bath, find a comfortable sleeping position, and wake up to a clean house.

But my biggest reason for wanting to wait doesn't concern my vanity. I can't afford to have marriage change our love. Our Universe spins perfectly now, nothing more is necessary. My life with Z and the children has stopped the bleeding.

As a form of matrimonial encouragement or emotional black mail and manipulation, Zolton's grandmother has made me the world's most hideous maternity/wedding gown. It's huge and flowered. An acre-sized polyester moo-moo. Because she is Hungarian and speaks just a little English and because she's 88 years old and I'm uncomfortable arguing with old people, I only smile at her and stroke the dress as though I'm delighted. It's the wedding gown of my dreams.

There is another aspect I must consider. My entire family, except for my grandmother, and some cousins and uncles are dead. So, I don't have to answer to anyone. I don't have to face the disapproval of those I love.

Zolton, on the other hand, has a wonderful Catholic family that's very much alive. If we don't get married before this baby is born it will hurt them. I don't want to be responsible for a family rift. Z's grandmother, Eva, is more like his mother. She's also cheap steak tough and ridiculously stubborn. She has survived two World Wars and the Russian occupation of her country because she never backs down. Eva has already stated, like a loaded derringer, that our child will be a bastard if we do not marry. She actually used that word.

It's possible, in this instance, his reasons for wanting to get married in the next week are more important than my reasons for refusing. But, in this day and age it's politically incorrect for a woman to admit that. Why are his desires more important than mine?

Maybe, if I had a slow-drip IV of tranquillity for a couple of years I could tackle these decisions without writhing and whining.

But this happens to us all. We have trivial conversations about sandwiches, headaches and traffic, seconds later, a continent shattering event takes place. Your mother dies. Your baby takes his first breath. After your mother dies you still have to fix bologna sandwiches for your family. After your baby is born, you need to wash your hair. The world returns to beautiful trivialities.

My mother told me my father was dead while she was sharpening a pencil. She didn't turn to hug me until the point was perfect.

As Felicity pulls me to my feet I say, "I think the word your looking for is irony, not conundrum."

"Maybe," Felicity says, then leans against my shoulder and sighs impatiently. "Mom, you didn't answer. Did Zoltan bring me a snake yet? I really, really want a pet snake."

"No Honey, you need to give him some time on that one."

My knee pops under my weight and the weight of my third child. "You have enough pets, anyway."

"You shouldn't make us go to school, it's an important day and you might go into labor and need some help with the delivery. I read about a six year old who delivered his own sister next to a highway. That could happen you know, anything can happen." Felicity is really awake, popping and edgy. I have to touch her hair. It falls down her back like a glistening chestnut wave. Why do my children have beautiful hair and I have a thin, straight wheat colored shag? "What do you have today?"

"Library." She pulls a giant Snoopy sweat shirt out of her pillow case. It serves as her robe.

"Well, there you go, you love library. You're gonna have a great day. Get us some good books, maybe something on Russian ostriches who love yogurt or rare pumpkin snails."

She moves past me like a circus acrobat. "Mom, you're making those up," she whispers.

Bear whines and stretches, obviously well rested and ready to run.

She is in heat and really wants to get knocked up.

A year and a half ago I found Bear. She was a two pound fur ball chasing a frog on the shoulder of the highway, oblivious to the fifty-five mile an hour traffic, nearly blowing her over. Because the frog made a giant leap into my lane, I had to swerve in order to miss them both. I drove on, trying to forget the cute and stupid puppy. I made it a mile before I gave up and turned around.

Once I had the dog in the car, I had to make sure she didn't belong to anyone. She smelled horrible, probably from rolling around in road-kill. I stopped at two trailers and one house to ask if the stinky puppy lived there.

Finally, a skinny lady wearing a polyester halter top looked at the puppy with near loathing. "That's one of them wild puppies."

Tightening my grip on the warm and squirmy dog, I tried to ignore the smell. This woman looked like Cruella DeVil. It seemed possible she might rip the animal from my hands and throw it in a crock pot with a little onion and salt. "It's a wild puppy?"

She flicked her cigarette past my shoulder into the driveway. "Yeah, there's a bunch of them dogs that run around and have puppies out in the back." She nodded her bullet shaped head toward a shack in the middle of a field. "We're gonna start shooting them if they get into the god damn trash anymore."

I nodded, as though sympathetic. "So you don't mind if I take this one?"

She laughed, showing her long skinny teeth. "Suit yourself." As I walked away she coughed then said, "Hey, be careful going up the driveway. That hole in the middle is a bitch."

Clutching my 'wild puppy' I nodded my thanks as she closed her trailer door.

Bear is pretty wild now, but it's hormonal. This is my first time to suffer through this wretched aspect of pet ownership. The adorable twelve pound slut has been clawing and whining at the living room door, trying to convince somebody to let her out. I can't blame anyone but myself. I put off getting her fixed. Last night I left her in the bathroom. But Felicity probably heard her moaning and scratching and let her out.

With coffee in hand, I walk out of the cluttered, dangerous room.

Mike talks to me from the living room. "Mom, James, in my class, has a cat that looks exactly like Socks the Cat, but James says he's a lot meaner. You think he could do commercials?"

Felicity is in the kitchen, getting some orange juice, she yells, "Suck the cat up in a vacuum cleaner?"

"Felicity," Mike hollers past me, "I said 'Socks the Cat' not 'suck the cat.'"

It takes Felicity a second or two to understand. She starts laughing. That gets Mike going. Felicity repeats her verbal mix up. "Suck the cat up in a vacuum cleaner." It sounds even funnier to them both the second time. I laugh, but they are nearly hysterical. Felicity holds her face so orange juice won't come out her nose. I've lost at least five, maybe ten minutes in my morning, get-ready-for-school-ritual.

I have too many theories. One is 'rituals are a crucial part of parenting.' Everyday parents must boss their children around, on schedule. If we don't say, "Go brush your teeth," their teeth will rot. If we don't say "Take a bath" they won't and then they will smell bad. If we don't say, "Do your homework" they will get bad grades. If we don't say "Drink your milk," they will live on soda. If we don't say " Go to bed," they will stay up past midnight. Children are, by nature, wild and dirty little creatures. At first, bossing my children did not come naturally. I've always thought it was rude to tell other people what to do.

But kids, at least my kids, won't brush their teeth or hair, do their homework or eat anything other than Ring Dings and orange soda unless I tell them other wise. Kids don't raise themselves and turn out alright. Parenting is exhausting because always being in charge and telling everybody what to do is exhausting.

As I fix Felicity a bowl of oatmeal and Z a cup of coffee, Mike comes into the kitchen. "Do we have any hard-boiled eggs?"

"Gross, no. What do you want with eggs. You hate them, don't you?"

"I don't know," he shrugs. "I'm just in the mood for them. Maybe for dinner?" he looks at me hopefully, but all I can do is crunch up my face in response.

7:15 a.m. I leave Z's coffee on the bed side table, then a manhunt begins for the lost car keys and Felicity's missing hiking boot. I lower my round self to the floor so I can look under the couch for the boot. I hesitate before sticking my hand underneath. What if there's another post-it note waiting for me.

Closing my eyes I take the plunge. Nothing there but Legos, cd cases, a condom wrapper, dust and a pencil. I stuff the condom wrapper in my robe pocket. Obviously I haven't vacuumed under there in a long while.

After taking a deep breath and pushing, I discover I can't get up. It's too early and I'm too big. Fine. I'll stay right here, on the living room floor. I'll stay here and conduct traffic. I can get everybody ready for school and out the door from this vantage point. "Mike, have you got shoes on?"

"Yes ma'am."

"Let me see." I cross my legs and arch my back. My spine feels like a guitar string.

Mike appears wearing a pair of high top Arkansas Razorback sneakers.

"Teeth done?"

He grins.

"Will you do me a favor?"

"Sure."

"Help me get up."

He stands over me and offers his hand. With an exaggerated assortment of grunts and groans, I struggle to my feet. Then I grab Mike, hug his shoulders and mess up his long hair. "Mom, I need a permission slip to go to the museum next week."

He doesn't care that I messed up his hair. He only brushes it because I tell him too. "All right, get me something to write on."

I sit down to think, then write, "Mike can go anywhere, at any time with anybody except the Devil. Sincerely, Liz McDade."

Mike laughs and tosses it to Felicity who is sitting at the dining room table. "Mom, they won't get it. You want me to write it and you can just sign your name?"

"Fine," I say, "nobody appreciates my cutting edge humor."

Felicity takes a bite of oatmeal. "Damn Mom, the teachers take Satin, damnation and redemption really serious."

"Don't cuss, honey. "Why is she talking about damnation? That's a big statement for a kid who weighs sixty three pounds.

She is chewing. Her blue eyes get big as she shakes her head in innocence. "I didn't cuss."

"Yes, you did."

She shakes her head some more, the spoon frozen in the air, full of oatmeal.

"You just said damn Felicity, we both heard it," Mike says flatly.

"Forget it, everybody," I raise my hands to stop the debate. While Felicity finishes eating, I pick out her clothes. It's easier this way and we both have full veto rights. She's exceedingly picky, not about how things look, but how they feel. Getting her ready for school is a little like dressing the Rain Man. Socks are our biggest problem. . The line over the toes, the elastic and the heel all have to be perfectly straight and snug. A sagging sock can make her cry with frustration. This can be very trying. If she doesn't outgrow it by the time she's wearing pantyhose I'll have to be committed.

"How'd I do this time?" I ask, holding up a pair of jeans and a big pink shirt with buttons at the neck and some velcro epaulets.

"Not that shirt Mom, please, my hair gets caught in the sticky stuff."

"Ok, fine." I locate a purple Tweety Bird t-shirt and denim vest. "How about this?"

She nods, stirring her oatmeal and humming a little song I don't recognize.

After eating five or six bites, Felicity carries her bowl into the kitchen, then absently drops it into the sink as though sleepwalking. There is a huge clatter. Did she break anything? My little zombie is totally unfazed by the crash. I check the clock 7:08. We are running out of time, so I ignore it.

"Hair time." I announce then sit down in my big chair and pull the milking stool up in front of me. Just a few months ago she could sit in the chair with me but we don't both fit any more.

Before she will sit down for the brushing, she has to find 'her brush,' the soft pink one. Then she has to locate the right kind of hair tie. The ties Zoltan uses on his pony tail don't work with Felicity's hair, they loosen up too quickly, then she has a lopsided and off center braided ponytail dangling from the back of her head. It's apparently a very bad thing.

"Hair we go," I say, trying to sound cheerful and optimistic but like 90% of the mother and daughter teams in America, this is the low point of our morning. Felicity, who has always been very mercurial, loves having long hair and her hair is beautiful. But she hates having it brushed.

"This could be a hair raising event," I say, trying to distract her from the brush.

She gives me a snort of laughter and rolls her eyes.

Suddenly she bolts out of the chair and squeals. "You pulled!"

"I'm sorry, I hit a tangle. Sit back down," I pat the chair.

"No, that's enough, don't brush anymore, please."

"Honey, you can't go to school like that. You're hair looks so scary. I've got to brush it. Now, sit down. I'll be really, really careful."

"I know, you think I look like a street Urchin, that's what your mom used to say to you."

The brush is suspended mid-stroke. "You're right. B. Wallace did call me a street Urchin. Did I tell you that story?"

Felicity just shakes her head and says, "I know lots of stuff. Mom, please don't brush anymore," She is able to stand up and summon one fat tear, the size of a marble. It glistens as it rolls down her cheek.

"Felicity, I didn't pull that hard." I wait but she doesn't move. I grind my teeth and say in a hushed voice, "If you don't sit back down and let me finish, I swear we're going to cut it as soon as you get home from school. If you can't take care of your own hair or at least help me, then your not old enough to have long hair, Felicity. That's just the way it is."

My blood pressure is rising and I'm getting depressed. I haven't really eaten anything yet, except half a kiwi, so my sugar level is low and it's too early in the morning to sound this mean.

Without speaking she comes back to me and sits down with her arms crossed. She tries hard to hold still because she doesn't want her hair cut, but her right foot still twitches and she snivels.

The hairs on my arms are about to stand up. We run through this scenario at least three times a week.

I finish as quickly as I can. There's one tangle underneath but I decide to just smooth some top hairs over it for now. I'll work on it tonight, when she's slippery with conditioner and in a better mood.

"Your lucky I'm not my grandmother, Marva. Once she brushed my hair so hard I had to get stitches in my ear."

I remember feeling exactly like Felicity does right now.

"Really? Purple Marva did that?" Felicity asks, suddenly feeling better.

"No, not really, but she was wicked with a hairbrush."

When I was little, my grandmother, Marva, loved to brush my hair. But she would always shake her head and make that 'tsk, tsk' noise. Then she'd say something like, "It's such a shame you didn't get you father's hair, it was so thick and pretty."

I adored Marva, but hated it when she brushed my hair.

Marva loved the color purple. She wore purple, hose, dresses, and blouses, gloves, pajamas and lip stick. She even had most of her shoes dyed purple. She was very active on the Southern social scene and matching shoes and handbags were crucial. Marva also had long fingernails. When she brushed my hair she would part it with one nail. I'd cringe and try to squirm away. Even at six or seven years old, her long fingernails seemed ancient and gnarled. I was always afraid there was something old and crusty stuck under there.

Aside from her fingernails and hair brushing technique, Marva was lots of fun. In 1968 she bought a dark purple Cadillac convertible. She'd drive around town on Saturday afternoon picking up her grandchildren. We'd pile into the back seat, skinny and sweaty. Sometimes when there were too many grand kids, she'd even let us sit up on the top of the back seat. We'd sing 'Froggy Went a Courtin' as we rolled through town.

I tell Felicity about Marva songs and clothes and even about her fingernails as I brush. The stories distract and calm her until we are buddies again.

When I was seven or eight Marva married a man named Charles. He came from a good family in St. Louis, had a neat little yellow Camero and a golf handicap of five or six. Nobody realized he was a remittance man with a nasty temper, especially when he was drunk.

After they'd been married for a couple of years, Charles was in a car accident. He broke his shoulder and was told, at the age of 65, he couldn't play golf anymore. His universe collapsed, as did his personality. Golf and socializing at the club were the center of his world. Without them, he had nothing.

Charles put on a bathrobe and didn't leave the house for almost ten years. He became a vile tempered recluse with poor hygiene. His finger nails were longer than Marva's and he never washed his stringy gray hair. His temper festered, and my joyous purple grandmother had to live with constant verbal abuse.

Poor Marva was stuck with Charles. She'd spent all her money on purple things and needed him because of his pitiful cash.

Once Charles turned ugly and sour we, the grandchildren, stopped spending the night at Marva's. Charles skulked around and cursed too much. My cousin, Jake, and I didn't really mind him all that much. Children are sometimes very good at ignoring, literally tuning out someone they don't like and have no use for. Charles never became an important factor in our lives. We didn't love him, we never even liked him, so we pretended he wasn't there. We only talked to Marva, only looked at Marva, only acknowledged our grandmother's voice when we were at her house. He was nothing more than a harsh whisper, a breeze in the curtain. This infuriated Charles and sent him into screaming, cursing rages. We were banned from Marva's magical old house because we would not look at or listen to Charles. Life had been a lot more fun when she was a widow.

My Aunt Sarah tried to kill Charles when I was nine. She moved in with the unhappy couple for a month because they both had the flu and Marva sprained her ankle trying to mow the lawn.

Charles would stand too close to Sarah when he yelled, droplets of spittle flew from his toothless mouth as he ranted and complained. He hated the world, himself and anyone that happened to be in the same room. For hours he stalked through the once happy purple rooms, cursing Sarah and my grandmother. He never let up. He told Sarah, who was a 50 year old paralegal, she was too ugly to ever get a husband of her own. He told her she was stupid and pathetic, he spit on the food she made, then threw all of her make-up in the toilet because she left it on the bathroom counter.

Aunt Sarah was always a scratcher. When she got angry or frustrated she started itching, everywhere. There was nothing wrong with her, she just scratched, uncontrollably when people became overly emotional. Charles saw her scratching her scalp as they argued.

He accused her of having head lice. He said she was a filthy street slut then called the Health Department to report her condition.

Sarah wanted to leave, but how could she abandon her mother with a man like Charles? Something had to be done.

The afternoon before Sarah was supposed to leave, she hatched a plan, made some egg salad, then left it on the back porch, in the 103 degree sun for five hours. While singing Disney songs, she always sang Disney songs when she was in a good mood, Sarah fixed Charles a lovely egg salad sandwich on soft white bread for dinner. She used plenty of mustard and pepper to cover any questionable flavors.

Her plan almost worked. Charles got sick, sick enough to go to the hospital for a week. But the bastard didn't die.

I don't tell Felicity this Marva story while I'm brushing her hair.

"What about your Mom, when you had long hair did she hurt your head too." Felicity asks, hopefully.

"Not that I remember, my mom wasn't much of a hair brusher. She was concerned with other things."

"Yeah, I know, like the substance of a man's soul."

"Exactly," I say, "How did you know that?"

Felicity shrugs her thin shoulders and I finish her ponytail. "Do you know what those words mean?"

"Of course. Well, all except diction."

"Diction has to do with your choice of words, how you use them and how you say them. Did you learn all that in school?"

Felicity shakes her head, "No, no way. I just know them. Somebody told me."

My daughter finally smiles at me oddly, teasing me with a secret. "Mom, if you and Zoltan get married can I change my name to Szabo. I want the same last name as you guys and the baby."

"If that's what you want, that's wonderful. I know it will make Z happy."

"I live here, with you, so I should have the same last name because we're all together, right?" Her willingness to change names should teach me something. I'm hanging on to my last name no matter the cost. I will hurt the people I love the most just to preserve the heritage of my dead people. That's so stupid. I should cherish the living, not worship the dead.

But it's so hard to let go of my glorious dead people. I've been trained, since I was a child to elevate my heritage. Once my family died, they all took on a magical air which, of course, made living people seem pale and flawed. The only bad thing my family ever did to me was leave me behind.

Felicity instinctively knows there's everything and nothing in a name. She loves Zoltan; she's with Zoltan; she wants his name. She wants us all to marry him and take his name.

I hug her from behind, resting my cheek on her cool, silken hair.

We are almost ready to leave for school.

I'm getting anxious. We need to get rolling so I can go to work.

I am a bookie and work for a famous red neck numbers man named Hurlie. He gets very upset if I don't pay my players off within 48 hours after the week's end. Hurlie closes our week out on Thursday night, after the NFL game. So, I have to deliver and pick up everybody's money by Saturday afternoon.

I only work football and basketball, pro and college. I tried baseball one season, but it was an unbelievable pain in the ass. There are baseball games every day, all day, on the east and west coast. And the odds change with the pitcher.

Being a bookie is a remarkable profession that I'm almost proud of. What a shame it's a felony in most states. But last week was the end for me. I have to give it up. Being a bookie with a baby isn't feasible. Even though most of my work is done at home, the phone rings constantly. Somedays I get 200 calls, and I can't miss one. And a guy calling to bet $500 on Green Bay doesn't want to hear a baby crying.

It's all about numbers and if I make a mistake giving a line or writing down a bet, I'm stuck with the consequences. There are always guys who want to argue about my line, or call after kickoff, trying to sneak in a last minute bet. They claim they couldn't get through. Too bad, next time call earlier. I start answering the phones two hours before the coin toss. The lines change when betting gets too heavy on one side or another, or if Hurlie hears about a pulled groin or bruised ham string.

Looking around the house, I make an announcement to Mike and Felicity. A maternal proclamation. "Everybody has to pick up two things and put them away. I need help today. Then get your backpacks and hit the door," I am the loving drill sergeant.

The living room and kitchen are a mess despite their pickup efforts. I don't know how this happens every morning.

Bear scratches feverishly at the door. She wants out. I've had nights when I felt like you do right now, Bear. Show some self control. Fred, our pet goat, is bleating next to the front door. He's hungry. He's always hungry. When we bought him he only weighed twenty pounds. We thought he was a pygmy goat. Now he weighs 110 pounds and butts the door with his head when I'm late with his feed.

Looking out the window, I am horrified to see a pack of dogs in the driveway and yard. They range in size from a ten pound black and white hair-ball, (probably a Cockapoo mix) to a gargantuan Rottweiler. There are several, nondescript mutts with long, short, curly, straight fur. And they are all waiting for my sweet Bear to come out and dance. No wonder Fred is making noise, there's a canine, bachelor party on our lawn. Who knows if they want to eat him or fuck him.

My dog is in heat and I'm about to have a baby. This isn't fair. How did all those dogs get our address?

I'm not up to explaining Bear's reproductive urges and all the dogs with hard-ons to the children, so I stop them both. "Let me see your teeth again."

They grin.

"Oh no. Look at the plaque. You both look like you smoke a pack a day and just finished eating a peanut butter sandwich. Disgusting. Go back and brush one more time, with some muscle this time."

As soon as they are out of sight, I step outside and start throwing handfuls of gravel and dirt. The dogs seem pretty unimpressed, so I find four rocks the size of chocolate chip cookies. Because of my stomach, I can't get any real distance, but my aim is fair. I hit a shaggy brown and white dog in the butt. He looks at me and moves reluctantly into the bushes. A fat black dachshund waddles after him. Waving my arms like a great, flightless bird, I throw more rocks. The horny dogs scatter and are momentarily out of sight.

Fred, is confused. Usually, I'm throwing rocks at him.

7:36 a.m. Sticking my head back in the house, I yell, "Come on guys, we've got to go. Get you're back packs, come on." Bear is out of the bathroom. She tries to bolt through the open door but I block her with one foot, then roll her backwards.

The kids emerge, running full speed and laughing. Mike still has toothpaste on his lips and Felicity's shirt is soaked.

Dogs are cowering in the bushes with wet and hungry eyes and we pile in to he car. I honk the horn five times to keep them there.

Every thing is fine. Deep breath, slow down, count to ten. 'How are you doing in there, child of mine?' I ask my womb. Everybody is cheerful. Felicity starts singing "Just sit right back and you'll hear a tale, a tale of a fateful trip," The theme to Gilligan's Island.

"Stop singing." Mike says in the back seat.

"No," she gives him a satisfied smirk.

Mike leans forward and covers her mouth with has hand. "No singing, it's too early. You'll make me hurl." Suddenly he jerks his hand back. "Gross, Mom, Felicity licked my hand." He wipes his palm furiously on the car seat.

Felicity starts singing again, "with Gilligan, the skipper too, the millionaire and his wife." She stops to dig through her backpack. "I've got a note from my teacher in here. You've got to sign it."

As we roll down the drive way, Felicity sticks a yellow-post it note in the middle of the steering wheel. I hit the brakes. There is a tingling in my fingers and the car suddenly seems unbearable hot. I can't read what's written on the paper. I can only see the yellow square.

"Read it to me please," I whisper.

"Ok," Felicity says. She thinks reading the note is part of her punishment.

Without removing the post-it she says, "Please discuss inappropriate language with Felicity. She's a smart child but I am growing increasingly concerned about her language and the odd subject matter she discusses."

"Get that piece of paper off my steering wheel, please." I say and take my numb foot off the brake. "What odd thing did you say?"

Felicity looks out the window and says, "Our pet Guinea Pig died over the weekend. These stupid girls were crying so the teacher said, Math Man has gone to heaven. You shouldn't cry. Then I said, 'If Math Man committed suicide the Catholic church would say he's in Hell, but maybe that's not the real truth. Maybe he's just in purgatory. Justin, who sits next to me asked what purgatory was and I told him it was a place that wasn't heaven and it wasn't hell and you went there to get punished for your sins and all the crappie stuff you had done while you were alive and then maybe God would let you into Heaven. The teacher didn't seem mad or anything, just kind of freaked.. Knowledge and understanding religion are good."

"Man, Felicity, how can you go off like that in class. You're such a freak." Mike says, disgusted but not very surprised.

"Felicity, how do you know about purgatory and the Catholic church's stance on suicide. We're not even Catholic. You know our church doesn't believe you have to go to Hell for killing your self. It's not a good thing but it's not a mortal sin." Maybe Nadgymami, Zolton's grandmother, told them about purgatory. She's the only practicing and devout Catholic Felicity spends a lot of time with.

"I know," she says, sounding a little bored.

"How do you know all that? Who explained it to you. Was in Nagymami. My throat is dry but I keep on staring at the road.

"I just know it Mom, I don't know how. Nagymami would never talk about suicide with me. She thinks I'm too young to understand anything major. Will you sign the note? I'll get detention if you don't." She sounds so young and worried now.

I want to go back to Gilligan's Island. My hand shakes as I sign the little yellow post it note without looking. I feel as though I'm signing off on something, committing or accepting.

There is a very real possibility I might throw up now. "Would you sing the Gilligan Song for me again?"

"No Mom," Mike hollers.

Turning on the radio, I listen to some yearning, deserted woman pleading for love, telling some guy that life without him is worse than death. The song is so different from my world, it has no relevance. I turn off the radio. "Guys, listen to me," slowing the car down, getting serious about what I'm saying. "If it hurts, there's a good chance it's not love. Love is supposed to make the world an easier place to live. Good love doesn't make you pierce your nose or stay in a dark room for days and days waiting for the phone to ring. If love is doing that sort of crap to you, if it makes you crazy and miserable, get rid of it. If love hurts, I promise you, you don't need it."

"Zolton told me if a woman hurts me more than once, she's not worth having," Mike says.

I check his expression in the rearview mirror. "He did, huh?"

Felicity likes this. She eats up any conversation concerning relationships or love, boyfriends, girlfriends, husbands and wives. "If it makes you be stupid you should just go out and get another boyfriend, right Momma? You and Zolton don't make each other crazy."

"Not usually, honey," I say.

From the back seat, Mike leans forward, sticking his head between the seats. This is rare, he's taken his seat belt off. Mike is usually Mr. Safety Guy. He brushes a piece of glitter from last nights art project off my cheek. "Mom, why are you telling us this?"

"I just want you both to know. Are you listening, Felicity?' Grinning, she nods at me. "People get confused all the time. They don't realize they can walk away and start over when they fall in love with somebody that hurts them. Your gonna have boyfriends and girlfriends soon enough and I don't want to forget to tell you this."

"You know what we do at recess, Mom?" Felicity asks.

"Tell me what do you do at recess?"

"We chase boys till they scream. We should be afraid of them but we're not, they're afraid of us."

"Chase boys till they scream." I say on mom response auto pilot. I'm seeing post it notes everywhere, on trees and squirrels, houses and cows.

"Probably they're afraid you're gonna lick them." Mike says, sounding just like the big brother he is.

Felicity is looking out the window again. "Momma, do I get to be the flower girl when you and Zolton get married."

"Sure, but it won't be for a while."

"Will Daddy come?" she asks.

"No, honey, because we're not getting married for a while. "

"Why can't he come?"

My kids are deaf. Why not? She wants to know why not. Because this isn't Chuck's family, because this isn't his world. It hasn't been for years and years. I'd never think about him but the kids remind me sometimes. "He's too far away Felicity."

"But he loves you, he'd want to be at your wedding."

I look at Felicity closely, wondering if she's serious. Sometimes I forget, she's only seven.

"Felicity, think about it," Mike says. "It would make Dad really jealous." Mike can say things I can't, and he states the facts succinctly.

All Felicity says is, "Oh," then asks, "But when?"

"When what?"

"Mommmm, when's the wedding going to be?"

"You're killing me child. I don't know, not for a while." I turn the radio back on hoping to change the subject.

"In the jungle, the quiet jungle, the lion sleeps tonight." Both of them howl like wolves. My ears may start bleeding.

And we are about to have a third child so our chaos will increase mightily. I turn the radio back down. I want them to understand and agree with me. Somebody has to be on my side. this isn't the right time to get married, not for me anyway. Surely they will understand that our world is too good to change. "I really want to wait until after the baby is born to have the wedding. Then I can wear a decent dress and dance. What do you think?"

"So what's more important Mom, a decent dress or a decent wedding?" I stare at a slice of Mike in the rear view mirror. Mr. Sanctimonious. Where did that come from? I won't answer him. I'll pretend he didn't say anything at all.

"Are you going to wear the dress Nagy mami made for you? " In a deep voice she whispers to Mike, "the giant dress." She smiles too sweetly. Then I hear her say, "The dress that's as big as a Toyota, no as big as a football field, no, no the dress that's bigger than the Little Rock airport." They're both laughing now and squirming like puppies. "What if Mom got big enough to fit in the dress? She'd be so huge, oh man, she'd squish us all." They are laughing again. The car is full of free-floating hysteria.

"Come on, give me a break. What if I were very sensitive, you might be hurting my feelings. Poor me, poor huge me. Let me tell you, I was much bigger when I was pregnant with you. You were both bottle sucking monsters in diapers."

"We're still monsters," Felicity yells, delighted with herself. This is the same kid who, moments ago was explaining Catholic dogma. Something is wrong. Those did not seem like her thoughts or words.

INVISIBLE BRANCHES

I try not to think about B. Wallace and the yellow post its, instead I listen to the news. We are approaching the 40th Anniversary of Desegregation in Little Rock Public Schools. If mom was alive she'd be so excited, ready to march in Little Rock all over again. The news has been filled with black and white photographs and film footage of the nine black teen-aged students who faced the screaming, hate-filled white mob Little Rock's Central High in 1957.

Little Rock is just fifty miles away. This happened in our back yard. Those nine black students looked so young and frightened. The girls all wore dresses, heavily starched and their smooth faces were drawn tight, saintly with fear. The boys wore simple button down shirts, their good pants. They held their books too tightly. They only wanted to go to school. They all looked handsome and smooth and brave in the face of raw hatred and death.

Why did those white adults hate the black children? How could they? I know the words. Ignorance breeds fear and hatred. That's why the white people, my people, acted so horribly. I've heard the words a thousand times, but I still do not understand, not really. It hurts me, embarrasses me to look at the photographs.

Those nine black teen-agers were escorted into Central High School by the 101st Air Borne. Troops with machine guns walked them through the screaming spitting mob. Even if they wanted to, the children couldn't turn around and leave. The mob of hundreds had closed in too tightly behind them. They had to walk on, into the mass of writhing, screaming faces, distorted by hatred.

Those nine students have all gone on to do more remarkable things. They are doctors and lawyers, writers and educators. Did that horrible year effect them in a good way? make them better?

Those frightened teen-agers returned to the all-white Central High, which is a grand and imposing building, day after day. They allowed themselves to be called nigger, they were tripped, smacked, slapped and spit upon by ignorant, stupid, white people.

I think about the parents of those children. The pain of knowing your own baby is walking into such vile abuse, would be unbearable. Any parent would rather give themselves up to torture than allow someone to hurt their child. The agony and fear and pride of the mothers and fathers at home is difficult to grasp. My mind does not want me to imagine their feelings.

It's because of the Little Rock 9 and Orville Faubus that my mother hated Arkansas. She carried a sign around Central High for nearly a month. It said, "Children are Children." She was screamed at too, one woman even slapped her but no photographers took her picture. A state trooper called Daddy and told him to come get his wife before she really got hurt. But Daddy didn't move, he just sat by the phone and waited for her to come home.

Mom walked in front of Central High with her sign for 14 hours on the first day of the rioting. When she came home she did not speak for nearly an hour. And when she did her voice was soft and deadly. She shook her head and whispered, "Ignorant bastards."

Daddy fixed her a bourbon and water then rubbed ointment on her hands, which were blistered from holding her sign. Then he pulled off her shoes so tenderly, she almost smiled. When he saw the quarter sized blisters and blood trapped inside her hose, he walked to the phone and called our maid Iolla. He told her to call a cab and come back to the house and help him take care of B. Wallace. Michael Justice believed in equal rights too, but he didn't have mom's vicious sense of dedication and fury. He always helped any man, black or white, who showed up at his door and asked for help. But he would never stand in the heat and rain and allow people to scream at him. Yes, he felt everyone deserved equal rights but, what he really believed in was B. Wallace.

So, that night he wrapped her wooden sign handle with foam, bought her some gloves and tried to understand why she had to march, day after day after day.

The Little Rock incident almost took mom's voice away. She simply had no words, but I would hear her at night, as she lay with my father, crying because nobody would listen to her or listen to reason and she was so very angry. Brilliant as B. Wallace was, she had tunnel vision. She turned on everyone who happened to be white and had any political power. She became a reverse bigot, hating nearly the entire population of Arkansas.

Every state has a racial horror story, a moment of historic shame, when gross stupidity and rage drowned out compassion, intelligence and morality.

INVISIBLE BRANCHES

The nightmare at Central high left B. Wallace depressed and angry. In some ways she should have seen the desegregation as a victory. In the end the racists and red necks lost. But the pain of the battle left her bitter.

During the racial turmoil in the 50's my grandmother, WaWa, had a black cook and a maid. For almost sixty years, these women took care of WaWa as though she were a piece of bone china, for sixty years. Louella spent four days a week at our house and two days with WaWa and Iolla filled in at my grandmother's so there was somebody with her everyday except Sundays.

My grandmother loved to tell the story about Louella and Iolla protecting her, when the violence erupted in Little Rock. They were afraid her car would be attacked in the evening, when she drove them home from work. Louella, told WaWa, "It's not safe for a white woman to be driving alone in a colored neighborhood right now."

Wawa said, "Oh nonsense. I've been driving you home for years. Your people know me."

"But they are mad, Miss. Wallace. The young people are acting crazy. They turned a car over and set it on fire last week, just a block from my house. And it belonged to a Mexican lady, not even white. She told a bunch of young boys they should quiet down and act right or they'd get everybody in trouble."

Wawa said, "The poor woman. I didn't read anything about that in the paper."

"No ma'am, it wouldn't be in the paper."

"Well, are you sure you're safe there?"

"Yes ma'am we're all right."

Wawa finally relented. For three months she paid Iolla and Louella's cab fair back to the black neighborhood.

But the cab driver would not actually drive the women home. He would only take them as far as the small grocery store on the out-skirts of the neighborhood. From there they would walk the ten blocks home. Wawa was very proud of herself and told all her friends how "her girls looked after her."

Several years after the desegregation of Little Rock, Mom tried to get, Louella, enrolled in a swimming class. We lived on a lake and had a swimming pool. Louella needed to know how to swim.

Nobody wanted a Negro in their pool. So, B. Wallace decided Hot Springs needed a black community center with a pool and class rooms. There were articles in the paper and on the 6 o'clock news. She solicited businesses for funds. Then the phone started ringing. In the middle of the night people called her a nigger lover, mechanics never had time to fix her car, there were even problems at the grocery store. They found reasons not to deliver to our house anymore.

Again, Louella was worried. She asked Mom to stop fighting for the pool. She was afraid for our family. B. Wallace, of course was fearless and truly pissed off. She pushed and pushed and pushed until there was a pool.

But my parents didn't get invited to a party for almost three years and Daddy lost several high profile civic design jobs.

One day, as I sat on the kitchen counter watching Louella frost some cupcakes, she told me she was still holding her breath, waiting for the other shoe to drop. She was sure somebody would eventually pay dearly for that pool.

She was right.

7:56 a.m.. We have four minutes to get to school before the first bell. We stop at a yield sign. Mike says, "Mom, I forgot my lunch."

"Charge it Buddy. I don't have any money with me.'

"Can I charge mine, too?" Felicity asks.

"No, you've got your lunch box right here."

"No fair. Here Mike, you take mine," Felicity throws her lunch into the back seat.

"Yeah, like I'm gonna carry a Barbie box into school." The lunch box flies forward and lands between Felicity and me.

I'm still thinking about Little Rock. Pulling a legal pad out from under the seat, I start scribbling notes to Felicity and Mike's teachers.

I write "I hope you will get a chance to talk about Central High and the Little Rock 9. If we don't teach the kids about these extraordinary events, who will? Thanks. Liz" There are only two black student in Fountain Lake. For that reason our teachers ignore the world shaping racial events. Still, I have to send the note. I fold each piece of paper up and hand them to the kids. "Give that to your teacher. Ok?"

They both nod. My antics are not new to them. Probably the school thinks I'm hormonally imbalanced.

Felicity is looking really serious, finally, she says, "I want you to do it now. You should go on and get married to Z. Then he'll be the baby's daddy as soon as it's born."

She's still thinking about the topic that's important to her. I hesitate, trying to figure out her logic, then realize, because I haven't fully explained to my daughter about the importance of sperm in the creation of a baby, she thinks the baby only gets a real daddy if there is a marriage. I've waited too long to tell her about sperm.

Using the rear view mirror, I glance at Mike in the back seat again. He's trying really hard to ignore us, and not to laugh. He's also waiting to see what I'll say to Felicity. He catches me looking at him and ducks out of sight.

I study Felicity's shining face. She knows how a baby grows in the woman's uterus and she knows all about labor and how the baby gets out. What I haven't told her is how the baby gets in there in the first place. I'm just not ready. She is, I'm sure. But, I hate thinking she'll know every time Z and I say were going to take 'a nap', or lock our bedroom door early in the morning, we're actually rolling around naked and sweaty and pushing.

We've almost reached the school. Mike says, "So get married before the baby is born, ok Mom? Felicity is right."

Air leaves my lungs. My shoulders sag.

It seems I'm sighing all the time these days. Maybe the baby is taking my air. Maybe my lungs are shrinking. Maybe I'll just hold my breath for a while. "I think the baby will be able to call Zoltan 'Daddy' no matter what."

Felicity is getting excited because we've almost reached the school. She gathers her back pack and lunch box and unlocks her door. Then says, "You'll look beautiful when ever you get married. It's ok if you're big."

"It's not my size holding me back Felicity. That's not why I don't want to do it now. It's not a fashion thing." I just contradicted everything I said earlier.

She shrugs. "Ok."

I stop the car in front of the flat roofed school building my father designed thirty years ago. The roof leaks now and the tall skinny windows look dated; but I can still feel him floating through the building. He is in the atrium with it's big windows and the interior planter boxes and skylights. My mother's spirit feels so different from Daddy's. when I feel Daddy, it's a good thing, comforting and clear. Right now, Mom feels threatening, like an impending thunderstorm.

Felicity puts one hand on my belly. Her elegant fingers are so long and brown. It seems, just a few days ago, she had stubby little hands that gripped my sleeve or hand when she was afraid. She leans over until her face is almost touching my stomach. "I gotta go to school now. Bye."

I give her a quick kiss and push a stray strand of hair behind her ear. "I love you."

8:00 a.m. Felicity is out of the car and running with her back pack. She melts, like warm chocolate, into a writhing pack of brightly dressed kids.

"She's such a suck up," Mike says laughing as he slides out. Then he leans in the window to offer me a kiss.

"I know she is, but I like it sometimes. Don't use the word suck. I love you, have fun today."

The second morning bell rings, loudly. Children run in mass to the school building, skinny legs, thick brown hair and joy. They are perfect. I glance at a lady in a green Pontiac behind me. She's smoking a cigarette. A thin gray trail of smoke drifts out the car window and filters into the world. Is she also feeling joy as her child runs inside? I don't know. She doesn't look overwhelmed or blissful; She looks kind of pissed off. Maybe she's not a morning person.

Driving away, I think of Z, I hope he's still in bed so I can crawl in next to him.

I put my left hand on my stomach. Braxton-hicks contractions makes me suck in a deep breath. My skin is so hard and tight. How is it possible that I'm not cracking open, like an over ripe tomato? Pulling up my shirt, I check my own flesh. My skin is so taunt and thin, there are blue veins crisscrossing my bloated belly and my once beautiful belly button is sticking out, like a gross flesh knob. I rub my stomach but avoid touching my own navel. Who would guess how stretchy skin can be? It's disgusting and wondrous.

There's a great big baby, arms and legs, head, back and butt, in my stomach. There are fingers and toes, ears and knees in there and I still have room to eat an entire Big Mac.

Heading home, I slow down as I approach the pasture with the cows. I love looking at them, especially when they are leaning against the fence, trying to eat something just out of their reach.

The bull, a massive black fellow, is doing a lot of posturing this morning and several gangly calves nuzzle their mothers for milk and attention.

God could be that fine black bull today, standing in the middle of the pasture, indomitable and unchallenged, with the damp grass against his legs. If I were God, I would like to be that bull for a little while, to have such an enormous and strong body, huge horns and a swishing tail, to be feared and loved by the cows, snorting around in the early morning sunlight. The bull stares at my car as I drive past.

We live on Park Avenue, in Hot Springs, Arkansas. It's the same street President Bill Clinton grew up on. Of course Clinton was born in Hope, Arkansas, a tiny town that grows a lot of watermelons, in the southern part of the state. But he and his mom moved to Hot Springs when he was in second grade. He stayed in Hot Springs until he graduated from High School. But the President and his press secretary and the press corps rarely talk about Hot Springs. This is not a good town for a President to call his home town because we have an infamous but colorful reputation. Since the mid-1800's Hot Springs has been known as a gambling hot bed. Though gambling was illegal, we had dozens of bars and casinos. All the giant Chicago mobsters hung out here, including Al Capone, Lucky Luciano and Onie Madden. Even while Clinton was growing up here, the Hot Springs economy was built around thermal baths and gambling.

Our house is actually eight miles outside the city limits in a rural, red neck community called Fountain Lake. I doubt Capone or Clinton ever made it out this far. Too many cows and not enough buxom, bright eyed women.

Our house sits at the top of a steep, dirt, driveway. A canopy of bushes and trees and yellow honey suckle have formed a tunnel over the drive.

I have a garden at the top of the driveway. I can inspect my tomatoes and pumpkin and strawberry plants as I park, but they are looking pretty scraggly now. Summer has roasted most of my plants and Fred has eaten the rest.

Zoltan bought this house and ten hilly, heavily wooded acres ten years ago. The hill the house is on is laced with quartz crystal. In the morning light, our land sparkles and shines.

Z has been 'fixing the entire homestead up' for years and someday it's going to be really lovely. But right now, it's a work in progress. The rooms are large but confusing. There's no flow because we have too much eclectic clutter, an old barber shop pole and my father's 1937 five-cent Coca Cola machine, beautiful Victorian chairs that don't match anything (especially our life style) and a massive three foot silver candelabra my grandmother bought in France. A steamer trunk his grandmother brought on a ship from Budapest to Ellis Island and our post card collection.

Inside and out, Zoltan has nearly a half dozen projects in progress. The bar, which separates the kitchen from the dining room is almost finished. The tile work around the beautiful Jacuzzi he installed is 95% complete. The shower we built with antique glass blocks is 75% finished and the backroom, with it's stone fire place and vaulted ceiling, still has naked sheet rock walls and a concrete floor. I use that room as my office. I'm sure we'll be done with everything in 6 or 7 years.

I have friends who think I'm insane. They shake their heads and say, 'Girl, you've got to get that man to finish those jobs." They are right. But bitching makes me miserable. And I am a lousy housekeeper, so nagging at Zoltan about his unfinished projects would be a little hypocritical.

Z works 50 to 70 hours a week. He gets one day a week off. When a man goes to work at 11:00 am and comes home at 11:00 p.m., it's tough to bitch. I don't want to wreck the little bit of free time he has. So he skips from job to job every time he has a day off.

In keeping with red neck tradition, Zoltan never throws anything away. There are two rusted out 1958 truck cabs on the hill behind the house. They've been here since long before Z. bought the property. He has a shed full of broken television sets, chair frames and wood scraps. I don't care as long as I can't see the stuff when I drive up to the house.

My "Zolton theory" is simple. Because, fifteen years ago, when he was just 25, he lost all his worldly possessions in the fire, everything from silverware and jewelry to the dog, dog house and posters, he now has to save everything, even if it's crap.

I sit in the car, looking at the house. The air is lovely this morning. I listen hard, hoping to hear the bull snorting. Fall is close. It will be hot by 10:00 a.m., but right now it's only 65 degrees and the world glistens with dew and promises.

Glancing at my own stomach, I say to my unborn child, "Hey, baby, just wait till you see this place. It shines in the morning."

Fred the goat is really mad at me now. I still haven't fed him.

He throws his black and white head up and down, barn yard indignation.

There are still three dogs I've never seen before hanging around. Where do they come from? How can they smell Bear, who's been inside for two days?

This business of being in heat is truly revolting.

"Baaaaaa',' Fred says again. He doesn't believe I will ever feed him. He walks to my car door and waits for me to get out. I'm worried. One of these dogs is going to get restless and bored and attack Fred. I scratch his black and white head. "Relax, I'll be right back."

Fred looks at me with his huge, unblinking eyes. He has long lashes and his eyes remind me of a computer, or a drawing of a snake's eye, unerringly one dimensional.

His skinny back bone is even with my hip. One of the stray dogs barks and Fred bolts. He runs in a giant circle, around the yard, then up the hill. Fred runs as though he is built of tinker toys. He's got long bones and fat joints so his gait is disjointed, but fast and happy. Fred bounds over Mike's bike, skids around the basket ball goal, then leaps on top of a stump. I can hear cartoon sound effects, 'Boing, boing boing.'

Suddenly, Fred stops. His legs buckle and starts bleating as though he's terrified to move. He sees something on the highway. I wait for him to stop but he is frozen. As I walk down the driveway the smell of something burning passes me in a breeze. A thin trail of gray smoke drifts into our bushes then turns black and noxious. Something is on fire between the highway and our yard. It occurs to me I should get Z and dial 911 but magnetic curiosity pulls me forward.

The sound of flames crackling assaults the morning air reaches me before I cross the cattle guard at the bottom of the driveway.

The image is so odd, it takes me a moment to understand what I'm looking at.

Our mail box is on fire.

From the bottom of the 4x4 post to the top of the curved metal box, there are orange and red flames. Even the open, barn-like, door and tiny metal flag are burning. Flames surge like hot waves from inside the mail box, rising two or three feet into the fresh day. My Time Magazine is curling up and burning, the glossy, four color photographs create psychedelic flames.

Fred is nearly screaming, so I throw a rock in his direction. He is startled out of his fear and runs away.

There aren't any cars on the highway, no strangers lurking in the bushes.

"Zolton." I'm yelling but he cant here me. At first, I try to jog up the driveway, but that's impossible, the baby won't allow such behavior, so I walk, as quickly as I can, to the house, without ever loosing sight of the mailbox\torch. My heart pounds furiously but my skin feels cool and numb.

Z is sitting on the couch in a pair of gym shorts. He is furry and dark, like a bear, especially in the morning. But he smiles and softly says "Hi." His voice is raspy from Marlboro's.

All I can muster is a choked whisper. "The mail box is on fire."

"The mail box is on fire?" he asks and blows into his coffee cup.

I shake my head up and down. My mouth is dry and tastes of charcoal. Slowly I find my volume, "Our mail box is on fire!"

Z looks at me with a funny expression then sees the rising smoke behind me. "Holy fuck," he mutters as he runs past me wearing nothing but his boxers.

The outside faucet makes squeaking sounds as Zolton cranks it open. Dragging the fat green hose across the yard, he looks like a nearly naked fireman. He doesn't run down the driveway, but crashes through the bushes and down the embankment instead. He hates fires.

The smoke changes in color almost instantly. He yells across the yard, "Everything is ok, you didn't call 911, did you?"

Numbly, I shake my head.

After ten minutes Zolton climbs back through the bushes dragging the hose.

Smiling, he says, "Well, the mailbox is toast, it's still standing but not for long. Are you ok?" He squeezes my hand and smiles. Droplets of water cling to his chest hairs and he smells of smoke.

"Yeah, I'm ok, but somebody intentionally set our mailbox on fire, honey. That's not good."

"Kids, teen-agers on the way to school. I did dumber things when I was in high-school."

A flaming mailbox doesn't seem like a high-school prank to me. It seems more like a message. It's not too different from a burning bush. Somebody is trying to tell me something. But I don't say this to Z this.

Z's boxers cling to his skin like Saran wrap and I have to touch the water on his chest to see if it's as cool as it looks. He catches my hand, kisses my fingers. "You're shaking."

"Our mail box was on fire."

"I know," he smiles. "But it's over. It was nothing, Liz. We're ok." When he pulls me close and rubs my arms I can feel the mounting tension in his body. He grinds just a little and his wet body cools me.

"You like all this, don't you?" I whisper into his ear.

"Fighting fires is pretty exciting. I bet there are a lot of satisfied firemen's wives out there."

"You know, I believe you've got testosterone poisoning," I pretend to feel his forehead for a fever. He just smiles until I raise one finger. "I'll be right back." Before I got pregnant "I'll be right back," meant I was going to get a condom or my diaphragm or a contraceptive film. Not anymore.

Now, because my bladder is the size of a pinto bean, I go to the bathroom, then stop in the kitchen and drink a glass of juice to get the burning taste off my tongue.

Today's paper is on the kitchen table. There are three large black and white photographs of those horrid white people screaming and spitting on the black students in Little Rock 40 years ago. I stop to study one of the pictures. I stare and my mother, B. Wallace, stares right back at me. It's absolutely her, I even recognize the dress, which was a light cotton, black and white checked shirtwaist. That dress was old when I was a child but she never gave it away. I touch the newspaper. Mom looks hot and angry and beautiful. In the picture, there is a state trooper standing next to Mom, looking disgusted and a short fat white woman yelling in her direction. But B.Wallace isn't paying any attention to her, she's looking up, at me. "Mom?" I whisper to the paper.

She keeps on staring at me. Finally I am able to look away from her eyes. She is holding a sign, but it doesn't say, "Children Are Children. It says "Do What's Right." What's that supposed to mean? Why is she carrying the wrong sign?

Why was I always told she carried a sign that said "Children are Children."

"Zolton, did you see the paper?"

I try to get to him quickly. "Did you see the paper? My mom's in the paper, look."

I toss the front page on the couch then sit down, "That's her, right there, look." I am mesmerized by her face. She's still looking right at me, her eyes startling clear. I can even make out her pupils and handsomely arched eyebrows. She's watching me, waiting for me to understand something simple.

"Unbelievable," Z studies the picture then flips the paper to read the story. "You'll have to cut this out. Forty years later and she's still making the front page."

"Isn't it odd that she's right there, looking at us? First the post it note, then the mail box and now this. She's subtle as a cow." He doesn't seem to catch the significance.

"Your Mom's dead, Honey. She hasn't been doing anything to you. Mothers can't bug you once they are dead, That's a rule." He smiles at me, trying to lighten things up. "It's a retrospective Liz, and it's great they picked this picture. But don't read so much into it."

Zoltan puts his feet in my lap and I rub the dark hair on his legs. "I guess I should go on and knock the mailbox down. I'll get a new one on the way to work."

I touch Z too often, his hands, his face, it doesn't matter, I just need to make sure he real and here. Many times I disguise my touches as hand holding or hugging but the truth is I'm feeling for his warmth and life. Even though most of the people I have love are dead, I still ache to feel their skin. My love goes out to invisible beings drifting above me. Daddy had huge hands and square fingertips, B. Wallace had thin cool fingers and Daniel always felt like summertime.

Just as I manage to coax all Z's legs to go in the same direction, he says, 'You've got to relax. I can call in today if you want. We can just hang out and watch bad T.V."

He's right. I close my eyes briefly and breath. Relax. Everything is fine. The baby and I are healthy, the kids are wonderful and I love this man with his feet in my lap. These are the things I must focus on.

"No, you go to work. I'm gonna need you even more in a week or so. And I've got to finish up with Hurlie." Z begins reading the paper until I interrupt.

"Bear's in heat and I'm worried about Fred out there with all those dogs. If we tie him up he's too easy to eat," I press the sole of his foot to my belly, so he can feel the baby kicking.

Z is a very large man. He's nearly 6'4 and weighs between 230 and 250 pounds. When we watch National Geographic specials about animals and the narrator says something like, "This handsome male weighs nearly 250 pounds," I always look at Z and compare the shape and distribution of muscle.

Z wiggles his toes at my belly.

The washing machine starts to agitate our dirty clothes. It makes a steady squeaking sound like people having sex on a bed with old springs.

There is a sudden clattering outside. Something bumps against the house. Fred suddenly appears in the window, a barnyard phantom. We have three feet of stone work on the side of the house. Our goat is walking on the narrow stone ledge and looking in the window. He presses his thick lips to the glass, trying to eat the African Violets he sees inside, on our window sill. His lips spread out, pink and shiny with spit.

I forgot to feed him again. Poor Fred.

"Hey, Goat Boy, how you doing?" Zoltan yells. Fred presses his funny lips against the window in response. Z says to me, "Granny called."

"Oh yeah?"

"She wants to have lunch, Lizard."

"I love it when you call me by my reptilian name. But tell me she doesn't want to have lunch today."

"'Fraid so. She needs water and has something to tell you. Are you up to it? I'll call her back and tell her you're too tired if you want." He rubs my arm with his foot.

Closing my eyes, I stick my lip out in a minor league pout. I love his grandmother but already know what the dreaded topic of conversation will be. "I'm just afraid if she starts pushing again about a wedding, I'll blow up. She's already got me making decisions I don't want to make. She wants me to have a wedding when I don't want it, in a dress I don't want to wear. My God, the only thing at this shameful little ceremony, that I want is you, the rest of it is absolutely what I don't want."

"I know. It's ok if you get mad at her. She wouldn't understand anyway." He smiles sadly and sits up to push my hair out of my face. "Your make-up is all runny." We both stare at Fred. "It'll be O.K."

"'That's just it, I want something better than O.K. The reluctant bride and groom deserve more than O.K. It's like we're in a time-warp. We're lined up for some prearranged marriage with both of us digging our heels in and everybody else is waiting at the church. God, I wish we could have something both of us wants."

"I'm not digging my heels in. I want you and I want the baby and I want to get married. And I want to be married to you for the rest of my life. I want to be with you until I take my last fucking breath. I love you, so marry me."

My blood is too thin now and races through my body. There are waterfalls of blood splashing into my heart. Closing my eyes, I whisper, "Please don't do this. Please Zolton. I don't know how I can get you to understand. I love you, I love everything about you and you're asking for the one thing, the only thing on the planet, that I can't give to you. Why can't you just walk away from it? Don't ask me to get married. Ask for anything else and I swear I'll give it to you."

I touch his hair and his beard. He does not pull away. I can keep on breathing. He leans his face into my palm and looks right into my eyes. 'That's the third time I've asked."

"Second. The first time can't count, we'd only known each other three months and you were drunk."

"I wouldn't have asked unless I meant it."

"Why do we have to do this now?"

"You're being a bitch, you know that, don't you? We should get married because we love each other, you're very pregnant and it's time. And I'm not asking again. It hurts too much getting shot down. You let me know when you're ready."

He's serious now. Maybe I've gone too far. I've almost said things to him that I will never be able to take back and Zoltan, when pushed too far, can be unforgiving.

When he is really wounded and angry there is an ancient blackness in his eyes.

"I love you but everybody is blackmailing us, Z. That's not why we should get married."

"I don't care about that. And Granny doesn't have anything to do with the fact that I just asked you to marry me and you said no."

I'm causing this man that I love pain. He wants a nice wedding, out doors with all our friends. He wants to put together a reception that will last for hours and everyone will eat and drink too much. But I don't trust marriage, as an institution. It certainty doesn't keep anybody together.

I say, "We are perfect right now, as we are, Zolton. Why do we have to change?" He's having to pay for my screwed up emotional baggage. If I was a normal person, a right or righteous person, I wouldn't do this to the man I love.

"Besides," I continue, starting to cry, "we don't have the money right now. We need to buy baby stuff and pay doctors, not buy wedding rings."

I'm trying to make pitiful excuses and my words sound as though they are coming from a cave. A steady torrent of tears roll down my cheeks. God I hate all this. Everything is so hard. Looking up, I ask "Can we be done talking about this right now?"

"I'm done until you say otherwise." He kisses me on the forehead. Then spins the gold band on my right hand middle finger. It's my Mom's wedding ring, so soft and old, it's worn down and nearly as thin as a rubber band.

A spider web like thought spins across the back of my brain. It's nearly invisible but it's there, and growing. Maybe Mom is trying to tell me that getting married would be a bad thing. Maybe she knows something bad will happen if we marry, and she's trying to protect me. That's what all this is about.

A funny taste rises in the back of my throat, as though I've been sucking on a penny. I don't want to be haunted, I don't want my mother to interfere with my life, but how can I ignore her? If she is trying to reach me, if she's going to all this trouble to get my attention, she must have something important to tell me. My mother was not the sort of woman who would casually venture back from the dead, just to see what's going on. My father, Michael Justice, would want to test his power. He would want to stretch the limits of death. But mom left this planet on purpose. Her suicide was strategic and intentional. Only something really horrendous could bring her back. This is all about protection.

Studying Z's profile, his beard and ear, the corner of his eye, I push back the idea that something might happen to him if we get married.

Holding hands, Z and I are quiet. Fighting is exhausting, for both of us. And when we finish the fight, I always wonder where to go next. What topic can we approach? If one of us gets up, leaves the couch, the other will be left, alone, so we sit together, silent and tired, but together.

Finally, I try to perk up my voice. I bury all thoughts of B. Wallace for my sanity's sake. "I bought a new bra yesterday."

He smiles a little, knowing exactly what I'm doing. "Can I see?"

Unbuttoning my top two buttons, I flash him. This bra is one full size larger than the last, but it's a soft and shiny shade of pink.

"Oh boy," he says and starts working on the third button. His fingers are so beautiful, the thought of loosing him sends a zinging feeling through the back of my skull. I play with one of his long dark curls. It forms a perfect ringlet. "they say, firemen are horny all the time."

He nuzzles until I pull away "Are you seriously interested in having sex? Right now, with me?"

"Always. Some sort of sex, anyway."

"I don't know if that's revolting or beautiful. Look at me, I'm huge. You can't possibly find this sexy. You can't look at me and think about sex."

"It's something different. I just want to feel you and you're beautiful all the time and especially now, because you're all worked up and your face is sort of red." Zoltan rubs my breast with the back of his hand. I am touched and look further into his brown eyes. I see the earth and I see a man who's not afraid of anything. He'll still love me, he'll still think I'm beautiful, when I'm 80, even if I don't get a nose job or liposuction or a face lift. What a remarkable sort of love.

He begins unbuttoning my shirt again, "Besides," he says, "there are still a couple of angles left where you don't look that pregnant."

"Fred is watching. Isn't that kind of kinky having a goat watch?" I say.

"Good for you Fred."

As he moves on me and through me, I want to give him everything. I want to be as much as I can, for him. And in return he gives me his world.

His beard is soft on my skin and I smile into his hair. My tears dry, leaving nothing but a little salt.

Chapter 3

10:00 a.m. Zoltan puts on his starched chef's jacket and hounds tooth pants. They remind me of Mom's dress in the newspaper photograph. I study the picture again, her stern and beautiful expression and the sign, "Do What's Right." At some point we are all supposed to know what is right.

In order to quiet my thoughts, I lower myself to the kitchen floor with the vacuum cleaner hose and a toothbrush. For twenty minutes I work on the A.C. filter. Scrub and suck, scrub and suck. This is not my nesting instinct. Fall is the only time I ever want to clean. Tiny dirty details pull me and I can't get anything else done until I've erased the dirt and dust. I do this because Fall will force us to close all the doors and windows soon. We'll be sealed into our home for six months with the same dirt and musty air.

When the A.C. grate is nearly pristine, I get on my hands and knees then use the vacuum cleaner like a cane to I push myself upright.

The phone rings. Breathlessly, I answer, "Hello."

"Hey Good Girl. You ready to work?" It's Hurlie, my employer.

"I'm on it, Old Man."

Hurlie snorts, "I'm old, but I could give it to you better than you've ever had."

"You're old and disgusting. And I'll be happy to retire."

"Yeah, well, we gotta talk about that later, I still think you're making a mistake" he coughs then asks, "Anything new going on in your neighborhood?" He's sucking on something like a toothpick or straw. Dogs bark wildly in the background. Hurlie grunts, then there is yipping and whining. He must have thrown something at them.

"Nothing new, not really anyway. Just swollen ankles." I would never tell him about my mother or the mailbox. He would perceive it all as weakness and a lack of concentration. .

"Nothing, huh?" he sounds strange today, almost thoughtful or at least reticent. Maybe the idea of losing me is bothering him more than

I thought it would. Finally he says, "So, what did you get this week?" Because Hurlie is terminally paranoid, he always asks me for my final figure first.

"We're up $2,500, I'll bring you $1750."

He drops his receiver suddenly and hurts my ear. He's shouting at his dogs to shut-up. When he comes back he panting a little. "Seven fifty for a weeks work. That's pretty good money, don't you think? You're gonna miss the money, you know. You gonna need it to feed that new kid of yours."

"We'll be ok, Hurlie, we have some money saved up."

"Yeah, but you're not a girl who can sit around and bake damn pies. And you don't wanna put too much pressure on your old man, making him work all the fucking time."

"Listen, don't start grinding on me, Hurlie. I've got too much to do today, including getting your money picked up, so lay off." I'm trying not to get angry. "We'll be ok. I've got a plan."

"A plan huh? It don't have nothing to do with a anonymous crime stoppers does it? No man or woman gonna put me away. You know that, don't you Good Girl?"

"Gimme a break Hurlie, Jesus Christ. What do you think I am, stupid."

"You know what they say about shit," he says.

"What do they say, Hurlie?" I might as well humor him.

"It happens."

"Shit happens, that's the best you can come up with? Nothing is going to happen to us. Z and I have everything under control."

He makes a noncommittal sound, "You never know, Good Girl, you just never fucking know what's gonna happen. You're whole world could catch on fire and blow up tomorrow. Then you'll be needing me and my money."

I change my position. What is he trying to say?

"Hurlie, do we have a problem?" I do not have time to play his games. Because of the baby, Hurlie is drifting out of my realm of focus. If there is something I need to do for him, he needs to speak up now.

"We've never had a problem, Lizzy, have we? What makes you think we got one now?" He laughs and coughs, then his voice changes.

"But things change, don't they? You never know what the fuck is gonna happen next, so you gotta take care of business. My business. "

"That's not a threat is it, boss?" My throat is dry and the baby's wiggles make me miserable.

Hurlie's tone is diving. He sounded like this a year ago when he virtually locked me in the office of one of his clubs for an hour and a half. He ranted and railed about some scummy player who tried to get him busted. The police had Hurlie on tape accepting bets and on video delivering cash. The only thing that saved the old man from going back to prison was his legendary web of connections. Hurlie has so many city and state officials on tape, humping around with his girls and anyone of them will swear they've been seeing a judge or cop just to cause trouble. Hurlie also has somebody reasonably important on his payroll in nearly every county. Last year, when they did get him on tape, Hurlie, told me it cost him nearly 100,000 thousand dollars to make the evidence disappear.

Oddly enough, six months after the same stupid player tried to get Hurlie busted, he was killed while working in a liquor store in Kansas City. It looked like a pretty simple robbery except for the fact that the guys testicles had been cut off and shoved in his mouth.

Hurlie Webb has been to prison once, years ago, and he's irrationally paranoid about getting set up and being sent back. Arkansas State Penitentiaries are notoriously unpleasant places.

"I don't know what the hell you want to call it Lizzy. I'm just saying things can change, your old man could loose his job tomorrow, hell he could have a wreck and not be able to work. Anything can happen. That's all I'm saying. You call it what you want. Now go pick up my money and think about what I'm sayin' You call me you have any trouble. You know all you need to know to take care. And don't forget to drink a lot of that cranberry juice. It's good for your kidneys. One of the girls at the club told me to tell you that."

"I'll talk to you later Hurlie." I hang up, then slowly waddle into my office. What's going on his creepy head? He's getting too bizarre, even for me. But I think, I pray he's just venting. I've never felt really threatened by Hurlie, though he gripes and bitches constantly. But I've worked with the man, I've lived in his dank world long enough, to know if he is threatening, I have a very real problem.

Hurlie has never been slow to follow up on a threat. God knows, I don't want a fight with Hurlie, it would be a loosing proposition no matter what. Over the years I've seen him do god-awful things to people who got in his face at one of his clubs.

Once Hurlie gets mad, he's incapable of reining in his anger. If a woman slaps him, he will punch her. If a man is thrown out of his club, he'll probably be beaten in the parking lot, often times by Hurlie himself.

Since I've know him he's had a wicked limp, like a peg-leg pirate, and when he gets pissed off and violent that bad leg moves so quickly like some merciless hatchet.

I've tried to explain Hurlie to Zolton before but they are such different men that there is no understanding. Hurlie is a wolverine ripping apart a carcass. He literally does not have the ability to stop himself, until someone drags the body out of his sight. Even when a man is down on his knees in the club's parking lot, spitting up blood, and gasping for air, Hurlie will always kick him one more time, in the face and ribs, just to see the body rise and jerk.

The baby kicks, a flurry of heels inside my stomach. It's hard to think about Hurlie and my precious new child at the same time. Hurlie and the baby in the same thought make me nauseous. Purity and filth, heaven and hell, fresh milk and cigarette butts.

These feelings about Hurlie are one of the reasons I'm quitting my job, despite the money. For the first year of the baby's life I must be there and focused, emotionally, physically and spiritually, 24 hours a day. It's part of my maternal predisposition. For a year after giving a birth, I raise my wings and shut out the rest of the world, except for family. It takes me a year to memorize every cell and pore, toenail and hair. For a year I'll have very little interest in anyone other than the baby, Felicity and Mike, Zolton and Eva on good days.

I don't know if this tendency is right or wrong, I don't care. It's simply how I have children. And I can not have Hurlie and his players interfering. They are inconsequential. I haven't tried explaining any of this to Hurlie, I don't care if he understands or likes my reasons for quitting.

The baby flutters again and I sing a little of my grandmother Marva's old lullaby. "Oh mother how pretty the moon is tonight. 'Twas never so cunning before." My voice cracks and is too deep in the morning.

The baby likes my song.

In my office, I look through some notes. Like a member of middle management, I'm a little bored. There's a big window right in front of my desk. Two squirrels chase each other up and down a skinny pine tree. Everything out there is light brown, the color of dried mud. I could watch the squirrels all day. I'd love to be a squirrel, or maybe an otter.

I make two lists on a legal pad. After sorting through sheets with old figures and names I've already taken care of, I throw them into the fire place.

I've got almost $4,000 to collect and just $1500 to pay out. My heart picks up a little. I do like thinking about my cut which is 30% of the $2500 dollar difference.. I don't really have to be a bookie. I've got a Masters in Anthropology from The University of Georgia. If I wanted to, I could go to work as a High School teacher or accept a position at the local Community College. But teachers in Arkansas are woefully underpaid. Starting salary of a full time Arkansas High School instructor is about $22,000 dollars. If they needed me at the Community College I'd make about 28,000. Maybe I'd make it to 30,000 after eight years and I'd have to have my children in day care every week. It's pretty sad.

My average yearly income with Hurlie is $39,438 dollars. I work roughly 20 hours a week and I've never had the children in day care. I've never missed a school play, I'm almost always available for field trips. I'm good at what I do.

One of my legal pad lists has this week's bets and the other is the late list with just one name. He shouldn't be much trouble. Jackson is an attorney for a local spring water company. He owes $550. He thought he had a hot tip and put a nickel down on Kansas City two weeks ago. He's been ducking me ever since. But that's typical. He's a regular bettor who whines when he loses and shoots off his mouth when he wins.

He's good for the money, eventually. Jackson just thinks this is all part of the game and he figures, since I'm a woman, it's ok to jerk me around, especially when he owes me money.

He'd bleat like Fred if I slow-played him after a winning weekend. But Jackson loses so often, I don't mind playing his game. Besides, this is the last time I'll have to deal with him.

In the end, he knows he has to pay and Hurlie always come out ahead.

I need to handle Jackson today, though. It can't go on any longer. There are options. I can hound him with a semi-threatening tone till he ponies up the cash. If I arrive at his office, nine months pregnant, and looking a little desperate, secretaries will talk. Jackson knows this. So, I won't have to do it. I dial his number and hold my breath while the phone rings. It's his voice mail. I leave a message using my sweetest purr. " Hi Jackson, it's Liz. I know how busy you are so I'll stop by your office after lunch. If you're not gonna be there just leave an envelope with you secretary. Thanks."

In less than five minutes the phone rings.

It's him. "Hey Kiddo, how ya doing?" he asks using his black velvet lawyer tone.

"Magnificent. How are you?"

"Same as always, busy as a one armed paper hanger in an ass kicking contest."

We both laugh at his joke.

"I don't want you going out of your way, Liz " he says. I drum my pencil on the desk top. "I'll leave the money with the bartender at The Jazz House this afternoon, wouldn't that be easier for you?"

"You don't want me going out of my way?" I try to sound sarcastic.

"Yeah, I worry about you, working so hard and being so pregnant. You don't let Hurlie push you too hard do you?"

"You worry about me?" I repeat, using my cool and distant business voice. I punch some numbers on my adding machine for effect. "Hurlie's not the one who pushes me."

"So when's the baby due?" He's nervous now, concerned that I'm pissed off and won't let him bet any more or that I'm not passing his name on. He's wondering about who's going to take his action when I'm gone. Shopping around for a good bookie can be tough. And by the time he finds one he can trust, the season will be over.

"The baby is due today; but I'll stop by the bar before going into labor."

He laughs too much. "Perfect, I appreciate it Liz, I really do." He sounds well educated and pitiful, all at the same time.

After adding the Jazz House to my list, I consider my stops. It's an odd array, but I like picking up cash after a good week.

The final stop in my booking career will be tomorrow or the next day. I'll go by Hurlie's trailer and give him his money. Then I'll be done. He can deal with the Jacksons of the world. But how can I reassure him, so he doesn't worry about me rolling over.

I try to think like Hurlie.

It's not good. If I were Hurlie I'd rather not have anybody floating around town that knows too much. Somebody with all his information is an obvious threat even if he's trusted them in the past. Hurlie is an instinctive man. Trust in another person is not part of his emotional or intellectual person. He'll feel better if he has something on me, that's why he's threatening me.

In a perfect Hurlie world...I'd still be working for him... or I'd disappear.

After all these years it doesn't matter how much money has passed between us, he doesn't trust me, he doesn't trust anyone. So I can't trust him.

Looking at my legal pads, I try to refocus.

Hurlie and I have been winning for almost a month now, so I don't have to subtract anything from my take. Last week I made $914 and the week before that $1186. It's been a good run.

Last month I went three weeks without getting paid because all my bettors were winning. That can be demoralizing. If Hurlie looses money, I don't get paid, he just gives me the money to pay my guys off. Then, we have to win back the amount he looses before I'm in the black and taking a percentage.

The reason Hurlie makes me pay off within 48 hours actually make sense and it's a matter of pride. We have to set the example and standard. If we pay quickly, we can expect to be paid in a timely fashion. It's also a matter of pride. He wants people to know he pays faster than any other bookie in the state because he's got so much fucking money, more than any other numbers man around. That's the message he's sending when he pays off $15,000 dollars cash, in thirty minutes. Hurlie, always wants bragging rights.

After forty five minutes of fooling with numbers, I open the door so I can see Zoltan sitting in the living room, on the orange couch. I wish I wasn't pregnant so I could take off my clothes, walk down to the couch and climb on top of him. I desperately want to feel him, to inherit his warmth. To hold him inside of me until he goes even harder, until his entire body flexes, his fingers hold on, as though searching for my bones and then he releases, and looks into me with eyes the color of thyme.

But I can't do that now, it's too late in the morning and I'm too far along. I have to wait.....for weeks or months. It's ridiculous and unfair. Pregnancy makes me horny but how desirable is an extremely pregnant woman?

I try to think of something else. I push the word penis out of my mind.

I think hard, then focus on the couch. I hate our couch. It's so wretched-retro ugly. One afternoon Z and I left the house with $500 to buy a new couch and we ended up spending it on a cam-corder.

Maybe I should get up right now, find that cam-corder and film Zolton's broad back, and dark hair on our ugly orange couch. His black ribbons of hair swirl out from under his base ball cap and down the back of his white coat. He's reading a cook book, studying something very intently, with an unlit cigarette in his left hand. Without looking away from his book, he takes a lighter out of his coat pocket. He flicks it, but stops just before touching the flame to the cigarette. He's still holding the lighter, the flame does not waiver, finally he leans forward, I hear him say, "God damn it," as he lights a scented candle on the coffee table instead of his cigarette.

I love him. I love his back and his hair and his concentration. He's trying so hard not to smoke around me.

I need to stop looking at Z and get back to work. I need to finish my numbers.

This is the first job at which I've excelled, and now I have to give it up. I never intended to be a bookie, but it pays well and fits in with my schedule. My first year I only handled the football cards and took 15% of the winnings. Then we dropped the cards, too much paper work, and I started taking straight bets, teases and parlays. Hurlie gave me 20% of our winnings and last year he bumped me to 30%.

Z stands up, puts his books back on the shelf, then walks over and stares at my stomach. "Are you ok?" Is he talking to me or the baby? I answer for both of us.

"We're fine. What were you reading about?"

"Artichokes and portabellos."

"What about them?"

"Well, Marilyn Monroe was the first Queen of the Artichoke Festival and tonight I'm serving crab stuffed portabellos with an Escoffier sauce."

"My God, that sounds good. The kids and I will be dining on something like macaroni and cheese this evening."

"I'm sorry. I'll bring you a plate." He smiles and there is peace in the room.

When the phone rings I'm not sure I want to pick it up.

An older woman with a fine accent says, "Liz McDade please."

Zolton kisses me on the head and whispers, "see ya," then adds, "Megeszem a kis szivedet," and cracks open a can of beer.

I cover the phone with my hand. "What did that mean?"

"I eat your little heart."

I smile at him, "Have a filet day."

Breathing, I try to take in enough air for me and the baby. Z hesitates before leaving, looks at me and smiles. He's thinking I'm beautiful, it's all over his face. How can that be? Then, as he walks out the door, he turns the lock on the knob so I will be safe while he's out.

This tiny gesture moves me.

I take one last breath of that man so I will have him inside me all day long.

There is a buzzing inside the phone. I concentrate. Something is wrong. The phone is making odd droning noises, then in the middle of all the static, I hear someone, a woman, say, "Don't do it, please" The tone is light but serious, a gentle warning.

"Hello. Don't do what?" I say loudly into the phone. Goose bumps crawl up my arm and I shudder.

Suddenly the line is clear. "Liz? It's Helen Houston. I'm sorry, I had to put the phone down for a moment. Were you waiting long?"

"Helen, how are you? I thought I heard somebody else say something."

"No no, dear, there's no one else here and I just picked the phone back up. There must have been trouble on your end." She dismisses me, but I know I heard somebody.

Helen Houston was an old friend of my mother's. At the age of 70 she's still one of Arkansas' wealthiest, most elegant women. Mrs. Houston might be the last great example of creative Southern aristocracy. Her thick hair is still very dark, almost black and always beautifully coifed. She frequently wears red and has in inexhaustible collection of lush cashmere capes, that flow behind her like flaming wings. When Helen walks into a room, it is filled.

This striking and enormously wealthy woman, is a sculptor. She works in bronze and creates heavy, decidedly masculine, abstracts that do not fit her stylish and lofty manner.

"Liz?"

"Helen, it's so nice to hear from you."

"'It's been so long since we last spoke. I should have called months ago. How have you been and how are those precious children of yours?"

"They're just perfect and glad to be back in school," I say.

"Oh, they all get so bored by the end of the summer, don't they, dear? I thought my grandchildren were going to drive me out of my mind by the end of August and I love them with all my heart. They are such rascals. I have sixteen grandchildren, now. Catherine, who married my Richard, had twins! Lord, she gained 60 pounds and the twins only weighed four pounds each. She's shaped just like a summer squash, the poor girl. Can you imagine?"

We both laugh and carry on for a few minutes and then Helen is ready to really talk.

"Liz, I'm calling about your mother."

I resist the urge to say, 'she's still dead.'

"You're calling about Mom?"

"I still miss her so."

"Yes ma'am. So do I."

"B. Wallace was a brilliant woman. Hot Springs didn't know what a brilliant woman could do until your mother came of age. She taught the men in this town a thing or two. Hell, she taught us all a thing or two."

I have to swallow hard. Mom would like hearing Helen say these things. "I miss her everyday, Helen."

"Oh, I'm sure you do. And that's why I'm calling. I have a wonderful surprise for you. I've been so concerned that she doesn't have a marker of any sort. Or, if she does, I'm not aware of it."

"I'd never try to hide Mom from you, Helen. You're right she doesn't have a..." I hesitate. "She doesn't have a tomb stone or anything like that. You know we cremated her."

"Yes. I knew that. But we all thought perhaps you would like to have a testament to her influence, here, in town."

"I have her here, with me," I say.

"I see. Well, that's good. But are you going to keep her her, always?"

"Well, she seems comfortable enough," I quip.

"Yes, I understand, but haven't you considered putting her someplace permanently?"

God, I love Helen Houston. She's rich enough to be blunt. If she weren't rich she'd be rude.

"I like her here, Helen."

"Oh, I see, you have a nice urn." I'm not sure if it's a question or a statement. I decide to keep my mouth shut. There's no reason to tell her the absolute truth. I glance up at the small cardboard box sitting on top of my father's 1938 Coke machine. That's where my mother is. There are a couple of pounds of ashes in a plastic bag in that simple white cardboard box.

That's how the funeral home gave her to me and I've never gotten around to buying an urn. They're so expensive and none seemed to match my mother's personality. I shopped around, looked at dozens of styles that weren't right. Now, I kind of like having her in the box, she seems so accessible.

I don't think Zoltan knows she's up there. But I do. I look at the box all the time; sometimes I even talk to her a little. I can always ask the box. But she never answers. It's like thinking out loud when someone is in the room but doesn't answer. But I can't actually open the box because the ashes weird me out. They are a lot chunkier than you'd expect.

"An urn is fine," Helen says. "But we all miss her. So, last year

Louise and Jill and I got together. We hired Raymond Hewet to design a monument, a fountain really that's to be constructed outside The Community Center, in her honor. We'd like to put her ashes there and then she'll have a place. It's a lovely design, but of course your input is vital. We'll have a reception and it would be so sweet if you would say a few words. We're planning on starting construction in two weeks."

"Construction?" I am stunned, flattered and outraged.

"Oh, that's too big a word really, it's nothing so large as to be embarrassing. Raymond's design is very simple and quite handsome. I think Betty and your father would like it. Your mother started The Center, and so many other things, as you know. It's a wonder. She deserves some sort of recognition."

"A plaque would be fine Helen, really or a donation to The Art Center, that would be good."

She laughs, a deep and throaty sound. "I'm sending a courier over with the plans this weekend. Don't say anything until you look at them. Then let us know what you think. It's not too late to make a few changes."

"Helen. Honestly, I'm touched, I'm just not sure."

She stops me and says, "Liz, don't say another word. Just take a look at the drawings and then call me. We can have lunch early next week. I know how busy you are with the children."

Numbly, I nod into the phone. "Thank you Helen."

Hanging up, I crash like a cinder block back into my chair. I'm under assault. Everybody has ideas, really helpful pain-in-the-ass ideas. "Zolton!" I yell, hoping he hasn't left. I think back. Yes, he kissed me while I was on the phone. The house is unnervingly still.

I look at Mom's box. She could have played Katherine Hepburn in A Lion In Winter and Betty Davis in All About Eve. Fierce, brilliant and mean sometimes. A beautiful and tough woman playing a man's game in a man's world.

"Well Mom," I say to the box. "Now I understand what you're doing, sort of.." The box doesn't respond. "Ok, Would you mind telling me how serious your threats were? Do the right thing, I get it." Tears are streaming down my face but I don't remember when they started. Why does Mom have to work me now? The baby rolls.

I wait, but she still doesn't answer and I guess I'm glad for that. As much as I miss Mom, I don't really want to hear from her.

After my mother's stunning and dramatic suicide, I heard a lot of theories about people who kill themselves. Apparently, because suicide victims die in such unhappy and unsettled ways, sometimes they come back to haunt. Many 'experts' feel suicide victims (victim is not the right word for my mom) have a hard time going on to the next life because their exits are so angry or sad and they leave so much unfinished and unpleasant business behind.

According to Florida State Law I even had to tell the people who bought Mom's Boca Raton condominium that she had killed herself on the porch. That way, if she came back to haunt the apartment, they could back out of the real estate deal. It seemed like the real estate commission was expecting her.

But I don't think B. Wallace wanted to come back. She was so happy to go, so ready to leave this world and life, that she would never hang around, unless...

Shaking my head, I try to convince myself that I'm being hormonal and absurd. Mom went to such great lengths to kill herself. But she did warn me, she always told me there was one thing she'd come back for.

And now, Helen Houston is investing herself and her fortune in Mom's memory. Helen doesn't know what my mother's note said. She doesn't know I swore I would never bury her in Arkansas. She doesn't know that's the one thing Mom said she would come back to stop. Maybe I should show Helen the yellow post-it suicide note I found on her bathroom mirror that says, "My darling, please don't forget on Wednesday, June 2nd 1991 you made me a promise. So remember, if my dead body ever touches Arkansas dirt again, I swear to you Sweet Heart, I'll haunt you for the rest of your lovely life. Throw me in the ocean, keep me in the freezer, but don't you bury me in Arkansas. Love, Mom" She sounded like Brier Rabbit. Her handwriting was sloppy and shaky, her drunk script. But she was absolutely right about the date and the promise.

Mom was always good with contracts and details.

Pressing both hands against my stomach, I wait to feel the baby move. I'll never leave my babies. I'll never threaten to haunt them if they don't follow my orders. Mom told me she was going to kill herself. She dropped hints, some subtle as tornadoes, some just a tone or note she hit after two or three or nine cocktails. Her hints were very matter of fact. She wanted to protect me from horrible shock of suicide. And she wanted me to understand I hadn't failed her and she wasn't trying to get away from me. She simply couldn't stand life without Daddy and my brother, Daniel, anymore. And she couldn't live with the bitterness and hatred she constantly hauled around like a 20 pound sack of onions. Mom had lung cancer and emphysema too, but they wouldn't have dragged her down for another five years. If she stuck around she could have seen Mike and Felicity learn to count, go to school and ride their bikes.

I forced Mom into a rehab program. I dragged her to therapy, but in the end, she did exactly what she wanted to do.

She cheerfully killed herself because she loved me and Daniel and Daddy and because she was still so pissed off at God and her lumbering racist home state.

On a fine South Florida evening, she put a gun in her 60 year old mouth, pulled the trigger and abandoned me.

I knew she would do it.

Still, when the Boca Raton police called and said, "You're mother is dead from a gun shot wound," I dropped the telephone and crumbled to the kitchen floor.

I picked the phone back up with grotesque hope, "She was murdered?" I asked.

"No ma'am. We're pretty sure it was self inflicted."

The moment I understood she had gone on, without me, I wanted to call her. I wanted to dial her number (305) 395-0080, as I had that morning, and report the days events to her and discuss the repercussions. I missed my mother with every cell and blood vessel and artery. For a time, every drop of blood that reached my heart was lonely.

Breathing was no longer an automatic. I had to consciously tell my body to suck in some air. I wanted to be dead with Mom, just so I could see her one last time.

395-0080. I loved that number. It gave me peace and became my mantra. At traffic lights I would recite it over and over and over again. During the week following her death, I dialed it a hundred, a thousand a million times. Muscle memory took over, so I could dial 395-0080 without looking, without thinking. My fingers were a blur when I was trying to reach my mother.

I'd sit and dial over and over. Some time's I'd push it manually, sometimes I'd hit radial 20 or 30 times in a row. I'd let the phone ring and ring and ring. Such an empty and endless sound when you know there's no one home. As it rang, I would imagine each empty room in her condo. I would walk from room to room, looking at the impression she'd left in her favorite chair after years of sitting, the lush and faded orange carpet, the lovely cream colored linen sofa, her ashtrays and perennial copy of John Brown's Body and The Master Builder. I'd imagine the two or three lipstick stained cigarette butts in the crystal ashtrays. I could see the little bit of Florida dust on top of her sculptures.

I would sit, with Mike, my beautiful sleeping son, who was only 3, on my lap, listening to the ringing, waiting for her to answer the God damned mother fucking telephone one more time. "Come on Mom, pick up. Just one more time."

And now, Helen wants to bring all this back to life. Unknowingly, she's about to summon my mother's ghost.

Or maybe it's too late. Maybe Mom is already here.

"Listen B. Wallace, I love you but please don't do this to me, not now. I've got to stay sane and strong." I stare at the box, wondering what it is I'm supposed to do? What does she want, what was it she wanted that I could never give her?

Mom's ashes and I are alone in the house. It's just us. Finally, I clear my voice and take a breath. My hand is shaking so hard that my fingers beat out a rhythm on the desk. I swallow and something hard enters my blood.

For a moment, I am stronger than she is. My mind sets. Slowly, I lock my hands together in my lap to stop the shaking and say, "There's one thing you have to understand. You have to, leave Felicity and Mike alone. Don't touch my babies or I'll wrap you up in a Confederate flag and bury you under the God-damn Arkansas state capital."

Thinking about Mom and her ashes, her death and gun shot wound, the bullet entry and exit, thinking about the way ice clinked against the edge of her glass, the way she tried to laugh but always ended up coughing into a Kleenex, can't be so good for me or the baby. So, I force myself to stand up and start cleaning.

First, I scrub the tub and bathroom sinks. While in the bathroom, I do my best to avoid looking in the mirrors. Every time I do, I am startled by my size and shape. Even after all these months and all this weight, I do not expect to see a woman with my face and a body the size of a refrigerator. Even the amount of fabric required to cover me is a surprise. There are not bits and pieces of a pattern but the entire swath. So, I don't look into the mirror, I lower my head and keep cleaning. I sweep and mop the kitchen floor.

The air in the house is disturbed. There is a feeling here that does not belong. I am tempted to look over my shoulder three times because I can feel somebody standing so close to me, but I will not give her the satisfaction. Not today. I vacuum with tornado fury, and feel vindicated as pennies, legos (which I usually avoid because the tiny plastic building blocks are so expensive), pen caps, rocks, dust bunnies and hair bands, disappear under my mighty Dirt Devil. The racket blocks out every sound in the house. I can not hear the telephone, the radio, the air conditioner.

After an hour, I get a cramp, low down on my right side, so I sit on the couch and rest with my feet on the lobster trap coffee table. Now, I'm ready for a shot of nasal spray and a two hour nap. My nose is all stopped up and I'm so sleepy. Maybe it's the baby that's tired. I put my hand on my belly and close my eyes.

If I could breath, I'd be able to smell my pine fresh house. This cleaning business is very unusual for me. I'm usually a pretty messy person. When I was pregnant with Mike and Felicity, there was a joke that I put the cap on the tooth paste and that was the extent of my nesting instinct.

My eyelids feel weighted, but I don't think I want to be alone, in the house anymore today. Besides, if I let myself take a nap now, I'll blow all my appointments. I want to drink a cup of coffee just to wake up, but I've already consumed today's quota.

I shuffle to the kitchen, fix a glass of ice water in a giant plastic Michael Jordan slushy cup. After drinking half, I take my shirt off and stand in the kitchen with my giant stretchy shorts, ugly bra and massive protruding white belly. I don't look anything like Demi Moore when she was pregnant. After a couple more sips, I lean my head back and pour a good bit of the freezing water down my neck. God damn it's cold. I suck in and dance backwards as the water rolls, like a Montana mountain stream, between my breasts and across my stomach.

Chapter 4

10:57 a.m. It's not even noon, how is that possible. The digital car clock insists I take note of every single passing minute. How is it I've already packed several days into this one morning? Driving into town, I have a sense of purpose. My shirt is still sticking to my damp stomach, but that's not such a bad thing. Sometimes, I have to surprise myself. I have to do something stupid and MTV like so I don't get bored living in my pregnant skin.

My brain hums, full of thoughts and ideas, emotions and love. History and present, fiction and fact flow like a river fed by many tiny streams. Now that I'm out on the road, I'm not frightened.

I turn on the radio. Marvin Gaye sings "Heard it Through the Grape Vine." I saw a documentary on Marvin Gaye a while back. Barry Gordy and the Motown machine made Marvin sing too high back in the 60s and 70s. It almost wrecked his voice. In the 80s he dropped a couple of octaves with hits like "Sexual Healing."

The air-conditioning blows on my neck. Zolton kissed the same spot this morning. I touch it with my finger tips. When Z cooks and it's unbearably hot in the kitchen, sometimes over 120 degrees, he'll dip a towel in ice water, then wrap it around his neck. The chef theory is, the blood, which is close to the surface of your neck, is cooled as it is pumped up to you brain. I can almost believe this. Zolton first decided he wanted to be a chef when he was 15 and living in Detroit, Motown, Motor City, Zolton's home.

Marvin Gay sings on, "I bet you wonder how I knew, about your plans to make me blue, with some other guy you knew before. Between the two of us guys you know I love you more." It's that opening bass line that always gives me goose bumps. Zolton likes Marvin Gay but, like many immigrants, he sometimes has difficulty dealing with minorities. When he meets a black man or woman, one on one, there are no barriers. But blacks in mass immediately put him on the defense. Some ancient hostile mode is stirred and he is always ready to fight.

His family had to work their way up from the bottom of the food chain in a Detroit ghetto. Because they couldn't speak English and because his name seemed so odd to them, Z got beat up a lot by the older black kids at school, his bike was stolen, he was thrown down two flights of stairs and slammed into the corner of a brick apartment building.

Zolton and I talk about his prejudice and my over-active liberal conscience. We almost argue, but we both understand that we are different people with different thoughts and stand down in respect. He acknowledges that his prejudice is wrong. We are both learning and changing, little by little.

His prejudice is different from the redneck ignorance and assumption of superiority. Most of the men and women here, who didn't want my mother to build a pool, who screamed at those children in Little Rock, who today still hate blacks, have never, in their lives been threatened.

Maybe prejudice is the same, no matter what the reason. Maybe Z's is just the same as the KKK assholes.

I don't like thinking about that. But Z acknowledges that prejudice is wrong and he doesn't want our children to feel as he does, to carry that fear and blindness in their hearts. He does not tell them about his childhood in Detroit. He teaches them to be honest and brave and fair to all people. He doesn't pass his prejudice on.

That's the difference.

Marvin is gone.

Right now, sitting in the car, I don't feel pregnant. I just feel like a woman with a legal pad full of crap to do. I check my list again. There is comfort in a good schedule. Diana Ross sings "Stop, In The Name Of Love" and the glowing October sun shines through the windshield. I feel alright.

As long as my belly button doesn't touch the steering wheel. How I miss my perfect indented, spiraling belly button. Men used to compliment my navel. No more. "See what you've taken from me, baby."

The drive into town is 14 miles, green and gorgeous and rural. I honk my horn and "Joe Bob the gas kid" waves as I drive past Daisy's

Fountain Lake Grocery.

Arkansans have faults. Most of the jokes you hear about the state are true. Many of us are obese, illiterate, smokers and chewers of tobacco. We have too many teen pregnancies and not enough libraries. The sons and daughters of this razorback loving land have very poor dental records and rank 48th or 49th when it comes to wearing seat belts, eating lean meats, green vegetables, finishing high school and recycling. But, all in all, Arkansans are pretty friendly. We'll usually let you use our cell-phone if you've got a flat tire.

Our men spit too much and rarely open doors for ladies anymore, but the state is still truly beautiful. According to my Rand McNally Road Atlas, almost 50% of the Arkansas is still heavily wooded. There is space here. We don't have towering peaks or pounding oceans, but we do have pastures with glorious oak trees, brown and white cows and twisting creeks. We have thick rolling forests, with secrets and shadows, deer and elves, mist and bears; we have tree-lined dirt roads, ponds and rivers, trout, catfish, raccoons and honeysuckle. And I pass it, all of this, every time I drive into town.

The city of Hot Springs lies in a valley, between a number of very old, gently rounded mountains. They are my mountains. They are not the massive granite or snow capped monoliths you see out west. My mountains, the Ouachitas, are part of the Zig Zag Mountain Chain. They are the oldest in the country, worn down and smooth, like the rubber soles of old sneakers. My mountains are more like tree covered camel humps, flowing, into one another. Lush and green, they do not intimidate or awe, they are not grand. Instead, they comfort with their gentle beauty, like a pretty woman in the morning. These mountains cradle me.

There's no traffic today on Highway 5. The baby and I make good time. The first church I pass, at the Buck Snort Bridge, has a new message on it's plugged-in sign.

"It's easier to build a boy than mend a man."

I flip open my notebook and write this down with a burnt sienna crayon. I always keep crayons handy, especially around the telephone. Unlike pens and pencils, if I see a crayon, I know it will write.

I started collecting church sign messages a few years ago.

I wonder, does somebody make a living coming up with these

things? Is there a really cheesy, born-again ex-Hallmark employee out there with a gift for sacred word play.

Surely, all these preachers aren't coming up with their own material.

The next church, which is close to the Mule Hill Flea Market, has a very special sign, it spins, slowly so they can put a slogan on each side. Twice the preaching in half the time. Their minister must have a lot to say. One side says, "You have insurance, but do you have assurance?" Almost witty. I slow so I can read the other side. The sign spins and there it is, "God is like a elephant, He never forgets and always forgives."

What's that supposed to mean? Why would the minister put that up there? Why does an elephant need to forgive. I write that one down too, just because it's so stupid. Not everything means something important.

But the word "elephant" stays in my mind. I say it out loud, toying with the syllables, using different accents.

Breathing in through my nose and exhaling loudly, I will find a story. The stories of my history and heritage are the most important things my family left for me. They are my heart and history. Telling myself our tales, visualizing each detail has become my life force.

Touching the tiny gold elephant on my necklace, I feel better. I am protected by elephants. My parents left them here for me. But what does that sign mean.

1932 Depression Love

B. Wallace, (she was called Betty when she was a girl) and Michael Justice fell in love when they were in third grade. Actually, Justice fell first. When he was just nine years old he asked Doc Blue, Betty's father, for permission to walk Betty home from Jones School. It was 1932 and the depression had the country on its knees. Because Justice's father was an architect, and nobody was very interested in building anything, his family suffered greatly.

Justice was the oldest boy in his family and he took himself and his responsibilities very seriously. He worked three jobs around town. He delivered the morning paper on his sister's bike, bagged groceries for eight hours every Saturday at Newman's Food Palace and stacked firewood with his Uncle every day from 4 p.m. till dark. He did all this to help support his family and he expected to be treated like a man, not a boy.

Still, Michael Justice, with his soulful eyes and callused hands, was only ten years old and not so experienced in the ways of love.

After three weeks of walking Betty home, Justice suspected his romantic campaign wasn't going very well. He was ready to pledge undying love and she was still talking about tether ball and spelling words. She wasn't falling in love fast enough, in fact it seemed to him, she wasn't falling in love at all.

One winter afternoon as they walked, Justice couldn't stop staring at the side of her face. He liked the way her mouth moved and she squinted her eyes a little when she talked about something she didn't like. Betty was a beautiful girl, but not in the same way that other girls were pretty. As they walked he realized he even like the way she wore her glasses.

Despite the depression, her family still had money, but she was so stern. She got so mad when she thought other people, especially girls in their class, were being stupid. And she was ruthless, just like a boy. She never ever let anyone else in the class win a spelling bee or math quiz. This did not make Betty the most popular girl in third grade.

After much thought, Justice decided it was his family's lowly financial situation causing romantic trouble. Betty's father was a very successful surgeon; obviously she was accustomed to bigger and better things. Her family still had everything, a big house, hunting dogs, two beautiful horses and a new car.

Justice tried showing her special things. But she didn't spend a minute looking at his prized arrow head collection. And the model air plane he wrapped in newspaper and gave her one Saturday morning before going to work at the Food Palace made her laugh in a snooty sort of way.

Michael Justice even tried buying her gifts, a box of candy and some hair ribbons, but she didn't seem impressed. They ate the 12 pieces of candy together as they walked home from school. Then she threw the pretty heart shaped box away, right in front of him! (After seeing her home, Justice ran all the way back to the garbage can on Central Avenue and pulled the pretty box out for his sister.)

Puzzled as to how to win Betty over, Justice stood next to the school bell tower waiting for her one Friday afternoon. It was early spring. The air was warm and fresh, full of green light and honeysuckle. When she emerged with a group of girls, his heart gave a funny little jerk that made him frown.

She wasn't paying attention to the girls she was walking with, he could tell. She was looking at him and he stared right back. With one hand in the pocket of his heavy brown corduroys, he leaned against the bell tower and tried to appear casual.

Slowly, with his books slung over his shoulder, he walked toward her. Finally she smiled. But he thought it was the wrong sort of smile. Justice knew this smile, he had a damn sister who looked at him that way all the time.

One by one, the other girls ran off giggling and shrieking.

Betty and Justice were left alone. 'She thinks she's better than me,' he thought. 'thinks she smarter and acts like she's older.'

And then he blurted out, 'My birthday is in March, you know. I'm almost a year older than you."

"So what?" Betty said swinging her books.

He watched his own ragged shoes as they walked up the street then said, "Gimme your books."

She let him take them.

Justice was so depressed and nervous he couldn't speak. He was sure she thought he was a gump. His mouth was dry and sticky. And he wondered if his tongue was really swollen.

If he looked at her, he was sure she would see how nervous he was. So he pretended to be absolutely fascinated by the picket fence they were walking past. Still, he could see the bottom of her dress. It was pretty, with navy blue and dark gold vertical stripes that were just a little bit shiny. She and her mother went shopping in Little Rock and Memphis so she always had different dresses from the other girls in school.

They'd walked almost two blocks without speaking. Michael Justice had never had a girlfriend, but he knew walking, without speaking, wasn't good. He could feel something uncomfortable settling between them. 'She's trying to decide if I'm good enough,' he thought. Then he panicked and started talking, just to make an impression, just because he couldn't stand the sound of their foot steps anymore.

"My Uncle owns a circus," he lied.

"He does? Where?" She looked suddenly interested.

"Oh, it's not around here. It's too big for here. It's in...Texas."

"Does he have clowns and everything?"

"Oh, he's got everything alright," he took a deep breath, thinking his story was going pretty well.

"Like what?" She was smiling.

The boy had to think. He'd never actually been to a circus. Every time one came to town he tried to save up enough money but his mom always needed groceries or something for the baby. He tried to remember what he'd seen on the circus posters hung all over town.

"Well, there are clowns of course and trapeze people and midgets and tigers and horses, ten white horses and he's got elephants."

"Elephants? Really, that's wonderful. I love the circus elephants. They've always been my favorite. Especially when they stand on their head. There are quite coordinated considering their size. Don't you think?"

"He's got eight elephants," Justice continued. He was starting to like this and it was getting easier. "Eight elephants, and you know what else?"

"What?"

"He's pretty old now, and when he dies, I get the elephants because I'm his favorite nephew. I get all of them. So, when I get married I'm gonna give my wife half the elephants. She'll get the four girl elephants and I'll keep the boys, because they're bigger and a lot harder to handle."

The story grew, like technicolor kudzu, as they walked. Justice almost believed he had an uncle with a circus and Betty was enraptured.

As he spoke, describing the sparkling costumes the girls wore and the silly antics of the clowns with their huge feet and funny honking horns, she began looking at him differently. She wanted to believe him. She wanted him to have something wonderful.

On that day, a deep green vine touched each of them, sprouted a leaf then grew a little more. And over the next forty years that single vine grew into an enormous, all consuming plant that wrapped it's rich and beautiful tentacles around their home and the trees, the fences around their houses, the children and neighbors and city. Everyone was pulled into the octopus like love.

My mother, always claimed she married my father under false pretenses. She never got her elephants.

So, every year Daddy gave her an elephant on their anniversary, for Valentine's Day, Christmas or on her birthday. Some were silver, some crystal, one was made out of paper mache by a boy at an orphanage across town. On Mom's 40th birthday, Daddy put a tiny gold elephant in her cup of coffee.

After her suicide, when the police found my mother's body on the condominium porch, all her elephants, big and small, old and new, were gathered, in a semicircle, around her lounge chair.

The authorities didn't know what to make of the situation. But I understood.

She had pulled the old herd together, one last time, to see her off.

Chapter 5

Two pickup trucks loaded with late summer watermelons from Hope, Arkansas are parked across from across from BobBob's Catfish House. Hope has always been the watermelon capitol of the world. It's also the town Bill Clinton was born in; but he grew up here, in Hot Springs. When he was running for office he kept saying, "There is a place called Hope" and we'd all roll our eyes and think about watermelon.

There is a hand painted sign in front of the store, 'RED AND YELLOW MELONS.'

My grandmother, WaWa, is 98 years old now, and lives in a nursing home. She used to love yellow watermelons. I loved eating them with her when I was little. It was the only time WaWa, who was always an absolute lady, slurped.

I pull over suddenly to buy two yellow melons. Dust clouds swell behind my car. There is a lovely similarity between my belly and all the melons. A very fat woman wearing a worn yellow dress and stained apron, sits on a folding chair. A fly lands on the big stain and walks around to inspect the rest of her apron.

I must stop looking at her or I'll get sick.

The lady watches me as I thump a few melons. I don't actually know what it is I'm listening for, but ritual is important. Finally, I pick two. One for E'va and one for WaWa.

The woman doesn't offer to help me carry the melons to my car. I don't need any help, but her fat lack of manners bugs me. After giving her a look that she doesn't notice, I pick up one melon, cradle it in my arms and let it rest on top of my belly. Then, I have to put the watermelon down, on the ground, before I can open the car door. Finally, I pick it back up and roll it onto the backseat.

The bitch doesn't even notice as I go through this watermelon dance, twice. I'm almost finished and she says, "Well you should of said something if you needed some help," as though she's been listening to my thoughts. This gives me goose bumps. I give her a tiny smile/smirk and I slam the car door. These better be the finest fucking watermelons in the country.

Driving away, I see her shaking her head as though she's heard that thought too.

Driving away, I force myself to breathe deeply. My heart slows and the muscles in my neck loosen. Rude people piss me off, way too much. I study the passing Arkansas landscape. Half the houses in this area have satellite dishes, floating around their roofs like captured and tethered UFOs.

In front of the church next to the old stone bridge, I slow down. There's an ancient spinning grist mill and two donkeys on the church property. Today the church sign reads, "Sign broken, come inside for message." That one is a little too cute for my taste, but I write it down anyway.

A cloud of flavor hangs over Micky's Barbeque. The air is thick with hickory smoke. The baby kicks my ribs. Maybe it's a sign. She's a true razorback and already wants barbeque.

I pass the city limit sign. Park Avenue, this winding road that squirms into historic down town Hot Springs, is a wonderful street. I can track the city's story, from beginning to end, in just one mile of this tree lined old neighborhood.

There's the Clinton house and Stubby's Bar-b-que where the President ate ribs when he walked home from school. There's the old Vapors nightclub, a famous casino from Hot Springs high rolling Dean Martin days. Everybody from Phyllis Diller to Sammy Davis Jr. hung out at the Vapors. Behind the Vapors there is a steep and rocky ledge. Hot water from the 24,000 thousand year old springs have made a tiny steaming waterfall that drips constantly. This mystical hot water brought Indian tribes to this valley hundreds of years ago. Today, thousands of visitor still come to Hot Springs to take baths in our perfect, 142 degree mineral water.

A little further down Park, there's the tall, run-down, turn of the century home which Al Capone used as a hiding place for his gang's women and children. Capone always stayed at the Arlington Hotel, but he kept his family and those attached to his men, in a nice house on Park Avenue.

Hot Springs has grown away from Park Avenue. Everybody moved into condos on the other side of town, next to the lake. The gingerbread on the Victorian homes has begun to rot. Beautiful old houses in the area need paint and there's a smoldering crime problem.

Cheap motels sit next to the beautiful mansions. Crack heads and exhausted looking hookers work the same four blocks, every day. One of the girls always wears up-your-butt cut-offs and a tuxedo jacket. She has a tiny baby. Sometimes I see her sitting on the bus stop bench, rocking her baby and swinging one of her shiny black pumps on her big toe.

A block from the Piggly Wiggly Grocery Store, I spot Saint Mary walking slowly, on the shoulder of the road. I pull over, in front of the old black woman. She trudges, with her her head down and her right arm pulled close to her body, as though wearing an invisible sling.

Throwing my door open, I struggle out of the car, then look back and smile at Mary, who is trying to hurry a little. But, she can barely walk.

Her body is crumpled by age and some unnamed illness. Mary has very little hair. Her dress is old and too big for her, but she is radiant. She looks at me as she limps toward the car and smiles. Her face glows.

"Hang on," I call to her. "Let me get the door for you."

Smiling, she nods over and over and I open the door. Mary has to push herself in backwards. Then, using her left arm, she nearly picks up her leg to get inside the Mustang.

When I wedge myself back in, behind the wheel, Mary looks at me and smiles. "Baby, baby, baby, baby, baby."

"That's right. I'm having a baby." She saw me a month ago and said the same thing.

Mary rocks a little and I ask, "Are you going to the Piggly Wiggly?"

She shakes her head and nods for me to drive on past. "Baby, baby, baby, brave, brave, brave, brave, brave."

"You think I'm brave or the baby is? Maybe we both are. Actually, I'm the coward in the family." I laugh. And keep watching her because she'll nod when she's ready for me to stop or turn.

"Brave, brave, brave," she says more softly and smiles at me with such a beautiful warm light that I suddenly feel rested and calm.

"I'll try to be, Mary. You smell really good today. You're wearing perfume. It's pretty."

She pulls a new bottle of perfume from her worn brown purse.

"That's very nice. I like it," I say.

She squirts a little in my direction and fills the car with the sweet smell. Then she nods at a small, storefront grocery that caters to blacks. I pull over and before I can get out to help her, a business man, in a dark suit and paisley tie opens her door. I recognize him from the bank. He presses some money into her hand, then helps her get out. "You need me to take you anywhere Saint Mary?" he asks and slams my car door shut without looking at me.

I wait for a minute with the windows down, airing the car and watching her. As I pull away, he leads her slowly into the grocery store.

Saint Mary, that's what she's always been called. I pick her up and give her rides because my mother used to, when I was very young.

When Mary was a girl, just 15 she was raped and became pregnant. Her pregnancy was fine, but when she went into labor, there were problems. the little boy, cried just once, then began choking. He died in Mary's arms.

Four other women watched as Mary, still naked and weak, fell out of bed and onto the floor. With the limp baby in her arms, she started praying. She begged God to take her instead of the baby.

She told God to take the beating from her own young heart and the air from her lungs and give them to her baby. She curled up around the dead baby boy and prayed without ceasing.

The ladies tried to pull Mary up and get her back into bed, but she wouldn't move. Shaking their heads they stepped back. Then the baby boy started crying. Mary offered him up to the ladies then slumped over, dead.

The baby was fine. A perfect, squalling little boy. But Mary was gone. After a doctor confirmed her death, she was taken to the local black funeral home.

Mary's mother, Sila stayed with her sweet daughter's body all day and night. Sometime around 3 a.m. she fell asleep with her head resting next to Mary's hand.

At 6 a.m. Sila woke when she heard something. A soft kitten like mewing. And then she heard her daughter cough a little and say, "Momma, I'm alive now."

Since that day, seventy years ago, that girl whom God listened to, that unselfish child who offered her life for her baby's, has been called Saint Mary.

Now that Mary is so old, she is taken care of by her entire community. If you have a dollar in your hand, it's good to give Mary fifty cents. Every preacher agrees, God has called Mary's community to take care of her. And so they do.

And it is known that when Mary speaks and especially when she gets stuck on words, what she says is always true.

She gave me two words, two good words today. One I do not understand. Baby and brave, brave, brave. Why did she give me the word brave? And she gave me a little bit of perfume.

My first three stops are quick, in and out in five minutes. I pay Davy Jones $150 dollars for a winning three team tease and pick up $25 from an old man who sits on the corner selling newspapers and yo-yos with President Clinton's face on them.

I stop by the Jazz House, a nifty restaurant and bar located in what used to be the old Texaco station. The restaurants bathrooms are still outside and require a big key. The bartender hands me an fat envelop and asks if I want anything to drink.

Everybody else I see wants to visit, especially because I'm pregnant and retiring. My fourth stop at a pizzeria / head shop called Hernando's Fountain (because Hernando DeSoto supposedly discovered Hot Springs) takes less than thirty minutes. I visit for a little while, count the $550 dollars they owe me, drink half a glass of herbal tea, eat some barley soup, then waddle on.

I've stopped arguing when I'm given food. People just like to feed a pregnant woman. It seems to be a fundamental Homo sapien instinct.

Only a few more stops.

I dream as I drive, making a mental list of all the things I want but can't have because I'm pregnant. After the baby is born I will take a dangerously hot bath, wear slinky full length body stockings and have raunchy jungle sex with Z. Then, I'll lie around on my stomach (something I haven't been able to do comfortably in four months) drinking beer and eating mounds of raw oysters.

When you are pregnant people assume your thoughts are gentle and pure, like a soft focus baby powder commercial. I see no reason to dispel this belief, so I sip my juice or milk, and smile sweetly while rolling naked with my lascivious thoughts.

Surely nobody will try to feed me at the next stop. The Gator Ranch on Whittington Park has been a cheesy tourist institution for 102 years. It's only a block from WaWa's nursing home, so I'll take care of business then take my grandmother her watermelon.

I park right along a chain link fence in front of the largest gator pool. Hundreds of alligators lie around in big pools of tepid water. There's also a petting zoo on the hill with llamas and deer and pigs, ostriches and emus.

The truth is, the general public is more sophisticated than it used to be. We like laser shows and giant water slides and beautifully maintained natural habitat zoos. Because alligators are general pretty sluggish animals, they don't entertain the masses much any more.

Sitting in the shade, with my legal pad on my lap, I watch a momma deer and her tiny spotted fawn for a moment before I notice the elephant. As quickly as my stomach will allow, I climb out of the car to look more closely. There's a baby elephant in the petting zoo. He's never been there before.

I hurry to the chain link fence. All the llamas and emus walk slowly to the other side of the pen but the baby elephant looks at me with his big ears flapping. It's a hot day, he's trying to stay cool He starts walking to me. I study the huge toenails on his strange, flat feet. There's an elephant, right here, next to me at the Gator Ranch. Where did he come from? He seems pretty skinny but healthy, his small eyes sparkle. He stands a few feet from the fence and stares at me with his beautiful trunk, slightly raised. How old is he? His backbone is even with my shoulders. God, I've watched enough Discovery Channel and National Geographic documentary on elephants but I can't remember how quickly baby elephants grow.

"Hi there, " I say and extend my flat palm. At the sound of my voice the other animals in the pen back further away, but the elephant raises his trunk. His nostrils quiver, shiny and damp. He steps closer and reaches over the fence with his trunk. Ignoring my palm, the elephant taps me squarely on the head, as though trying to get my attention.

I laugh and his trunk waves elegantly over me. "What are you doing?" Gently and with great precision he strokes the top of my head again using the very tip of his finger like nostril.

It's an astonishing feeling, he is so gentle and sure of his moves. The baby and I have been consecrated. Reaching up, I try to pat his trunk but he will not allow it. He lifts it, just out of my reach and only touches me again when I lock my hands together behind my back.

"What are you doing here, elephant?" He does not answer but rests his limb like trunk solidly on top of my head, as though he's tired.

"Where's your ma'ma?" I look around, maybe I missed seeing a 6000 pound mamma elephant.

There is a rustling in the bushes 100 feet away. The elephant touches my cheek with his trunk, his skin is warm and dry, then slowly steps backwards and walks to the other end of the pen, closer to the noise.

I can't help myself, I have to follow him. He stops to toss some hay piled in the corner and then I see her. There's a little girl standing on the foot trail behind the pen. She's skinny with glasses, a yellow poka dotted scarf on her head, smooth shorts and brown Mary Janes. This little girl, who looks strangely dated, is staring at the elephant, almost smiling, suddenly, she looks over her shoulder, into the woods. Maybe she's waiting for somebody. I recognize her profile and her polka dotted scarf. It's my mom, B. Wallace.

I watch and she touches her horned rimmed glasses. What is it she's looking for? I step forward, onto the dirt path. The instant my shoe touches the dirt path, I understand where this trail leads, to my mom and 1934. The sensation is startling, frightening and exciting. Pulling my foot back, I pray this feeling will all stop because I really want to run up the trail with B. Wallace. I want to see what she sees and know what she knows.

My mom grew up on an affluent street call Prospect Avenue. My Dad was raised here, on Whittington. West Mountain, this mountain, separated their homes and their neighborhoods and their lives.

When Daddy was in 4th grade he started running over West Mountain two or three times a week just to visit Betty Wallace Lore. He followed a deer trail that started behind the Gator Ranch and ended up just 50 yards from Mom's backyard.

Betty's father, Doc Blue, wasn't too pleased by the notion of this scruffy little boy running over the mountain all the time to see his daughter. He told the maids Michael Justice could only visit with Betty once a week, on the back porch. The rest of the time my father was told she was too busy to visit.

The maids felt sorry for the ragged but undeterred boy, who was so obviously in love. On the days he wasn't allowed to visit with Betty, they secretly gave him a bag of cookies and jar of milk for the trip home.

Forty five years later, when the lawyer read the final sentence in my father's will aloud. B. Wallace and I did not hold hands, but our fingers were just touching. We heard my father's voice, not the lawyers when he read, "Scatter my ashes on West Mountain. I'll always be running through those woods, trying to reach my girl."

Of course it's Betty standing on this mountain path, staring at the elephant. Maybe she's been looking for Michael Justice.

Slowly, the little girl turns to look at me. She doesn't smile or frown or wave, she just looks at me and I suddenly feel very old and fat. What does this child, my mother, see when she looks at me?

"Betty?" I can't stop myself from saying her name.

She tilts her head to one side then steps behind a large pine tree. She's so skinny she completely disappears.

"Betty?" I move closer to the tree but I still can't see her. I can hear her moving a little. My fingers trace the outline of the lumpy tree bark as I peek around the trunk.

Saint Mary is sitting in the dirt holding a small cloth bag with one hand, her bad arm is pressed close to her body. I look around for Betty, but she's gone.

"Mary, it's you." I lean against the pine tree, in need of support. "How did you get over here so fast? I just left you on Park Avenue."

Mary is staring at the the baby elephant too. She nods in his direction. "Die, die, die, die."

"Die? The elephant is going to die? No, he seems fine."

She shakes her head up and down over and over again then reaches up to me. Taking her warm and dry black hand, I help her to her feet.

"What's wrong with him?"

She's already shuffling to the pen and does not answer me. The elephant trots over when he sees her her. He stands sideways and presses his entire body against the chain link fence until wrinkled gray skin pops through each hole.

Mary touches him through the fence link and laughs. She only has a few teeth. The elephant does not pat Mary on the head but allows her to stroke his trunk. He searches for her touch. They are happy to be together.

For nearly ten minutes I watch them. But I know I'm not supposed to be here anymore. But I do not want to leave the elephant. I stand next to Mary, the elephant touches my huge belly once with his wondrous trunk as though he's listing to the baby with a stethoscope. Mary likes that. She nods to him over and over and rubs my stomach with him. Then he turns his attention and trunk back to Mary.

I will ask Mr. Bagby, who owes me $1005 and owns The Gator Ranch, about the elephant.

Mr. Bagby never talks much, just gives me money or takes his with a nod. I always feel guilty because I can't draw him out.

Last week I tried to make small talk, I said, "Those are beautiful shoes. Alligator skin?"

He nodded.

I pressed on. "Do they use the same animal for both shoes and the belt?" I failed miserably. He furrowed his deeply wrinkled brow, then picked up Henry, a green eyed baby alligator he keeps in an aquarium for tourists to handle. Henry rolled his bulging eyes at me. There was a different Henry last summer, but he choked on a chicken bone and died.

Today, I will make Mr. Bagby talk to me about the baby elephant.

Walking into the souvenir shop, I will myself not to hold my breath. The smell of the ancient alligators and their swampy pools permeates the air. I say "I saw the new addition in the petting zoo, he's wonderful. How old is he?"

"Year and a half," Mr. Bagby says and he sounds a little sad as he walks to the cash register and pulls out an envelope for me. "Not mine, though."

"He's just visiting?" I ask and take the envelope.

"Yeah. Belongs to Jungle Land up in Jonesboro. Got some kind of disease, contagious, can't be around other elephants."

"Who's treating it?"

He shakes his head and produces a tupperware container filled with enormous eyedropper and plastic syringes without needles. "But there's nothing to be done."

"What do you mean?" I ask incredulously, "He's not gonna die, is he?"

"Most likely. I got a new vet coming over from the Memphis Zoo this week to take a look at him but..." He doesn't finish his sentence and puts the massive box of elephant medication back under the counter.

Mary was right, the elephant is going to die. Damn. I stop myself from making an elephant grave yard comment. "I'm sorry," I can't think of anything else to say to Mr. Bagby. Our conversation is over. Leaving, I add "Take care of yourself." He nods. He's sad too. Mr. Bagby never liked people nearly as much as he likes his animals.

Once outside, I take deep breaths of the fall air. There is an ancient, rotting smell and then it gets stuck in my nasal passage as though I've inhales a clump of moss.

The smell and the thought of the baby elephant and seeing Betty on the trail, make me want to cry, but I will not.

With one hand on my belly, I snort like a bull. That doesn't really work, so I walk down the block to an over burdened Magnolia tree. Reaching high, I pull a branch down, so I can bury my face in one of the giant white flowers and fill my head with the lemony scent.

As I get in my car, I can see Saint Mary and the elephant. She's inside the pen now, though the only way to get in is through the souvenir shop. Mary is sitting down next to his hay pile. He is standing very close to her, his big front foot nearly touches her outstretched legs. She has something cupped in her good hand and is letting him touch or smell it. It's Betty's yellow polka dotted scarf.

I want to go home and hide, but I'm not sure that will help and I'm afraid to be alone. God knows what will happen next, so I might as well push on.

My dear, sweet grandmother Wawa's nursing home is only two blocks from the Gator Ranch. It's not until I park the car outside the flat building it occurs to me Betty might have been looking for Wawa, her mother.

I heave the watermelon out of the backseat. But Wawa is gone, her body just happens to be here. What ever it is B.Wallace is doing to me, or trying to tell me doesn't have anything to do with WaWa, I don't think. Somebody as old as her is out of bounds, even for Mom.

I manage to push the front door buzzer with my elbow. They have to keep all the doors locked now because patients wander off.

An 86-year-old man with alzheimers walked out last year and the Police and Forest Service finally found him two days later in the woods three miles away. He was sitting on a rock with four candy bars and a can of Pabst Blue Ribbon and a Grape Nehi. Nobody ever figured out where he got the rations.

A big eared attendant opens the door for me. "Whatyagot?" he asks, patting my watermelon.

At first, I take tiny breaths, testing the air. Sometimes it smells fine, like pine cleaner and other times the urine smells gags me. It's a nice enough nursing home, the staff is kind and they keep it clean but there are good days and bad days.

The lobby and hallway are lined with old people sitting in chairs. They are all so white, marked with rising blue veins. The color is horrible. The sitting and waiting, for nothing, is horrible. They are not speaking to one another, they really aren't even moving. Some smile at me and I try to wave and say, "Hello there," very loudly. One man yells, "Hi ya there girly, girl."

Nothing B.Wallace can do to me is worse them this place. It's a warehouse for the living dead. Hell, if I can take take this I can take anything.

Sometimes I bring Mike and Felicity. This makes a lot of old people happy.

Many of the residents reach out to touch the children as we walk past. Once Felicity said, "This must have been how Jesus felt." Perhaps their almost desperate reaching is unconscious. They just want to touch warm brown skin, kissed by the sun and so full of life. They reach out, hoping to make contact with life, one more time.

If it scares the kids they hide it well, they say hello over and over and smile but they stay very, very close to me.

How could God do this to me? I think as I pass an old woman

sleeping in a wheelchair. She is toothless and her head rests on the back of the chair. She makes a gargling sound as she breaths. I try not to look, but can not help myself. Her open mouth looks like a black pit that will suck me up.

Here they come, the thoughts. This is the blackness I fight. But sometimes, I can't keep it down and the anger eats me up for a few minutes then pukes me back into the sunshine.

What sort of cruel irony did God intend. He took my family, fine and shining Father and Daniel and Mom. He ripped them away from me and left me here with WaWa in a sea of the living dead.

I can not swallow. Tears blur my vision and I must stop with the watermelon in my arms. Well, it's not going to work, God. Whatever it is you were trying to do to me, it's not going to work. I'll fucking get through this.

The baby kicks at the pressing weight of the watermelon. It makes me feel better.

Usually, I don't talk to God. I've got nothing to say. I think about Him, but we are not on speaking terms anymore.

The rage passes almost as quickly as it arrived. I can't go into WaWa's room feeling so hateful. She's been screwed by His cosmic plan too.

Forcing myself to smile, I move on.

Wawa's room is right across from the nurses station.

Somebody says "Ohh look what you brought, how sweet."

I rest the melon on the desk top. "Can you get me a knife and a plate, maybe a paper towel?"

I back through her door then turn, she is in bed, and the television is on too loud. The Price Is Right. Shut up Bob Barker.

If I were speaking to God I would say a little prayer right now and ask him to let Wawa remember me, just one more time.

When I try to put the melon on the dresser, it almost slips out of my fingers. The dresser is to high for me so I turn and place the giant fruit gently on the end of Wawa's bed, between her feet.

"Hello, who's there?" she asks.

"Hi Wawa, it's me, Liz.."

"Liz?"

"Yes ma'am Liz, your granddaughter."

"Well how nice of you to come to visit." She stares up at the ceiling, her blind eyes wide open. Thick cataracts have covered her eyes with a blue and milky white veil. She pats her blanket a little then sighs. After a moment Wawa says, "I'm sorry dear, what did you say your name was."

"Liz. I'm your granddaughter. I brought you a surprise today, a yellow water melon."

"How wonderful of you, a yellow watermelon, I love melons. How did you know that dear?"

"We used to eat watermelon together, Wawa." The nurse comes in smiling. She has a knife and a large tray and a pile of napkins. Without speaking, she cut's the watermelon into slices then takes all the seeds out of one piece for Wawa.

"What did you say my name was dear?" Wawa asks.

"See if you can remember."

"Victoria?"

"No ma'am."

"Mary, Guinivere?" she is almost coy, not realizing all the names she thinks might be hers were once queens.

"No. You have a pretty name, and it's got 9 letters. I was named after you."

"Victoria, is that my name?"

"Your name is Elizabeth and so is mine," I explain.

"Is Elizabeth still on the throne, she's been there so long. You know, Mary Queen of Scotts had a little dog that lived under her gown. What did you say your name was?"

"Mine is Elizabeth too," my throat tightens.

"What a lucky coincidence, we have the same name."

"I was named after you because you are my grandmother."

I laugh a little, at our funny game, though it is so sad my heart flutters and flops like a dying bird.

"Elizabeth" she chuckles. It is a deep Southern sound that warms me, though I can barely stand to look at her. "Elizabeth what?"

"Elizabeth Lore."

"Oh, good." she said, content as a cat. "Well thank you for coming to visit, Dear" She doesn't have a clue who I am, but her impeccable manners never fail.

"I have something for you," I say and I put the slice of melon in her empty tapping fingers.

"Oh, is this a watermelon? How nice." She takes a bite and laughs a little.

"Do you remember when we used to sit on your side porch and eat watermelon?" I always loved eating watermelon alone with Wawa because it was the only time she would slurp. Then she would try to spit a few seeds out, but she couldn't spit. She would take a huge breath and blow, but the seeds always landed on her knees and we would laugh and laugh and swat at the sugar hungry flies.

"No dear, I'm afraid I don't. I had a nice home?" she asks and a little juice rolls down her pale chin.

"You had a wonderful house Wawa. Big and white with green shutters and high ceilings. There were three fireplaces, and a butler's pantry. You lived there for 60 years. Doc Blue built it for you." I want her to remember every thing, please let her remember my life, our lives before all of this. If she remembers, just one last time watching fourteen year old Daniel play basketball in her driveway or the way Daddy and I looked when he tried to teach me to fox-trot in her living room, if she can remember with me I'll know it was all true. My life was real. Maybe the taste of the yellow melon will tickle some precious summer circuit in her brain. Maybe if she tastes the sweet and juicy meat, she'll remember holding my hand as we picked bitter cherries from her tree when I was so young and she was my Wawa.

Maybe, as the watermelon dissolves on her old tongue, I'll have her back for just a moment. She'll say my name out loud, one more time. Then I'll tell her about the baby. And Felicity and Mike so she'll know we are here for her, she's not alone on this planet and some part of her will always go on. I'm the only one left, except for you Wawa, so please remember with me and I will know forever.

I'm asking a lot of one watermelon..

She takes another bite and smiles a little. She smiles every time she tastes the sweet meat but that's all. "Oh how stupid I must be not to remember my own house. Was I always so thick, Dear?"

"No ma'am. You've always been very intelligent, very smart and wise. You still are."

"Wawa, you call me. I must be so old, ancient or you wouldn't call me wise. I'm an old owl," she says and she's wondering why I call her Wawa.

She is finished eating. Without saying a word, she leans her head back in her pillow and waits for me to take the melon away. Before I can even wipe her chin and throw the rind away, she is snoring softly.

I can't go back in time. I know that. Staring at Doc Blue's portrait hanging over her bed, I feel better. Something touches me and I know I have more in front of me than there was behind. I don't need Wawa's memories to make my world real. I have every day, with my family and that's enough.

I turn to sit in her big straight back chair but there is something already there, covered by a thin cotton nursing home robe.

My heart slams inside my chest. Jesus Christ how can you do this to me Mom? I'm trying to take care of your mother. It's a yellow watermelon. Stepping back I can only stare at the melon and at the blank yellow post it note stuck to the top. A decapitated head wouldn't have frightened me half as much.

Walking backwards, I make it to the other side of Wawa's bed. After ringing the nurses button I wait but do not look away from the melon.

When the nurse comes in she is smiling.

"Where did that come from?" I point at the melon, like Donald Sutherland in Invasion of the Body Snatchers.

"I don't know," the nurse says and walks across the room. She pulls the post it note off the rind and looks at both sides.

"Has she had any visitors today, or yesterday, anybody this week?"

"I'll check the visitor list but I'm fairly certain she hasn't had anyone except you in months. Besides, this melon is still cold so somebody must have dropped it off recently. Do you want to take it home with you?"

Hardly able to speak, I just shake my head and croak, "you keep it." I reach for Wawa's hand. It is cool and too soft and she does not respond. But at least it's there for me. squeezing the hand a little I breathe. It's just a watermelon, it was just an elephant, just a yellow post it note. It's mom, there's no doubt but a quilt of knowledge touches my shoulders.

It's Mom, B. Wallace really is trying to get my attention. Well, you've got my attention Mom. I'm listening so go ahead and say whatever it is you need to. My mother would never hurt me and her ghost won't hurt me, she's just trying to tell me something.

I touch my own shoulder. It's so warm, as though I've got a fever. Maybe there really is a quilt or shawl resting on my shoulders.

If I don't address this situation logically and with a brave heart, I'll lose my mind. I've got to give birth in a few days and I have children to love and take care of. I can't go insane right now.

Ok, so what is it B.Wallace is trying to tell me? What does she know that I don't. Maybe there are two things she's trying to tell me, she knows I shouldn't marry Z. or our world will get screwed up and she still doesn't want her ashes buried in Arkansas. It has to be one of those two things, or maybe both.

Maybe I'm squeezing Wawa's hand too tight. I loosen my grip, then place it on top of her blanket.

I've got to get out of Wawa's quiet room. B. Wallace's presence leaves me thirsty and unsettled, as though she's taking something from my cells. Maybe she's just lonesome. If that's the case, I need to push her away.

For the sake of my children, I can not let my mother draw me in.

Chapter 6

11:30 a.m. After thirty minutes in the nursing home with Wawa and the watermelon, the beauty of Whittington Park seems absurd, like a digitally enhanced postcard. The greens are too bright and the creek, which runs through the middle of the park, sparkles too much. The magnolia trees have too many flowers, it doesn't look real.

My other grandmother, Marva, raised my short and tough father on this street. I stop the car in front of the house he grew up in. It's boarded up and abandoned now. The roof sags and the front porch is caved in, forming a splintered 'v.'

I wait in front of the house with the car windows down. Maybe my father is here now, maybe that's why Betty was looking for him.

Closing my eyes, I listen. Finally, I can hear something, children laughing. But it's not my parents. It's just kids from the neighborhood. They sound just like we used to when we visited Marva in this house. We'd play T.V. tag and catch crawdads in the creek using old bacon and string. Marva's house was next door to the Showman's Club, a private establishment for retired carnival and circus people.

Once, when I was seven, Marva fell down her living room stairs. She couldn't get up and whimpered so much, my cousin Jake started crying. We tried to pick Marva up but that made her cry even more. Finally, Jake and I ran next door, to the Showman's Club.

The only person there was a midget clown from a small traveling circus. When we ran in, screaming and panting, he was on his knees, trying to fix a television set. He didn't ask any questions, didn't say a word. He jumped to his feet as though he'd been expecting us. His tools clattered loudly on the tile floor as he ran out the back door with us.

What a strange sensation it was, running next to that short man, who's name I didn't know. I watched all our legs as we sprinted, at full speed, across the gravel parking lot. Jake and I were barefoot, but didn't feel the rocks. The midget was a little smaller and much wider than we were and he was wearing long pants. I could see that his legs were much shorter than ours, but moving fast, faster than our bony, brown, seven-year-old legs. He beat us to Marva's back door. I watched the back of his square head disappear into the house just as we reached the bottom of the porch steps. He was exactly the same height as the door bell.

By the time we got inside, Marva was trying to sit up. I was so happy there was another grown-up to relieve us of responsibility. And then we watched, stunned and silent, as he scooped up our diminutive grandmother and carried her to the purple couch. He carried her easily, the muscles in his back and shoulders pressing hard against his work shirt. The midget carried my grandmother in his short, muscular arms, like a miniature Rhett carrying Scarlet up the stairs.

There's no one here in this house now, no people or spirits, power or answers. It's just an old house that needs to be torn down. I must move on.

My next stop.... Jim Bob's Parking Palace.

"Every Body Gets Their Own Space At Jim Bob's "

I like Jim Bob, he's a goof that always makes me feel better.

I pull up to the tiny, red brick booth, Jim Bob is reading a racing form, wearing khaki shorts, a white button down shirt, untucked with the sleeves rolled up. His black, high top Air Jordan's are propped up on a stool. He's not wearing any socks.

I toss a penny at Jim Bob just to get his attention. "You're feet must smell horrible by the end of the day."

He closes the racing form, "Sweet as horse shit, honey." He grins.

I grimace.

"And my closet smells like old bratwurst. But I kind of like it. Let's me know I'm home. I've been waiting for you, Darlin'."

"I bet you have. How's business?" I put the car in park.

"Merrily, merrily, life is but a dream," Jim Bob sings, then adds, "All three lots have been full for a week. There's a golf pro convention at the Arlington, 300 guys with bad pants and beautiful back swings. And there's a mental health workers group at the Majestic. Those people give me the creeps, but they always park right between the lines, never drift into any body else's space."

Jim Bob used to be a pretty good lawyer, when he wasn't at the track. He took care of social drunk drivers and divorces. Then he inherited three downtown parking lots from his uncle and became a parking czar. Jim Bob soon discovered sitting in his tiny brick booth, studying the racing form and taking money from tourists, was almost as profitable and a lot less stressful than being a lawyer.

Folding his newspaper, Jim Bob says, "Liz, are you married? We could have dinner this weekend. Honest to God, I'd rather spend my money on you than give it to that ugly bastard, Hurlie. I'm a great date, hold doors and nibble ears. How's that sound? I could fall in love with my bookie, that would be almost as good as a Sunday morning blow job."

Because I'm in the car, it's possible he's forgotten, or never realized I'm pregnant.

"I'm so in love right now, Jim Bob, I don't know what to do with myself when he goes to work."

"Well good for you," he says sincerely and takes a slurp from his Orange Crush. "A grand thing, love is. You still with that big-ass chef, huh? Guess I shouldn't piss off a guy with a knife that's bigger than mine. He's got a really big knife, doesn't he?"

I nod and my heart warms just a little thinking about my big-ass chef.

"I met a little girl from L.A. last week. She had beautiful ankles, like a race horse. I let her park for free, no charge, this space is on me." He winks and laughs, then throws a fat white envelope through my car window. He's a cheerful and steady looser. There's almost $2,000 dollars in the envelope. Last week Jim Bob won $55 dollars from us after placing $4000 dollars worth of bets. Sometimes, I wish I could convince Jim Bob to make straight bets. He might win once in a while. Instead, he goes for the three team tease, which means he has to pick three teams and I give him an additional ten points in their favor. This sounds like an easy way to win but upsets and teases bets have made Hurlie a rich man.

"Hey Liz, I know it's none of my business but Hurlie's not giving you any shit is he?"

"What are you talking about? What sort of shit?"

"I just heard some talk that Hurlie's not taking your departure too well. Hell, nobody likes loosing a good employee. And you know how he's always been a little...extreme."

"Hurlie and I are just fine."

"Glad to hear it, Darlin'. I was just checking. You be careful out there and brave too."

What an odd thing for Jim Bob to say, totally out of character. Surely he hasn't really heard anything. He's messing with me. 'And brave too' why did he use the same word as Saint Mary? Bravery is only needed under truly adverse or dangerous situations. Do I need to be brave? Am I in danger?

After making a u-turn around his Joe Bob's, I head on up Central Avenue.

I park in front of an antique light pole, adjust my bra, then count out the money I owe Gideon Sinclair. Forcing myself out of the car, I lock then double check the door and waddle two blocks up Central to Josephine Tussand's Wax Museum. George Bush and Ronald Reagan shake hands. Clinton, Mae West and Lizzy Borden are kept in a separate window.

I hate these wax people, so skinny and pale. Even busty and smiling Mae West looks tense and scrawny. A man could never get a hand full unless he aimed directly for her bosom. Bill Clinton's head is too big and he looks strangely like Jimmy Carter.

If Mae gets any closer to Bill Clinton, she'll suck all the meat off his bones. Little Red Riding Hood looks as though she's suffering a vicious bout of PMS.

None of these underfed characters look very American.

The wax museum building, with it's purple canopies and magnificent Romanesque arches, used to be The Southern Club, a lavish casino. Every great American 20th century gangster threw some dice in this joint.

Wawa's husband, Doc Blue, always carried a pair of Southern Club die in his pocket for luck. With Lucky Luciano standing next to him, Doc Blue had a winning night here in 1928. Those dice and some Chicago money, financed the charitable medical empire he began building the same year.

With my eyes squeezed shut, I stand in front of the Southern Club. I can feel people walking past, they are wondering about me, wondering if the pregnant lady is alright. I am dizzy, but I'm just fine.

INVISIBLE BRANCHES

Central Avenue swirls.

I step into a time warp pot hole. Looking around, there's no doubt I'm caught in the 1920's. I touch myself to make sure I'm still pregnant. Men in double breasted suits holler happily inside the Southern Club, and there is the high sweet sound of a woman laughing and teasing. She must be blond. A black man in a tuxedo calls my name, "Miss Liz?" A trumpet player inside blows, St. Louis Blues. A little girl and a black maid wearing a starched white dress approach me. The girl is only five or six, serious looking with glasses. The maid squeezes her hand tightly and pulls her to the far side of the sidewalk, away from the Southern Club. But the little girl wants to look inside the sparkling building.

The maid says, "We got to get home to you're dinner, Miss Betty, now come on."

B. Wallace. I look more closely. It is my mother. Look at her go. She has very short and shiny hair and wants to argue with Francis, her nanny. I know she cut her hair a few weeks ago in the garage with a pair of pinking sheers. She wanted to look like her daddy, Doc Blue. This act of five-year-old defiance made WaWa cry for days and days. Her little girl wanted to be like her Daddy not Mummy. Betty heard that story a hundred times.

Suddenly Betty pulls Francis' arm and they both stop. She turns to look at me, angry and pleading, disapproving. Her eyes look ancient and drill into my soul and she just stares. I can not move. Francis is tugging on her hand, but Betty does not look away from me and she does not blink.

Finally, she says something, please let me hear it.

"What?" I say loudly.

Betty closes her eyes, as though making a wish and lets the nanny pull her away.

A breeze surrounds me with magnolia and I am tempted by their world, time is willing to suck me backwards like a tornado made of cotton balls. I will be wrapped up, encased and spun around and then I will be the laughing woman inside the Southern Club or perhaps Francis, Betty's nanny.

I open my eyes. There are no dapper gangster or beautiful laughing women. No rolling dice or long black cars. Only tourists eating ice cream and staring at the jaunty wax figure of Louie Armstrong. His trumpet shines in the mid-afternoon sun.

Why am I seeing all of this? I am not afraid, but I must be close to something I've never known or seen before. The ghosts of my family have always kept memories so close for me, they push the memories into me, bump them against my elbow so I have to look. I have to pay attention. But this is different. The memories are moving into my blood. Mom doesn't want me to look at her, she wants more than to refresh my memories. She's got a mission.

Gideon Sinclair, the undertaker like manager of the wax museum, breaks into my thoughts. I owe him over $900 dollars this week. That's why I'm standing here, on Central Avenue.

"Are you alright Liz? You been standing there a good long while." He sounds like Goober on "The Andy Griffith Show."

"Hi Gideon, I'm fine, just a little warm." I hand him the last fat wad of money in my pocket. His long fingers are cool and pale. I try not to touch them. "Nice call on that Saints game. You're the only person I know who can tell what that team's gonna do."

"Everybody has to win sometime, even a Saint. Only dumb shits believe in the status quo."

"I'm not sure winning a game because you kick a 23 yard field goal in a 0 to 0 game is much of a win."

He counts the money slowly, right there in front of me as he speaks. "It's not how, it's how many."

I want to slap him. What the hell is he thinking counting cash on the street. I let it go because this is the last time I'll deal with Gideon. Next week he'll be somebody else's problem.

Light dances on Louie Armstrong's trumpet again. Something looks different about the window today.

Gideon says, "We had to give Armstrong a new horn this morning. Bitch cost about the same as my rent."

I nod. "So that's what it is. Well, if anybody deserves a new trumpet, it's Satchmo. What happened to the old one?"

Gideon starts counting the money again, then puts the bills in numerical order. People passing by watch. He says, "Louie's old horn got stole. I don't know how, but some little puke disappeared it right out of the window. This lady on the street came in and asked me if it was Idi Amin or Martin Luther King Jr. in the window and why was he holding his hand to his mouth like he was coughing."

"Gideon, I gotta go."

As I walk away he yells, "You heard anything about the Monday night game?"

I smile and act as though I can't hear him. What a turnip head.

Lumbering like a pot belly pig in need of water and shade, I head back to my car. Central Avenue suddenly seems very long. I'm cranky and exhausted. I try to focus on the lovely details of the historic buildings, Palladian windows, pressed metal facades and domed roofs.

Hot Springs National Park runs along either side of Central Avenue. Magnolia trees stand in front of eight exquisite and ornate old bathhouses, all built between 1893 and 1923. This was the first property in America to be set for Government protection by the President in 1832.

My body is going to break down before I reach the car. The cramps in the back of my thighs feel like spider bites. I hobble. Only ten more steps then I can drive to the Medical Center and enjoy the comfort and humiliation of having my vagina and uterus examined by a man wearing rubber gloves.

Chapter 7

11:55 a.m. I'm on time. Slowly, I walk across the black asphalt parking lot.

The air-conditioned waiting room feels nice. My skin cools. I wish I could lie down on the couch and take a little nap. I give the pretty but uninterested nurse my name, find a magazine, then sit.

Forty five minutes pass. I've stopped trying to look composed. I've got things to do.

They don't care. Pregnant women are supposed to sit around with benign, cow-like expressions exuding serenity.

Well, fuck that. I hate waiting for this doctor.

Pregnant women should have their own planet, a place where there are plenty of pillows so we can always have one supporting our backs and legs and one tucked between our knees. Pregnant Woman World would be a land of enormous air conditioners, so we never have to get that nauseous and sticky, suffocating feeling. And there wouldn't be any panty hose on our planet, only long flowing dresses and giant soft T-shirts we can wear without underwear.

I play this game for a minute or two but it doesn't help. Why does the waiting piss me off so?

I start reading again, but my palms are sweating. The strange and waxy paper *Time Magazine* is printed on sticks to my skin. I wipe my hand on my shirt.

Taking a deep breath, I try to fix my face. I don't want to unconsciously glare at the other women in the room. My mother used to fuss at me for that. Once, when I was eight or 9 we went to an oriental restaurant Mom looked at me over her uncracked fortune cookie and said, "Please, stop looking at me as though you find me utterly repugnant. You look like a fishwife boiling cabbage."

I had no idea what she was talking about or why she thought I was looking at her like a boiled cabbage. I was so confused and frightened by her sudden defense that I simply didn't speak till we got home. Then

I looked up the word repugnant, in the dictionary. Sitting on my yellow and pink flowered bedspread, I cried and cried. I sobbed into my hot-pink pillow, as only a adolescent girl can. Why did she think, I thought, she was disgusting and horrible?

Finally, with swollen eyes and my dictionary clutched in my hand like a bible, I dragged myself downstairs to ask B. Wallace why she thought such a thing.

She didn't even look at me as she poured herself a bourbon and water. "You were glowering at me," she said lightly. Then she turned and squinted her eyes at me.

"That's how I was looking at you?"

"Yes," she said evenly, with an undercurrent of Tennessee Williams.

"I was squinting?" It was a question/statement.

"Like a judgmental mole."

I understood then. The time had come to confess my great secret. I think I probably sighed and rolled my eyes; then explained I wasn't giving her the 4th grade version of the evil eye, I needed glasses. The school nurse had already sent three notes home, telling my mother to take me to the eye-doctor. But I tore them all up. I moved to the front row in class, then scooted my desk forward another two feet.

"I wasn't making faces at you mom, I just can't see you. Last night when Daddy showed me the big dipper, I couldn't see that either. I'm sorry you thought I was being ugly."

She kissed me on the cheek and touched my temple. I loved her cool bourbon breath and beautiful fingers. "I'll make an appointment tomorrow," she said and then we both laughed as I made another funny face at her and she walked into the other room.

The same week, there was an episode on the Brady Bunch with a nearly identical plot. Jan had to get glasses and cried a lot.

Getting glasses meant I wasn't Marcia anymore.

It wasn't until I was in college and working on a freshman human psych project that I realized how sad and paranoid my mother's reaction was.

Over and over and over again I have vowed, sworn and willed myself not to do this sort of thing to my children. I will not be that way, for their sake, though I can feel the sharp edges of sarcasm and defensiveness whirling in my veins.

A family gremlin.

12:46 p.m. It's still Friday though I feel like I've been sitting around this fucking waiting room for a month. With one hand on my stomach, I ask the baby to ignore any of these angry feelings he's picking up.

A nurse appears in the doorway and calls my name with an officious smile. She has perfect teeth, Mary Tyler Moore hair and three inch black heels. The bitch, she should not be allowed to wear those in an OBGYN office. Obviously, she's not from The Pregnant Women World, a place with a bathroom for every woman and shoes made entirely of elastic. There's nothing stretchy or forgiving about her pseudo-snakeskin heels. They are sharp little things you could use to pick the meat out of a pecan.

I follow her shoes until she stops at a scale and motions, like Carol Merrill. Please step up. She starts me at 150 then slides the little weight over. She doesn't say anything, just writes my weight down in the chart. I can't remember what I weighed last time. I try to peek, but she snaps the folder closed and says, "This way please."

I follow her into an examining room where I put on my ugly yellow gown then shuffle into the bathroom to pee in a blue plastic cup.

Sitting on the toilet, I wait some more. Nothing. I must pee in this cup. Finally, I turn on the water and manage to perform, just a little.

As I climb onto the examination table with my backless dress and clean white socks, I check my watch. I really hate waiting in here because there's nothing to look at but shining and intrusive instruments. I know at any moment a man will come into this room. I will lie down, lift my legs way up high and be completely exposed. He'll see all that I am. He'll see more of me than I have ever seen.

I check my watch again. Now I've been waiting an hour and 15 minutes. I'm way past annoyed. Still, my composure is Zen like.

Dr. Jones steps into my room with a dignified smile. He has no idea I'm ready to leap off the examining table and choke him with his own stethoscope.

Smiling, he looks at my chart. "You've lost six pounds, Liz."

Because I'm a well trained American woman, I instantly feel proud.

"A little weight loss in the last few weeks is normal but that's too much. You must eat. The baby needs everything you can give him. Try eating a lot of little meals, all day long. Alright?"

I nod dutifully.

Actually, I like Dr. Jones, he's a fine old fellow with an arid sense of humor. Sometimes, I can't tell when he's joking because he always makes his jokes when I can't see his face. He'll say something droll when my knees are up in the air and he's looking at my cervix, That's when he announces, "You have plenty of room here, Liz."

I feel my face redden. What's he mean by that? Does Zoltan think I have 'plenty of room?' That doesn't sound good.

Then he peeks up, over my white gown with a wry smile, "Everything looks great."

Because this is my third child, there's very little for him to tell me. Thus far my pregnancy has been so perfect it's boring. The baby has turned, her head is down now, that explains the pummeling my ribs have been subjected to. The Doctor measures my stomach with a tape measure.

"Every thing is perfectly normal. Your blood pressure is a little higher than usual but that's fine. Anything unusual?"

"Well, yes actually, I had some bleeding this weekend. And I've been feeling funny."

"Really? Was it heavy?" He's looking at my chart with mild interest now. I've done something, finally.

"What did you do this weekend, anything strenuous?"

"No, not much."

"Have you been having sex."

"I shake my head. "Not really."

He catches my blush. "Sexual activity?" He sits down on a little stool and the nurse leaves.

I'm embarrassed to the point of being paralyzed. "Mild sexual activity without penetration?" he asks.

"That's a fair description," I stare at different things around the room.

He puts my chart down. "That's probably it, then. I suspect your placenta is a little low and the stimulation, especially if you had an orgasm, brought on the bleeding. Nothing to worry about though. The baby is fine. Be happy. If, in fact, you did experience an orgasm, you and your husband," he checks the chart to find my husband's name, "Zolton, are part of a small and fortunate percentage that take part in pleasurable sexual activity after the sixth month. But you need to be careful, no stimulation for a week so we can make sure this clears up."

Yes, I'm lucky I have orgasms. That's what he's trying to say.

I make a clucking sound. "Poor Zoltan, first he had to give up cigarettes at home, now this."

He laughs and crosses his legs. "You know, I just read that women who swallow their husband's semen during pregnancy have lower blood pressure."

A tsunami of embarrassment blasts through my brain. He's talking about blow jobs. "No kidding," I feel the blush rise from my throat and spread across my face like a crimson tidal wave. I laugh nervously. "I'm sure Zoltan will be happy to hear about that." I check my watch. 12:55 p.m. How do I suppress the urge to run screaming from this exam office?

The doctor stands up. "I just want to know where they find volunteers for studies like that."

I laugh because this oral sex conversation with my old doctor is ridiculous. I laugh because I'm stunned and embarrassed. I'm also interested. Low blood pressure is a good thing.

"What was the other thing you mentioned, feeling funny?" he asks.

"Funny feelings" I correct him. Why did I mention this to him, in the first place? "I keep thinking I'm in strange places. Everything around me changes for just a few seconds. I hear people and songs." Dr. Jones steps closer. He holds my lids up and looks into my eyes as I speak. He's been chewing Juicy Fruit gum. He pinches the skin on my wrist.

"Nightmares, strange dreams are common during pregnancy."

I shake my head, "This happens when I'm awake."

"Do you get dizzy?"

"Sometimes. But... these feelings, they are more like..." I'm about to say the word visions when he interrupts.

"Liz you are dehydrated. You need to drink at least half a gallon of water every day and juices too. Coffee and sodas don't count. I need to see you in three days. Call me if there's any more bleeding or cramping."

I nod. Not enough water, that's why I'm watching my mother's childhood take place on Central Avenue as I try to conduct a simple business transaction. Water, yeah, that's it Doc. I nod and smile some more.

"Let me ask you something, are you planning on having any more children?" His question surprises me.

"I don't know, why?"

"You know, there are a lot of birth control methods now that are extraordinarily simple and effective. I see you've used condoms in the past, films, you've never been on the pill?"

"No, I'm worried they'll make me fat."

"You're using antiquated information. Birth control pills won't make you fat unless you eat too much. You keep taking your vitamins and drink, Liz. You'll be fine."

Dr. Jones is a fine old guy, but holy shit, he doesn't ask any of the right questions. How can he make a diagnosis without knowing me. Even a bad doctor should figure out I'm suffering survivors guilt. A smart doctor might figure out it's something more. But not Dr. Jones. He just wants me to drink more water.

I'm ready to go. He never knew my mother, he doesn't know what she's capable of. He can not help me. B. Wallace is warping my world and the doctor wants me to drink a half gallon of water a day. Mike's advice for eating kiwi has a better chance of helping me get through this.

He thinks I've had enough children and wants me to get my tubes tied.. Three is enough. He's probably right. But he doesn't know what I know.

My children, my love for my children, keeps death away. Sometimes, the only thing that binds me to this earth, the only little string that keeps me here, is the love of Mike and Felicity and this baby. Without them, I would float away, melt into the tree tops and clouds and be gone.

It's all too alluring.

To bad my love was not enough for B. Wallace. It was not enough to keep her from Daddy and Daniel. She loved me and I loved her, but they outweighed me and the pain here on earth gnawed at her will to live. I wanted to be enough for her, I tried to love her enough to keep her here, with me. But there wasn't enough of me. I don't want to leave my children until it's time, until they are all old enough to stay here alone with love of their own.

I can not tell the doctor this.

I hurry to get dressed then try to walk quickly to the front desk. I want out. This clinic is too big. Five doctors and a herd of nurses. It's an ovarian uterine factory. Everybody smiles but, after all this time, nobody knows my name unless, they look at my chart. They don't know who my children are. That's not right. God knows, child birth is a fairly personal experience.

The only nurse in this clinic who actually takes an interest in my world is Rachel, the financial counselor and book keeper. Zoltan and I don't have insurance and she worries about us.

Chapter 8

1:30 p.m. Z's grandmother, E'va, stands in the door, impatiently waiting for me. She looks at her watch. I know what time it is. I'm five minutes late.

She is dressed up, her beautiful silver hair pinned in a bun. Dangling, onyx earrings catch the afternoon sunlight. The dark stones flash.

Her eyes move back and forth, from my car to the mountains in front of her home. The street she lives on runs along the bottom edge of West and Sugarloaf Mountains. There is a sweet curve, where the two mountains meet. It dips down low and dark, like a fat woman's cleavage. Fog hangs in this dense pocket every morning, but is always burned off by 9 or 10 o'clock.

E'va watches the sky and mountains, so she will know what to expect from the day.

I am captured by her knowledge.

At 89, E'va is beautiful. She still has a cunning I-beam strength. If allied forces arrived on her door step tomorrow, she would bake loaves of gorgeous bead and fix a kettle of goulash to feed them all.

She has an ancient strength and cunning that comes from centuries spent on the same land. Her blood line, like Z's, is so pure, unadulterated by anything other than Magyar blood. Sometimes, I feel I have corrupted their rich heritage with my well breed mixed bag of Scotch/ Irish/English.

This old woman has a magic. When she cuts herself, rich soil from the edge of the Danube river flows. And then the cut heals at an astonishing rate.

My grandmothers were blue bloods, DAR and 17th Century Dames, but they did not heal quickly. They could trace my family's arrival in America to the early 1700s, but they could not turn grapes into wine and I do not believe they could ever save themselves during a military occupation.

"Szervusz," she says, Hello.

'Szervusz,' I respond. 'Hogy vagy?" How are you?

She chuckles, pleased that I am making an attempt to learn Hungarian. "You come inside now, you will eat. I have goulash and nice bread."

I want to whine. I also want some wine. But I can't have either. I don't want to eat goulash. I'll throw up. There's too much in my body right now, including another human being. I can't put anything else in there.

"Wait" I pick up the melon and hold it out for her to inspect.

She hurries to me. "For me something?" She asks.

"It's a yellow watermelon."

"Watermelon," she repeats. Taking the big fruit in her arms like a baby and walking inside. "I do not know this word waddermelton." She says as the screen door slams. "You come inside."

"But we are going to lunch E'va, why eat now?" A futile grandmother question in any language.

Granny is already dishing up a bowl of the rich meat, gravy and spatzel. There are potatoes too, the size of thumb nails, which she grows in her garden.

She approaches me then bends down to speak to my baby. "Hello szervusz hogy vagy kis angyalom?" Hello, how are you my little angel?

"You eat," she says to me and pushes the bowl across the table. After watching me take a bite, she puts two sprigs of parsley next to my potatoes. The parsley roots dangle off the edge of my plate. "A petrezselyem jo' neked!" The parsley is good for you. I just look at her, nod and keep chewing.

She taps her temple impatiently, until a strand of gray hair falls from her bun. "For your blood, it is good."

"Ok," I say, and nibble on the fresh parsley then hold one of the tiny leaves between my front teeth. Crisp and green, it leaves my mouth feeling nice. It reminds me of this morning's kiwi.

Knowing she won't let me out of the house without eating more, I take five bites. "Ez nagyon jo'!" I say slowly with a smile. It's very good.

"Koszonom." Thank you.

The last bite won't go down. I chew some more and take a deep breath. My throat is constricting. After sipping some water, I try to swallow the goulash again. Finally, when E'va turns away, to search for her house keys, I spit the last bite into my napkin.

"That was wonderful. Thank you." I hold the door open for her. As we step outside the car makes an odd hissing noise and the baby kicks like a mule.

I play with a smooth rock in my pocket. Z gave it to me last week and I've been holding on to it ever since.

E'va holds my arm as we walk to the car. She clutches a paper bag in one arm and glances at me sideways. I know what she is thinking. E'va likes me and she loves the baby in my belly, but she wonders, what sort of woman I am? Why won't marry her grandson? Why won't I give this baby a proper family? Why do I want to be pregnant and unmarried. She thinks I am odd, to choose a shameful situation when there are other options. She likes me, but knows I am strange and my life has been tainted. When she first heard that most of my family was dead she crossed herself and looked away. For nearly a week she could not make eye contact and then she asked Z if he thought I was cursed.

Now, she is concerned for her grandson and talks to God about me, she prays that I won't hurt Zolton, that I won't have his baby then disappear. Because I am so odd, she worries I will shatter his world.

What E'va doesn't know is that I will never upset or harm this piece of heaven, this refuge I've searched for since I was a teenager.

This is the first time since I was old enough to drive, that I've had security and happiness, love and good sex, all at the same time. And I'm going to do my best to give all these things back to Zolton.

I have found love and I will do everything necessary to keep it safe, even from myself and my self-destructive tendencies. I want to be happy and that is why I will not marry Z.

I know Eva's bag is is filled with pastry, strudel and hussar choke, but I can tell from the shape there is something else in there. Fluffy stuff.

She hands me the bag.

"Apple and cabbage strudel I give to you." Pride shimmers in her dark eyes. She knows she is the strudel master.

"Cabbage?" E'va always makes wonderful apple and walnut strudel for us. She spends hours stretching the phyllo dough across her kitchen table, until it is so thin, we can literally read a newspaper through the dough. When she had restaurants up north, food critics from Chicago and Detroit wrote glowing reviews of her pastries, using words like sumptuous and old-world to describe E'va and her desserts.

I wonder if they liked her cabbage strudel.

"Cabbage, men like it so much," she says. "It makes them more." She gestures, flexes her thin arms at an odd angle. This means strength, I think.

I put the bag on the hood of the car and peek inside. The stiff brown paper smells of flour and pastry, apples and cabbage. What am I going to do with cabbage strudel? The kids won't touch it.

There's also something fuzzy inside the bag, a faded leopard skin animal print thing. Hmmmm. I pull out the soft yellow, brown and black material. E'va, the ultimate recycler, smiles,

"It is a..." she touches her head. "What is the word, it is a ...for your legs, when it is cold."

"Oh, a lap robe," I rub it against my cheek. It has button holes, a satin lining and faded label on one edge. It's an old coat she's taken apart and turned into a lap robe. It's so soft and smells good.

Under the lap robe there are a bunch of bras, at least a dozen. They are not new, but seem to be in good condition. Black, white and beige, plain and lace, most have underwire. I hold a giant black one up. The cups are big enough to hold cantaloupes. All the bras are different sizes. I look up at her and smile, "Bras? These are for me?"

"Egan," she nods, "you take." She pulls a pretty black one from the bag and holds it up by the straps, so the cups point at me, accusingly.

"See," she says and pushes at the center of the cup with her finger. A little square flap falls open, right where my nipple would be. She peeks at me through the opening. Smiling, she opens the center of the other side. "For you and the baby, see? Now you can feed him." She holds her arms in front of her chest as though rocking an infant.

I reach out and touch E'va's nursing bra. She has carefully sewn a tongue of velcro to the top of each flap. "They are amazing. How wonderful, E'va. Thank you. Nagyon sze'pen koszonom."

She pulls another bra from the bag. "You see, I don't know how to do it first and I use a button. But, no good. See." She holds a white bra with a button in the center of each cup in front of her own chest. Her fingers are slightly misshapen by arthritis, but move expertly across the fabric. "The buttons, too big and the baby might suck it." We laugh.

"You know, these are so expensive at the store."

"Yes they are, all bras are." Briefly I consider asking where she found all these old bras. There is no way we'll get through this conversation.

I take the bag and smile. "You are so smart. Thank you. They'll be wonderful."

"Szivessen," she says. I give with my heart.

She is smiling as I put the bag in the back seat.

E'va puts her purse on the floor of the car, then picks up a big plastic carton with half a dozen green, one gallon wine jugs. She points to four more jugs next to her kitchen door and I load them into the back seat.

I have to close my eyes, when E'va gets in the car. As is the case with many older people, sitting down is a choreographed free-fall and I'm always, certain she will hit her head on the door then fall out of the car.

E'va doesn't close her eyes, she watches me screw myself in behind the wheel. Maybe I make her uneasy too.

I catch myself groaning softly, as I arch my back then start the car. What's happened to me? I am not a person anymore. I'm a freaky cartoon character, a giant belly with legs. I thought the baby and I could live comfortably in one skin, but it's impossible. I touch my stomach and pout in defeat.

The baby kicks with the joy of victory.

One block from the house E'va taps the window and makes a 'tch tch' noise at a woman watering her yard with one hand and clutching a tiny Shitzu named Mr. Beau Jangles under her arm.

The woman's name is Ivy. She and E'va had a horrendous fight a few months ago when E'va found dog poop next to her peach tree. E'va was sure it belonged to Mr. Beau Jangles because it was such a tiny pile.

They haven't spoken since.

E'va asks, "We get the water? and the flour from the store."

"Sure, the grocery store, which one?"

"First we go to the Harvest Foods for flour. Forty-nine cents one pound and then we go to" she waves in the direction of the Shopping Super Center until I say," Kroger."

"Yeah, yeah,' she says, smiling and hopeful.

We were supposed to have lunch, now it's two grocery stories and water. "Yeah, fine," I grumble with a smile.

She fumbles with her seat belt. Arthritis in her left arm makes the strap difficult to pull.

A baby in my belly makes the job difficult for me too.

We stop in front of Harvest Foods. I park in the fire lane but do not get out of the car while she goes in for her flour.

I wait with the air conditioner blowing in my face and the radio playing softly. Rod Stewart sings Maggie May. I almost fall asleep with my head tilted back and my hand resting on my belly.

I used to feel guilty when I let her shop alone, but not anymore. We are both happier this way. E'va gets cranky when I take too long pushing the cart up and down the isle. And she gets furious when strangers touch my belly. Her eyes darken until the pupils look like flaming raspberries. Now, I wait in the car for her

My thoughts float. I wish I was back in school. Talking to my smart, stoned and narcissistic friends.

I hear E'va's voice outside my window.

A gangly blond bag boy with acne, has pushed the shopping cart for her. His shorts are monstrous and hang well below his knees. The waist band rests on his skinny hip bones. I can read the make of his boxer underwear.

Opening the glove compartment, I pop the trunk. The boy heaves bags of flour into the trunk. They make a dull thud, as though Joe Peci is throwing a body into my car. How much flour did she buy?

"No, no," E'va scolds "Throwing is no good. They break, you are not good. Don't throw." Shaking her head, almost sadly, she gives him a quarter. "Next time, I help you. I show you how so you do not hurt your back."

The Kroger grocery store is less than a mile away. Again, I park in the red fire lane. "Do you want me to come in with you?"

She shakes her head and reaches for the door handle. "No no no," her voice trails off. Thin and foreign. She walks so quickly towards the big front doors then yanks a cart impatiently and starts pushing past the manager's booth, like a very old bolt of lightening.

Wawa had most of her groceries delivered. Aldridge's Razorback Grocery, a mom and pop store, was the oldest, smallest and most expensive grocery store in town, but they took care of my grandmother after my mom moved to Florida.

Someone honks behind me because I am blocking their exit. I drive forward ten feet, roll the windows down and turn the car off. I can still see the grocery store door and I watch for E'va.

She emerges from the store and walks directly to the place we were parked before. She stops and looks around, fear distorts her face until she sees my car and waving arm.

"Why did you move?" she says through the window.

"I had to."

"I could not find you," she says angrily, "I thought you were gone." Leaning over, I open the door for her. "I am getting so old. I do not know what to do in this world."

She gets in, clutching a plastic grocery bag.

"What did you buy?" I ask just to change the subject.

Triumphantly, she extracts a stalk of celery with a huge and hairy root ball attached. It looks like a giant deformed testicle.

"This I will grow," she says proudly, stuffing the fine and hideous plant back into the bag. Then she hands me a bag of Hershesy's Kisses.

"I am a rich lady today, I have chocolate. You give them to the children. Chocolate is good for them, for the heart," She thumps on her own bony chest with her finger tips, "And good for the lungs too."

"And this is for you," she says and presses crisp bills into my hand.

Before I even unfold the bills, to see how much she is trying to give me. I start shaking my head.

"It is for when you get married." Her eyes glimmer with sneaky joy.

Ten one hundred dollar bills. They are excitingly crisp and textured.

Poking the money back into her purse, I say, "You can't pay me to get married, E'va. I don't except bribes, not today anyway."

"Not paying you but you will need money for the children. It is gift for if you get married."

Turning left, I head up Prospect Avenue. We pass, WaWa's, beautiful old house. I can't help myself. I have to slow down and look at it carefully. Three grand Colonial stories, painted white with forest green shutters and three brick chimneys.

I say a little prayer. I ask, Doc Blue, who's been dead for forty years, to please come back and take WaWa. He must take her out of that nursing home.

How could Doc Blue leave, his bride, his wife, his love, behind? I try to keep annoyance out of my voice when I pray for him to come get WaWa. But as far as I'm concerned he's abandoned her. If he carries any weight at all in the after life, he should get his ghost down here and do something about the situation.

Suddenly, like a deflated balloon, my thoughts mellow. E'va is looking at the house with respect. I touch my stomach. The baby is quiet.

Things are ok. Really, my world is fine. I have love and we are all safe. I am overwhelmed by a sense of calm. My heart slows and I feel all wrapped up. Dead or alive, B. Wallace won't hurt us, she's just trying to get some point across.

WaWa, really, isn't unhappy in her nursing home. It's just her living conditions that make me uncomfortable.

Maybe Doc Blue is here with her, all the time. Perhaps that's why Wawa is happy in the horrible nursing home. Doc Blue is responsible for her startling and easy mental absence. So many of the other residents at the nursing home are angry. Spewing hateful words, cursing and spitting, hissing like cornered badgers at those who try to help them and at those who put them in that awful place.

WaWa is always calm. Her room is tranquil. Maybe Doc Blue can't get her out, so he is staying with her until God lifts her up.

Maybe... I feel better thinking this might be a possibility. I was weaned on Doc Blue stories. What a fine strong man, fine doctor and fine human.

Doc Blue died before I was born. But WaWa kept his medical bag right by the front door for 30 years after his death. Every night when I stayed with Wawa, I would lay in bed, kicking at my sheet and waiting for a breeze to push through my room. WaWa would sit on the edge of my mattress and tell me how it felt to have Doc Blue in the house, as though he were Jesus Christ. She would close her eyes and describe each sense, his smell and slow, even foot steps. His voice was smooth like melted fudge and his smile was soft and comforting. She told me stories of his youth. In 1894 he turned 7. That summer he hit his Negro friend, Eli, in the head with a rock. They both knew they would get whoopings so Doc Blue plucked a boll of cotton from the field, covered it with black shoe polish and stuck it in the bleeding hole.

When Eli was 23 he borrowed $500 dollars from my grandfather and turned it into a lumber business worth more than one million dollars. Legend has it Eli was the first black millionaire in the state of Arkansas.

During the depression, Doc Blue allowed patients to pay him for treatment and surgeries with sacks of potatoes and turnips, fresh plucked chickens and hunting dogs.

I am responsible for this family history. If I forget the stories or don't share them with the children, our history will die. That's another reason I need to stay here, in this life, with the kids.

Looking at Wawa's big white house on the hill, I whisper, "Doc Blue, please come get her. Take her home with you so she will be beautiful again. Please."

Everyone, if they truly love, says a prayer like this at some point. We all have to say good-by. We all desperately want to say good-by. Still, when the moment comes our hearts are collectively crushed. Life is not for the faint hearted.

E'va touches my arm. "You and Zolton get married. Why not? I not understand?"

All I can do is shake my head as we drive away from WaWa's house.

E'va and I don't speak, as we roll over West Mountain. The road winds and curves like a fire hose. I watch for Betty, though I know she's not here.

Like the rest of this town, West Mountain belongs to me, my history was created on this fine little hump.

There is a sign that says, "Caution Falling Rocks." When I was just five or six years old, Daddy told me there were Indians on West Mountain trying to push boulders on cars as they passed under ledges. I was terrified we would have a flat tire on the Mountain and the Indians would stone us while we tried to jack up the T-Bird.

"This looks nice, always, like Budapest," E'va says, clutching two water jugs in her lap.

The heavy magnolia trees give us a rich green shade. We are the only ones at the spring, so we get to use both taps.

Sparkling water pours from the middle of the mountain like a liquid gift from the gods. For a moment, I let the water run onto my palm then roll between my fingers, encasing each digit in a cool, bubbling glove.

We each fill one of the big green wine jugs, then E'va starts to speak. This spring has always been our place. When we are here, alone, she talks, she tells me stories in broken English. Her life's adventures and sorrows flow as though she is speaking to the mountain.

In the 1950s the mighty Russian ego awoke again. It was time to expand the empire and Hungary was one of the first countries consumed. The tiny country asked America for help but the United States was unmoved by the Hungarian pleas. She tells me she will never forgive America because our President let Russia eat Hungary.

While E'va speaks, I think about B. Wallace. She was mad at the South, E'va is still angry with all of America. The bigger and more powerful you are, the easier and more enjoyable it is to hate you.

During the '50s, E'va says, she was married to a very clever and handsome man, Kristof. He was a professional soccer player and they had a family.

When E'va realized Russia was on the verge of an invasion, she and Kristof collected all their money and started buying wine, thousands of gallons.

She touches me on the arm, "Oh, so much wine, everywhere, everywhere, in the kitchen, the living room, in the cellar and closets." E'va made her own wine too, in the kitchen of their small house, outside Budapest. She put up nearly 1000 gallons of her raw and fruity peach and apple wine. "Twenty one days is all it needs, not so long when you see a war outside the window. But it is a long time when you are thirsty."

While the wine was ripening and E'va was hoarding, she sent Kristof, into the fields with a post hole digger. When the wine was ready, they filled hundreds of wine skins, then buried it all in the holes Kristof had dug. They hid their wine from the filthy swilling Russian soldiers in a cow pasture.

Once it was in the ground, E'va asked her brother-in-law to bring his herd of cows over to graze. She wanted them to stamp on the earth and cover her freshly buried mounds with piles of dung.

Survival and success, were E'va's way of sneering at the Russians. They could take her country for a little while, but she would never let them take her strength. She buried that sweet and potent wine, then waited for the tanks.

Now, looking up from the rushing water, she smiles at me. The dappled light filtering through the magnolia trees makes her look younger. Her eyes match her ebony earrings. "I did not know if I am going to live." she says. "They killed so many, so many in my village. One solider, he wanted to cut my finger to get my ring." She shows me her naked and frail looking ring finger, then holds it as though a soldier might still appear and cut it off.

We fill four more jugs, watch the water for a little bit, then she tells me Russians were so much worse than the Germans. "But if I lived, I would have money. You always need very much money. Having no money is worse than war because you are alone when you are poor. When there is war, all people are together and sad."

E'va's plan worked. The soldiers did exactly as she expected. Once they invaded Hungary, they began to drink. They drank all the wine they could manage and what they did not drink, they destroyed. Hungary was a dry land.

Budapest was occupied. Tanks blocked the way to the local market. The Americans said they were not coming to help, so the Kremlin relaxed, fat and confident and dangerous. Some tanks were pulled back and the soldiers started laughing at the angry and beautiful Hungarian women. That's when E'va and Kristof started digging. Every night they dug up dozens of wine skins, then the next morning, they sold it to their thirsty countrymen.

Picking up one of the jugs, filled with water, E'va says to me, "I didn't make them pay too much, though. I don't hurt them more. But they pay enough."

E'va keeps talking. She wants to tell stories today. Thirty six days after the fall of Budapest, Kristof was killed by a Russian soldier during a neighborhood soccer game. Kristof was the goalie. He taunted the Russians because they couldn't score on him. Laughing, he gave them free shots; he danced in the goal box and he stood on one foot and still stopped their best shots. He laughed at them and called them little girls with big guns. The final score was 9 to 0. After the game Kristof slapped one of the soldiers on the butt and said, "Good game my pretty little red woman." E'va smiles a little and shakes her head. "He never knew when he make people too mad with the jokes.

The soldier slammed the stock of his rifle into the back of Kristof's head, then walked off the field with his team. Kristof died that night, just before dinner. E'va says, "then I knew I would take the family far to America."

"Where did you and Kristof get the idea to bury your wine?"

"When the Nazis soldiers were in Hungary there was no wine because they drank it all. The Russian soldiers did the same thing. Soldiers are soldiers. And I said if any soldiers ever came back to Budapest, I would be ready. Soldiers are the same."

"You're too tough, E'va," I say, screwing a cap on another bottle.

She smiles a little and her eyes flash, old and merciless. "Yes."

E'va is so unlike the vulnerable and gracious women I grew up holding hands with. My grandmothers saw hardship, they struggled through the depression, knew the pain of sending their men off to war, and they buried their families.

But E'va is an entirely different sort of soul, grown from a different soil. Her dirt is darker and has buried more bodies. She marched past Nazis and Russian tanks and inner-city gangs in Chicago and Detroit.

We finish filling the jugs. They are wet and heavy. I pick up the biggest carton full of jugs. E'va eyes suddenly go cold, "No, no, no, too heavy. The baby, you must think." She tries to take the carton away from me. She pulls, but I resist.

"E'va, I'm fine," but she is dead serious and really pulling hard now. Looking into her black eyes is like staring down a small caliber gun barrel. Still, I can't let her have the carton. I can't let an 89 year old woman take a fifty pound load away from me. I'm suddenly afraid if I let go she will fall over backwards and hit her head. What if I accidentally kill Z's grandmother. Jesus Christ, I'm fighting with an old woman on the sidewalk. Which is stronger, pregnancy or age?

"Please, E'va, I've got this, really I do."

"'No, it's too heavy for the baby."

"Here," I say, "We'll put it down together, ok?"

We stare at each other for a moment. It is a face off. The carton might as well be Zolton. Finally, she lets go, angry and frustrated. She turns and shrugs in true disgust. I hand her the biggest glass jug. "It's not too heavy now, I'm fine, I promise."

She is still angry, but takes the jug and sort of race walks to the car. Then she turns around and takes another bottle from my carton, just to prove her point.

WaWa would never pick up anything as heavy as a grocery bag. She would just stand next to heavy things and people would always pick them up for her. WaWa had an elegant queenly magnetism which forced men to be kind and helpful, to honor and serve her. And she would never stop thanking those men who helped, so they always felt good about doing her will.

Once we are back in the car, E'va is quiet for a little while, obviously annoyed. Then she says, "You must take care of the baby."

"I am E'va, but you shouldn't try to carry things that weigh nearly as much as you do."

"I carry heavy things. I have no baby."

"I know you can do it, but that was dead weight. You could hurt yourself. I'm sorry I upset you."

She crosses herself. "Don't say that word, dead. Sometimes it is to close and you don't want it to know you are here."

Glancing in the rear view mirror, I wonder if E'va knows how close death really is, that's it's looking in our rear window, keeping tabs on me, wondering what's taking so long.

Finally, I add, "At least we got the water."

Arguing with an old woman is wrong. It makes me miserable and I feel guilty. All old women win when they argue with me. Even when they are wrong.

"The water is not the important," is all she will say for nearly a mile.

This woman drives me crazy, I mean really pisses me off. I've never felt this way about an old person. I've always adored and obeyed and taken care of my old people, but E'va will not tolerate such behavior.

As we drive past Wal-Mart she says, "I need a button. Do you need things at Wal-Mart?" Fighting doesn't really bother her. It's a good way to work up an appetite.

Trying to win her back, I lie and say I do. We will come back after lunch and shop.

Slowly, I drive down Central Avenue, hoping my hands will stop shaking before we reach the restaurant.

Because she is an old woman with arthritis and an accent, E'va is constantly underestimated. Hurlie is underestimated too, because he looks stupid and has a limp.

I must be careful.

Driving towards the restaurant, E'va says with her soft voice and heavy accent. "Zolton, he works too much for what they pay? Is it enough for the hot in a kitchen? Do they know how hot it is? He could get an office job. He could teach. He is too old now for this. You make him change."

"But he's happy doing this E'va. I don't want him to change if he's happy," I say, parking the car.

We both get out, then I stop and try to hide behind a large potted plant. I can't take another step until I fix the underwire in my bra. It's poking my ridiculously large breasts. And the bras I have to wear now are atrocious looking, huge and white. As long as I'm hiding, I might as well fix my underwear too. The front pregnant panel is hot and itchy. Should I just pull the elastic over my knobby belly button or keep it all low down?

As soon as I have this baby, I'm going to buy a dozen new pairs of underwear. Little slinky ones in hot colors. I've always hated thong underwear, they make my butt muscles clinch up all the time. But maybe I'll try them again. I'll wear anything that's not like these, big and ugly as the state of Texas.

E'va watches me wiggle. I guess she knows what I'm doing. I'm too huge and miserable and itchy to care.

"Zoltan should do more," she speaks to me, though I am hiding behind a bush.

"Maybe he wouldn't be happy doing more. And I like him happy." I smooth my shirt over my rearranged underwear.

"You need more money. For the children. He's young, he can do more. The post office."

I laugh, trying to figure out how to respond with my limited vocabulary. She likes the idea of his working at the post office because it's a government job, secure and steady. But Zoltan isn't a post office sort of man.

"Everybody always thinks they need more money," I say, "And it's true, we are always broke," Hell, I might as well go on and say what I'm thinking. If she understands, wonderful. If she doesn't, to hell with it. "E'va, I grew up with money, I've had money most of my life. I'll have money again. I'm not worried. What Z and I have is more important. He already works sixty hours a week. I can't push him any harder. I don't want him to be unhappy. If he's miserable, we'll all be miserable. We get by and we like each other and we're happy E'va, that means something. Zoltan makes good money, we just have too many expenses."

I could go on but she is shaking her head like a dog with something in its ear. She wants me to stop. "I do not understand." She walks away, annoyed again and disappointed. She thinks we are both weak.

She stops to say something more, but I'm not really listening. I'm adding things to my mental "when I'm not pregnant list." When I'm no longer pregnant I'll walk around in front of Zoltan naked. I'll vacuum and talk on the phone and do the dishes without any clothes on at all. I'll take a bath so hot my skin will itch and steam will rise from my hair when I emerge from the water.

Z's family is a perfect example of "The American Dream." After the Russians tried to swallow Hungary, his mother and father and E'va came to America. His mother was already pregnant with Zoltan, so he was conceived in Hungary and born in Detroit. They started out desperately poor and worked their way up to upper-middle class in less than 15 years.

Looking at E'va, I am reminded of the baby elephant at the Gator Ranch. Gray skin and wrinkles. But the elephant seemed a lot more understanding. I wonder what sort of funeral arrangements E'va has made. I'm not mad and hoping she'll die soon but I hope we don't have to go through some ashes ordeal with E'va too. What am I going to do with Mom, what can I do, what does she want me to do. Maybe she just wants me. Why shouldn't I let them build a little monument. Mike and Felicity will be so proud. She'll be remembered. Looking around, I half expect to see my mother.

Ashes to Ashes, Dust to Dust....Ashes Ashes we all fall down. Why risk it? I'll just leave her on the coke machine.

Zolton walks out the front door of the restaurant. His whites are still clean. I love seeing him; my heart speeds up just a little. How is it that I have the love of this big, handsome man? He offers his hand, kisses me and says, 'How's it going?"

"We're fighting."

"Is it bad?" he grins.

He walks to E'va and kisses her on both cheeks "Szervusz. Hogy vagy?" He gives her a scolding look which she ignores.

"I think our relationship will survive," I say shrugging.

He looks in the back seat of the car, "What's in the bag, strudel?"

"Yeah, that too. Use your imagination."

We are moving very slowly towards the restaurant door. He rubs my shoulder. "Who won the fight?"

"I think it was a draw."

He holds the front door open and as I pass by he kisses me again on the cheek. "Good for you. Sometimes you gotta be tough."

Zolton and E'va are so similar, they love each other deeply, but they argue. Love lets them do that. He and E'va are bone to bone. Nothing is hidden, so they are allowed to fight.

Because his parents were busy trying to learn English and finding jobs when they arrived in America, E'va raised Z for nearly eight years.

She taught him Hungarian before anyone taught him English. The Detroit school system didn't know what to do with a little boy and his strange language. So they sent him home from kindergarten with a note that said he could not attend public school until he learned how to speak English.

Zolton did not return to school that year. Instead, E'va bought a television set. Everyday the grandmother and grandson sat and watched black and white shows like "Red Skelton," "Leave it to Beaver," "As The World Turns" and the nightly news with a note book, a Hungarian dictionary and an English dictionary.

When they went to the neighborhood market, E'va drew pictures and wrote down the names of the fruits and vegetables, then asked the manager how to pronounce the words. After one year Zolton was fluent in both English and Hungarian and was able to enroll in first grade.

There has never been any doubt that E'va only wants good things for her boy. She taught him to speak and now she wants him out of the kitchen and married.

If B. Wallace is here to keep me from marrying Z. she'll have to go head to head with E'va. I can't win.

"Come" E'va motions for me to hurry, then finds a booth she likes and settles in.

Zolton is holding my hand and we walk, together. I watch his shoes. There is a tomato sauce stain. He needs new shoe laces.

A crab like cramp works its way up the back of my calf. I wish he could sit down and rub my leg for me. He addresses my belly, "How's that garlic smell to you?"

I sit down in E'va's booth. My stomach touches the edge of the table. This is not a good feeling. Fortunately the table is not too heavy, so Zolton scoots it it toward E'va. The sudden noise startles her, then she understands.

"You need room," she says. "It it a boy, I think."

"Maybe."

"There are too many women in America. Boys are good now." She stares at my torso as she speaks.

I chew on my tongue until it feels like taco meat. She says some of the most god-awful things. What if the baby is a girl, will E'va still love the child?

The waitress, a heavy set blonde, approaches the table and smiles. E'va says "For us, three schnapps."

The waitress looks at me and says, still smiling, "three glasses of schnapps?"

I shake my head. "E'va, I can't drink that much. It's not good for the baby. Will wine be alright?"

She waves the girl away. "Yes fine."

"If it is a boy you will be eight days late. Boys are lazy and do not want to come out and go to work. If it is a girl you will be a little early. The girls are in a hurry always. But you have a boy. That would be good."

She looks around the restaurant. "They need to paint."

"Yes, they do." I look around the tiny restaurant too. There are hanging Chianti bottles, framed pictures of gondolas and heavy white plaster Italian statues of half naked Renaissance men.

"Italians, they have too much of everything. The country is like that too." E'va says.

Zolton comes out of the kitchen. His dark hair is pulled back. The contrast between his black beard and tan arms against the heavy white cotton coat always gets to me in a very primitive way.

E'va moves over so he can sit down but he's looking at me. I scoot over too, so he can sit down next to me. This all feels very immature but I don't care. I'm pregnant and needy. The world must revolve around my body and my family for now.

Because of his beard and mustache, sometimes it's hard to tell when Zolton is smiling, but it's always there for me, in his eyes, a dark brown shinning.

He holds my hand as he speaks to E'va in Hungarian. Then she answers. She has a lot to say. Talking to Zoltan is a crucial outlet for her. E'va still thinks in Hungarian, so he is the only person with whom she can freely and thoroughly express all her thoughts. She is constantly held back and limited by her stumbling English.

And so I am quiet as they rattle on in this bizarre and extraordinarily complex language. Two waitress come and stand by the table for a moment. They just want to listen.

Americans always assume English is the most difficult language. Wouldn't that make us superior? Well, it's nothing compared to an ancient middle European language.

A very skinny and country waitress looks at me, "I didn't know he could talk like that. What are they talking?" She puts a basket of garlic bread and three glasses of wine on the table.

"Hungarian."

She shakes her head. "I never head anything like that. I thought maybe it was Russian."

E'va raises her glass. She makes a toast to Saint Stephan and then says, "Prosit."

The wine fills my mouth with white flavors. I don't want to swallow. "Who's Stephan?"

Zolton takes a gulp of wine then checks his watch. He leans back and yells to his bread boy, "Joey, check the oven." Then address me. "Stephan was the first king of Hungary."

E'va says to him, " Olyan jo' kiraly voit, hogy a Pa'pa szente' avatta."

Z says to me, "He was such a great King that the Pope made him a saint in 1005."

He listens to his grandmother. She is animated and intense. I recognize the term Magyar which means Hungarian, but it is very pure. All Hungarians wish to be Magyars but they are not, True Magyars were great horsemen and descendants from seven original tribes that roamed and terrorized the Western half of Europe.

Zoltan and E'va are Magyars.

As E'va speaks, she pushes the silverware to the side and leans forward on the table. She stares deep into her grandson's eyes. He is being pulled into her ancient story and for a moment, belongs to her. They are going back in time, searching for the wild and dangerous Magyar ancestors who still fill their veins.

Late at night, when our house is dark and silent, I listen to Zolton breathe. I can hear his history; I see horses and campfires and men with tangled black hair sweeping across the continent, full of the earth and power. He wakes up hot and intense, still smelling of camp fires.

Sitting in the restaurant, I try not to react as E'va takes him, though my natural instinct is to touch his hand and draw him back. Then, suddenly, she runs a finger across her own throat, someone must be getting killed. She sweeps her hands across the table. This seems to be a sign of inclusion, everything is being brought together.

"There were seven tribes of Magyars," he tells me though he's still looking at her. "...barbarian's on horseback. They drank wine mixed with blood and made goulash in the bladders of goats. All of Europe was afraid of them. The were great horsemen who murdered and burned their way across the continent. Stephan brought these tribes to Christianity. Until that time the Magyars didn't have a country of their own."

"Sounds kind of Klingon," I say and Zolton nudges me with his elbow.

Once E'va is finished telling us about King Stephan, she raises her glass again and says, "to King Stephan. Maybe you name the baby Stephan?"

We touch glasses and drink.

My hand is shaking a little and Zoltan notices. "You need to eat."

"That might be a good idea."

"I'll have you done in five minutes." He says, then finishes his wine and stands up.

E'va says something else to him in Hungarian. He answers and they both look at me for a second.

I feel like a cow.

She nods at my belly. Zoltan says to me. "She wants you to drink two glasses of red wine a day. She thinks it's good for the baby, it'll give him thick red blood. I told her you didn't want to do that, your doctor doesn't believe wine is good for babies. She said we were wrong. So I told her this was your third baby and she only had one, so you probably know more than she does." He kisses my cheek, smiling. "I'll be back with your lunch. You girls have fun."

We are silent for a moment. I need an uncomplicated topic. Goats are easy. Kecske. I tell her how big Fred, the goat, has gotten. I hold my hand out. "He's taller than the table."

She says, "You should eat him now, before he is so old and tough."

"No, he's a pet, E'va. The children would be so sad if we ate Fred."

"America is a funny country. You have a goat for a dog."

We both eat some garlic bread. I tear it in half and E'va folds it then bites the heart right out of the center. "Garlic and butter, it is good." She swallows then leans forward on her elbows. "I want to give you money for buy wedding rings."

"No, you know I can't let you do that. If we need to buy wedding rings we can get them ourselves."

"Do you have them already?" She sounds so hopeful I almost want to lie to her. "Maybe you wear your mother's, she's dead, yes?"

I nod, but the thought of my mother's wedding ring, of her thin and eloquent fingers makes me close my eyes. I can smell the expensive lotion she covered her hands with. Sometimes, as we knelt to pray in church, Mom would cover my hands with her own. The scent would swim through my brain as I talked to God, certain he would always love and care for me. Why did you abandon me? You were supposed to watch over me, God.

Then I hear his voice. "I always have, Liz. I always will," God says to me, while E'va finishes her wine. God is in my head or in the next booth, his voice warm and smooth as a creamy soup.

My head jerks up. E'va chews on a new piece of bread. She did not hear God. Looking around, I realize there aren't any men in the dining room, not even a bus boy.

I hear something powerful and hushed in the air. Twisting around, I check the next booth. The air shimmers. God's seraphs or cherubim are here. His guards have arrived so God is on his way. These are not the fat-faced angels sold in Hallmark stores. They are mighty, untamed creatures with unlimited power and grace. They can destroy or save every soul. Their mass and glory fill the restaurant, their wings and hooves and throats pass through us. No one notices, though E'va looks up and smiles a little as a wing sweeps across her face,

The seraphs melt into the shimmering air and God says, "I don't care for everyone in the same way. All lives and loves are different." I have never heard this voice before. It is perfect and complete.

E'va smiles a little. There is butter on her old lip. "Your mother's ring would be nice, I think."

INVISIBLE BRANCHES

I am relieved when Zoltan returns, carrying two plates.

He sits down next to me and I rest my forehead on his shoulder for a moment. "I'm hearing voices, Z."

"No kidding, who? I thought I heard George Burns, once."

"I'm serious. I just heard God, He spoke to me."

Zolton holds my face in his big hands. "Relax. Everything is gonna be ok. You need to eat and you need to drink more water and you need to go home and take a nap."

He sounds like the doctor, full of well intended, irrelevant advice. But maybe he's right. I could be blowing all this way out of proportion. So the Gator Farm has adopted a baby elephant. Saint Mary wants to take care of it, she likes elephants, and there's a little girl hanging around on the mountain who looks just like B. Wallace. An unseen visitor delivered a yellow melon to Wawa and Felicity is suddenly saying stuff no 8 year old should even think about. As I list all the events I might be blowing out of proportion, tears push at my eyelids. It's not in my head. There's too much. Church signs and post it notes and the fact Helen Houston wants to bury my mother's ashes in Hot Springs.

I nod because I do not want to scare Zolton, but there's no doubt B. Wallace is here to tell me something or to push me into action. I just don't know what it is I'm supposed to be doing.

But I don't want Z to think I'm loosing my mind. I'll try to explain everything to him later, maybe tonight when he gets home and is soaking in the tub.

Our lunches are beautiful, food art, grilled salmon steaks (E'va always eats fish on Fridays) with shimmering rivers of apricot sauce. There's also a bit of potato, swirled like soft-serve ice cream with tiny flakes of fresh parsley and basil. A kiwi fan stops the apricot sauce from running into the potatoes.

"Pretty plate," I say softly to Z.

"Thanks, don't forget to eat the kiwi."

"I know, Mike gave me the potassium and vitamin C lecture this morning."

"I just got the salmon." He pokes at my food with a fork, then takes a huge bite. He leans back happily, "It's there."

He watches me, waiting for me to take a bite too. But I make him wait. I hesitate because I love watching his face at this exact moment.

When it comes to food, he's so full of expectations and concern. I do the same thing sometimes, when we are having sex. I take him to the edge and just when he's about to fall over the edge, I pull back and watch his face.

Under the table, he rubs his hand on my thigh; his calluses feel like little leather footballs. I take a bite. The flavors are exquisite. New and fresh, fruit and fish. It's perfect.

E'va says something in Hungarian and his hand stops moving on my leg. His fingers stiffen, then the two of them, fall into a word pit. Some crucial conversation swallows them and I am left alone with my salmon. As they argue, I feel as though I am standing on the rim of the volcano, watching the lava bubble and boil.

The conversation heats up quickly. My name is spoken twice, surrounded by words I do not understand.

I squeeze Zolton's hand. "What are you talking about?"

"The baby."

"What about the baby?" His grip is tightening and he's leaning forward, then thumps the table with his fingers and sighs heavily. He looks away but doesn't see the dining room or waitresses. Neither E'va or Z speak. Zoltan is dark with anger. E'va is, without a doubt, on a moral high-horse. She's stares at him with those hot black eyes.

In a deep and hushed voice he says, "Te lehetetien vagy. Most haggya'l bennunket magunkra!"

Then he looks at me. "What's the exact due date?"

I put my hand on my stomach. The baby's kicks have been fluttering, like a guppy. Happy and warm. Her feet have settled high and to the right. Since he's turned and heading due south, this might be a punch instead of a kick. I want to be away from both, E'va and Z. The baby and I should not be here with them when they are talking about us. I should leave for a couple of weeks, curl up and have my baby, alone. Let them fight without us.

I look at Z He profile is dark, his ancient eyes are the color of wet slate. He is fearless and will always protect me. He is standing guard now, I know that. I must trust him to guard our fortress and life. He's all I've got.

I can not do anything more than I am doing now. I can only protect my body and have this baby and try to stay away from my mother.

"Liz, what's our due date?"

"November 1st, tell her I'm due November 4th just to be safe."
E'va, speaks, then waves her hand in disgust.

Zolton drops my hand, says "Nem" to her very loudly. "She says if we don't get married the baby will be cursed."

"Cursed my ass." he laughs at her. "You're an old woman and you can't run my life." Then he says something else I do not understand. He's moved past passionate. He's hot and I hate not understanding.

They are finished with this argument. Our booth is silent. But Z is still very angry. E'va shrugs as though it's too late to help us. I feel a tremor in Z's hand, a twitching of anger. They both lean back in the booth. E'va begins eating again, scraping the tongs of the fork across the plate, then biting down very hard.

"It's good," she says, "what kind of fish?"

Chapter 9

After lunch E'va and I go to Wal-Mart so she can buy a button. We do not speak much in the car. I'm exhausted and she is old.

Five blocks from her home, E'va leans over and says to my belly, " Viszontiatasara, szeretiek te kis Magyar." I love you and kiss you my little Magyar.

As soon as we turn onto E'va's street, I see the smoke. It drifts up lazily then hangs in the tree tops. I slow down as she sits up. Clutching the door, E'va whispers "Oh my God."

Her ancient neighbors shuffle out of their homes, screen doors slam and dogs bark madly.

E'va's mail box is on fire.

Once the police leave, (they take the charred mail box with them as evidence) all the old neighbors roll up their hoses and go home. We call the restaurant. Z does not speak when we describe the mailbox. But I can feel his anger melting into the phone lines. The receiver nearly burns my hand. This has become personal.

"Liz, tell me what's going on."

"I don't know," I lie. He won't believe me if I tell him anyway. And there's nothing he can do to stop my mom.

Anger makes my voice crusty and my fingers twitch.

I leave E'va in a straight back cain chair on the front porch. She's on guard.

How could my B. Wallace do this? How could she terrorize an old woman just to get my attention. "What the fuck is wrong with you, Mother?" I yell in the confines of the sealed car.

Finally, because my hands are shaking so hard, I have to pull over and breath. Leaning the seat back, I stare at the interior light. Slowly, I count each breath as it fills my lungs. Time and space become one for me and I breath until the ringing in my ears stops.

I try to imagine what Zoltan and E'va said to each other at lunch. Nothing that pops into my head is very good. Maybe that's why B.Wallace set the mail box on fire. Maybe E'va said something really ugly about me. More likely though, Mom is just making sure I'm paying attention and fully understand.

Forget about the grocery store, the lawyers office, the post office and Hurlie. I've got to get to my children, my goat and ugly orange couch. I need to get out of town and onto the narrow two-lane highway headed home.

This feeling covers me like paint. I have to get home.

With the radio on and the windows down, I feel a little better until I actually listen to the news story being covered. Once again, the highlights of Arkansas' horrendous racial history are being recited. Nobody says anything about burning mailboxes.

The National Public Radio announcer tells me a story:

In 1927 Little Rock authorities defied a screaming lynch mob when they refused to hand over an African-American teenager, suspected of murdering a white girl. The mob wanted blood, so they broke into the jail and took a different black man. He was hung in public, shot 200 times, his body was set on fire, then dragged around Little Rock behind a car. When the Governor, John Martineau, finally sent in the National Guard they found one member of the lynch mob directing traffic with the dead man's charred arm.

Turning off the radio, I say, "Alright Mom, you win. There's no doubt about it. I understand, I'm not going to bury you here. I won't let Helen have any of your ashes. But you're wrong about this though. Every place on earth is contaminated. White men have been like this for fucking 2,000 years, Mom. I don't think Arkansas is any worse than other states and countries. But I understand this was your particular battle and your blood, so I'll keep you on the Coke machine. Just please, get off your fucking high horse and leave us alone." Sniffling, I wipe my wet face on my shirt sleeve. "I won't do anything, I swear"

The car is quiet. I run a traffic light just as it turns red, then speed up on the way out of town.

I must hurry and make sure our home is safe.

Five miles out of town the road construction begins. A skinny teenaged boy with a razorback cap and an orange flag waves at me to slow down. Highway 5 is being improved, widened a little, repaved.

We will have smooth shoulders to redeem us from our careless moments. I don't want the road improvement, I don't want my street to be changed at all. I'm afraid it will make everybody drive too fast. Making good time will become more important than the gentle rural scenery. We'll all be going too fast to take note of the pumpkin crop and the pretty angle of the tin roof of the Watson barn.

The road improvement will increase the value of our property. I consider this fact.

Marriage will theoretically improve the value of our relationship. But I'm afraid Z and I will start going too fast if we are married. We'll get lazy with our emotions, knowing that smooth paved shoulder of marriage will be there to give us a little leeway. We'll ignore the details, forget to take in the scenery as the trip slips past.

The baby kicks with more energy than I have and my entire attention is suddenly focused on my belly. The skin tightens with a contraction, it seems I will split up the middle, like a dropped cantaloupe.

The barbequed mail box has fallen over. Its charred 4 x 4 wooden post is black but has stopped smoking.

Once I turn up the driveway, I have to support my belly with one hand so it won't bounce too much. The jostling makes every stretched abdominal muscle constrict again. Everything, including breathing, makes my flesh tighten.

Fred stands, poetically, between the tire swing and hammock with a pair of my shiny red underwear in his mouth. The wind must have blown them off the clothesline.

This is my home. Fred waves our banner and I feel better.

Fred responds suddenly to the sound of my car and bounds down the hill, a bouncy black and white streak, then stops right in the middle of the driveway. He stands in profile, the wind ruffling his short coat. "Baaa," he says, dropping my underwear and showing me his flat toothed overbite.

As I climb out of the car, one leg at a time, the phone starts ringing, inside. With one hand on my extended belly, I shuffle as fast as I can. I hate being pregnant. It's hard. Just before the machine picks up I grab the receiver.

"Hi Mom, it's Spider man."

"Mike, what are you doing calling? Where are you?" I'm panting.

"I'm at school. I broke my web and don't have any insurance."

"You broke your leg?"

"No, I broke my web. It's a joke, Mom, I'm I spider."

"I'm too pregnant for jokes, Mike. I'm getting confused. What are you doing?"

"I'm in the nurse's office, she left for a minute, so I thought I'd call and tell you my real new joke and check on you. How are you feeling?"

"Fine, I guess. You're gonna get in trouble for using her phone," I say.

"Naaa, I can hear her coming down the hall. Ok, how do you make your Kleenex dance?"

"I don't know, how?"

"Put a little boogie in it. Hey, I gotta go." He hangs up suddenly.

I lie down on the couch and while I'm trying not to fall asleep again because I know I'll dream about flaming mail boxes, I wonder why he might be in the nurse's office. He didn't sound sick.

Chapter 10

Squeaky brakes. I hear them. That's the school bus. With my eyes still closed, I begin to count. I'll be able to hear Mike and Felicity's voices when I reach 45 and then they will open the living room door carrying back packs. My children are my home. My home is here. "Hi Home," I say to them happily.

"Hi mom," they both respond. The house is filled and I feel better. My soul has arrived in a big yellow bus.

Mike isn't smiling. He hands me a pink slip of paper. I don't bother reading it. "They caught you, huh?"

"He plunks down next to me and puts his head on my belly to feel for the baby. "I'm really sorry Mom. It was stupid. Please don't get mad." Then he grins. "The note isn't mine, it's Felicity's. So what happened to the mail box?"

"Just teenagers and some stupid sort of prank. What did she do?" I open the folded piece of paper.

In a teacher's handwriting it says, 'Felicity continues to use language that is not permitted on school grounds. Please call our office on Monday to make an appointment with the principal. Thank you, Mrs. Bryant."

I look at my daughter. Fat sparkling tears are just about to spill from her eyes. Before I can speak she says, "I'm so sorry Momma, I didn't know the teacher could hear me. I thought I was just talking to my friends."

My heart is torn. "Honey, it doesn't matter that the teacher could hear you, what matters is your mouth. What did you say?"

She shakes her head.

"You might as well tell me, Felicity."

"I said Al Gore was a butt muncher."

"The Vice President?" I'm trying not to smile. "Why did you call him that? I don't even know what it means."

"I hate the way he looks. It's gross," Felicity states and plops down next to me on the couch. "He creeps me out."

"You are in huge trouble Felicity. I'll start with two weeks being grounded and tell you the rest after I talk to the principal."

"I'm so sorry, Mamma." She stands up then shoves Mike and runs to the kitchen. Then she yells. "Joy Burns got a bra and wore it to school. She thinks she is so old and so hot. It's gross."

"Really, does she need it? " The idea of my baby wearing a bra makes me kind of queasy.

Felicity comes back and sits next to me with a cup of strawberry yogurt. "She let me try it on in the bathroom. It was so uncomfortable. I thought I was gonna choke or something. And it's not like she's got anything to put in it. She's just kind of chubby and now she just thinks it's so mature, as if...." Felicity rolls her huge blue eyes.

"Second grade and wearing a bra. Seems a little premature to me." Felicity looks disgusted then puts her hand on my stomach.

Mike kicks off his tennis shoes. "Can we please talk about something else?" he whines then runs and slides like a hockey player, into the kitchen.

Felicity tries to pull me to my feet. "Let's go outside. All those machines are getting close. Maybe they'll pave our driveway."

By tomorrow I'm sure the back hoe, shovel, grater and gravel truck will nearly be blocking our driveway. All the equipment, huge and yellow, is in front of our neighbor's pasture, 150 yards away right now. The size and sounds of the heavy equipment is awesome and exciting. It's the grinding, rumbling sound of progress.

While Mike and Felicity wander around in the back yard, searching for the clippers and a rake. I look across the road, being careful not to focus on the mailbox, and practice my breathing.

We have a beautiful and rustic view. There is a perfect pasture on the other side of the highway, with patches of yellow wild flowers, four huge oak trees and it is all surrounded by a knarled old barbed wire fence.

The kids and I putz around in the yard for a while. I want to make certain the road crew can see the stone steps, circa 1920, leading up from the street to the front of the house. I don't want them running over part of the house's heritage with a back hoe.

Everytime a new piece of road equipment is started, all the frogs and birds become silent. Waiting for this machinery is like waiting for an invading army. Is the ground vibrating a little? Can I really hear construction workers shouting? It's all so ominous.

But today there are other noises too. I stand over Felicity, who is making grass angels. This time, I pull her to her feet. She's wearing red pants, a red t-shirt, hiking boots with red socks and her favorite necklace. It's just a piece of leather with hanging doodads, sea shells, an arrowhead, an old Hungarian coin, a tiny bell, an egg-shaped river stone that's been drilled through and a little gold ring she outgrew when she was three. Somehow, Felicity has befriended the high school shop teacher. Anytime she finds some extraordinary new trinket, he drills a hole in it for her.

"Listen to that," I say. We are all quiet. Felicity holds her necklace so it won't jingle. And then they hear the strange sounds too.

Cows, lots of cows are mooing. They are excited. And there are car horns and people shouting. Mr. Ray's herd must have wandered onto the highway. Sometimes, they push through one of his gates searching for fresh grass. I love his cows. Their heavy presence is comforting. At night, when he moves them to the front field, I can smell the manure, heavy and sweet, in the night air.

We all listen to the commotion.

Mike says, "Steaks for dinner tonight, huh Mom."

"You don't think any of the cars will hit the cows do you?" Felicity takes my hand.

"Everybody probably just wants them off the road, but the honking might be making it worse."

We are all silent, straining to piece together a story from the sounds. Then I realize, I'm listening past the cows. I'm waiting for another noise, something, it's out there, heading my way. The heavy equipment cranks up again and drowns out the cows. I try to analyze my feelings, what is it I'm waiting for? Not the baby, as far as I'm concerned, she's already here. I've just got her in a holding pattern. And I'm not waiting for love, it's definitely found me. So, I shouldn't be waiting, I've got it all. I've arrived, so why am I looking to the distance, certain something is on the way?

Felicity moves closer to me. "You smell that?" she asks.

I sniff. "Smell what?"

She is cautious before speaking, looking out across the land then she stares into my face and smiles. "It's like perfume and a circus, hay and elephants and popcorn.. I like it. And it smells really close, too."

I let go of her hand. "I can't smell it Felicity. I don't know what you're talking about."

"Don't worry Mom, it's a good smell. It doesn't mean anything bad is coming."

"How do you know that Felicity? You can tell what a smell means?"

"I just know."

Mike shrugs. "She's been saying she smells a circus for a week now. She's just trying to be weird, Mom.' He picks his clippers up again and starts working.

Felicity tries to saw through a branch. After a moment she gives up, hands me the saw and says, "Forget it." Then she sits down cross legged and picks up a pretty but dead moth. It is white and nearly as big as a dollar bill. "Can we save it to show the baby?"

"You'll have to keep it for a year or two. And then the baby will just want to eat it."

This makes her laugh. She's shakes her long dark hair down and looks like a child from a pre-Raphaelite painting. "Oh well," she says to my belly. "Maybe next time, kid." Then she picks up the beautiful dead moth and tries to fly it to Mike, like a paper airplane. The moth disintegrates mid-flight, then loses both white wings when it hits the grass.

Fred trots over, grabs the remainder of the moth's body and runs off. Felicity laughs even harder. She falls back into the grass and holds her hand to her mouth like a microphone. "Flight 305 has just been eaten."

Mike looks at me, then hacks away at the bushes again. He's getting sweaty. His hair is damp and sticks to his lovely brown back as he holds the clippers over his head and tries to reach a branch I know he'll never get though.

It's all here, with my heart. Felicity and Mike and the baby and the land. I couldn't ask for anything else, so what am I waiting for? I look to the sky. What have God and B. Wallace got going on.

This feeling for something unnamed is almost a longing, a physical sensation that twists my soul and maybe my lungs just a little, as though I'm homesick for a place I've never been before. If a baby was denied his mother's love or her milk, this might be how he would feel. Searching and empty.

Sometimes, I have this same feeling after an orgasm. For almost a year I thought the yearning, the wanting and waiting was a thirst for milk. Once I sat cross-legged and naked in bed, and tried to describe this to Z. But he didn't get it. He nodded as though he understood, but I knew.

Z and I would have sex, then I would drink a glass of milk. It seemed like my body and soul wanted to backup and return to the basics. But milk didn't help. And the feeling, the prickly twisting of my inner-self, continued especially after great sex.

C.S. Lewis is the only other person I've heard describe anything that sounds remotely like my feeling. He thought it was a longing to return to heaven. His theory was we were once with God, in heaven, and we desperately want to be there again, even if we can't remember. We want to be wrapped in the wings of an angel in the white light and beauty of His protection and perfection. The ultimate case of Homesickness. Once there, with God, our pain will be gone.

So, after having an orgasm, maybe I am closer than ever to God. This is my theory, not Mr Lewis'. I've always thought a woman's orgasm was a pointless and perfect gift from God. It serves no purpose, but there it is, doing nothing but making me feel good. Is there any thing else in the human condition that doesn't have a reason for existing?

I long for God after sex. This makes as much sense as needing a glass of milk.

The mooing cows have moved on, the honking has stopped. Slowly, I lay down in the sun-warmed grass. My back cracks, then shapes itself to fit the gently rounded surface of my planet. I groan in relief. The twenty-five extra pounds spread out across the lawn. Grass tickles the back of my legs and a stick pokes my side. But I belong down here, with the earth and dirt. Can the baby feel the lush green warmth of her beautiful little planet?

Our yard has always felt strange and sacred to me. Even the kids are aware that there is something special here. The roundness of the planet takes hold of our bodies and we know we are lying around on a big ball. If we were Indians, I would make this a holy place.

Mother Earth, Father Dirt, please soak the soreness from my bones. A brilliant ray of sunlight sucks the ache from my face and my skin warms. I consider spending the rest of the day lying on my back in the yard. Why doesn't my body feel as well constructed as it once did? My bones, tendons and ligaments are all akimbo, misconstrued and lacking alignment.

I want to take a bath so hot I could cook corn on the cob.

"Soon, my burden will be taken from me," I say aloud and Mike flops down next to me. He puts his face too close to mine and squints at me.

"What did you say?" he asks. I study the enamel on his front teeth. His teeth look too big for his face. Pretty soon he will grow into them.

"Soon, my burden will be lifted." I say again and scoot away from him just a little. They are like puppies who wedge themselves between your legs.

"What's that mean?" He reaches out and touches my nose. "Did you know you have a spot on your nose?"

"Yeah, it's been there for a while."

"What is it?"

"I think it's just a big freckle. I hope that's what it is." In the summer I'm always afraid of skin cancer on my nose. What if my big freckle turns into a cancerous spot and they have to scoop it out. Then I'll have a pot hole on my nose.

Felicity walks over on her knees to join the inspection of my nose. They are both leaning in very close to my face, they start to laugh. Felicity says, "Your face doesn't look any different even though you're big. That's good, isn't it Mama? My teacher's face got too fat when she was pregnant."

"No fat face for me. Did you guys brush your teeth today? Your looking a little yellow in there."

They are both silent but still grinning. Felicity falls over on her side and lets Fred smell her forehead. He nibbles at some of her hair until she starts laughing and rolls away. "He likes the smell Mom, it's that flower shampoo you bought."

Mike walks over and pats Fred's boney back. "You're a big petunia head, Felicity."

"Go brush your teeth right now, please. I'll stay here," I say, suddenly concerned about their dental hygiene.

Mike kneels down next to me. "Oh, man. Can't we wait till we go inside?"

"Nope, I'll forget about it if you don't do it now. Like Mohammed Ali said, 'We must fight Mr. Tooth Decay.'"

Felicity grins. "So, what's a burden?" She does this all the time, backtracks for the meaning of a word or phrase even though the conversation has changed completely. I have to down shift and refocus to figure out what she's talking about.

"A burden is something heavy that weighs you down."

"Like rocks in your pockets?" She says absently.

"Yeah, like rocks in your brain, I mean rocks in your pockets."

"Like a secret you've got to keep?" she asks.

I look at her. Her face is smooth and inquisitive. Another a strange thing for her to say.

"Yes, sometimes a secret can definitely be a burden. Do you have a burden.?"

"I am burdened," she states and I am impressed at her conjugation. My heart is haunted. Where are these words of hers coming from?

"Go on inside and brush. It won't take you five minutes if you just jump up and get it over with."

Felicity stands up, then starts running backwards across the big green yard. Fred chases her sweet smelling hair.

Mike moves more slowly, doing his reluctant cowpoke saunter, then sprints past Felicity and Fred.

Without sitting up I yell as loudly as I can, "Use toothpaste."

Felicity screams something I don't understand and they holler happily at each other, then I listen as they disappear into the house.

The world is silent again, except for an occasional passing car.

They have fun. We have fun. I thank the sky and the grass and the trees around me.

Sometimes, when I watch them, I think I know exactly how God feels when he looks down at us. I will always be devoted and hopelessly in love with my children.

They can grow up and leave and fall in love with their own children, but I will always belong to them.

I understand why B. Wallace had to die. She could not live with her shattered heart. She could not live on this planet without her Golden Boy, Daniel. When Daddy and Daniel took their love away, she had to follow them to a sweeter place.

I wasn't enough to keep her here.

Does she miss me as much as she missed them. Maybe she doesn't miss me at all because she's right here. "Is that it, Mom?"

A car pulls up the drive way. It is a very new, very red Jeep. The white walls are still clean. It's not anybody I know, unless Hurlie got a new truck.

My heart perks up and I am suddenly hot. What if the sheriffs department or the FBI have been tapping my phone calls? After all this time, maybe the they figured it out and they've come to bust me. Son-of-a-bitch, ready to give birth and going to jail. I haven't burned any papers in three days. There's a truck load of evidence sitting on my desk. They'll get Hurlie too and that's a dangerous thing. I'm toast. There is a rolling in my bowels. My muscles seize up. It's the ultimate Braxton-hicks. This is a cramping I haven't felt it in a long time, but I recognize the feeling instantly. This is a physical manifestation of an emotion and knowledge.

This is Fear.

"Ok," I say out loud as I push my enormous body into an upright position. One, two, three, I grunt then rise with very little grace. No doubt I look really funny from a distance. I begin walking across they yard.

The jeep with its tinted windows idles in my driveway. What are these people waiting for?

By the time I reach the basket ball goal, which is right in the middle of the yard, I'm panting. How embarrassing.

When the door swings open, I am surprised and relieved. Grinning ridiculously because of my relief I squeak, "Hi there."

It is Jean Luc, a painter who lives and owns an extravagant art gallery down town.

I'm not getting arrested, today.

Jean Luc is renowned. Collectors from all over the world travel to Hot Springs just to visit this Frenchman and his posh gallery. He does not feature his own work in his gallery, instead he shows that of other French and Nordic artists. His work hangs in larger, more exclusive galleries and major museums.

Once, I saw one of his abstract paintings behind a man in Forbes Magazine and last year there was a column on Jean Luc's work in Time Magazine.

Well, here Jean Luc is, standing in my yard, five acres of redneck heaven. He smiles as he watches me waddle.

I smile back at him because he not a law enforcement officer. He waves, then begins walking toward me with his hand stretched out. He has a beautiful smile and shaggy blond-gray hair. He's a large man, probably sixty years old and aging nicely. I can not imagine why he is in my yard.

Fred emerges from the woods because there is a stranger in his sanctuary. Please God, I hope Fred doesn't jump on the Jeep and destroy that shiny paint job.

"Hello, hello," he calls to me, his French accent is thick. He takes the cigarette that is dangling from his bottom lip and flicks it fifteen feet.

"Hi there Jean Luc."

"I came to see you."

"I see that."

"How are you feeling?" He asks, smiling but with concern in his liquid brown eyes.

"Just dandy." I'm waiting. I am wary. He must want something but I am also curious and flattered that he has driven all the way out here and up my muffler eating drive way to see me.

"How is the baby?"

"Oh, the baby is just great. He's got the easy part, swimming around all the time."

"May I feel?" He holds his hand out, but waits for me to nod before placing it on my hard belly.

I close my eyes, as I always do when some one touches my stomach because I don't know where to look. Seeing a hand on my body that doesn't belong to Zoltan or the kids is unnatural. His knuckles are not like Z's and the pressure points are different. Jean Luc pushes with his fingertips. Zoltan's entire palm and every inch of his fingers melt into my flesh.

Suddenly, much to my surprise, the baby shifts mightily, then kicks three times, very hard.

"My God," Jean Luc immediately places his other hand on me. It nearly cover the entire surface of my stomach. "How does that feel, when the baby kicks?"

"I like it. It reminds me that I'm not in this pregnancy all alone. Sometimes I get a little sore, when she kicks a vital organ or the same spot for hours, but that's ok."

He nods, in a solemn French sort of way, then stares at his own hands spread across my stomach. The baby kicks again. I look at Jean Luc's hands and my belly. What's this, what's going on in there? This sort of thing never happens. My baby is not a show kicker. Maybe it's the French accent.

"Walk with me," he says offering his arm.

I accept his gallantry. I wonder where we will walk, to the pump house or around the basketball court, perhaps.

"I have a proposition for you, would you like to listen?"

"Of course." Because he is using so much charm the proposition must be extreme. He must want something big.

As we walk, Fred watches us. He knows if he jumps on the car I'll pick up a rock and nail him.

Jean Luc is looking at Fred too. "He's too old to eat now, you know. He would be very tough."

"He's actually a pet." All of Europe wants to eat Fred.

"I see," Jean Luc says without judgment. "I was told there will be a monument soon for your mother. She was an artist?"

"Theater, Mom loved the theater. She acted, directed, produced. Anything, as long as it took place on a stage. But that was a long time ago, Hot Springs was very different then. Nobody gave a rat's ass for the arts twenty or thirty years ago."

"It is not so different now, but your mother, she persevered in the name of art."

"How did you hear about her?"

"I have heard her name mentioned several times. She had a great deal of influence and her reach was powerful. But surely you, of all people realize that."

"Perhaps," I say. What's he talking about? I'm still unable to decide if Jean Luc is just jerking my chain. Maybe he wants me to trust him so he's going on about B. Wallace. Maybe he's looking for a bookie and doesn't know how to ask if I'll take his action. It's also possible I'm really paranoid and should be pleased anybody remembers my dead mother.

"From what I've heard it is good that she is being honored," Jean Luc says.

He makes B. Wallace sound so grand, a Southern Joan of Arc with a proscenium arch. She would like that.

"Who is designing her monument?"

Ahh, it's the sculpture he's interested in. "To be perfectly honest, I don't remember. I heard about the plan for the first time this morning. You probably know more than I do?"

He nods thoughtfully. "Perhaps you are right." It is an odd thing to say and then he continues. "I came here today to make a proposition."

"There's more?"

"Of course." He smiles and I am tempted though I'm not sure by what. After knowing Jean Luc for three years I've decided I like him but I don't trust him.

"A proposition. How kinky, I've been getting so few recently. Men don't flirt with pregnant women you know, and it sort of hurts my feelings."

He smiles again and strokes my arm. "Well then, you should like this offer very much. There are a few of us, who work together on Thursday nights. We would like for you to model for us before you have the baby. When is it due?"

"A couple of weeks.."

"Good then, that will give us time. You will be beautiful."

"You want me to model. Nude?"

"Of course."

The heat of my blush creeps up my neck and nests, like a warm bird, on my cheeks. I grin with embarrassment, then laugh.

I can see myself in a stark and brightly lit second floor studio, naked, sitting on a straight back chair. It's very hard and cold against my exposed butt. My stomach is so large my breasts rest on it. My belly button sticks out and, because my stomach is very, very pale I can see tiny blue veins through my skin. As the baby moves her foot I watch my skin roll, slowly, like an undulating snake.

My back hurts, I can't get comfortable in the chair, so I squirm. The artists surrounding me all look up from their sketch pads and sigh impatiently. I'm not supposed to move.

"Your mother would have done it, I think. She was brave," he says.

"I'm not my mother. And this has nothing to do with bravery. You have no idea how self conscious women are when they are pregnant. My body is a wreck. I'm flattered but this is an easy offer to turn down."

"You are beautiful," he says, touching my face with the back of his fingers and I turn away slightly. "You are not so provincial are you? I was sure you would appreciate the importance and beauty."

"Yeah, yeah. But my liberation is only a facade. Actually, I'm a real prude."

"That is too bad." He sounds genuinely disappointed.

"I'm flattered by the offer, though."

He kisses both my cheeks. His lips are dry and supple. And all he says to me now is, "How do I get out of your drive?"

Fred watches Jean Luc roll slowly down the driveway. He seems disappointed, as though he missed a fine opportunity.

I walk back to the far end of the yard to pick up the saw and clippers. It's getting dark. I listen intently, for anything. But the world is silent, except for a couple of crows. The heavy equipment has stopped for the night.

B. Wallace. My mother, even dead, there's no way I can out think her.

What the hell am I going to do now? I really would love to bury B. Wallace's ashes somewhere. Having a place, other than the top of the Coke Machine, to visit her would solidify things and give me a sense of closure. I'd like to stand in front of a marker, stare at her name, etched for all of eternity in some heavy rock. I'd like to talk to her, the way normal people do in graveyards. I could put some flowers out on her birthday and that would make me feel good, help me remember things about her. Gravestones are important, especially for the living.

But that's not going to happen. She's not giving me the opportunity to make a choice. I simply must live with her decisions.

We are all looking for control and power. I know that's what I want right now, so I'm jerking Z around, proving I have a little control over something. And it seems to be what Mom is fighting for, even dead. Control.

The white men in this state made sure the blacks never had any control and they tried to do the same to B. Wallace, in a more amiable way. But the outcome was the same.

Bitterness and hatred.

Mom obviously still thinks burying her body in Arkansas will signify a victory for the Arkansas home boys. She is afraid the 70-year-old good ol' boys who smirked when she was named high school valedictorian and fought her because they didn't want the black community to have a swimming pool, will get the final satisfaction.

She still thinks they will stand over her grave and say, "Well fellows, we finally won. Betty came home so she must not be mad at us anymore."

The afterlife must not be so heavenly for my mother, or she wouldn't be messing around with petty crap like this. That's the true tragedy in her suicide. Even now that she's dead, my mom is being eaten up by the same rancor and bitterness.

Peace, tonight, I will pray that God will give her a little peace and allow me some clarity.

Walking toward the house, I realize just how much I want this memorial. The very idea of a structure in my mother's name fills me.

If I let Helen build a monument for Mom, I could show it to the kids and tell them about their grandmother. I could drive past and try to understand.

5:15. The day is slowly coming to an end. Thunder moves in from the west. The sky directly overhead is still blue, but the horizon is dark and the wind has picked up. It's a western front. Most of our storms roll in from Oklahoma or Texas.

A few leaves fall from the enormous old oak that towers over the house. I remember, like every kid on the planet, standing under big old trees when I was young, waiting for the wind to blow so I could try to catch leaves. I'd spin with my face tilted to the open sky, laughing and grabbing until I was too dizzy to stand.

With one hand on my big belly, I stop under the mammoth swaying oak. I look straight up at the shivering leaves. They rustle and shimmy like skinny flappers in a breeze. Then the real wind pushes through and I get the mother-load of falling leaves. Because my stomach is so big and my balance so poor, I don't spin. Instead the leaves swirl for me and I am lost in the motion.

Some one down the road is burning leaves. The smell is orange and brown. I look at the house and am assaulted by panic. What if something is going on in the house, with the kids. What if B. Wallace decides to burn down more than mail boxes. Maybe the kitchen is on fire, God only know what B. Wallace will try to do next.

I run for the first time in five months.

When I slam through the living room door, Mike looks up. He is sitting in the middle of the living room, sorting basketball cards. Of course everything is fine. There's no fire. The air is safe.

Felicity is hiding under my desk, talking to her friend, Cody, on the telephone. Her "Grease" video is on the VCR. A young John Travolta stands on top of a car singing "Greased Lightening."

Michael says numbly, "If I have to listen to this movie again, Mom, I'm gonna blow up the television. Who pulled up in the jeep? I was watching you from the window," he asks.

"Just business." I sit down at my desk, pretending I don't know Felicity is underneath. She whispers into the phone, "I've gotta go."

I shove my feet under the desk, nearly hitting her, then kick off my shoes and wiggle my toes.

"Oh it feels good to stretch my stinky feet. But they sure do smell bad, I can barely stand it. They smell like a dozen dead skunks on the side of the road. They smell like rotting eggplant and tofu casserole. My feet smell like a big dirty championship wrestler with b.o. who's been eating a rotting seaweed eggplant, road-kill skunk and tofu casserole."

Felicity starts to giggle.

"What are you doing under there, girl?" I extend my hand and she puts the phone in my palm.

"Dying from the smell of your feet, Mom." She crawls out, wobbles then falls over. "I'm dead, see what your toes did to me. You must have some sort of toenail fungus problem."

She makes a gagging noise as I stare down at her. She goes on and on and on.

"Enough." I say. She gags again and adds a little writhing. "Felicity, enough. Please stop."

She stops making the noise, is silent but still pretending to be dead on the floor next to my chair.

I stroke her beautiful hair. "Will you get me the phone book? It's in the living room."

She crawls across the floor. Picks up the phone book and brings it too me in her mouth, like a dog, fetching a stick.

I'm looking for Helen Houston's phone number and my hand sticks to a left over Jolly Rancher watermelon candy one of the kids spit out and left, stuck to the cover.

Felicity barks and shakes her head like a cocker spaniel.

The phone rings and I jump a little. "Hello."

"How'd it go out there, Good Girl?"

"Went fine Hurlie." I spin in my chair and face the desk. "I'm almost done."

"Naaa, you'll never be done. You can't leave me now, we're making money."

"I'm leaving. It's time for me to stop, Hurlie. Don't make this hard."

"I haven't made it hard, yet. But you need to think about the consequences and about the security."

Deep sigh. Hurlie is flexing on me and I must deal with him now, before it gets out of hand. "I can't do this anymore. I've explained the reasons to you. I'm sorry your upset but I'd be a lousy employee. Z's job is secure, we'll be fine."

I listen as he lights a cigarette. "In this fuckin' economy, you never know what could happen to a business. Then you'll be wishing you still were working for ol' Hurlie. The world's a crappy place but I always took good care of you, didn't I?"

"And I appreciate that. Hopefully it's been a symbiotic relationship. I've brought you some business and you've been fair with me. But Hurlie, I'm gone, so don't bother trying to scare me into staying."

"Lizzy, I'm not trying to scare you, honey. I'm just saying anything can happen especially to restaurants, grease fire, bad wiring, Hell, the health department could walk in and shut the place down, happens all the time, and then how would your old man take care of your pretty little family."

I try to swallow, but something is caught in my throat. Gulping a little, I smash the anger and fear back down, so Hurlie will not hear it in my voice. I can't let him see or sense fear.

"As soon as I'm finished collecting tomorrow, I'll come out to see you. I've got to go now." I hang up before he can say anything else. The phone is slippery in my hand and my right foot twitches uncontrollable.

Felicity crawls down the two steps into the living room and barks at Mike. He ignores her until she barks very loudly, right in his ear. They begin to wrestle and are laughing so hard I know someone will get hurt in just a moment.

"Stop it, right now, please." My voice is thick.

They stop instantly and stare at me. Clearing my throat, I try to smile a little and cover the anger and fear in my chest. "I need a break, ok. It's been a rough day."

Hurlie was threatening me. I know too much and I've made him too much money. Going after me would be too obvious. But Hurlie has never been known to be a subtle man.

With the phone cradled in my lap, I close my eyes.

I'll deal with Hurlie tomorrow. He must be bluffing. But, I have to make certain Z. doesn't hear about any of this. He'll immediately go on the offense, he'll over react and threaten Hurlie. He'll take Hurlie out before I can stop him. Then I'll have a real nightmare to deal with.

The phone rings again, while I'm still holding it. It's too loud and startles me. What if it's Hurlie? I need to be prepared. My words must be strong, ready and right.

I say to Mike and Felicity, " You guys be quiet while I'm on the phone."

"Hello?"

"Elizabeth, it's Helen."

"Helen, hello." I laugh breathlessly into the phone.

Thank God, it's only her.

Helen suddenly says, "Just a minute dear, there's someone at my door." I hear her doorbell ring again in the distance as she puts the receiver down.

Fine, this gives me a minute to think. What can I say to her that will derail her plan? There needs to be true understanding of B. Wallace on my part before I can pass it on. Can I possibly hope Helen will understand that I'm afraid my mother will keep on haunting me and tempting me, maybe for the rest of my life, if I bury her under a monument in Hot Springs? There's no Hallmark for this occasion.

Waiting for Helen I push the computer monitor back a few inches and it flickers. The computer is off. I put my hand on the back of the monitor, flip it on then off. It flickers again so I unplug the damn thing. The screen goes from black to color.

Just as I push the on/off button at the bottom of the monitor, I am pulled inside by the beautiful heartbreaking clarity of the story on the sixteen inch monitor. A smell assaults me, yeasty and pungent, like a healthy food store.

Good Bye

"Hang on. I'm coming," I yelled as I brushed my long hair. It was nearly down to my waist then. The brush felt good on my scalp. I stopped to re-button my midriff shirt.

Mom yelled from her bed room that I needed to hurry up or I was going to miss the school bus again.

I shoved both my hands in the front pockets of my jeans and forced them down lower on my bony hips. My stomach was tan and heartbreakingly flat, my belly button a perfect inward swirl. I want the world to see everything. I walked out of my bedroom with its orange shag carpet and waterbed, and smiled at my father.

Daddy was standing in the kitchen cracking raw eggs into the blender. He was wearing a dark pin stripe suit. His dark brown hair still damp and parted on the side.

"That's so gross, Daddy," I said and poured a glass of orange juice.

He winked at me and shook tabasco sauce into the blender, then added three tablespoons of various protein powders, ginseng, a clove of garlic, honey and some milk.

That's where the smell was coming from. The protein powder stinks. I always hated it. Daddy turned on the blender.

"I'm glad it's good for you, but it's too disgusting." I whined at him and studied my own smooth reflection in the mirror hanging over the breakfast table. "You know that stuff has wrecked the blender. It smells like mold all the time, no matter how many times we wash it. Mom bought a new one last week at the mall, it's just for normal stuff."

Michael Justice turned off the blender, filled his glass, raised it in a toast then drank the goopy liquid in one gulp. It clung, white and foamy, to his mustache.

I kept talking, despite his stoic silence. "But if that's what you want, I hope you have a good time. I've got to go, have a good day." He leaned forward, so I could kiss him good-by but I backed away, laughing, "No way, that stuff smells disgusting. Maybe Mom will kiss you." Grabbing my school books, I flounced out the door.

My father, Michael Justice, died that afternoon, while I was in algebra class.

I touch the computer screen. Why didn't I kiss him good-by?

After his funeral, Michael Justice came back to visit Mom a few times. Maybe this is a competition between B. Wallace and Daddy. She might be haunting me just to prove she can. Mom always hated being outdone. Maybe haunting is a tradition in our family.

I can not look away from the computer monitor, which has a new,

Rorschach pattern dancing across the screen. Now it looks like a theater marquee and the picture becomes devastingly clear.

"Mom, I remember this too well, you don't have to walk me through unless you really want to. It was just the two of us. B. Wallace and I were alone in the world with our misery."

There I am again, still only fourteen. Skinny and beautiful in an odd way. But I look so tired. Mom and I were both in the kitchen, surrounded by massive flower arrangements and platters of food, meat and cheese. I picked the petals of the flowers and drop them on the counter. Daddy's funeral was the day before but we still haven't put all the food away.

Mom put a filter in the coffee maker. Slowly, as though moving underwater, she poured a pot of water into the back of the machine. As the coffee pot fill with dirty brown water, she watched. It took three or four minutes before she realized something is wrong. There was a glass of burgundy next to her coffee cup. She picked up the coffee can and slowly looked inside.

"We are out of coffee," she whispered, and her hand began to shake so she put the can down.

"We're out of toilet paper, too."

Mom smiled a little, then I giggled. She giggled too, then we both laughed so hard we started crying.

She drained the glass of burgundy. "The grocery store."

I nodded.

"I'm not going alone, " she stated.

"Alright," I agreed. There wasn't enough life force left in either one of us to accomplish the mission alone. Together, we almost equaled a whole person.

We both pushed the shopping cart through the store isles. We bought toilet paper, coffee, carrots and for some reason, two cans of vienna sausage. The fact that the kitchen was already stuffed with processed meat never occurred to us. The trip to the store took less than a half hour. With our grocery bags in hand, we walked silently from the car to the kitchen door. While standing in the sun, waiting for mom to find the key, I heard a definite and inappropriate noise. Nudging Mom with my elbow, I said, "What's that?"

She stopped digging in her purse and turned her head a little. "I don't know, some kind of motor, I think."

"God, I hope it's not the smoke alarm."

She began digging frantically. The sound continued, strange and steady. Her tiny and aged hand shook violently as she unlocked the door.

I dropped the grocery bag and shoved the kitchen door open, fully expecting to find flames or a burglar.

I was ready to fight any situation to the death.

But there wasn't a burglar and there wasn't a fire.

The blender was on.

It had been pulled to the center of the counter, it was empty, but the top was on and the blades whirled away. The sound seemed extraordinarily loud and filled the kitchen like a tidal wave.

Mom didn't move. She just stood in the doorway with her mouth slightly open. I sat down on one of the tall stools and we both stared at the noisy blender.

Finally, I looked at B. Wallace. "Should I turn it off?"

"I don't know."

We were quiet again, until I stood up and slowly walked toward the counter. I looked at the blender setting. The puree button was pushed down. Reaching behind some cook books, I unplugged the screaming appliance.

Mom smiled just a little, a tiny light flickered in her eyes as the tears started. "He's showing off, you know," she said and there was love and awe in her voice. Then she walked to the blender and put her hand on the plastic side. She stroked it and said, "I can't believe you'd leave like this, then come back just to tease me. Michael Justice, you are such a bastard."

There was never any question as to who turned on that blender. And from that day on Mom kept it on her bedside table between the lamp and ashtray. The screen is black again.

If Daddy would come back and haunt Mom, just for fun, there's no telling what she might do to me, given a real reason.

My mother might set the standard by which all other ghosts, spirits and poltergeists are judged.

So what should I tell Helen Houston with her handsome memorial fountain?

If I turn her down for fear of my mother's ghost, she will think I'm an idiot. She'll also think I'm selfish to rob my children and this city of their heritage.

I like Helen. I don't want her to think ill of me.

But I'm no match for my mother.

When Helen comes back to the phone, I am startled. I'm still not really prepared.

After a moment of pleasantries, I get my thoughts together, but she stops before I can get to the meat of the conversation.

"Liz, let me ask you this. Is it true you're pregnant? I haven't seen you in so long, obviously."

"Yes, I am. Very."

"That's wonderful dear, I didn't even know you'd gotten married. Well congratulations. Do you know if it's a girl or boy yet?"

"Don't have a clue."

"Really? I think that's wonderful, it should be a surprise. There are so few in the world. I think God wants to keep us guessing. Will you be breast feeding?"

Ahh, another one of those questions everybody lobs over the net. Asking about breast feeding is the verbal equivalent of putting your hand on my stomach. I never ask other women about their nipples. I don't even think about other women's nipples very much. But now it's open breast and nipple season. Any question is fair. No doubt Helen has a breast feeding opinion.

"Yes, I'll be breast feeding for a while."

"Good, good, I'm glad to hear that, but not for too long dear. After seven or eight months that's enough, don't you think? Certainly once the baby can walk it's time to stop. You need your freedom and I just get so uncomfortable when women start unbuttoning their blouses in restaurants. It's not a problem if they would just be discreet, a baby blanket or a shawl over their shoulder or something. Don't you think? But I come from the old school, ancient as a dinosaur, I know that. And I really don't think babies should be out in public too much until they are four or five months old. There are just too many dreadful germs and dirty people wandering around. And good lord, it seems the dirty people are always the ones that want to reach out and touch your baby."

She's absolutely right. "Yes ma'am."

Well, tell me about your husband. I'm sure he's adorable."

Should I tell her or should I coast? Perhaps, if I tell her I'm living in sin she'll get disgusted with me and forget about my mother's memorial.

"Actually, Helen, I'm not married."

"You're not? Why on earth not? He doesn't want to?"

"He wants to. I'm the one holding out."

"Well that puts a new twist on things. Good for him. But really you must get married Liz. For the baby."

"The baby won't care, at least not for a while. I don't want to get married while I'm pregnant. I want a pretty wedding, one that I can enjoy without swollen ankles. I just hate the idea of a shotgun wedding. We'll get married eventually," I blabber on without thinking.

"Every thing you said is bull shit, Liz. You simply must, I know you hate hearing those words. You love him don't you?"

"I adore him; I love him unconditionally."

"Fine, fine. It's simply the right thing to do."

"Why, Helen? Why is it wrong to wait a couple of months? Why do I have to back down when I feel so strongly about this issue."

"This is an intangible thing, like love itself. Accept it, stop trying to convince yourself it doesn't matter and get it over with. Sometimes you don't have to know why something is right. It's a little like going to church. Have your children been baptized?"

"Yes."

"Well there you have it. Why did you have them baptized?"

I can't answer.

Anything I say will make her case stronger. "You should have been a lawyer, Helen."

"Yes, I know, but I'd rather get important things done. I'm an artist. Anyone can be a lawyer, not everyone has talent. Now, back to the meat of the matter. You never thought for a second God wouldn't accept your babies into heaven if they weren't baptized did you?"

"No."

"But you had them baptized anyway because...?"

"I wanted to do that, and that's the difference." I know what Helen wants. She wants me to say I did it because it was the right thing to do.

"Am I giving you a headache dear?" she asks innocently.

"Yes, how did you know? I'm sorry Helen, I just have so much on my mind."

"I understand, I give people headaches all the time, Just one more word. Prioritize dear, you must sit down and decide what is most important to you and what fits with your true understanding and vision of the universe. Now then, let's change the subject. About the monument."

I can't tell her, not just yet. The plans for the monument are supposed to arrive tomorrow, I'll explain the situation and Mom's presence tomorrow night when we speak. This phone call has already been too weighty for me and I'm exhausted. The baby is pummeling my ribs like a boxer trying to rob his opponent of all breathing ability. I need to lie down so the baby will swim or shift or take a nap.

I run my hand through my hair then look at my fingers. There are at least ten stands trapped between my fingers. Great, now I'm going bald. In previous pregnancies my hair was always in beautiful shape. What's the problem? Scratching my belly, I wonder.

Outside the big living room window, the wind blows through the pines on the west side of the house. The pines and oaks sway as the storm rolls in. The squirrels are all gone and Fred has jumped onto his window sill perch. He's pressed flat against the window hoping the eaves will keep him dry. He takes a few tentative steps, his cloven hooves tapping. He tries to bite and lick through the glass. Stupid Fred. He does this every day. I make a mental note. Someday I'm going to put a great big African Violet plant outside, on the ledge and let him have at it. He shouldn't go through life wanting something he never gets.

More leaves fall from the trees and the rain begins. Fat drops thud against the glass. Everything outside the window is gray, the air, the sky, the rain, the trees and the ground. How impressive the complete absence of any other color is. Even the red and gold leaves have vanished in the murky ocean of wolf fur colored rain.

Maybe, someday I'll be able to bury my face in that soft and colorless fur. It will be impossibly soft and smell like my grandmother's stole. Maybe that's what death will feel like.... Imagine the joy of feeling nothing at all.

I can't let myself have thoughts like that. Is this what Mom is doing to me. Making me think about the comfort and ease of death. B. Wallace you must stop, you can't do this to me.

The storm's energy is building. "Helen, the weather has really gotten ugly here. I better hang up." My hand shakes so I put it under my thigh.

"Yes, yes that's right. I'll call tomorrow. Good-by." She hangs up suddenly, without much ladylike pomp.

Mike has gone into his room.

Suddenly, there is a musical explosion in his room.

Felicity, who's been sitting on the couch working on a cross word puzzle says, "Jesus Christ, Mike turn that down." She sounds like a fifty-year-old Long Island divorcee.

The music continues, so loud I can hear the bass notes in my bones. My ear drums ring and sizzle. When I was six, my brother Daniel got a new stereo. He let me wear the huge and heavily padded headphones then turned "Blood Sweat and Tears" up so loud my eyes watered. But I didn't want to take the headphones off. The music sounded pure and close. I laid down on the floor and fell into "Spinning Wheels" while Daniel sat at his desk doing his homework. Every now and then he would turn around and check on me. He'd smile and I would wave back. The trumpets ripping through my brain. That day, I experienced my first headache.

Louella put me to bed, with a cool rag on my forehead, still I smiled remembering the power of the music, Daniel's grin and the way his blond hair hung down over the collar of his shirt.

My brother was proud of me that day and called me "his little rock and roller." Nothing was better than making Daniel proud.

I only had Daniel for a little while. And there are so many things about him I can not remember. That hardly seems fair. What did his toes look like and how did his voice sound. I've lost those memories. Everyday I lose another piece of my brother. His memories drift to the bottom of the lake. I do know, if Daniel were alive today, he'd tell me to bury Mom. He'd say "screw the spooky shit and do what you want."

Where is that brother of mine now?

Michael opens his bed room door and runs out to get his file folder. The music is suddenly twice as loud. I can not recognize the cd he's listening too.

I'm afraid of time's passage. It might do to me what it's done to WaWa. If I forget, I'll have nothing.

The notion of losing everything, the way I've lost Daniel, makes my heart and lungs and throat constrict. I wait for the baby to move so I can try to feel some comfort and company.

But I know too much. Sometimes, the worst imaginable things do happen. They happen to me. God has taken everyone I love away from me before. What if He does it again? He could, I know He could. What if he takes these people, these faces and voices and hands, and He leaves me alone with nothing but air and time. He could take my Felicity, my Mike, my Zolton. He could take my baby.

If He does that, I will draw my elephant herd around me and move on.

The rain rolls across the house in waves, pounding and thrashing. Like a maniac trying to get through a locked door.

Maybe I'm just hungry. I try to remember the last time I ate. It's 7 p.m. now and I had lunch five hours ago. A bowl of Zolton's cream of Mushroom soup might help fight my sudden melancholy.

But Felicity starts screaming. She runs out of the bathroom laughing and screaming and pulling up her pants. Her eyes are the size of poker chips. "There's a snake in the bathroom."

"There's no snake." I say flatly, but I'm already trying to stand up.

"There is a snake!" she screams as she hops around and points toward the bathroom. She's gone into her Carol Burnett hyper-drama mode.

However, judging by the size of her eyes, I guess there really is a snake in the bathroom.

I'm getting a little excited now, too, but I'm too huge to move quickly. This frustrates Felicity to no end. "Come on Mamma, hurry, he'll get away!"

"Let's hope so," slowly I push myself past the chair. "What kind is it?"

"How should I know, it's a snake, long, skinny. I asked for a snake and I got one. That's what I prayed for, remember" she hollers at me.

Slowly, I peek into the bathroom. It takes me a minute to understand what I'm looking at. "Oh my God," I whisper.

Mike is backing me up. "What? Is it a copper head?"

They are both trying to peer around me but I'm too big and nearly fill the door frame.

"There's a bunch of them." I peek again. There, on my shiny white tile, are five or six little black snakes with yellow rings around their necks. They are all squirming but not moving very fast. It's hard for them to get traction on the tile. As I watch, another squirms out of a tiny hole in the grout under the sink. "Oh, my God, it's another." Now

I'm getting kind of freaked out. It's like one of those 1975 cheap nature-on-a-rampage movies. SNAKES IN THE BATHROOM! "They're just ring necks, they can't hurt us," I tell the kids but my heart jack-hammers.

"Cool," Felicity says but neither one of them wants to storm the bathroom first. "My prayers are coming true. Somebody in heaven answered my prayer. Talk about good service."

I actually like snakes and catching one wouldn't be a problem but a wad of snakes, a gang of snakes in the bathroom, that's kind of pushing my limits. I close the bathroom door in order to think. "I don't think these snakes are the answers to your prayers, honey."

Felicity pulls on my arm and then sort of hugs me and spins around my torso. , not listening to a word I've said.

"Oh boy," I crack the bathroom door and take another look. They are still there, writhing and twisting on my fairly clean floor. I wish they would just go back down that little hole. But that doesn't seem to be their plan, so I will do battle with snakes in my bathroom.

"Ok, kid are you ready for this?" I say to the baby in my belly.

No answer.

"Fine, be that way."

"Mom, stop talking to the baby. If we catch them we can take them to school."

"Great, this is just beautiful." The pool of tiny slithering reptiles rearranges itself. I want to call Zoltan. I want to tell him to come home and help me deal with this unfortunate situation but it's 7:00 o'clock. No doubt he's dealing with dinner snakes of his own, waitresses and Chicken Fontaine orders.

"Ok, Mike, get me one of the big coffee cans under the sink."

"Felicity, I guess we need..." I look at the snakes. What the hell do I need?

"I guess I need a spatula."

The kids disappear into the kitchen, obviously delighted that I'm taking matters in hand. I am the general, they are my foot soldiers and we shall capture the harmless reptile enemy.

When I open the bathroom door the snakes don't seem interested in going anywhere. They just wrestle around one another in a black and slippery ball.

How should I do this, try to scoop them all up at once with the spatula or chase them into the coffee can? Hummm. They are actually pretty small, about as big around as a baby's pinkie and as long as a ball point pen. They mean me no harm, just want to dance on my bathroom floor.

"Ok, you guys go around and get on the other side so they can't squirm back behind the toilet."

I approach the snakes, then try to bend over. I can't. Because of my mountain like belly, it's impossible for my to bend over and get the snakes, so armed with my coffee can and spatula, I lower myself into a squatting frog position. But I'm too far away from the snakes and I know I can't stay balanced like this for long. I give up and get on my hands and knees. The tile is cold and it seems as though my belly might drag on the ground.

I don't want to do this. I don't want to crawl around on my hands and knees chasing little snakes.

"Get ready," I say, then try to move quickly. That's a joke. Using the spatula, I flip the snakes toward the coffee can and actually capture two. The other three make a break toward the kids. Mike grabs one and tosses it into my can, but Felicity accidentally squishes one with her knee. The center of the snakes tiny body is flat and wet.

"Oooooo" she says then starts laughing and crying. "I'm sorry, oh, Mom, I killed him." She starts to get up, but the dead snake hangs from the knee of her pants.

"It's ok honey, you didn't mean to." Using the spatula, Mike peels the smashed reptile off Felicity's pants then dumps it into the toilet. I look in the coffee can. The snakes squirm inside on the the shiny silver surface. One stretches nearly three quarters of its length up the side of the can, trying to escape, but it'll never make it. I shake the can and he falls back inside with his brothers and sisters.

I look around. The last snake is gone. I crawl toward the toilet and look behind. Nothing. My back is starting to hurt and the baby is kicking with vicious accuracy at my belly button. I pick up the bath mats. No snake. I nudge the plunger and toilet bowl brush. The snake has vanished.

"We lost him. Maybe he'll come out later." I have to sit down before I can push myself into an up right position. My knees are aching from the cold hard tile. Felicity takes the can from me. "You need some help getting up?"

"That would be nice."

She puts the can of snakes on top of the toilet, then both my children take a hand and haul me to may feet. "Thank you very much," I say, trying to regain some of my dignity.

Felicity holds the can and grins, "Here Mike, you want to hold them?"

"Maybe tomorrow," he says.

I sit down on the toilet, let my legs flop out in front of me and I lean back. Then, with my best Jewish accent I say, "What did I ever do to deserve this. Tell me, God. I'm here, I'm huge and you give me snakes, explain this to me, Lord."

Mike looks at me and grins. "That's good."

"What was it?" I ask him.

"A politician guy from New York?"

I close my eyes. "Close enough, you better watch out for the A.F.L.C.I.O." I say then take his hand and press it against the skin next to my belly button.

We both wait. Then our baby begins to kick, every two seconds. It's a foot. One two, kick, one two kick, one two kick.

"Feels like a punter."

I smile at him then lean further back on the toilet.

"Can I take one of the snakes to school tomorrow, Momma?" Felicity asks.

"No, we need to let those guys go free, they'll die if you try to keep them. Come here, feel this."

I stand slowly. My knees crack. That never happened before I was pregnant. What if my bones just collapse from the weight, cave in like straws. Felicity puts her hand on my stomach, in the same place Mike was touching and I study my reflection in the mirror. I'm looking kind of yellow these days and I should color my hair. But what if the chemicals get into my milk.

The baby suddenly rolls and presses her butt against Felicity's hand.

"You know what that is?" I ask.

"Her back?"

"Maybe, but I doubt it. Guess again."

"Oh no," Felicity jumps back, laughing. "It's a baby butt."

Mike stares into the mirror and makes gruesome faces. "Why did all the snakes come in at once?"

"The rain maybe. It must have washed them out of where ever they were living." This notion gives me the creeps because it means there may be more snakes down there and they might squirm into my bathroom again. Getting out of bed and walking into the bathroom will be a nightmare. And I do a lot of walking to the bathroom in the middle of the night. What if I step on one in the dark or they wrap themselves around my toothbrush or hide in the toilet paper roll?.

Felicity wanted snakes and here they are. My prayers are rarely answered in such short order.

"Felicity, find a lid for the can and punch a couple of little bitty holes in it. You can keep them until tomorrow."

It takes me almost a half hour to locate a bucket of grout in Zoltan's work room. Then, using a table spoon, I get back down on my hands and knees so I can stuff every hole find with the goopy white stuff.

The storm has blown over; the rain stops. I look out the bathroom window. The world is soggy and limp.

Mike and Felicity are building a Hot Wheels city in Mike's room with intermittent fighting.

I listen to them until Felicity comes out of his room laughing. She sees me and becomes sheepish, wondering what I heard.

What do people without children, without families listen to? I have forgotten. What does joy sound like in an empty house? I know exactly what my joy sounds like. It's the tapping of tiny silver pieces going around the Monopoly board. It sounds like spelling words, like Felicity sounding out a word, slowly almost painfully. M-I-G (she pauses) H-T-Y and then looking at me to find out she got it right. It sounds like the brakes on the school bus. I can't imagine my life anymore without the volcanic color of joy.

I sit down and think about the baby. I really need to hurry up and have this child because I'm tired. Sitting down, I wait, I will myself to go into labor. Nothing happens, so I guess I need to think about dinner. According to one of my baby books, if I rub my nipples for three hours a day I will probably go into labor. But I have to rub continuously, with intensity. I don't have three hours to spare and that kind of seems like cheating. I'll just wait it out.

7:30 p.m. Mike and Felicity start their homework. I want to take another nap, but I must try to think about dinner.

It'll be pizza and peas tonight, that's the best I can do The snakes took all my energy and my calves are cramping.

Mike lies on WaWa's large green oriental carpet in the middle of the kitchen floor and reads a chapter of Arkansas history to me. Hernando DeSoto treated the Ouachita Indians horribly. He cut off the noses of two braves so the rest of the tribe wouldn't give him any trouble.

Suddenly feeling guilty, I call the nursing home to make sure WaWa is ok. The nurses assure me she's sleeping.

"Has she had any visitors?"

The nurse makes an odd noise. "You're the only one that's visited her in months. Was she expecting somebody?"

"No, just checking," I say and hang up without saying good bye.

What if this happens to me. What if I get old like Wawa and end up in a nursing home, staring at the ceiling with blind eyes. Mike and Felicity and their children will visit me once a week but I will not remember them or us. B. Wallace, is that what you were avoiding? WaWa makes a pretty good case for suicide. It's best to die before things get really ugly.

The room is warm and silent. The baby hums in my body, growing, waiting, sleeping sweetly. Felicity knocks the sugar bowl off the bar with her elbow. The white grains spread across the brown linoleum. She jumps off the bar stool so quickly. "I'm sorry mamma, I'm sorry. It was an accident. I'll clean it up." She is about to cry.

My heart flutters sadly. Maybe I've been yelling at her too much. Maybe I've been sharp and cutting without realizing it. My mother had such a quick and frightening temper, sometimes I have to concentrate to rein my own in.

"It's ok Honey, relax. Sugar is cheap. The broom is out on the front porch. "

She runs through the living room and out the front door. Mike has stopped reading. We both hear Felicity's laughter.

"What do you think it is?"

He stands up, "Maybe more snakes."

Felicity walks in holding the broom. All the straw has been hacked off, so there is only a long stick and two inches of yellow straw nubs.

"What happened?"

"Fred was eating it," she smiles.

"What?"

"Fred was eating it. He ate the broom," Felicity repeats.

"Not a chance. Are you serious?"

She hands the useless stick with nubby straw piece to me.

Mike says, "I forgot to feed him this morning. Sorry."

I scratch my belly again and sit down at the kitchen table, too tired to stand. "Maybe tomorrow night we're eating out, tonight you'll have to live on frozen pizza."

Mike looks up from his book, "Excellent. Where?"

"I don't know, maybe Ed's."

My daughter says suddenly, "Chicken city, chicken city, chicken city." She starts bobbing her head and scratching in the sugar with her foot.

"What are you doing Felicity? You're making me nervous."

"She's a chicken, Mom. She call's Ed's Chicken City," Mike explains.

My back hurts. Everything has become a problem.

It's this time of day when my heart aches too, and my blood slows sadly in my veins. Z's absence hurts. Chefs must work when the rest of us live with our families.

Chefs feed the world lunch and dinner, so they can't eat with their families. But he was a chef before he met me.

If Z were here I'd feel better, safer about Hurlie and B. Wallace. I'd have my crutch. If I marry him, then we might get divorced and I'll lose him, lose my ballast. I can't lose anything else, not yet.

Ohhh, that's a new excuse, I need him too much to marry him. Even I know this is not a healthy situation.

I won't marry him because I don't want anything to change. I'm a big fan of the status quo, so I'll do whatever it takes to keep things, to keep us, just as we are, right now.

That's my decision. I won't bury my mother and I won't marry Z. These decisions should make me feel better very soon.

After dinner Mike plays a computer game and Felicity takes a bubble bath in the jacuzzi. She stays in the tub for nearly an hour, drinking orange juice and playing with several action figures in the towers of bubbles.

While Felicity splashes around, I go over my numbers from this afternoon. The phone rings twice. I hesitate before saying hello then realize I'm dreading the sound of Hurlie's voice. Apparently I'm afraid of him.

Hurlie doesn't call. That worries me too. It's only players, wanting any early lines on the Sunday games.

I've told them I'm all done being a bookie, but they don't want to believe me. I even hooked them up with Charlie, who's worked for Hurlie out of a news stand for years. But changing bookies can be painful and worrisome, like changing dentists.

I wash Felicity's long hair then we brush it with conditioner. "Mom?" she says, her voice distant as fog.

"Yes."

She just stares and me and smiles. I know she's trying to think of a question now that she's got my attention. "Do I get to invite some of my friends to the wedding?"

I continue brushing. "What wedding?"

"You know what wedding."

"You're right. I'm being intentionally obtuse. Forget the wedding." I'll side track her with a word she doesn't know just to avoid the wedding topic.

"Obtuse? What's that mean." She falls for this every time.

"Obtuse. It means being stupid or slow on purpose." I pour a pitcher of fresh water on her head and watch the white suds slip away from her dark hair.

"If I used that word nobody at school would know what I was talking about."

"You're teacher probably would."

"Can I invite my teacher to the wedding? Can Mrs. Hobson come?" She made it back to the topic. As the kids get older my subterfuge work less and less.

"I don't know when the wedding is going to be, Felicity."

"Nagymummy, said it was going to be next week."

My eyebrow begins to twitch. I stop working with her hair. This sort of thing has the potential to push me right over the edge. I want to call E'va and tell her she has no idea what I'm going to do. How dare she assume I'll get married next week. It's none of her fucking business.

'And 'Zoltan wants to get married before the baby is born."

"I know that, but we still haven't decided. However, you'll be one of the first we notify and you can invite one friend."

I finish her hair and as Felicity gets out of the giant tub she says,

"Mom, are you gonna tell us a story tonight?"

"No."

"Why not?"

"I'm in a bad mood and it's already 8:45."

"Tell us a story about your mom, please. Once the baby is born you'll be too busy."

Felicity's works me like a deck of cards and she's still my wide open child, her thoughts, opinions and emotions dangle like ear rings. Everything she thinks and feels comes out of her mouth, instantly. This purity of emotion is probably dangerous. I worry about her teen-age years.

But, in this situation, she's absolutely right. I'll have less time to tell stories when they baby is born. I look at her beautiful and clever face. "You're good."

"Shannon at school, told me you won't love me as much once the baby is born and I'll get jealous. But I know that's not true. Isn't that a really mean thing for her to say?"

"It seems kind of pathetic to me." I touch her cheek. "I could never love anyone more than I love you," I say wrapped her in a great big blue bath towel, I hug my wet daughter. "This is our baby. This baby is going to give us all more love, not less. Instead of me, Mike and Zoltan loving you, you'll be getting love from me and Mike and Zoltan and the baby. This baby will love you so much she will drool love on your shirt when you hug her."

Felicity smiles then says to my stomach. "Hello baby, baby, baby, baby. How's it going in there?"

"Go get into your pajamas, tell Mike to brush his teeth."

"But Felicity," I call and she pokes her head back in just as I stretch out, slowly, on the bed. "You guys don't give me a tough time tonight. I'm really really tired, ok?" I might cry simply because I'm so tired and huge. How can God do this to women with a clear conscience? My grotesque twenty-five pound growth is killing me. Right now it doesn't feel like a baby, it feels like a tumor. There's no telling what's happening to my spine.

After kissing everybody good night, I stand in the silent and darkened house.

I don't know what to do and I'm afraid of the future. Tomorrow could be bad.

INVISIBLE BRANCHES

My body hums as I lower myself onto the couch. Hummmm, I can feel the electricity and the baby in the silence. When Mike and Felicity finally go to sleep, the house deflates. When the kids are in the room, I am blinded by their presence. Everything else is lost in their shadows.

The phone rings and I hesitate before picking up the receiver. There's no one there, just silence and I start to cry. There's no safe place for me anymore, Mom has contaminated my refuge with her newspaper photographs, watermelons, snakes and flaming mail boxes. She loves me so, that I am afraid of my life. There's nothing anyone can do to make her stop. She will have to leave on her own.

After checking on the children one more time, I walk out to my car, barefooted. The night air is fresh and cool because of the rain. I climb in behind the steering wheel, pull the door closed and hit the lock button. The air in here smells of plastic and stale french fries but I am safe. I can do anything in this car, go anywhere and nothing can touch me.

With my seat reclined, I watch the moon disappear behind bulbous clouds, then re-emerge, fat and white. I think about driving on endless highways. I sing "Stop In The Name of Love," to the baby, watch a spider walk across the windshield wiper, listen to the farm report on the radio station and pray Zolton will get home quickly and safely. Holding on to the black steering wheel with both hand, I pretend I'm driving fast and recklessly. I think about the freedom of heaven. Then thoughts, new thoughts begin to snap and pop in my mind, like hot oil in a skillet. Heaven. What if my mother isn't in heaven. What if suicide sends you to hell and this is a whole new and horrible B. Wallace I'm dealing with. I've always believed in everything. So, what if.....

Staring through the darkness, I watch Mike and Felicity's windows. I will see her if she wakes up. Sparks and stars dance in and out of my line of vision. The baby kicks, reminding me why I am here.

After nearly an hour headlights slice through the darkness and I hear his rumbling truck. Before Z gets to the top of the driveway I climb out of the car so he won't know I've been hiding.

I lean casually against the hood of the car and smile when he gets out of his truck.

Zolton is home and he smiles. Black tennis shoes, black jeans and a white chef coat with a big tomato sauce stain on the sleeve. His hair pressed down from sweat and his base ball cap. He's carrying all sorts of stuff, a file folder under one arm, a styrofoam to-go box and his red tool box full of knifes.

"I'm freeee," he says in a funny voice. "I don't have to turn on a fucking stove for ten hours. And I brought you food. It's after eleven, Lizard, what are you doing out here?"

Ignoring the question, I hold the front door open for him. "What a man. Bring home the bacon, fry it up in a pan."

He puts the to-go box on the table in front of me then takes off his coat, wads it up and pitches it across the room. He reeks nicely of onion, garlic, maybe a little white wine. "You smell like chicken Francesca. I could eat you."

"Please, help your self." He falls into the couch, and I sit down too. "Actually, that's what I brought you. You haven't been eating enough." He opens the container proudly and there it is, Chicken Francesca, a dish he created two years ago. A single chicken breast stuffed with cheese, ham, egg plant and artichoke hearts covered with a very light breading and an exquisite red basil sauce. It's as big as a soft ball. "How much did the doctor say you gained?"

I pull an artichoke heart free and bite it. "I'm not telling."

"You lost six pounds. I called the office. Now eat."

There is a flaming red welt the size of a veal cutlet, on the soft skin of his right forearm. Zoltan gets burned all the time, usually by oven racks or broilers on busy nights. But this is a new burn pattern.

"It was stupid." he says as I touch his arm. "I don't even want to talk about it." I pull my feet up on the couch and he briefly rests his head on my knees. "I was trying to show Julie how to saute. Sounds simple? It is. She had a couple of chicken breasts going, they were just about ready to turn and then for some un-fucking-believable reason she decides to do the big toss, like she's making a pizza. One breast and two ounces of four hundred degree butter landed on my arm. I swear, the chicken melted into my skin. I had to peel it off. Tonight was her first night on the stove. She's been a bread and salad girl for almost a year."

"Did you put anything thing on it?" I study the wound. It's purple and pink and puffy. There is already one pecan shaped blister.

"No. We were busy as hell. The wheel was wrapped with tickets and we had two new waitress and one was in tears by 7 o'clock.."

"Did you say anything to Julie, you didn't fire her did you?" I'm thinking about Julie. Eighteen years old with a two year old baby boy. She lives with her parents or a boyfriend .

"No, I didn't say anything. She felt bad enough." We both stare at his arm. Tentatively, I touch the puffy pink skin surrounding the burn.

He twitches. "How was your day? Tell me something good."

I love it when he says this. He listens to the bizarre details of my world. "I got most of my collections done and Fred ate my broom, as you know, our mail box turned into a torch and so did your grandmother's."

He sits up.

I nod, ashamed because I know all this is my fault.

"Why didn't you call me?"

"There wasn't anything you could do and your day was ugly enough. I'm so sorry, Z. But E'va is ok." I close my eyes and add, "I know who's doing it but there's nothing we can do."

"There is something I can do. I'll break their fucking arms and it'll be tough to light a match."

I shake my head. "It's my B. Wallace, I'm telling you, she's doing all this." I hear my own voice and it sounds stupid.

Z takes my chin in his big hand. The smell of garlic is overwhelming. "Your mom isn't responsible, Liz. You've got to stop saying that. You know it's not your mom. Please don't get all wacked out on me now, Lizard."

'Well, how about this? They have a baby elephant at the Gator Ranch, and I'm almost finished with my collections. Hurlie doesn't want me to quit."

"Too bad. You need a break. He'll get over it."

I nod, wondering if he will.

"I'm almost done but the idea of being unemployed is weird. It makes me nervous," I confess.

Z stares at me, his focus forces me to concentrate on his eyes and the safe space he creates for us. "Don't be nervous. I'll take care of us, we'll be ok." I've never known Z to go back on his word. That's very important right now. I have to believe in him, like a squirrel trusting the branches he doesn't see, but knows are there.

I nod. "The doctor said the baby is all ready to go, his little head is pointing south."

"Glad to hear it." He puts his hand on my stomach. "Keep up the good work in there," he says to my abdomen. We are both still. The baby only flutters, but that's enough. Zoltan breathes and a little bit of the day's tensions slip away.

I watch his fingers creep toward me and he takes my hand. "I don't understand your reasoning about anything but Liz, will you please marry me, woman?"

Blood rushes to my brain and he rubs my legs. "I should be rubbing your feet, you're the one that's been standing up for the past eleven hours."

"Yeah, but you need special consideration. Look at the load you gotta carry."

He continues rubbing, then works up to my calves. His hands are huge and make my legs look diminutive and feminine. Knots of tension dissipate. He says, "How about this idea. We get married next week at the courthouse with Mike and Felicity and Granny. Then have a major wedding event later on. We can invite everybody, take lots of pictures and the baby will even be there, with the kids, in the wedding party. This doesn't have to be so hard, you know."

He doesn't understand, but he's trying and in a just and fair world, that scores points.

Thinking hard, I realize I don't know the right words to pry his mind open. I can't think of a sentence that will help him understand my fears. They will scare him, he'll think I'm losing my mind. Everything sounds small and hollow and feels gargantuan.

My voice is tiny when I say, "I love you too much to get married right now and I don't want to have a wedding while I'm pregnant."

"Unbelievable horse shit. And you realize you keep changing your reasoning, proving that even you don't understand what it is you're doing to us. You're starting to fuck with me, Lizzy. Can't you just stop?"

My mind sizzles like bacon. I want to fight back. I want to use words to prove him wrong. I could do that. Tie this argument up in meaningless words. But he's right. He's right. My intangible fears are screwing up our relationship. Sometimes I wonder why Zolton stays here, with me. I can never seem to make things easy for him and God knows he deserves an easy love.

For nearly ten minutes we don't speak. We just lean on one another in the half darkness.

"I'm sorry," I whisper into his neck.

"If you were really sorry, you wouldn't do this. You'd say yes. Why does it matter? It's between you and me. It doesn't concern anyone else. Getting married will change things, it will make us stronger. Why can't you believe that? Its our life and our marriage and our baby. You're pregnant, so what? You're scared, well so am I. We'll be scared together, we've done it before. I'll marry you even if you are a chicken shit."

Looking at the coffee table, I realize the newspaper with mom's picture is staring at me again. B. Wallace's dark, newsprint eyes flicker with indignation and frustration. She wants to speak. How did it get down here again? Maybe the kids moved it. "Just don't give up on me Z. please."

Shaking his head, slowly, he is suddenly serious again. "I'm too tired to talk about this right now." Z leans back into the couch and closes his eyes. "I'm not asking you anymore because I'm tired of getting turned down. Ok? You let me know if you change your mind."

My words and breath stop for an instant. He's serious and will not ask again. Z never, ever bluffs. This saddens me so. He's giving up.

Now, for the first time, I'm certain of one thing. This is not what I want him to do. Obviously, I've been more manipulative than I realized. Have I just been playing games? I don't think so.

If I think about my actions, it's possible I've been enjoying his pursuit. I'm pregnant right now, so I don't think of myself as highly attractive. I've got two kids already. I'm a little under-employed. The fact that Zoltan wants me, even after all these years, makes me feel good. It makes me think, 'I must be a wonderful catch, otherwise, why would he be chasing me?'

Every woman wants to be chased.

Oh, God, I hope I haven't been torturing him just to feel better about myself. That would make me a real bitch.

"Will you look at something with me?"

I hold out my hands and he pulls me to my feet.

"Getting pretty heavy."

"No kidding." I keep his hand and we walk into the kid's room. I nod at the coffee can on Felicity's desk. "Check it out."

"I don't think so."

"Go on and look. Don't be a weenie."

Until the kids and I moved in, Zoltan didn't know the cardinal rule of child rearing. 'Never look in a can or box with out being properly briefed.' It took him a few months to learn this lesson; during that time he was surprised by lizards, lady bugs, frogs, a mole, tad poles, crickets, and a sparrow. He moves toward the can. "What is it?"

"Go on and look."

He picks it up and hands it to me.

"Fine, I'll show you." I peel back the plastic lid. "Snakes! Lots of snakes."

"Where'd they come from?"

"That's the problem, Mr. Homeowner. They were in the bathroom. They squirted out of a hole between some tile. We only caught three out of five."

"The other two are still in the bathroom?"

"Well," I say, "one got away and the other got squished in the excitement."

He looks in the can again. "I miss all the fun. You can close the can now."

With a sideways grin that makes his mustache twitch, he says. "You want to play foozball? Just one game?"

"Sure, we can work out some of your flaming mail box snakes in the bathroom my wife is really pregnant hostility."

"It has been a day, hasn't it?" He says thoughtfully

In the kitchen, Z pulls a bottle from the freezer. He pours himself a huge shot of E'va's schnapps, drinks it down, then comes to me and gives me a wet kiss on the cheek. Now he smells like eleven hours of sweat, garlic, onion, distilled fruit and alcohol. It is a pungent assortment and confuses me momentarily. We stare at one another, up close. I can see each hair in his beard and follow it back to the follicle. There is a tiny scar on his bottom lip from a racially motivated-bicycle accident that took place when he was eight. I study his thick black eyebrows. "You are very furry."

He runs his hands over my breasts then touches my neck. "I'll give you three points," he says hoping to draw me into the game and sounding a little like Mike.

We take our positions at the foozball table.

The little plastic men, skewered by metal rods, on the 4 and a half foot table have complicated lives. I always take the right side with

Larz, the blond European soccer playboy.

Zoltan has Raul, a South American soccer champion who works with the underground and is desperately trying to save the rain forests in his home land.

We started playing foozball a lot when pregnancy made quick sex cumbersome and kind of embarrassing. It gives us something almost physical to do together and lets Zoltan blow off some steam after a day in a 112 degree kitchen surrounded by high school dropouts.

I score the first point with a wicked bank shot. Before my pregnancy, I was a better player. My body doesn't move with any power or grace now, and I have to stand too far away from the table.

Zoltan answers my single point with three untouchable shots.

Every time he scores, the ball makes a solid whump sound against the back of the goal box. I love that sound.

He takes off his shirt. His chest is so broad. Hair curls in tight black ringlets right in the middle. "Turn around," I say.

He does and flexes, so I can admire his biceps and back muscles.

"Ohh baby. I'm happy to report there's no hair back there yet."

"My shoulder's are in good shape." He flexes his upper body.

"And your stomach looks massive and strong."

He pokes his belly out and thumps it like a watermelon. "Massive, no kidding. I'm turning into a fat boy. At least my navel is going in the right direction."

"You've got a long way to go before you qualify as a fat boy." We are still thumping the ball back and forth but without a great deal of focus. After he scores another shot, I say, "I've got something to tell you."

"You're pregnant?"

"Yeah, well that too. But sometimes, when the children were little..."

"Yesss?" He stops playing.

"Sometimes, when my babies get dirty faces and hands in public, say there's chocolate smeared all over their cheeks, I get a really serious urge just to lick their faces clean."

"Cool."

"Well, yeah, I think it's cool and it makes so much sense. I want to lick their faces and clean them up just like cats do to their kittens."

"That's ok honey. You do what you've got to do," he says then scores with a straight power shot.

I shoot but miss, get the rolling rebound and shoot again. Still no score. "Helen Houston called after you left today. She wants to build a shrine for my mother."

"A shrine?' He scores again. I'm losing.

"Ok, not really a shrine but something close. They want to put her ashes in a monument outside The Center, you know because she sort of started it."

"That's great."

We play and I do not speak.

He says, "What's the deal. You're not happy? B. Wallace finally gets a place of her own."

"B. Wallace doesn't want a place of her own, not here anyway. Honey. She'll haunt me. I think that was all this is about. Everything that's happening is coming from Mom."

We play for another minute or so without speaking. Foozball is actually a pretty noisy game. The ball rolls across the table, is slammed against the sides and against the end of the table. The sounds echo in the silent house and I am always surprised when the kids sleep through our games. "You've been talking to your mother?"

I shake my head. If I try to form my thoughts into words, I'll start to cry.

Z is still waiting for a punch line or an explanation about my haunting mother. But I don't know how to explain her in a way that will make him take it seriously.

"Do I really want to know about this?" he asks. He still doesn't believe in the weight of this situation. But who can blame him?

"Probably not, but Mom's bound to get you, too. So you should be prepared. You know, she might haunt you, just cause you're in same house as me."

He smiles at me a little. Actually, I can't see his lips or teeth but I can tell by the way he's tilting his head and there's a rich glint in his eyes. Reaching over, he presses his hand to my forehead as though taking my temperature. When I don't smile at his joke he says, "You're serious?"

I nod.

"Ok," I finally say, stepping back from the foozball table. "Here's the deal, in fifty words or less. My mother always said if I buried her in Hot Springs she'd come back and haunt me. She said it a lot of times and I believed her. Her skinny little CPA ghost is probably just looking for a reason to stir things up. Zoltan, I honest to God, think she'll come back and fuck with me. Actually, I think she's already here. Probably she's not dangerous but my nerves are shot and I'm just not up to being haunted. I need to focus on the baby and you guys, not my disgruntled dead mother."

"You really think she's here, now?" He sounds so sad for me.

"Think about it Z. Wierd crap has been happening all day, starting with the post it note this morning. I know you don't think my mother put it on our wall but who did? And who else would torch our mail box and E'va's. And did I tell you about the stuff Felicity's been saying and how she prayed for snakes last night."

Z stares. Once again he is a man trying to decide if the woman he loves, who might some day be his wife and soon will be the mother of his child, is insane. "Let me ask you this. Do you believe in ghosts?"

This is a tricky question. We stare at each other while I think, I believe my father turned on the blender after he died. I believe my Mom, might find a way to come back and bug me. So, I guess I believe in ghosts. I feel sorry for Zolton. I never make his life easy. "Yes, I do. You don't believe me, do you?"

He squinches up his face. "Not really. But I almost believe that you believe it."

I shrug and take a lame swat at the ball. It dribbles around without power or enthusiasm.

"You're gonna let Helen build the monument aren't you? That's important. You should be proud. And think about the kids, Liz. Their Grandmother did great things in this town and somebody remembers. You can't take that away from them. It's not fair."

"I am proud of her. That's not the point."

"It is the point. You're afraid of all the wrong things. You're scared of marriage and honoring your mother. Doesn't that sound just a little skewered? I'll tell you what you should be afraid of. Number one, the fact that we don't have insurance is pretty fucking scary. You should be afraid because everytime you answered the phone for years you committed a felony. And there are some of your players you should be really afraid of and giving birth should be sort of scary. But none of that bothers you. You are the bravest woman I've ever known. So what is your problem with getting married and burying your mom?"

I can not look at him. He's brought my fears together and put them right in front of me. I can not avoid their simplicity and gravity and stupidity.

After drinking another shot of Granny's Schnapps he looks at me again, shakes his head then walks into the living room.

Chapter 11

11:07 p.m. My legs are getting weak and my body must be horizontal. Z watches "Star Trek" in the living room.

Slowly, I put on one of his giant T-shirts then stretch out on our bed.

I roll from my back to my side, wedge a pillow between my knees. After flipping the pillow three times, looking for the cool side, I call to him. "Will you please just sit here with me till I fall asleep?"

Silently, he comes into our bedroom and lies down behind me. He's still wearing his jeans. His beard is soft and furry on the back of my neck. Draping one arm over me, he rests his big hand on my belly. The baby does not move. But our hearts are beating nicely.

I am safe. Closing my eyes, I'm not nearly so confused because I know this is all I need.

Finally, sleep wings into the room and takes me.

For hours I sleep without moving, as though I have been taken captive. Then my mind frees itself and becomes a gum ball machine. It's 2:04. I stare at the green digital clock, trying to dive back into the sparkling pool of unconsciousness, but there are thoughts and ideas and visions packed into brightly colored individual packages.

Will Mike and Felicity feel left out when the baby arrives?

I need to get my car tags renewed.

We are out of coffee filters. I've been using paper towels for three days.

Did I eat an orange today? I don't want the baby to have spina bifida.

Have I been drinking too much coffee?

What if labor is too long and painful. Can I take it? I hate pain.

What if they decided I need a C-section? We can't afford that. Think of the ugly scar it might leave.

What if Z gets tired of waiting for me.

Why is it I don't want to get married? I want to be with him forever.

What the hell is my problem?

What time is it? 2:24

When was the last time I changed the sheets?

What if the baby has a huge birth mark on her forehead like Gorbachov?

My hair is gonna turn gray soon. Maybe I should try a new color.

Can I color my hair while I'm breast feeding or will the chemicals leech into my milk?

What if I can't get back into shape after the baby is born.

I haven't checked my butt lately. Is there cellulite back there now?

We need to buy a play pen.

I used to flirt with men all the time. I had a gift. Even when I was married before, I was thinking about other men. I could feel the heat of sex rising up, curiosity. What would it be like. I don't have those thoughts anymore. I never want to be with anyone but Z. I don't even think about anyone but Z. He's the man for my life. I love him.

So why don't I want to get married?

Have I been paying enough attention to the kids school work?

Did I feed the animals tonight? I need a new broom.

What time is it now?

Is the front door locked?

What if Z can't stop smoking and gets lung cancer?

Would I still live with him or move into a trailer next door.

Should I just marry Z and absolutely bury my feelings? I love him. I love him. I love him.

Do the kids know enough about sex? Do they know that Z and I had sex to make a baby? Oh my lord. What do they know?

Alright B. Wallace, what are you doing to me?

Should I let Helen build this monument?

Would you come back and bug me? What exactly would you do? You're not evil now are you? Surely not.

What time is it? 3:00 a.m.

Are we going to have enough money now that I'm not working?

What if I die, I don't even have any life insurance and then Z will have to raise three babies by himself.

Will Hurlie let me go?

He has to, right?

Why would Mom act so crazy? She didn't have to kill herself. We could have figured things out.

Why do I have to worry about her now?

Why am I so afraid?

The room is dark, tiny zaps of light streak through the black air.

I hear something coming in the darkness. Trying to touch Z for reassurance, I listen harder. A quick and even beat. A horse is galloping on hard packed dirt. Listening, I try to figure out what direction is it coming from. When did it get so hot? The taste of red dust settles on my tongue. Opening my eyes, I reach out and touch the barn I am standing next to. The sweet smell of hay and manure and fried chicken fill the air.

The chicken smells heavenly. I know it's golden brown and crispy. My mouth begins to fill with saliva. I want a thigh and a breast. Looking down I see a filtered cigarette butt. Benson and Hedges with a crimson lip stick stain. Mom has been here too. Maybe she actually brought me here, shoved me through a burp in time. She wants me to understand. I roll her cigarette but under my foot and listen.

The hoof beats are getting louder. I drum my fingers on the barn to the steady four count rhythm. There he is, in a swelling cloud of red dust down the road. My great-great-grandfather, Father John, on his new Arabian mare, Beauty. Sucking in a hot breath, I close my eyes hoping he'll go away. I know what's going to happen here today. Please, God, don't make me watch.

Father John is galloping Beauty slowly down the road. They look lovely together, smooth and elegant. He smiles and pats her arched gray neck, but they do not slow.

He was Doc Blue's father. He had 300 aces of farm land and was one of the first politicians in this area. He and a group of land and business owners ran things for years and years after the Civil War.

Of course Father John didn't have any slaves after the war, but three black servants decided to stay on with him to help rebuild. He paid them a little bit and gave them their cabins. But they pretty much kept working like slaves. The most remarkable thing about Father John was he encouraged blacks to learn to read because he wanted everybody to read the bible. He was unusual in that way and I suppose he must have been a decent man.

Sally, the cook, was one of the three who stayed. She was born on the other side of the county and worked for my great great grandfather most of her adult life. She simply couldn't imagine living anywhere else. Sally had a son named Solomon who worked in the stable tending to the prized Arabians Father John bred and sold in Little Rock, Memphis and Atlanta.

Father John circles with Beauty, they are heading back to the barn, now.

The mare is hot and frothy. Father John stops her right in front of the barn. His black riding boots are covered with red dust. Solemn runs out of the barn and takes the reins while Father John pats Beauty one more time, then dismounts.

"She's a champion, Solomon."

"Yes sir, she's as pretty a horse as I've ever seen."

Father John laughs, slaps Beauty on the rump then pats Solomon on the back, You cool her off good, boy. I put her through her paces today."

"Yes sir," Solomon says as he hauls Beauty's saddle off then throws it over the top fence rail. He know's he will have to walk her in the pasture nearly thirty minutes because she's so hot. He'll have to keep her out of the barn till she's cool and calm or she'll get sick. Some horses who eat and drink while they are still hot, die. Solomon has been hot walking since he was six. He hopes to be a blacksmith someday. He's proud of the fact Father John trusts him with every horse on the farm.

But Solemn is only ten years old and right now he's thinking about his mother's fried chicken. It's Sunday so, after Father John eats, Sally will give him a plate with two, maybe three pieces of chicken, potatoes, a biscuit and some greens. The smell is making the Solomon giddy with hunger and excitement.

As he pulls Beauty's blanket off, he suddenly remembers he was supposed to take his mother another bucket of water for the potatoes. He'll get a whooping if he doesn't get that water for her. Solomon puts Beauty in the first stall, next to the tack room. He pats her neck and says "I'll be right back, girl then we'll go out for a long walk." Solomon has loved Beauty since the first day Father John brought her home." Hey girl, I'll see if Momma's got any apples for you. Ok."

Because Solomon has been working all morning, there's already a trough of fresh water and two buckets of grain waiting for her. Beauty eats and drinks until she founders. The oats swell up in her belly and her stomach bursts.

Father John found Beauty dead, in the stall, after dinner.

He dragged Solomon, who was eating his chicken on the back porch, into the barn, threw him onto the dead horses bloated stomach, then beat him with an ax handle until he was unconscious. Before leaving the stall, Father John kicked Solomon one time, in the head.

The boy regained consciousness two days later. He was blind in one eye and he was stupid. Solomon forgot everything he once knew. He sat on the floor instead of in chairs and used his fingers to eat.

My great grandfather destroyed Salomon's brain.

He gave Sally $50 dollars.

Two years later Father John was elected Lt. Governor of Arkansas. Sally kept working in the kitchen and Solomon sat around on the back porch playing with bugs and humming to himself for the next 30 years, until Father John died.

The hoof beats are almost gone now. The barn fades under my hand. It's Z's back.

"Zolton, will you wake up?" I am shaking him.

"Do I have to?"

"I know what was wrong with Mom. I know where it all started. But I don't think knowing about it will make things any better. "

"Is this the story about the swimming pool and Louella's house getting burned down?" He's trying to wake up.

"No, no this is different but it's kind of the same. B. Wallace never got over this. It ate her up and she got a case of liberal guilt that's lasted more than a hundred years." I'm thinking that my mother must have felt she had to fight the old man's DNA or something horrible would happen. You know, maybe she was afraid she would turn into him. Whatever it was, she just couldn't forgive her own ancestors. Then she felt absolutely responsible for getting Louella's house burned down."

"Are you gonna tell me the story, Liz?"

"No, not now. It might bring it all back again."

I've got to find a way to put it all back into the past. It was her family. It was my family. They did horrible things. And somehow Mom felt she had to make up for them. She had to make it up to Sally. This was Father John's state. That's why she doesn't want me to bury her here, ever.

Z puts his hand on my arm. "Lie down Liz, you've got to get some sleep."

"I know. But I have to decide what to do."

"We'll figure it out tomorrow."

The warmth pulsing out of his skin soaks into my body like a heating pad. Closing my eyes, I wonder, will I ever go to sleep?

Thirty minutes later I get up to shuffle to the bathroom. There are fat and fully developed concerns in the center of my gooey brain rather than the comfortable night time fog. Three more times I rise during the night to go to the bathroom. Weighted by the baby and my cumbersome shape, I move like a very old lady elephant, touching things with the tips of my fingers, the jacuzzi, the sink, the towel bar, so I won't topple over. By 5 a.m. I am so exhausted I want to cry. I can't control my emotions and my body is a thing I don't recognize. Misery washes through my blood vessels. My knees and thighs ache. It's times like these that death sounds like a pretty good deal. My body is sore, my brain is sore, everything hurts. If God offered to wrap me up and carry me away right now, I might consider.. Getting back into bed, I rest my hand on Zoltan's shoulder. Even in the dark he feels brown. "Honey?" I whisper.

"Good night," He says.

"No, Zoltan. Not good night. I need you to get up when the alarm goes off and take the kids to school. Ok?"

"Ok," he mumbles.

"You'll have to get them all ready. Mike can make the lunches while you do Felicity's hair, ok?"

"Ok."

"And they both need to take picture money in. It's the last day. $12.95 each. Ok?"

"Ok."

"I love you." I rest my cheek on his shoulder blade. I don't want to marry you and screw up.

My stomach touches Zolton's back. I hate my stupid belly button. Can Z feel the baby when she kicks? I hope so. Somebody else should have to be pregnant with me.

"Liz," he says, "It's Saturday."

"Oh, then everything is different." I drift away, warm and safe and so full of life I can't roll over.

Chapter 12

Saturday

Sometimes in the morning, I wake up, and, for an instant, I don't know I'm pregnant. Then I see my stomach, rising under the sheet like Mt. Kilamonjaro, and I am horrified. I fear I've gotten grotesquely fat in my sleep. Then the baby rolls like the sea and it all comes back to me. It all comes swishing and sloshing back.

The first few minutes are the toughest. Every thing hurts, every bone and muscle, even my ankles and elbows and shin bones. I wish I could think of someone to call so I could gripe and bitch. Better still, I wish I had the sort of friends who take me out to lunch and give me silly little presents just because I'm pregnant. All my pals call me because I was their bookie and now they are getting ready for the Saturday afternoon games.

I'm feeling sorry for myself. Mike and Felicity are my best friends but they don't have the money to take me out for lunch. Maybe I should raise their allowance. Maybe I need some friends with credit cards.

I reassure myself so a monster case of self-doubt doesn't attack. My players are my friends. Maybe they will still be my friends when I'm through. Probably not.

Things get too muddled. Actually, after years of their phone calls, I know more about most of my bettors than I should. They tell me about their wives' face lifts and midnight hard-ons when they think about winning a big super bowl bet. I know when their businesses are slow and all about their teenagers in rehab.

Lying in bed, tears roll back down my temples and melt into my hair. I miss my mom and dad. I want them here with me now, to hold my hand and stroke my hair and maybe fix my breakfast. But they abandoned me. I am an orphan. They can't baby sit for me or come see me in the hospital and tell me how beautiful their grandchild is. It's not fair. I wish, when I was a teenager and Daddy was lying in the hospital

I'd said, "But Daddy, you can't die. I'm going to have babies and I'll need you. Please stay to see the grandchildren I'll give you."

I know I must be very tired because I'm getting so sad and I'm pissed off and blaming everyone for everything.

Angry and lonesome, I close my eyes and fall asleep again.

10:00 a.m. I crawl out of bed and drink my self indulgent cup of coffee. I listen to the radio. I'm a little ashamed that I was so bitchy with my parents this morning. After all these years, I still want them.

There is a note from Zoltan next to the coffee pot. "Call you later. Took kids to the Y pool. Pick up time around 2. Don't be tense. Get some sleep. I'll bring food home. Love Z"

He's already gone. I finally slept and missed my whole family. How weird it is to be in such a quiet place on a Saturday morning. If I concentrate, I can still smell Zolton around the house. Deodorant in our room, coffee and a cigarette in the living room. There are pop tart crusts on the counter. At least they ate something before leaving. I give Bear the crusts after she does a cute doggy dance.

I listen to National Public Radio and learn that Cigar, one of the greatest thoroughbreds in history, is sterile. Too bad Father John's Daddy wasn't sterile. But then where would I be?

Poor Cigar. They have injected his semen into sixty mares but no one is expecting a foal. His inability to produce any offspring is financially equivalent to a five story luxury condominium being destroyed, beyond recognition, by a hurricane. Fortunately, there's a 25 million dollar insurance policy covering Cigar's lack of sperm. I hope they are letting him actually mount a few of these mares.

Sitting down, I think about my list for the day. I only have two people to visit and then my book making career is finished.

Both of today's stops concern bears.

First I have to pay off Raymond SunBear and his wife, Mimi. Then I'll deal with Hurlie, who has a pet bear named, Ambush.

Slowly, I get dressed, blue shorts and white short sleeved button down shirt. Most of my shirts are actually extra large men's shirts. I refuse to buy maternity clothes with stupid peter pan collars, pink and blue bows and smock tops. Why does every one want to dress pregnant women like huge tooth fairies?

When the phone rings, I hesitate. Phone fear. What if it's Hurlie, what if it's Helen. "Hello."

There's no one there.

While I peel a banana, a chorus of barking explodes in the yard.

Bear answers with several sharp yips, then with whining. Finally, she begins scratching at the crack between the door and the carpet, in an effort to burrow her way out. She needs to be taken for a walk. I'm almost afraid to look out the door. God knows what's out there, but I must. I can't have a pack of dogs hanging out in our yard.

It's worse than I imagined. There are a dozen dogs, all lounging around like teen-agers on a pool deck. This is disgusting and dangerous. And where's Fred? He thinks he's a dog too and wants to hang with the pack. What if some bad ass Chow or pit bull shows up and rips his throat open.

Stepping outside, I pack all my frustration and hostility together into one piercing and primitive scream. I scream for years, leaves begin to fall because of my power. The sound is endless, has no beginning, middle or end. It echoes in the woods behind the house. The neighbors probably think I'm being murdered, but I don't care. Like a faucet that's been dripping and dripping and dripping. Finally, I've crank the handle and let the torrent out. My ears ring and my eyes water.

My scream ends The dogs are completely unfazed. They look at me and blink.

"Fine, have it your way." Cautiously, I step sideways down the front steps. I'm still barefooted, but I can make it to the garden hose. My extra weight makes the rocks hurt my feet more than usual.

I turn on the hose, then, with predatory accuracy, I try to squirt every dog in the yard. I soak three before they are out of range. My mission is a failure, but maybe their erections shriveled. The dogs scatter a little but, like jackals on the plains, I know they will be back.

If I do nothing else today, I will get rid of these dogs. I don't care if I have to set the yard on fire, I'll make them go away. I will have control of something.

Gingerly, I try to step around the biggest rocks and get back into the house to put on some socks and boots. I find the dog leash and snap it onto Bear's baby blue collar. She bounces and hops and jumps, exquisitely, like a wind-up squirrel, pulling on the leash as hard as her fifteen pound body will allow. I'm not accustomed to walking my dog, usually I just open the door.

This makes me feel good. I love a happy dog.

Lunging like a miniature sled dog, Bear tries to make a break for it. I hold on tight. "I'm shocked, you slut. Do you know how many of them there are out there?" She doesn't pay any attention to me. Her tiny body quivers in anticipation and her furry chest heaves. But I have the leash looped around my wrist. "Don't do it Bear, you'll end up like me, an unwed mother. And trust me, there's not a dog out there who will pay puppy support on time."

I drag her back into the house and find Mike's pellet gun on the bookshelf. I will handle this situation. The pellet gun is bulky and difficult to aim because it's so heavy, but I'll manage. Despite it's imposing size, the gun doesn't have any real power and won't draw blood, but it hurts a lot more than a b.b. gun.

A dirty golden dog with a long face and perky ears and a big fat black poodle pick up Bear's scent before she's out the door. Hesitantly, they slink out of the bushes, heads down, tails tucked, like they have any sense of shame.

This is surreal. Funky stuff that my dreams are made of. Half the dogs must be too big for Bear. The Rottweiler and Labrador don't stand a chance. They couldn't get it in unless they rolled over and she got on top. But there are a few with legitimate possibilities. A fat white short haired hound and some strange and tiny dog that looks a lot like a gerbil. It has ears shaped like Florida that drag in the grass.

My liberal arts education has not prepared me for this moment. But instinct has taken the place of education.

With confidence, I pump the pellet gun three times. These are obviously country dogs. As soon as I raise the gun to aim, they start backing off. But I'm quick and hit the Rottweiler in the left leg. He jumps a little, whimpers and lopes into the wood. After pumping up again, I tag the gerbil who has the nerve to growl at me before walking away.

Bear and I proceed. She will have her walk today.

I'm a pregnant woman, walking a tiny dog. We are surrounded, but I am armed.

I'm warming up to this, it's much better than screaming.

With surprising accuracy and very little remorse, I close one eye and aim at the hindquarters of a medium-size cinnamon colored dog that's been here for two days. He looks old and discouraged and obviously senses my semi-lethal intentions. But it's too late. I nail him right on the rump and he trots off with his tail tucked.

Fred shows amazing good sense and walks behind me. He leans

down and touches Bear's ear with his round, black and white, goatnose. I raise the pellet gun again then lower it so I can shoot from my expanded hip. There is a fine bong sound when the pellet hits a metal trash can. The remaining dogs scatter. "How about that Bear, no shotgun wedding for you today."

With a strange sense of pride and determination I walk Bear around our yard with the pellet gun in my right hand.

We pause in the shade of our magnolia tree, which is blooming furiously. Huge white flowers fill the morning air with their heavy lemon scent. There is a big 'x' carved into the trunk of the magnolia tree. Mike did that when he was six years old and playing pirate. After carving the big X in the tree, he climbed up and waited for Felicity to find him. Unfortunately, Felicity got caught up in watching cartoons and forgot to find poor Mike who patiently stayed in the tree for two hours.

The tree rustles in an unseen breeze and the X seems to pulsate. It is throbbing slightly until I drag Bear over and touch the trunk. Is it warm.. This X is just like...I have to let the texture of the tree trunk fill my veins and then I find the memory, so acute I feel like I've been slapped. With my fingers in the groves which form the carved "X" the scene takes me so quickly, I drop the big gun. It falls across Bear's leash. She yips as she is jerked helplessly backwards.

"There you are Mom," I say out loud. God, I love her. We are in line in a Boca Raton grocery store. I'm barefooted and the tile floor is very very cold. Mom has already been ravaged by emphysema, and consumed by bourbon and cancer. She's tiny and weak, so weak she had to lean against the meat refrigerator on the final isle. But she is still fighting, her eyes are quick and fierce. Still I love seeing her. I've missed her so much.

I'm holding a package of Roma tomatoes and Mom is leaning against our grocery cart. A fat bald baby happily leans out of his shopping cart to grab some candy and gum. Mom laughs again but it turns into an ugly cough and the sound frightens the baby.

I check our list, compare it to the stuff in the grocery cart, milk, cigarettes and artichokes. Mom stares openly at a huge black man wearing a shirt with a big red "X" emblazoned on the front. Above the X is the name Malcolm.

This guy must be 6'6 and probably weighs in at 275. His upper arms and shoulders are enormous. The man looks right back at B. Wallace, probably because she's an old white lady openly staring at his chest.

Suddenly, in her long ago theater voice, Mom says, "I don't see an American dream...I see an American nightmare...Three hundred and ten years we worked in this country without a dime in return." She's quoting Malcom X.

There is an excruciating moment of silence. I hold my breath, waiting for one of them to speak. Am I going to have to protect B. Wallace from this giant man in the express lane. Finally he speaks, so softly I lean forward. All he says is, "Alright Malcolm."

Mom shifts her weight, straightening her posture. "That doesn't mean I agreed with his entire doctrine."

"Don't matter. You listened to the man," he says.

"The truth is, I resented being called "a wicked race of white devils but..."

Her new acquaintance is almost through checking out. He turns to me before leaving with his plastic bag and says, without smiling, "You be good to her."

All I can do is nod. My feet are so cold they hurt. I put our groceries on the conveyer belt and I am back with my hand on the magnolia tree.

My feet still hurt.

Bear pulls me across the yard, but I'm thinking about Mom in a happy and confused gray memory haze. I never knew what was going to happen when we went out in public. It took us a few years to learn to breathe again after Daniel and Daddy died. But then, I thought we were happy, almost happy living together in the thorn patch of grief. But I wasn't enough. She left without me.

Bear is too excited to perform, so we trudge back inside. My feet are still tingling from the cold grocery store tile..

Sometimes it's so hard to keep on living. So hard to do the next thing, so I make lists. They remind me of step two and three and four, and they remind me of all the things I love. I must look at today's list again so I will remember to visit MiMi and Hurlie and pick up my life, my children and then, maybe, go into labor. Lists are good.

After walking around the house, turning off lights and radios, I collect my notebook and ledger and walk back outside.

11:13 a.m. Standing on the porch, I can see all of our front yard which rolls down to the highway. On the other side is the humpy lumpy cow pasture and then the dark green Ouachita mountains. The mountains are only ten miles away but they look cool and safe. There must be dozens of caves and dens out there, places to curl up and have a baby. That's what I would be looking for if I was a bear or wolf.

The world spreads before me like a quilt. From this vantage point I feel poetic, grand, tragic and blessed.

With determined steps I shall walk across mother earth with my kicking, squirming baby in my belly. When I was a child the priest would spread his arms before dismissing us from Sunday service. "Go forth now into the world to love and serve the Lord," he would say.

Looking at our charred mail box makes me thirsty. Pregnancy has taken all my water. I'm always thirsty. My tongue shrivels and sticks to the roof of my mouth. If I wait to drink, a strange and intense longing seizes my heart. It's so odd. I become dizzy, sad and depressed, as though my cells are dying and my body knows the end is near.

But today, I've left the house without my customary green jug of Mt. Valley Water, so I must stop at Daisy's Grocery to spend 89 cents on water. The water I'm paying for is almost identical to the stuff that flows from our well.

Daisy's parking lot is nearly full because it's a beautiful Saturday in deer hunting season and this is a popular weigh-in station.

Daisy's is the heart of Ft. Lake. Everyone must get gas and propane, peanut butter and milk, so we all end up here. It's also where county residents buy hunting and fishing licenses hang out and listen to the store's police scanner and sign up for the Volunteer Fire Department.

I watch the store for a little while and practice my breathing. Thirst squeezes my tongue. Nearly a dozen men, fat and skinny, bearded and clean shaven, short and tall are standing around in camouflage. One group is still pretty clean and getting ready to head out to the deer woods. There's a rusted Ford F100 next to the gas pump. It's caked with dried mud and there's a ten point buck tied across the hood. The dead deer's elegant legs dangle in front of the truck grill, his glassy eyes stare at the gas pump. One very fat man in filthy camouflage keeps patting the deer with his closed fist. It must be his. He is Mike and Felicity's school bus driver.

It's strange that all of these men match. Ten or twenty years ago they were all probably wearing Fountain Lake football uniforms together, now they all wear camouflage. Mottled green and black and gray patterns with leaves and branches printed on hats, pants, shirts vests and boots. They look like a giant pack of armed trick or treaters.

As soon as I get out of my car, my eyes begin to water. The sweet smell of the deer blood mixes with gasoline, spilled beer and sweat. I hold my breath and smile at the men simultaneously.

Walking into Daisy's I get very dizzy. The registers and check-out girls swirl in front of me, tilting to the right then the left. I lean against the shopping carts by the front door.

Linda, who is working the register, walks toward me just as the fluorescent lights start to blink. There is a man with a can of corn and a box of Tampons at her register, but she ignores him. "You're pale, girl, you gonna hurl? Was it that buck out there?" She puts one hand on my belly and the other on my forehead. "You need something to drink?"

I nod and try to smile again. I feel so wiggly, cool and hot. The grocery store is pale and bright, swirling and sinking. I am about to hit the floor. But I must not pass out, not here. If I do, I'll hit my head on the shopping buggies. Wrapping my fingers around the cool silver handle, I lower myself, so slowly, to the floor. The old tile is cold and gritty on the back of my legs, but I'm grateful to be here. Blood pounds in my ears like a snare drum. I pray for Zoltan. I want him to be next to me when I open my eyes. I need his big warm hand. Nothing bad is happening, but I need him.

I can feel people looking at me, probably thinking I'm going into labor, but there's no pain and no dampness between my legs. I need to smile at the people and reassure them that I'm alright.

Linda squats down with a plastic bottle of Hawaiian Punch "Drink this, you need some sugar."

My hand trembles but I drink almost half. A little dribbles down my chin and I try to wipe it away with my sleeve.

The man with the tampons and corn is still waiting. Finally, he takes five dollars out of his wallet, waves it at us, then places it on the scale, puts his groceries in a paper sack and says," I left the money over there for you."

She waves him off.

"You need me to drive you anywhere?" he asks me.

What nice people there are in this store.

"No, I'm fine, really. I just got out of my car too fast." I look up at him and smile. He is a middle-aged man who looks very tall to me because I'm on the floor. He shuffles his gray cowboy boots next to my knee.

"I'm ok," I say to Linda. "You need to get back to work."

"You want me to call your house?"

I shake my head. "Nobody home."

"Here, give me your hands." She holds both my hands tightly than on the count of three, pulls me up. She does not let go of me for several seconds and watches my face intently.

Suddenly, I shiver uncontrollably.

Linda rubs my arms. "Somebody must of walked across your grave."

This comment does not make me feel any better, but I smile weakly. "I'm fine really. See?" I raise my arms slightly to prove I will not fall over. "Actually, I came in for some water. I was thirsty."

"You're color is coming back. How long you got to go, girl?"

"Two weeks."

"No shit?" Linda's hair is the color of a tangerine.

"That's what the doctor said"

"Not a chance." She says, sizing me up. " Look at you, that baby's ready right now. This is your third, right?"

I nod.

"Any day now. Go home and mow the yard. That always puts me into labor."

I nod at her advice and she hands me a tall green bottle of water. "Here, go home. You can pay next time you come in. I don't want to see you dropping that kid right here."

I take the water and Hawaiian Punch. Linda holds the door open for me then walks me to the car.

"You sure you're ok to drive?"

I nod again. "Right as rain."

She walks back to the store as I turn the ignition key. What if Linda, the register girl, is right? She's got six kids, maybe she knows something. Should I go home and mow the yard? I don't think so. Really, I don't want to go into labor this afternoon. Something else, something besides the baby, is about to happen, but I don't know what it is. A fundamental, but pivotal event is going to take place, I just know it.

The baby suddenly feels low down, pressed, like a bowling ball against my pelvic bone, she might just fall out before I get out of the car. She wants to come out, wants to wriggle free of my body and cry, really loud, she wants to come out and suck and pull on my nipples until milk pours from my breasts and makes her strong.

And I am ready to look into his eyes and see a glimmer of the future.

With my eyes closed and the air conditioner blowing on my face, I consider my next move. I can't go home. Holding my day's list, I drink the rest of the Hawaiian Punch. I still have to go see Hurlie. If I miss him today, things will get even more complicated. Anything can happen between now and tomorrow. I have to deal with him today.

My body finds its balance. I'm ok. With one hand on my stomach, I say to the baby, "We're ok now. Don't' get all worked up. Lets get this over with."

I reach for my purse and a piece of gum. My purse isn't here. Turning, I check the back seat then under the front seats again. My purse isn't here. I must have left it at home. The key for the glove compartment is in my wallet and I've got over two thousand dollars locked in there from yesterday's collections.

I will stay calm. There's no reason to get worked up over a three mile detour. I'm feeling better, the Hawaiian Punch seems to be helping.

After two deep breaths, I remind my self to drive well, slowly and cautiously.

Big fat tears roll down my cheeks. I watch my own eyes in the rear view mirror. They are red and my eye lashes look puny. Mascara has formed a crescent moon under my lower lids. God, I have a lot of wrinkles, tiny lines form a miniature map on the skin around my eyes. It looks a little like Texas. No, there are more roads on this map. Up close, the skin around my eyes looks like a street map of Cincinnati.

They say women with expressive faces are the first to get wrinkles. I am proof of this theory. I guess I must laugh too much, cry and frown, sneer and smile. As a result I have wrinkles. Women with passion and grand emotion are the first to be marked by age. That sucks. The cold and passive bitches get to be beautiful.

Why would Z want to marry this face and this body? My thighs are chaffing, a bride shouldn't have chaffing thighs.

At least I've stopped crying. I sniffle at myself.

Fuck them all. I shouldn't have to make any big decisions right now, not when I'm this pregnant. I shouldn't have to deal with B. Wallace and her ghost or threats, and I shouldn't have to make any decisions concerning marriage. I'm not fit to make life changing resolutions. My hormones have me trapped in Space Mountain so everybody should just love me or leave me alone.

I could leave today, drive around for a couple of weeks with the credit card, we have six hundred dollars left on the Visa. First I have to deliver Hurlie's money though. He never gets beat, not even by a pregnant woman.

I'd check into a small, clean and quiet mom and pop hotel. When I go into labor, I'll call 911. They will take me to an emergency room. Maybe the paramedics can deliver the baby in the hotel room then leave us there, me and my baby alone in a warm, clean, quiet room. I'll have the baby and be fine. Then I'll go home.

I squeeze the steering wheel until my fingers cramp. They look bony and white, as though I have suddenly been stricken with arthritis.

There is a commercial on the radio for a nicotine gum that helps you stop smoking. "The power to calm, the power to comfort." I don't smoke but I defiantly want some of that.

When the Nicotine gum first hit the market I was going to school in New York. The gum wasn't legal in the United States but you could buy it over the counter in Canada. I desperately wanted B. Wallace to stop smoking. So, I drove 300 miles, crossed the border, bought 50 packs of the foul tasting gum, a sewing kit and a stuffed Kangaroo. Thinking I was very clever, I cut the Kangaroo open, stuffed the gum inside then sewed him back up. My childish plan actually worked. I successfully smuggled the gum across the border and into New York. Then I mailed the gum and the kangaroo to Mom.

I don't think she ever opened a pack. Nobody ever stops smoking for somebody else.

Thinking about Mom makes me sniffle again. I need to stop thinking about her so I won't cry.

The baby kicks happily.

Without turning on my blinker, I make a sharp left turn and thunder up our driveway.

11:45 a.m. The porch light is on. That's odd because I was the last to leave the house and I remember turning it off as picked up Bear's leash.

Maybe Zoltan came back home for something, but he's an absolute Nazi about turning all the lights off. So, why did he drive off and leave two electricity sucking spot lights on?

My purse is sitting on the front steps. There's no way I left it there. I never put things on the ground anymore because I hate bending over to pick them up.

The baby pushes with an elbow or maybe it's his skull, against my hip bone. As soon as I open the car door I can feel electricity in the air. This is a different house than the one I left a few minutes ago. Something has happened.

I'm being watched.

The tiny hairs on the back of my neck and on my arms stand up. Ready for anything, I look past the house into he woods. Listen, I must listen, I hold my breath and concentrate on sounds, leaves fall, a crow cries then flaps overhead. The creek is pretty loud because of yesterday's downpour. But there aren't any odd noises. Fred is standing next to the swing set eating a shoelace. He looks unconcerned, so I must be wrong. His ears aren't even twitching.

Strangely enough, there aren't any dogs lurking.

Still, there is something different. My back hurts so I twist and arch, hoping to release some tension. The baby doesn't like this move and kicks in retaliation.

It takes me a moment, then I realize there is definitely something wrong with the grass, right in the middle of the yard.

Slowly, I walk across the lawn. Another crow flies from a branch and lands twenty feet in front of me. His feathers so black they shimmer, silver and blue in the sunlight.

I stop. There are two perfectly round rings of dead grass in the middle of my yard. Each is about three inches wide and four feet across. Every blade of grass is dark and curled, as though singed. If I pressed a flaming hoola-hoop into the yard I might be able to produce something like these. There is a second dead patch of grass about the size of a dinner plate inside both rings.

Reaching down, I touch the wounded lawn. It's not warm; it doesn't burn my hand or make me itch. The grass is just dead. What could make such a pattern?

There is a whimpering sound coming from the bushes next to the driveway. My pregnant knees crack as I squat down again to peer underneath the bushes. Because my balance is not good, I must sit down all the way with my legs spread out in front of me.

There is another thumping and rustling sound and then I see four eyes, shiny and black. Two dogs are cowering in the bushes. One is the dirty golden dog I saw earlier, the other is a brown and white spotted hound dog of some sort. They look pitiful.

"You guys pissed on my grass and it burned up my yard?"

They thump their tails against the dry leaves.

For some reason I call them. These are the same dogs I tried to shoot an hour ago. I make clucking and kissing noises and speak sweetly until they crawl out of the bushes. Their tails remain tucked as they slink toward me. Both dogs are shaking and their hackles are standing straight up. They look like punk video dogs.

After scooting forward a couple of feet, they stop, refusing to come any closer.

"What's the matter?"

They don't answer. They just hunker down and whimper again. And then, as though asking to be excused, both dogs lower their heads and creep back through the bushes, then disappear into the woods.

Crop circles.

I've got crop circles in my yard. This is not a good thing when you are pregnant. All I want are a few placid days and tranquil nights, so I can bring my baby into the world peacefully.

Maybe Zoltan screwed up the yard fertilizer, or maybe a UFO landed in my yard while I was sitting on the floor at Daisy's. The aliens want my baby. Maybe teen-agers came over, burned up a patch of grass and hurt the stray dogs. Perhaps a freak solar blast fried my lawn and scared the dogs.

I try to stand up, but that doesn't work, so I roll over until I am in a crawling position. This baby must weight 30 or 40 pounds now. I'm gonna be one of those women in National Enquirer with the freaky giant baby.

With enormous effort and some big grunts I manage to get up.

Taking a few steps backwards, I realize the circles look like giant eyeballs. I'm being watched by my grass. I'm not scared, just annoyed. I'm too tired and to pregnant to be scared, anymore. Anything fucks with me and I'll kick it's ass. I have a baby in my body and true power. I back away a few more yards, surely I've missed something.

Grass, trees, house, bushes, car. There's something else. Bits of white stuff along the edges of the circles. I have to squat again, for a third time, in order to pick a piece up. It's egg shell. Not half a shell, but tiny pieces, somebody peeled a hard-boiled egg in my yard.

I hate hard-boiled eggs. In fact, since I got pregnant we haven't had an egg in the house. The very idea of a raw egg, that edible unborn chicken, makes me sick and the smell of hard-boiled eggs has turned my stomach since I was a teenager.

The unmistakable sound of a horse whinnying, cuts through the warm and weird afternoon silence. I've been sucked into an Arkansas episode of X Files.

Fred, stands next to my car. He is curious. He lifts his stupid but inquisitive eyes to the sky. I listen and hear the whinny again but this time I can identify something. It's the mare our neighbor, Danny, got a few weeks ago. He traded his 4 wheeler for a quarter horse with three white stockings.

I drop the egg shells. What could possibly cause marks like this in my grass and why are there egg shells?

There's something about hard-boiled eggs that I can't remember. The smell tweaks a memory but I don't want to dredge it up.

Walking slowly, slowly back to the house, I keep looking over my shoulder. Hard boiled eggs. I hate them. I really loathe the smell, but it is hanging on in my nasal passages.

Suddenly, an entirely new scent wafts into the forefront of my memories and rescues me from the eggs. It's nice. It's a perfume. An expensive green perfume that came in a heavy bottle shaped like a tear drop. Mom wore it for years. When we rode in a car or an elevator together that smell lifted me up and made me feel like I was on the very top of a tree looking down on the jungle world. I would close my eyes, weightless and surrounded by her beautiful, expensive smell and deep Broadway voice. Yendi, the name of the perfume was Yendi.

My mother is near, she must be. That's all this wonderful green smell makes me think of. Mom has filled the air around me. She's packed her bags and moved into my lungs, now she is my oxygen. Maybe there's more here, why should she stop with a smell and some alien inspired crop circles and egg shells. I look around, hoping to see something nice, hoping she'll speak sweetly to me or a white dove will flutter down from the heavens.

But there are just the burned circles. Big grassy eye balls, or maybe they are wheels and I should roll the fuck out of here.

Then the hard-boiled eggs come back to me, as though a water balloon has been thrown into my brain. Exploded and splashed, the memories soak me. Why did it take me so long to remember?

One month after Daddy and Daniel died, Mom tried to stop smoking. She was consumed by the notion that she would die too, and leave me alone in the world.

For weeks she peeled and ate hard-boiled eggs constantly. The peeling part gave her something to do with her hands. Hard-boiled eggs are compact and portable so she could take them with her. She kept an egg rolling around in her desk drawer at the office and in her bedside drawer. It's a wonder she didn't die of salmonella. My broken hearted mom peeled and ate eggs in the car, tossing egg shells out the window at stop lights; she ate them by the pool and while she pretended to watch television and cried because she missed her husband and son.

Hard-boiled eggs and bourbon kept her alive. They were the only things she could keep down.

The egg smell, which was everywhere, was revolting. Everytime she cracked a new one, I gagged.

I was so sad I couldn't speak, but the sound of her tap, tap tapping the egg on any hard surface then peeling the shell away, coupled with the nauseating smell almost drove me insane. I stopped speaking because words meant nothing compared to our pain.

I couldn't ask her to stop eating eggs. How could I take something else away from her when she'd already lost her husband and son, he life and her love. Her world had disintegrated, melted away so quickly and she didn't have time to say good-by.

At night, as I lay in my skinny, twin-sized bed with pink and yellow flowered sheets, I was overwhelmed by her grief and my own. I called out to Daddy in the darkness, begging him to come back and help me help her.

She loved Daniel so much, he was her child. Daniel had always been the one who could make Mom laugh. He could pick her up and spin her around in the kitchen when nobody else dared touching her.

For weeks, I thought her thoughts and writhed with her pain and tried not to breath through my nose so I wouldn't smell the eggs.

She had forced Daniel out of her body, raised him so well, bought him clothes and candy, watched his school plays and sent him to college, but she was never going to see him again, never going to touch his hair as he slept or hear his voice.

Never.

I thought her pain would kill me.

If I could never touch Mike and Felicity again, I would shatter like a pane of glass. No words would touch me.

Daniel was gone as though he'd never existed at all. Like a rain puddle that evaporates completely. And Daddy, the man she'd been with since third grade, was gone too. So he couldn't hold her in her sorrow or sit with her in silence, thinking of their beautiful, sleepy-eyed boy.

Her despair was so mighty, it swallowed us both.

Mom and Dad had grown up together, they had learned their multiplication tables together; they'd learned how to kiss and argue. But they never learned how to be apart. And when she needed him most, Michael Justice McDade The First wasn't there for her. For the first time in 40 years, he let her down.

After a month or two I was fairly certain my mother was dying too. And who could blame her? The eggs and bourbon made her smell like death. Her expression never changed. She looked exactly the same when she was swimming or cooking dinner, fixing a drink or peeling an egg.

If an egg meant something to her, I couldn't take it away. All I could do was sit and try to breath without smelling.

And now, as surely as I'm pregnant, my mother is in my yard. All this because she doesn't want to be buried in Hot Springs or because she doesn't want me to get married.. Well, I'm too pregnant to get jerked around right now, even by your precious ghost. My yard smells of beauty and motherhood and death and I can't take it.

I have a ghost and crop circles and a dog in heat. At least the first two took care of my dog problem temporarily. What am I supposed to do now?

Thank God the kids aren't home.

I start crying again but this time the tears are born of anger and frustration. I'm talking out loud, "This is supposed to be a beautiful special time for me, damn-it." My legs cramp and the braxton- hicks contractions make me wince. I gasp for breath. My chest hurts. I've been holding my breath unintentionally.

Leaning back, I breath hard and fast and stare at the sky. It's beautiful, the absolute color of turquoise. The trees around the yard make a swaying ring of green.

Why is she doing this now? I've told her I won't let Helen build anything at all, I'll keep her ashes out of our God-forsaken dirt and I won't marry Zolton. What do you want Mom. Give me a fucking clue, will you please.

I try to categorize my problems then realize, maybe I should focus on Zolton. It's his heart I need to watch out for. I was born into this crap but his only crime is loving me.

Eventually, the sky and trees and breathing make me feel a little better. Eventually my grass will grow back.

But I kind of like the idea of a monument for Mom. It's the first pure and relatively honest thought I've had in a while. "I, I, I, I, I, I want a monument for my mother. A great big one with her name etched in eternal granite. I want a monument that makes people wonder who she was. That's what I want," I whisper. I say those words out loud and that gives weight. For a moment, what I want is a spoken word and has significance. So I lean my head back and yell at the blindingly blue sky, "I want!"

How Shakespearean this is, in a puny sort of way. A moral dilemma has hatched. Calling all of this a moral dilemma is good, it gives me an easy handle on my decisions. Naming it stuffs the whole package of questions into a lunch box.

I will not be able to decide what to do about Zoltan or Mom standing around in front of the spooky lawn art. If I go do something, maybe get some work done, I'll be able to think. I can not stay here. This place has been taken over, so I will get back into my car and drive away. I'll drive away to deal with Hurlie's money and my friend Mimi, as though the world is progressing with an average spin. This is how the great women of my family have moved from one day to the next.

Driving into town, I focus very hard on the highway. I read every sign, gage each curve and consider each oncoming car. Driving is the only thought in my head until I am far from my home. Suddenly, as though poked through a time warp, I am parking a block from the exquisite SunBear Art Gallery.

Raymond SunBear is Mimi's fifth husband. They've been together twelve years, which is more time than she spent with the other four husbands combined.

Mimi and Raymond are rich. He literally makes a fortune buying art work on various reservations and selling it at an extravagant profit. They have three homes and more cars than I can keep track of. But Mimi's body is dying. She's still so beautiful in a rich, well preserved, way. But she's rotting from the inside. Everytime I see Mimi there's less and less of her. Ulcers are literally burning her up, they've started bubbling in her intestines and stomach. The pain leaves her balled up on the couch for hours. Her body, mind or spirit is rejecting life.

When Mimi's first four husbands got on her nerves, displeased or provoked her, Mimi divorced them, immediately. Her lawyer's number was #1 on the speed dial. She wasn't nice or loving or particularly kind. But she was Mimi and that has always had an effect on men. She did well in all the divorces and could have vacationed for the rest of her life. But Mimi fell in love with Ray, invested too much in this gallery and he's killing her.

Ray is a viper, conceited and handsome with his dark hair and beautiful teeth. He's charming and smart and dangerous. Mimi laughs sadly when she says, "Well, I got what I deserved. I fell in love with a man who's exactly like me."

Raymond Sunbear scares me. He's one of those men who can turn his good-looking charm on long enough to cover his venomous slow-burning anger.

He's a master of psychological warfare. I've seen him look at Mimi with such searing contempt and heartbreaking disregard, she just wilts. With his strong dark features and sparkling teeth, he flirts outrageously, with other beautiful women who come into the gallery. He doesn't care if Mimi is standing at his side.

Ray has had three affairs, that Mimi's knows of. One with Mimi's own sister.

What Ray really likes are threesomes, but he generally looks for that action in Little Rock and Memphis. He sometimes asks Mimi if she wants to join him, knowing she'll turn him down. He then knows his wife will spend the next 48 hours wondering who he's with and what they are doing.

I do not understand the power Ray SunBear holds over her.

Once, at a cocktail party, I told Mimi I thought Ray was a pathetic little puke.

She touched her wine glass too mine and smiled brilliantly. "I know honey, and I just love him so much."

I hate Raymond Sunbear. When he smiles at me, I'm afraid he's going to eat me up, then make a beautiful necklace with my bones.

If Mimi divorced Ray, I believe her sickness would vanish. He's put some sort of curse on her. It's his presence her body has turned against. But Mimi is afraid she'll end up trading her ulcers and burned up innards for a broken heart. And that is the one thing she is most afraid of.

Waddling down the street, to the gallery, I wonder, if I should talk to Mimi about my problems? Doesn't she have enough woe of her own? Are crop circles, haunting mothers and bitching grandma's what she needs right now?

Mimi meets me at the door. "Hey girlfriend." Her platinum blond hair is short today and she is tanning booth brown in a luscious green silk toga dress. The hem is slanted from the top of her right knee to the middle of her left calf.

Mimi wraps her arms around my torso as best she can and gives me a warm hug. Her bones feel tiny, like a sparrow. I could crush her.

"You look so brown, it's great." I hold my arm up, which is the color of a file folder.

She puts her arm next to mine. "I couldn't bear looking so pale next to Ray. Skinny and brown is always better than skinny and pasty."

"You're not skinny, you're svelte and you inspire me. Maybe I should go for the round and brown look."

Mimi takes my notebook and hooks her arm through mine. Being with her makes me feel Southern and European.

"You are not fat Liz. You're beautiful, beautiful and huge. You are a magnificent work in progress."

"God, I love talking to you."

Ray watches from behind his jewelry counter as Mimi leads me through the gallery. He smiles, flashing his magnificent teeth, but does not speak. Still holding my arm, Mimi takes me into their lush cinnamon colored Southwestern apartment.

"Great stuffing," I say, plopping into a love seat with brown and red and beige throw pillows. Everything in the room is perfect. The coasters, the woven throw rugs, the art, even the coffee mugs fit in. It's all coordinated with an air of casual expense. "Everything in here still smells new. How do you do that? I want to live in your rooms. They're so clean. Our couch is unraveling and I can't remember the last time I bought anything matching."

"That's because nobody lives here, Honey. You know that. Ray and I don't actually have a life. We exist. Sniff the air, you won't smell a single sign of life. This might as well be a furniture warehouse. You've got a husband that would die for you and those beautiful, beautiful children. Who gives a fuck what your couch looks like?" Her thin hand shakes just a little but she smiles with conviction.

Actually, I do smell something, mixed with the new fabric scent. I hesitate then say, "Z isn't my husband, you know."

"Yes, he is."

I shake my head baleful and stick my bottom lip out.

"Well whose fault is that? He's more of a husband than Raymond could be in a thousand life times. Have a ring, don't have a ring. Doesn't make any difference." The veins in her neck rise and fall. She's so thin, there's nothing much covering them. She seems exposed and vulnerable, as though her blood is right out in the open. Mimi should wear turtle necks.

I am struck by the word fault. It's a politically incorrect word these days. We are not supposed to place direct blame on anyone. But Mimi is right. The fact that Zoltan is not my husband is my fault.

The simplicity of her statement staggers me.

"Everyone thinks I have to get married before going into labor. I don't want to do it."

Mimi looks at me for a long time with stern kindness. She is appraising my situation and my face.

"I don't think I can give you any advice, honey. My husbands and marriages and loves have been so entirely different. None of my nuptials included two people who loved each other at the same time. Too bad, huh? You'd think after all my relationships and interdependences I'd be a fucking font of information." She stands. "Let me get you something to drink. You've got to keep your fluid intake up." She wobbles a little as she leaves the room and straightens her toga, making sure it doesn't hang up on her bloated little stomach or poky hip bones.

While Mimi is in the kitchen I look at the end table. It's covered with dark brown prescription bottles. She's been to a dozen doctors and tried countless medicines and diets but her body has turned against her. Nothing involved in her digestive track wants to work properly, so she is dying of something akin to malnutrition. Nobody can fix her, except Raymond.

Pretty little scented candles are burning on almost every tabletop. But they can not cover the smell of Mimi's death. She is surrounded by a gray haze. When did I start seeing those colors? I look at Mimi again, her air is gray, is see that as clearly as I see my own hand.

Sweet with familiarity, Mimi's smell makes me so sad. Mom smelled that way for a long time. It's not a bad smell, just wrong and full of regret.

Returning with a huge glass of cranberry juice, she says, "You can't leave till you drink it all."

"I'll spend the morning looking for bathrooms."

"It's a good way to make new friends. So, this is your last weekend working?"

I nod, not sure what to say. "It feels kind of strange. I hate letting go of things that have worked for me. You're the last person I'll be paying off, that should make you feel good." I pull an envelope with five hundred dollars out of my purse. Mimi always bets the over/under. This week she won on the over for the San Francisco game even though Hurlie set it at 56. I never thought so many points would be scored.

Mimi bets at least a thousand every week of football and basketball season. Last year, during the NBA play-offs she won more than 8,000 dollars from Hurlie. He was furious when he found out a woman was taking so much of his money.

Mimi grins at me mischievously, then suddenly shifts. "I've been stashing all the envelopes you've given me over the past four years. Never even opened one of them. And when I lost I paid you out of Ray's account. I told him I was buying CDs."

"No kidding, how much have you got now?"

The tip of her tongue appears as she mentally adds this 500 to her war chest. She looks so pleased with herself. "Forty nine thousand dollars."

"Oh my God. Have you got it in a safety deposit box?"

Mimi shakes her head. "He always goes to the bank with me. I keep it in pots and pans in the very back of the kitchen cabinets and in tampax and napkin boxes. It makes me feel good because I've got something he doesn't know about."

"That's beautiful, Mimi."

She nods, agreeing with me, then sucks in a sharp and painful breath.

"Are you ok?" I begin to move to her but she waves me away.

She laughs a little, though it's obvious she is in pain. Grimacing, she says "You know, I hate thinking about time and dates. I hate thinking how old I'm getting and how fast life is going. I'm nearly fifty. I never thought I'd be that old. My God, this year is almost over and it's been fucking miserable. I hate wasting a year being miserable. It's like throwing t-bones to the dogs. I wish I could just stand up and leave with you, leave his sorry handsome ass right now. We could go home and I'll take care of the kids while you finish being pregnant. I'll fix their lunches while you and Zoltan sleep late." She is hunched over a little, with her arm wrapped around her own waist. "Last night he went out with two waitresses who works across the street. They called me at 3 a.m. to see if I wanted to meet them somewhere for a drink. He just got home a couple of hours ago."

"Oh Honey, he's disgusting, Mimi. You have to leave," I reach for her hand. "Stop doing this to yourself. He's just a little piss ant who gets off on watching you suffer. Get your pots and pans and tampax boxes and credit cards and let's go. He's a fucking masochist who gets off on your pain."

"I know," she says and straightens up a little. But her face is still crumpled.

"Let's go then, right now. It'll be perfect. You can be my coach at the hospital. Zoltan gets too intense. Come on. I need somebody, especially during the day, and we'll have fun. I swear you won't think about Ray." I desperately want Mimi to come with me. I need her more than she needs me.

Mimi takes my hand but shakes her head softly. " Honey, I was just talking. This is my life, I can't move into yours."

"But you don't have to stay here, with him. You can change things right now. Make your life different. You must be thinking about it or you wouldn't be stashing cash. The rest of the year can be great. Come on with me, Mimi. Help me have this baby."

She hugs me. "I love him Liz, and I know that's a damn shame. Besides, I think he's starting to get tired of all the games."

"You're delusional, Mimi."

"I know. Now drink your juice."

A phone starts ringing. Mimi looks around, "It's you."

"Oh yeah, I forget." My purse rings and that seems so ridiculous. Zoltan got it for me a couple of months ago. "Hello."

"Hey. How you doing?" I smile just hearing Z's voice.

"I'm good, but it's been a Salvador Dali kind of day. I'm with Mimi. But you wouldn't believe what's going on at the house. Aliens."

Zolton's not really listening to me, he thinks I'm kidding about the aliens.

"Maybe it was aliens here at the restaurant too, but I doubt it. Somebody set the dumpster out back on fire. The police blocked off the street and we had two fire trucks out there for one dumpster fire. The flames were 30 feet high," he says and my palms get slippery with sweat as I tighten my grip on the phone.

"You had a fire?"

"The police are sending it to the crime lab. It smelled like somebody dumped a bucket of gasoline in to really get things going."

"I'm so sorry," I whisper.

"Why are you sorry, you didn't set the fire." Z. yells something to the dishwasher then comes back to the phone.

"I don't know what to do about her, Z."

He sounds annoyed. "Liz, this doesn't have anything to do with your mother. You know that." He's quiet then says, "It's Hurlie, be honest with yourself. I'm gonna find him when I get off and have a talk. He's no so big or bad that he can't be taken out. Don't go out there without me, Liz."

My heart hammers. "I'll take care of him, Let me just talk to him, Z. Please. You didn't say anything to the police did you?" If he gave the police Hurlie's name we are in for a new brand of trouble.

"What could I say? They won't find any proof and I can't tell them you've retired as a bookie and that's what's causing all this." There is a racket behind him and then Zolton says, "I'm not even finished tell you weird things honey. The reason I'm calling is because of Granny."

"She's ok?" I lean against the couch armrest for support. Mimi squeezes my hand and gives me a look.

"Yeah, I think so, but the Hot Springs Mountain Tower called. She's been up there all morning."

"E'va is up on the tower? Why?"

"I don't know. They said she was friendly enough. I know this isn't what you need. But can you go up there? Between the cops and the firemen and the customers I'm crushed with orders right now and it would take me 20 minutes to drive across town. They said she's being polite and seems to feel fine but they're worried. They think maybe she's praying."

"Praying? To God."

He laughs a little, "Most likely. Call me when you get there, ok and I'll come up if you want me to. That's all they told me." I can hear waitresses behind him, filling glasses, dumping dirty dishes into a dish pan and yelling out orders.

"Ok," we keep talking as I walk towards Mimi's door but I'm thinking about Hurlie. I don't know what to do. If I walk in accusing him, he'll puff up on me. If I even mention the fire, he'll know I'm scared and he's counting on my fear to keep me in the harness. I can't tell the police. I stop that thought before it goes any further. There are boundaries I mustn't cross. If I talk to the police I'll implicate myself, in years and years, of felonious activity. And then, we'll never be safe. Hurlie knows that...

Looking at Raymond Sunbear, I see more colors, red and black hues vibrate from his smooth skin. It's horrible. He grins like a skeleton, knowing Mimi told me about the pair of waitresses. 'Well fuck them all,' I say to myself, then I say to Z,. "I'll call you in a little while."

"Is everything ok?" Mimi wants to know what's going on.

"I think so, just more weirdness. If you'd come to my house to stay for a while all this would be a lot more fun. Weird is an adventure when you've got somebody to share it with. Please come with me."

She kisses me on the cheek as though she hasn't even been listening to my speech. She touches my arm with her cool finger. "Don't get overwrought. Find a word and keep it in mind so you don't get nervous. The baby's the important thing." If I had a coat on, I'm sure she would button it to protect me from the cold.

For a long moment, I study Mimi's face. It is a mask. She puts her hand on my stomach and I will the baby to kick for her. It works. He hits her hard with an elbow. My stomach bulges to one side. Mimi's face instantly lights up with a beautiful and instinctive joy. I hope she doesn't wait until it's too late to get away from Raymond.

"You've made a baby," she says, hugging me again and there is such warmth and love in her embrace I almost start to cry. For a moment this child in my body has overridden her pain.

I drive up Hot Springs Mountain too fast. Usually, I love the narrow and squiggley road that snakes through the forest, but today, the 24 turns and curves are in my way. Speeding up, hitting the breaks, then speeding up again. I must stop at a cross walk because there is a squirrel in the middle of the road. He stares at me defiantly, then hops slowly to the shoulder.

12:27 p.m. The Hot Springs Mountain Tower is a 216 foot concrete and steel overlook. Tourists enjoy paying $4.00 to ride the glass elevator to the top and look around at our beautiful town and surrounding mountains.

Why is E'va up here?

Entering the lobby of the Mountain Tower, it is obvious the staff has been waiting for me. A fat teen-age girl with painfully tight Levis walks over to me. The thick seams of the dark jeans are pulled tight along the sides of her huge thighs. How could she possibly sit down, how could her mother let her leave the house wearing those? How could her mother let that happen to her? She smiles at me like a nurse and asks, "Is she your grandmother?"

I nod.

"She's been up there a while, nearly two hours," she says as she walks me to the glass elevator. The girl holds the door open with her beefy forearm. Her fingernails are beautifully manicured and the color of a Christmas ornament. She has a ring on every finger and two on her fat thumb.

I look around before stepping in. Even the floor is glass. The elevator is shaped like a bullet. The ground races out from under my feet and I am suddenly high above the waving tree tops. My stomach rolls and the baby wriggles. Feels like a tango. God, I hope I don't throw up in a glass elevator. There are people down below, watching my ascension. That would be disgusting.

The girl says, "I talked to her for a little while. She told me about her grandson and showed me a picture with his name on the back and I saw one of his business cards from Georgio's in her wallet. That's how we knew where to call. She's so sweet. Where's she from?"

"Hungary."

"You want me to go with you?"

"No, that's ok. I'm fine."

"There are other people up top. My manager thought it might be good if we kept folks going up so she didn't think she was all alone. It seems like she really wants to talk to somebody."

I know exactly what this girl is trying to say. They kept people going up so E'va wouldn't find herself alone and jump. They are afraid she's up here to commit suicide, but E'va isn't a jumper. She's not a suicide. But they don't know that.

E'va is up here with a plan.

The moment the elevator stops, I see her. The wind is much stronger and strands of her hair have blown out of her silver bun. Her back is to me as she leans against the black railing, nodding her head, in absolute agreement with something, the wind or the swaying trees tops. Her colors, the blues and green, fade into the tree tops. I look toward the restaurant, thinking there might be some smoke left but the wind has washed everything away.

A family on the other side of the observation deck gets ready to leave.

"E'va?" I say softly.

She turns and smiles. "Hi," it's almost a whisper. Her accent carries the 'i'. She is holding her rosary.

"Servous, Hudge vudge?" I walk slowly toward her with one hand on my belly. When we are close, she takes my right hand and squeezes it. Her dark eyes are shining so brightly, like wet river stones. Sunlight dances in her beautiful silver hair.

"I'm ok. Kersinmin, yo." Good thank you.

"It's so pretty here." We both look out at the sweeping view. Sometimes I forget just how gorgeous my home is. My view becomes myopic, small things like buildings and streets, people and stop signs, fill my vision.

There are soft mountains rolling around on all sides of us, like green waves in the Atlantic. Each is covered by dense forests. To the west Lake Hamilton and Lake Ouachita shimmer, in the midst of all the trees, like a giant black mirror.

The city of Hot Springs looks tiny compared to the vast and gracious mountain range. Central Avenue, directly beneath us, is just a streak of civilization, a single thread in the middle of the carpet. This realization smoothes some of the rough edges in my mind. This world is much bigger than B. Wallace, Hurlie and my yard.

"I was praying." she says raising her Rosary.

I nod. "Do you feel ok?"

"I feel ok. I just want to ask God if you get married."

"Ohh, I see. Did he give you any clues?"

She chuckles and squeezes my hand. Her skin is warm and soft, there is life in her flesh. "No," she says. "But not married is no good, it's no good." She says something in Hungarian and crosses her self.

The wind blows suddenly and trees for miles and miles wave and sway. It feels as though we are on a ferris wheel. E'va makes a happy noise. "Are you ready to go home?" I ask.

"Ok. Maybe so," she says then pats her purse to make sure she doesn't leave it behind.

I take my cell phone out. E'va stops. "What is that?" Her curiosity is like a child's.

"It's a telephone."

She looks at me to see if I am joking, "No, that is telephone? It is in your purse?" She is incredulous.

I flip the phone open and she touches the bottoms. "Let's call Zoltan," I say.

"We talk to him now?" she asks. "This is an American phone."

I dial then I press the phone to her ear.

"Zoltan?" she says into the mouth piece then she looks at me.

When he comes to the phone they start speaking to one another rapidly in Hungarian. Smiling, she says, "Good bye, thank you for calling" and hands the phone to me.

Zolton is still on the line. "Did she tell you where we are?" I ask.

"On top of the tower," he says. "I love technology. I wish I was there with you."

"Everything is fine and we're heading home. She was just talking to God about our situation."

"Taking it to a higher power. Good for her. There wasn't a problem?"

"No problem except the elevator ride made me want to hurl."

"That's a nice thought. Call me when you get home?" His voice tickles my ear.

E'va has already called the elevator and is waiting for me. She's ready to go. Obviously she and God are finished with their conversation.

Maybe He's still here. Looking around, I speak softly to the wind. "I think I'm gonna need some help with Hurlie, maybe with Mom too. I'm not sure what your doing to me, but I need a little slack, please." Except for yesterday, I haven't prayed in so long, I haven't asked for anything, I haven't spoken to God in years.

The wind blows His response through my hair, but I do not understand.

E'va touches my arm and we step into the glass bullet. The elevator starts to drop. The tree tops and parking lot race toward our feet. Actually, I can't see my feet but I watch E'va's. She holds my arm and the side of the elevator for balance. "So pretty," she says. "Budapest like this. I think you would like it."

We are being swallowed by nature. There is a squirrel on a branch watching us as he holds an acorn. His bushy tail twitches but he remains. Without warning, the squirrel drops the nut, runs out on a branch so thin it is nearly invisible, then flies, legs spread, miniature gray head pointed, onto another tree. What faith that animal has, knowing those tiny branches will support him until he makes it to a thicker limb. Perhaps God has become that squirrel for a moment, enjoying the precision and near weightlessness of a squirrel's delicate but skillful body.

If I was God, I'd like being a squirrel for a little while.

E'va is not watching the squirrel; she's holding her rosary again and staring into space. "Did God tell you anything I should know, E'va?"

She shakes her head, refusing to disclose what the Creator of the Universe told her.

When we reach the ground floor she says, "You will see."

Walking through the Mt. Tower lobby which is filled with Hot Springs ash- trays, Bill Clinton playing cards and tiny replicas of Bath House Row, E'va smiles at the employees and shakes hands with the heavy teen-aged cashier. "She take me home now, this is my Grandson's wife. She will have my great great baby soon"

They all nod and smile and say good-by to E'va.

Driving down the mountain, E'va clutches the passenger door with her old hands. Blue veins bulge like twisting rivers, but she is smiling, liking the ride.

Chapter 13

Hurlie Vick lives at the base of Quapaw Mountain. His sleazy bars and strips clubs have allowed him to buy more than 500 acres of heavily wooded land. The first time I met Hurlie I felt as though I'd been pulled into a Faulkner novel. He's an easy man to describe, crude, with a fifth grade education, tiny eyes, a jagged temper and his intelligence is generally underestimated. Because he looks ignorant, has bad grammar, squinty eyes, and a pot belly, people assume he's stupid.

Hurlie uses their miscalculation to his advantage..

1:08 p.m. I pull into his trailer compound and honk. There are too many dogs, some are tied up, others are fenced-in, snarling and barking and lunging at my car. A huge rottweiler is tied to a run. A fat thread of drool hangs from one side of his mouth. He is not barking or jumping, but I know he is the dog I must keep an eye on. I can feel his growl in my bones. He wants to eat my baby.

His eyes remind me of Raymond Sunbear.

Maybe I'll never get out of the car.

Four trailers are arranged in a loose semicircle. Two are nice double-wides, one even has a cedar deck and hot tub. The other two are small and dingy, with tiny windows and skinny doors. Last time I was out here there were only three trailers. His neighborhood is expanding.

Ambush, Hurlie's 800 pound Grizzly Bear, is sleeping on a dog house in the middle of his chain link cage. He is draped, like a floppy bean bag animal, across the top of the little a-frame. His head is the size of my steering wheel. Ambush would be awe inspiring if he didn't smell so bad. Flies buzz around he coca-cola colored fur. All four of his paws touch the ground, though he's on the roof of the dog house. He looks at me with dull curiosity.

I honk the horn again and Hurlie limps onto the porch of the nicest double-wide trailer. Holding onto the cedar railing, he squints in my direction.

It takes a moment before I realize something is different about Hurlie today. I stare and wonder. He always looks the same, jeans, a plaid shirt and bright white socks. Finally, I realize there's only one sock. Shielding my eyes from the sun, I look again.

My god, Hurlie only has one foot. His pant leg looks normal, at least to the knee. But below the knee, his pant leg is limp. I've known this man for years, how could I have overlooked the fact that he's missing a leg? He's always hobbling but that doesn't mean anything. When we first met I asked him what was wrong, and he told me he got caught in a bear trap when he was 12. I thought he was kidding. I thought his leg was just messed up. But it's simply not there.

Hurlie only has one leg, one sock, one boot.

I thought I knew everything I needed to about my employer. Obviously, I've made mistake. Hurlie's first rule was 'the more you know about your players the less they can hurt you.' I should have applied that rule him.

"Shut the fuck up, Jesus Christ, I'm gonna shoot every god damn one of you," he yells and most of the dogs stop barking. Then he hollers to me, "Come on."

The dogs are still growling but I have to open my car door. Finally, I plant both feet on the ground, like an old woman. For an instant, I look at my shoes. Both of them. I need new laces. I hold the steering wheel with one hand and the seat with the other.

It's not too late, I can stay in the car, back up and let Z help me. I don't have to go inside. I don't have to take my baby in. But Hurlie isn't stupid. He's not going to hurt me, not here, not today. That's not how he operates. I have to go inside.

Hurlie scratches himself.

Almost everybody in town hates him and he doesn't care. Christians despise his strip joints. His clubs are ugly places with flashing lights, filthy carpet and underage girls humping brass poles when they should be doing their algebra homework. Bony, strung-out, thieving, men pay well-endowed women wearing g-strings to do table dances. These same women convince husbands to buy overpriced, watered-down drinks and $25 blow-jobs.

Politicians and law enforcement officials hate Hurlie because he buys and bribes his way out of everything. When a neighborhood garners enough power to force him out, he reopens in a new location a quarter-mile away.

Club, bar and restaurant owners hate him too, because he cheats and he makes money and he gives them all a bad reputation.

Now, Hurlie owns every strip joint in town, but two years ago there was some competition. Coincidentally, both rancid establishments burned down in less than four months. The Bad Cat Club, burned on Christmas Eve, then House of Red Hot Mamas went up in a tower of smoke and flame on Valentine's Day.

Nothing was ever proven, no warrants issued.

Despite the fact that he's one of the most hated men in Hot Springs, I've always considered him a friend, sort of.. He's been straight with me, paid me on time and he's never tried to screw me over. Now, I must look at him differently, like a pet that's gone bad. He's gross and a threat to my family. I will not let him have any part of my life. He's also missing a leg. I've seen him in several fights, but now I know he's a one legged man who can win an ass kicking contest.

As Hurlie waits for me on the porch, one of the dogs, a brown and white hound, climbs the front steps and leans heavily against his leg... his only leg. Leaning down, he scratches the dog's head then rubs his smooth ears.

"You too fat to get up these stairs?" I don't know if he's talking to me or the dog.

"I think I can make it."

"Well come on then. God damn, I got the air conditioner on."

I follow him into the living room. It's attractive with a high cathedral-like ceiling. The carpet and brown corduroy furniture are all new. Tightly shut blinds on all the windows keep any natural light out. An enormous, 52-inch television dominates the cool, dark room. ESPN.

There aren't any pictures or books, just a few neatly stacked magazines, including a racing form and Las Vegas tip sheet, T.V. Guide and a satellite manual, along with four remote control paddles and a blue steel 45. Three pairs of cowboy boots are lined up next to the front door and five brown felt hats hang over the couch.

Hurlie sits down in the Lazy-Boy, which is positioned squarely in front of the T.V., then hits the mute button. Now it's impossible for me not to notice his empty pant leg. It's just lying there. "I've been waitin' a long time for this."

"For what?" I ask, trying not to let him hear the fear in my voice.

He makes me wait before he says, "For you to come on out and visit me. Now, how much you got?" he says.

"Seventeen fifty." We're back to business.

"Supposed to have 2,500."

"I already took my cut."

He changes channels, "Not if you're quittin'. Nobody gets a cut on the last week."

"Bull shit. Stop grinding me Hurlie. I don't have time for it." I throw the envelope with his $1,750 on the table, beside his chair. He grunts again.

"God damn, I've always paid you good." He leans back in the recliner so he can pull a roll of cash from his front pocket. "You're making a bad mistake you know, trying to leave me. It ain't gonna work." He takes the $1,750 out of the envelope and adds it to the wad. the he changes his mind and peels five one hundred dollar bills off the top and tosses them on the table. "Keep that, for you're little family."

I'm not touching it.

Taking a deep breath, I say, "What do you mean exactly when you say 'it's not gonna work' Hurlie? I'm not trying to leave, I am leaving. I'm already gone."

He shakes his head then looks me in they eyes, his tiny cold eyes unmoving. "I'll tell you when you're gone, Good Girl. Things can happen that'll make you want to change your mind. Just remember once you go too far you can't take nothing back and things can't be undone. Some things are forever." He picks at his teeth with a tooth pick. "Sit down, why don't ya? You're about ready to blow. You know who the daddy is?" He almost smiles.

"Leave Zoltan out of it."

"What the fuck kind of name is that? You sure he's got a green card?"

"Fuck off," I say smiling, because this is the game we always play and I want to keep things normal.

"I don't see any wedding ring on your finger. Doesn't want to marry you till he knows the kid is his, huh?"

"You're so full of shit. I don't want to get married till after the baby is born." Why am I talking about his with him? How did I let the conversation swing in this direction?

"Why not, scared it'll be a little nigger kid?" He mocks me in a sickening voice.

The word nigger burns in my ear canal as though the tender membranes are being scorched with a wooden match. I touch the side of my face, thinking it might be warm. Outside, Hurlie's pack of dogs suddenly goes berserk, they bark and howl, we listen to the chain link shaking as they try to climb over their fences. Something must be out there.

Then I catch her scent. For just an instant B. Wallace is here, in the trailer. The room darkens, as though a cloud has passed over the sun. But there was never any sunlight in this trailer. Holy fuck, she's really, really close.

Standing up, I look at my enormous belly. It doesn't seem human. I hope the baby isn't listening. This isn't what either one of us should be focusing on right now. "I have to leave." That's when I see it, his artificial leg is leaning against the wall, next to his chair. "I really have to go."

"Sit back down. You look like you're about to puke. What's the matter, you never saw my leg?' I look at him for a long moment. His tiny eyes are too close together and his mouth is wrenched into a painful looking smile.

My hands are clammy and I wish I was back in my car with the a.c. blowing. "I don't know why I mess with you. Your not worth the grief or the money. And no, I've never seen you without your leg. The truth is, I didn't know you were missing one."

He's grinning now and reaches behind his chair to pick up the hard, flesh-colored, plastic leg. He waves it at me. "You want to touch it?" he laughs and my skin crawls.

"I've got to go."

"Oh come on. What's your hurry. We've been working together for nearly five years and now you gotta run off, like your scared of me. Shit." He puts the leg down. "Good Girl, you at least gotta' get me something to drink before you go. There's soda in the refrigerator. You can't leave a poor crippled man all alone after he gives you all that money."

"You didn't give me anything." I say walking into the kitchen. It's spotless, not even a dish in the sink, but there is another gun on the kitchen counter, a .32 snub nose along with some unopened mail.

Lifting my head, I try to find B. Wallace again. But she's not here anymore.

Hurlie yells, "I heard there was some excitement downtown today."

Holding the refrigerator door open, I freeze. He's watching me, waiting for my reaction, I can feel it in my spine.

"I didn't hear about anything." His refrigerator is nearly empty and pristine.

"You didn't hear about nothin' downtown today?" I hear him light a match. He wants to talk about the fires. "Get me one of them Mountain Dews."

I toss the soda to him so I will not inadvertently touch his hand. "Who lives next door? That other double wide wasn't out here last time I was here."

"The two shitty ones are for bands that come to town and need a place to crash and for the girls when their old man kicks 'em out and they don't have no place to sleep. The other one's for my mother. I had to put her somewhere. Her husband died."

"Your father?"

"Yeah."

"I'm sorry."

"He was a son of a bitch and sick as hell, hacking up all the time. And it was his god damn bear trap that got me my leg cut off. I ought go dig the bastard up and cut his dick off. Even things out, don't you think?"

"Your serious, about the bear trap?"

"What the fuck do you think?" He starts flipping channels again.

" What happened?" I can't help myself. I have to know.

"What happened? What do you think happened? The old man set bear traps in the woods where me and my brother hunted squirrels. I tripped, fell into his trap and it got my leg, just about tore it off."

"You were alone?"

"Yeah, 'cept for my dogs." He is staring at the giant, muted television set. Beach volley ball. But he's not focused. His eyes are there, but his thoughts are not. I can imagine Hurlie as a boy, lying in the woods, with his dogs and shredded leg. "The trap was chained to a tree so I couldn't drag it nowhere. I wasn't strong enough to open it and I knew wasn't anybody gonna look for me. Hell, the old man was probably glad as hell I was gone. Eleven years old and I damn near bled to death right there."

I wait but he is silent. Finally, I have to ask. "How did you get away?"

Hurlie looks at me for a long time, "drama's killing you huh? Why the fuck do you care anyway?"

"I'm just curious."

"Yeah, we get them like you down at the club, always curious, just want to watch, see how big the other guy's dick gets." He waits for my reaction but I just shrug. "I got stretched out far enough and used a stick to pull my gun over. Then I pried them jaws open a little and I got a rock wedged in-between so I could pull out what was left of my leg."

"You were just a baby."

"I wasn't a god damn baby."

"I'm so sorry."

"Not half as sorry as me. Hell." He pauses but does not look at me. "So I crawled on out of the woods to a gate for a cow pasture. My dogs they stayed right with me sniffing and whining and wanting to lick me. Took me a while. But I could see this farmer off a ways, bush hogging. He couldn't hear me and I was getting pretty shaky cause I was fucking bleeding everywhere. So I just wrapped my coat around my leg and layed down there in the grass and waited till he got done. Finally, he noticed the dogs just sitting there and come over to see what they were sniffing at. Probably thought I was a dead calf. I was passed out and when I woke up that old fuck was standing over me, chewin' and makin' face, like I smelled bad. He sorta picked me up. I was surprised he could do it, and got me on his tractor and rode me all the way to town. I was holding my leg and screaming cause it was a rough ride and hurt like hell."

I can hardly listen. The picture is too clear. My stomach feels so hard and the baby is so still. I wish he'd kick or roll so I could think about something other than Hurlie's leg.

"I knew, even when I was trying to get out of the woods that they was gonna have to cut my leg off. I didn't care, I just wanted it to stop hurtin'. You know in them movies when those fucks say 'do anything Doc, just don't cut it off. I don't want to lose my leg,' that's such bull shit. When pain is eatin' you up like a donut, you'd let them do anything to make it stop. Cut the fucker off, I don't care."

He is done and we are both silent.

Grunting, he leans back in his recliner.

"How'd you do it," my voice is gravely.

"Do what?"

"How'd you make yourself do it? Weren't you scared?"

"Hell yeah, I was scared but it wasn't like I had much god damn choice. I could lie there and die with my dick in my hand, or I could drag my ass out. What are you, stupid? You think I was gonna lie there and whine till I died? What kind of dumb ass pussy do you think I am? I was scared but scared is how you lose your god damn life, girl. Scared is how you lose everything." He sits up straight in his recliner and looks at me. "That's your problem."

"My problem?"

"Yeah, your fucking problem. You got more problems than a room full of whores."

"Oh, you're going to tell me what my problems are now," I say, leaning away from him, looking around the room so I don't have to see his face, which has turned to asphalt.

I need to go.

But Hurlie keeps talking, like an alarm that won't stop ringing until it's completely unwound. He's almost yelling at me. "You're always thinking about your choices, like your shoppin'. Well, sometimes you don't get a choice. Nobody ever said that to you did they?" These words sound like a challenge and a threat. "I didn't have much of a choice did I? You god damn debutantes think too much, now your sitting there thinking about me being scared forty years ago. What the fuck is wrong with you? You'd get so busy thinking, you wouldn't get your sweet little ass up out of the woods. And you think your gonna quit working for me just cause you're having another kid. That's so stupid it makes me want to puke, like this business is gonna get your little brat dirty. You're too good for it now, is that it? Working for me wasn't too good for you four years ago when you were dog dick broke. Was it?" He's staring at me and I'm trying not to cry or scream at him. "Look at you, hanging around waiting...that's what your doing, ain't it? You're waiting. Well you won't have to wait for very fucking long cause I'll make something happen. Something you won't forget, that's for God damn sure. No bitch walks out on me, not in this lifetime. Not till I say it's time for you to go."

I've got the doorknob in my hand but can't move. "Hurlie, I'm leaving. I'm sorry you're mad, but you don't know jack shit about me and I'm done."

"You haven't seen mad, girl. When I get mad, your pretty little world will be over. You hear me? And don't ever think I don't know about you. I know plenty, and I know you're not really walking away from me." He grins and my heart pounds. His mouth is a cavern, endless and black. I try to turn the doorknob but nothing happens. "Fucking broads all the time thinking they can walk away. "He laughs a little and I realize he's relaxing into his chair.

The knob finally turns and I say, "You don't take rejection well, huh?" Then I turn away and know it is a mistake before I finish the sentence.

He snorts and looks at me. I want to cover myself when he looks at my stomach, at my baby. All he says, so softly I can barely hear him, is, "Honey, I don't take rejection."

His mind has turned a corner and I'm in trouble.

"Hey," he hollers at me so suddenly I jump, "You want to hear the story how the dentist pulled three of my rotten teeth out?"

I nearly fall out the door. Heat and noise slap me. All the dogs jump suddenly, then their growling bleeds into a chorus. A vicious echo of barks and growls hits me again and sucks up my last breath. Every step, makes it all worse, my movement fuels their anger and rage. Maybe I should go back inside, but his laughter keeps me from touching the doorknob. The chain link fence shakes with their fury.

If I run they'll be on me, so I try to walk quickly, without showing my fear. Please God don't let them rip me open and kill my baby. Please don't let them eat my child. The dogs stand up on their hind legs and the fence bows toward me. Their teeth glisten in the sunlight. Both the rottweilers lunge against the chain link and a foamy spray of saliva falls on my arm.

Something moves in the bushes on the other side of the fence. It's moving towards me. God, what if one of the dogs is loose and moving around to get a better shot at me. Then, the bushes stop shaking but I can still see it, something, watching me struggle.

Frantically, I get in to the car, lock the doors and back straight out the drive way and onto the dirt road. A cloud of dust swells around the car.

How did this happen? When did my work with Hurlie veer into the throat of Hell? How is it I didn't see the danger? What's wrong with me?

My first instinct is to drive to the restaurant and tell Zolton everything. But I can't do that. If Z knows what Hurlie is doing and saying he'll track him down and kill him. He'll go too far and then I'll lose him forever.

The idea of not telling Z makes me feel so empty and shaky. For more than seven years I've told him every detail my life. We've never built separate worlds. There's always been us and the rest of the world.

I will not tell Z. Crying and shaking and so cold, I try to think what to do. I need somebody's help.

Though I'm sealed inside the car, I can still hear the dogs.

Why are they barking? I roll down my window an inch. The sound of Hurlie yelling at them filters through the trees. The barking sounds even more insane and then I hear a thundering snarl and roar.

It can only be the bear.

Chapter 14

As I drive to the YMCA to pick up Mike and Felicity, the sound of Hurlie's laughter and the snarling dogs washes through my head in sickening waves. Then something happens. There is an inexplicable, but absolute, lightening of my thoughts. A dark room is filled with light and some evil presence leaves me. I blow my nose, close my eyes and know everything will be alright. My family is safe.

I know everything is ok because I'm suddenly hungry. Hunger hijacks my body and I have no way of fighting it off. Getting something to eat is just about the only thought in my head. I run a stop sign and yellow light, I don't slow down and let a pedestrian cross. I have to eat.

My hands shake a little on the steering wheel. This sudden and profound need for food is primal. I will find food because the baby in my body must have it. Meat. I need some meat.

Fortunately, I live in America so I know there's hamburger close by.

At the corner of Grand and Central Avenue I consider my options. Burger King, Taco Bell or Wendy's.

There's only one car in front of me in the Burger King drive-thru. Good thing or I would have to beat the crap out of the drivers, tell them to get the hell out of my way, then move ahead in line.

The large menu sign board welcomes me and asks for my order.

"One Whopper please but I don't want any lettuce, tomato, pickle or onion on it and a big glass of water."

The sign recites my order with a questioning tone.

A nice girl with a pretty smile takes my money then puts my bag of food on her window ledge. Why isn't she handing it to me? I can smell it. My mouth waters. Still she doesn't not move, she's talking to another girl over her shoulder and waiting for someone to hand her a glass of water. They have a problem, they are out of straws.

I don't give a flying fuck about the straw. I need the food. My heart is thumping oddly, maybe I'm having a heart attack, but I force a smile.

"That's ok. I don't need a straw. I'll drink out of the cup."

"Really?" she says and picks up my bag of food. Then slowly, as though her batteries are running down, she extends her thin arm towards my car. I will be calm. I will not lunge through the window and snatch the bag away from her. I will not snarl or growl, though it is rising in my throat. The smell of the burger fills my car.

Finally, I have the bag and the paper cup of water. I accelerate too quickly then park in the Burger King parking lot. My stomach growls furiously. There is thunder in my belly.

I don't even bother putting the car into park. Instead, I keep my foot on the brake and dig into the white paper bag, which rips as I pull the hamburger out. Like a starving cat, I claw at the wrapping, then jam the burger into my mouth for the first bite.

I swallow too quickly. I have to slow down or I'll choke to death in the Burger King parking lot with a mouth full of Whopper.

Two more quick bites. The bread is so soft, the mustard and ketchup juices fill my mouth, wash over my tongue and calm my shaking hands.

I'm ok. I just needed some meat. Some protein. Now, I can actually put the hamburger down, take the plastic lid off the cup of water and drink. This body is mine, again. Hunger has released its grip.

Loneliness must be the cousin of starvation.

"How you doing down there, kiddo?" I ask my rotund belly. "Any of this burger getting to you?"

I have eaten the heart out of my hamburger and created a crescent moon shape. The next bite has too much bread and not enough meat.

The baby is still. Probably in shock and feeling bombarded.

Looking at the burger remnant on the crumpled paper square, I hear WaWa's voice. Her accent was so slow and southern and her flawless enunciation and grammar allowed many people to mistake her for English Aristocracy. God, what would she think if she knew I'd just run away from an insane, one-legged bookie. Nothing like this could happen in her world.

WaWa used to love going to Wendy's for a burger with nothing but mayonnaise. We would walk into the restaurant so slowly, because she was very old, and everyone would turn too look at the elegant old lady holding my arm. She would nod and smile softly, greeting her subjects, as we passed each table. We always sat next to the window so we could see West Mountain. After each bite, she put her hamburger down and delicately wiped her thin lips with the corner of the paper napkin. It took her nearly half an hour to finish. I would sit, poking my ice cubes with my straw and watching her chew.

One day, between bites, WaWa said to me, "Darling, you must always remember, it's unbecoming to eat anything in public you can not hold in one hand."

The man at the table behind her started laughing so hard I was certain he would choke.

Chapter 15

2:13 p.m. Felicity and Mike are still swimming in the 82 degree YMCA pool. The smell of chlorine assails me. Their eyes will be purple. My children look like lithe little seals, slipping through the water without friction or fear. They surface close to the edge. Water runs off their faces and they smile at me.

They smile at me.

This is a miracle. Seeing me makes them happy. How miraculous that I make these two beautiful water children happy. I do not need to do more. I'm not worried about B. Wallace or Hurlie as long as I can see my children.

I keep telling myself, 'Every thing is ok'.

Chapter 16

When we get home the baby begins to roll, performing an aquatic dance of her own. She is already in our lives.

Felicity gets out of the car then lies down on the hood. She has always loved the warmth of a car engine.

Mike stands by the headlight and waits for me.

I call to them, "Thing One and Thing Two, would you mind getting your stuff out of the back seat so we don't have mildewed swimsuits."

I almost forget about my yard problems. The crop circles are still here. Fred is standing in the middle of one, eating a piece of cardboard.

Felicity squeals and struggles to sit up. "Mom, look at the yard. What happened?"

"Oh cool. What are they?" Mike is already running.

He doesn't hear my broken voice when I say, "I really don't know."

"What are they Mom?" Mike yells again. Then, moves to the center of one circle. He stands with his arms stretched out and his head tilted back.

I want to yell at them. 'Stay away from my Mother's creepy message. I want them to come into the house, with me, but it's too late. Mike is now on his knees examining the dead grass and Felicity is lying down in the middle of one of the circles, waving her arms and legs as though making a snow angel.

Mike and Felicity do not see these things as a threat. Maybe I'm missing something. Still, I'm annoyed that B. Wallace wants to involve my children in this. If she's angry, she should deal with me.

How can children resist yard art?

"You don't know what these are, Mom?" Mike yells. He know's I'm holding out on him.

Slowly, I scuffle to the front door. Gravity pulls, I am defeated. "Please come in the house?"

"Why?" Felicity yells. She sits up in the middle of the circle.

"Just because I want you inside. It's my prerogative as a parent."

I sit down on the ugly orange couch and wait for them to appear. Exhaustion weighs down my legs. They will come to me. Surely the crop circles don't have any power over them.

3 p.m. I've got six hours to get through before Zoltan comes home and seven hours before bedtime. How have I allowed my life to become so onerous and frightening? If there's a puzzle out there in my yard, if she's sending a mystical message, I don't have the time or strength to unravel it.

Bear is scratching in the bathroom. She needs to go out. The crop circles have taken care of the horny dogs. At least that's a good thing.

Mike and Felicity come inside with their back packs. 'Those rings are so cool," Mike grins. "Has Zoltan seen them?"

I shake my head.

"Maybe it was some kind of worm."

"Maybe," I try to smile but I feel so wrong about everything. How is it I've screwed everything up?.

"Put your stuff away then take Bear for a walk, ok?"

"A walk?" Felicity asks. "What for? Just let her out."

"We can't do that."

"Why not?" Felicity has a right to wonder. We've never had Bear on a leash, but I'm not up to explaining this situation. Bear's in heat, how do I explain this? Truthfully, simply, honestly.

I can't do it right now.

Mike suddenly steps in, seeming much bigger and older, accepting the role of adult. When he looks at me, I see the eyes of a young man. He knows exactly why Bear has to be on a leash and he knows this is not the time to tell Felicity.

"I'll take her," he says. "We'll walk her around the circles, see what she thinks they are."

As they go out the door I hear Mike whisper, "She just needs some down time, she'll be ok."

They are worried about me.

Standing up, I watch them through the living room window. Bear tries to sniff every blade of grass in the yard. She's been locked in the bathroom and things have been going on in her territory.

Felicity runs around as though the rings are race car tracks. Fred follows. He stops every few feet sniffs, bites a little grass, then catches up.

I force myself to go into the bathroom to pick up after Bear. Things are pretty dry but she's destroyed the bottom five inches of the bathroom door with her scratching. She's also shredded an entire roll of toilet paper.

Accidentally, I see my own reflection in the mirror. I didn't' want to see myself. My eyes look huge and desperate. Surely that's not how I look, exhausted and pleading. I'm looking at myself in third person. There is yellow and gray inside the blue of my eyes and new lines between my eyebrows. I don't know if I can give this person what she's asking for.

I put on one of Felicity's fat stretchy headbands so my hair is pulled straight back from my forehead. .

Leaning close to the mirror, I study my face some more. My widow's peak is gone. How can that be? Where did it go? The upside down V on my forehead is gone. When I was a little girl, my grandmother, Marva, loved my widow's peak. She always told me it was a sign of great beauty. Sometimes, she would even push my hair back with her long fingernails and show it to her friends.

Now it's gone. My sign of great beauty has vanished. This is disheartening. I'm losing everything, my hip bones, my ability to make a decision and my widow's peak.

The front door slams. Bear's toe nails click on the kitchen tile. She laps at her water, pushes her empty food bowl around a little, then trots, like a light hearted pony, into the bathroom to look at me with her bright black eyes and perky, fury ears.

She prances sideways until I pick her up and carry her into the kitchen. Her long black hair is silky and warm from the sunshine.

Mike and Felicity are arguing over the last can of orange soda. I stroke Felicity's hair on impulse. It feels just like Bear's, only thicker.

Mike starts to rub my shoulders but I move away from him. He says, "There are messages on the answering machine. You want me to listen?"

"No, I'll do it." It makes me nervous. What if it's Helen Houston or maybe even Mom with a cryptic message. If I push the button, I'll have to listen and acknowledge. Maybe it's Hurlie laughing on the machine and then that particular thought vaporizes, like fog. He's not my concern anymore. That part of my life has been eliminated.

I punch the red blinking light.

It's Helen. Her wealthy and spirited voice fills the house. "Liz Dear. Oh, what was it, I know, a courier will bring you the drawings tomorrow morning. We'll have lunch together Monday and you can tell me what you think. Give my love to the children."

She hangs up and Felicity says, "Who was that? She sounded nice."

I'm trying to listen to E'va's message and don't answer Felicity. "Hello, this is the grandmother. We'll go to church tomorrow? Please in the morning you call me. I want to go to the church. This is the grandmother, Nagymumma. Good-by."

I get a Dr. Pepper out of the refrigerator, crack it open, eat a hand full of Bacos, waddle to the couch and fall into the cushions. The baby pushes hard on my right side. Maybe I'm having a monkey. Lifting my shirt, I can see his foot stretching my skin. I touch his heel, the ball of his foot and even a couple of toes. He's really getting crowded in there.

"It's time for you to come on out, huh baby?" I whisper. "I don't know. Everything is kind of a mess." I stroke his heel again and he does not pull back. "Have I told you about clothes? Once you come out you won't be naked and floating in that pool. We're gonna wrap you in clothes. Dry you off and cover you up. It seems to me that floating naked would be a lot more comfortable but you've got to come out. You're wrecking my body. I've got a fat ass and big hips for the first time in my life."

When I close my eyes, sleep tries to pull me away. "I love you so much. You're my baby and I'll keep you close."

He stops pushing, but I can still feel his perfect little foot. The house is quiet. I try not to breath too loudly because it will break the calm. Nothing but calm. My thoughts drift.

When a woman is her most unattractive, that's when a man should tell her she is beautiful. That's when she needs to hear it, not when she's all dolled up and looking hot. If a man tells a woman she is gorgeous when she thinks she is ugly, he can change her. He can make her beautiful with his love. Most men don't know that. I must try to remember to tell Zolton this later.

The world falls away as I dive into the sparkling darkness of sleep. It swallows my brain and fears, like a pitted olive. Some soon-to-be-mothers have lots of bad dreams, they see baby's with cricket heads or dream their house falls into giant sink hole. Not me. I am a fearless sleeper and dreamer.

Hours pass. I open my eyes then will myself to go back to sleep. While I am gone, making love to the darkness, wallowing in the nothingness, I am a bad mother and wife, still, nothing touches me and I feel secure. Why should I ever leave this place?

But there are noises. I think my children are trying to make a peanut butter and jelly sandwich. Somebody drops the jar of strawberry jelly on the tile, kitchen floor. They whisper as they try to clean up the gooey mess. With my eyes closed I am saddened because I know they are afraid of me, afraid of what I will say if I see the mess they have made.

So, I will myself to go back to sleep on the couch. I will not acknowledge the exploding jar of jelly.

When my eyes finally open, I really can't see anything outside the living room window, just the reflection of the dining room. It's dark out. I'm lying down on the couch with a blanket pulled up to my chin. My nose is completely stopped-up, but I am warm.

I listen very hard until I hear the radio in Mike's room. Where's Felicity? I listen again until I hear the T.V. in our bedroom. She's watching "I Love Lucy." Lucy and Fred and Ethel are talking. It's the episode where Lucy takes Little Ricky to the club in a stroller then dresses up like an Indian maiden.

7:12 p.m. I squint at the clock. Where did the night go? How long have I been asleep, three or four hours?

Reluctantly, I sit up. My mouth is dry because I was sleeping with it open. Pulling the blanket around my shoulders like an Indian shawl, I stand up and walk heavily into the bedroom.

"Hi there."

"Hi mama." Felicity bubbles. Lucy bangs on her tom-tom and does a little dance. Felicity says, "You were sleepy. Did you have a good nap?" she smiles at me. What beautiful eyes my daughter has. I stand in front of her and push her hair out of her face.

"I had good nap."

"We covered you up and checked on you. You drooled on the pillow a little."

All I can do is smile and sit down on the edge of the bed to watch Lucy and Ethel. Hopefully, I'll get some blood flow in my brain soon.

Felicity is on her knees next to me.

She jumps up and down a little, rocking the bed. I fight the urge to tell her to stop.

"So, you ready for dinner?" I ask as Felicity begins to bounce on her toes.

"Z left a message. He said he'd try to meet us at Ed's at 8:00."

"Really, that's perfect." I say, but I'm wondering how come he's getting off early on a Saturday night.

"We did our homework while you were asleep," she says proudly.

Mike appears in the bedroom doorway. "Hey, you woke up." He disappears before his words melt from the air. Felicity and I watch as he puts the milking stool under the silver chin-up bar. Stepping up, he strips off his shirt so we can admire his skinny arms and bony chest.

"Oooo, look at those rippling muscles," I say to Felicity.

He grins and Felicity falls back into the bed. "He'll never do it," she says, swirling her hair around one finger. Then she stops swirling and studies it for split-ends. Felicity is looking a lot like a teen-ager. Did that happen while I was asleep? Without even looking at Mike, she says, "I'll be able to do a chin-up before him."

Mike spits on his palms, rubs them together and grins sadistically at his sister.

"Hope that wasn't a hocker," she says.

I flick her on the back of the head. "I believe he will do a chin-up very soon."

Felicity rubs her head. "You always believe we'll do things. Mom's believe everything. What's that word you always use when I believe things that probably aren't going to happen? "

"Faith, it's called having faith," I say.

"No, that's not it," Felicity says. "It starts with 'g' and sounds like a fish eating something,"

Mike cracks his knuckles then stretches his back and neck. "Gullible," he states

"Yeah," Felicity looks at me now, "That's the word. Mom's are gullible."

"Moms have faith," I correct her. "I have endless faith in you. I have absolute faith, because I know you are magical. You are my gifts to the Universe and you're God's gifts to me." I have to swallow hard because I've almost made myself cry.

Felicity goes back to watching Mike, "Gullible, faith, so what's the difference? Mike still can't do a chin-up."

Mike takes hold of the bar and grunts like a 300 pound truck driver. His body starts to rise, a little, a little, he's moving up, up. It's so slow, I want to help him, push him over the bar. He's only got another two inches to go, he's past the hard part, but his arms give out and he drops back to the stool.

"I think you need to eat more protein. You need to eat animals, boy...hamburgers and steaks and raw eggs."

"Yeah, that's the ticket," he says out of the corner of his mouth, doing an imitation I don't recognize. But it sounds funny and I laugh.

"Well," I lay down on the bed. My belly obscures my view of Mike, but I can still turn my head and see Felicity. I could easily go back to sleep. "I think they serve protein at Ed's, and if we're supposed to be there at 8:00, we better get rollin'"

Felicity jumps off the bed, throws a pillow at Mike, who cheers victoriously. They love eating out.

"Chicken city," Felicity yells. "Mike, where did I leave my shoes? I could eat the ass end out of an alligator."

I sit up and almost yell, "Felicity, what did you just say."

She looks at me, stunned.

"Do you know what you just said?"

She nods her head yes. "I'm sorry, it just came out."

"Where did you hear that?" I demand.

"I don't know, I promise, Mom. I just said it. Can we still go out to eat?" She's about to cry.

I give her an evil look. "Yeah, we can still go out but I'm gonna think of a good punishment, something that will get your attention, Felicity. This has got to stop. You can't go around talking like that. You're 7 years old and sound like 40-year-old trailer trash. That's absolutely unacceptable. I love you too much to let you run around with a gutter mouth in 2nd grade. It may be cool in front of you friends but if any of your friends parents hear you talking that way they'll never invite you over again. I know I wouldn't. You understand that, right?"

She nods again, and steps into my arms. How did this happen? "You are grounded from the phone and from going to visit friends for two weeks and you have to clean the bathrooms, even the toilets, every day this week. That's your punishment. Now go find your shoes."

"Mooom," she bleats, but I just shake my head.

Walking past Mike, I pat his bare belly. Will mine ever be anything like that again? I look down at my huge bulging body. I doubt it. "Put your shirt back on and find your shoes, too."

By the time I emerge from the bedroom, Mike and Felicity are sitting at the dining room table looking a little smarmy. Their hands are resting on the embroidered red, white and green Hungarian table cloth Nagymummy made for us. Everybody is dressed, and ready to go, except for the giant glob of toothpaste on Mike's shirt and the fact that Felicity needs to brush her hair.

"Ohh, you look so prim. I didn't recognize you." They must be really hungry.

"Here's your purse," Felicity says and Mike jumps to the door.

"You guys are sort of creeping me out. Why are you acting like this?"

"Pods," Mike says, slamming the door shut. Using his T.V. announcer voice he says, "Pods have taken the real Szabo children, Mike and Felicity. We are the scary and polite children they left behind. But it's only for a limited time. This offer will expire, soon, very, very soon."

"Yeah, and we'll have a food fight in the middle of dinner," Felicity laughs, and throws herself into the back seat.

I do not allow myself to look at the yard. What can I do about it anyway? I don't want to see the lawn circles again. Maybe they will go away, all by themselves if I ignore them. Maybe they are gone now.

I have to look.

Moonlight lets me see the pressed dead grass shining in the dark fluffy yard. Wind stirs through the pines, a pine cone falls on my windshield and I jump.

Maybe if I tell Helen no, B. Wallace will be appeased and the rings will go away.

What am I going to tell Zoltan?

I don't have to say anything.

My blood pressure is rising. My face warms and my eardrums thump softly. I take several deep breaths and think about the evening air. It is soft, caught between cool and warm. Leaves shimmy against the ebony sky. Sometimes it seems the top of my head is missing and my brain gets mixed up with the atmosphere.

I wedge myself behind the steering wheel, hoping my brain is coming along with me.

Felicity is looking at me in the rearview mirror. Her brilliant blue eyes and those dark lashes. I can see thousands of thoughts flashing through her mind as she stares. Waving my hand at her I realize she's not really looking at me. Her thoughts have taken her. Expressions change her beautiful, unmarred face, over and over again. What is she thinking? What distant voice is she listening to?

Suddenly she looks up and gives me a haunted smile. "Something weird happened tonight."

"You're the weirdness," Mike says with a grin.

But Felicity doesn't hear him, she's looking at me. "What sort of thing?" I ask.

She shrugs, "I don't know, just something weird."

"You think I'll go into labor?"

"No, that's not it." She looks out the window again. Blinding headlights from oncoming cars slide across her face, making my child look like a model on a runway.

For ten years Mike and Felicity and I have been one entity, with several branches, traveling in mass. An octopus of family love. When we fell in love with Z, he became part of us. Now the baby is here, our entity will reorganize and we will rarely be able to have dinner at Ed's alone again, just the three of us. Instead there will be four and sometimes five. New tentacles.

Driving, we tumble back into our unusual silence.

The kids stare out the windows, watching the dark rural world slide past. Mike checks on me with a sideways glance. I think he's going to ask me a question. He studies the side of my face as we pass the junk yard and Daisy's. But there is only a wondering silence.

I turn into Ed's parking lot. It's a slow night. "Z's not here yet." I state.

"Why should he be? He's working, Mom." Mike opens his door.

"I know, but Felicity said he left a message that he was gonna meet us."

Mike looks at Felicity. "That wasn't Z. That was some old lady."

"What old lady?" I ask them both.

Felicity crosses her skinny arms. 'I didn't know, it sounded kind of like Z, to me."

"Forget Z," I interrupt. What old lady are you talking about"

Felicity's eyes glisten with tears. "You know, Mom. All she said this time was, 'For heaven's sake, it's all going to be fine, Liz. Let's meet at Ed's around 8, and then she hung up. She had a deep voice, like a man's almost and she coughed a little. I'm sorry I told you it was Z mom, I thought it was, sort of."

I leave the keys in the car. "Let's go inside. It's ok Felicity. Don't cry. It was probably Helen." I stroke her hair.

"You and Z should get married, Mom." Mike drops this statement like a cinder block of judgment.

I can not answer for a moment because I'm afraid I'll be mean. "Mike, don't push me please. You've got no idea what I've been though and having you toss off these little self righteous nuggets is just too much."

"Well, there's not much time and you're just thinking about it from your point of view. That's what you always tell me, I should try not to do." Mike The Agent, negotiating a better deal, negotiating for the future for himself and Felicity.

"This is bigger than you realize, Mike."

"Then there must be something you're not telling us, cause nothing you've said about wanting to wait seems like that big a deal. We're not little kids, Mom and this is our life too. So, just do it."

Just do it, like a Nike commercial. "Ok, you've got big reasons for me getting married, let's hear them." My voice is even, I will be rational.

"Ok. We love Z, he's our Dad, you love him, he should be your husband."

I look at Mike, I need to read his face but I'm a second too late. He's already looking at me, taking inventory.

"I'll consider your suggestion."

He lets me hold his hand walking into the restaurant which isn't too busy, there are only three other tables and a large party of women in church clothes, sitting in the corner.

Once again, hunger mugs me, despite the fact that I'm edgy and sort of spooked. I'm starving. Ed's smells just right, like a grandmother's kitchen. The air is heavy with flour and chicken and fresh, over-cooked green beans with onion and bacon.

There are family pictures hanging on the walls, somebody's father with a deer, a grandmother holding a baby on a porch, a young boy with a crew cut and flannel shirt sitting on a stump, surrounded by a pack of hunting dogs.

Mike and Felicity immediately find a booth and slide in on opposite sides.

"Come on Mom," Felicity pats the vinyl bench seat. "You can sit next to me." But I remain standing and smiling until they figure out the problem. I don't fit into Ed's booths anymore.

Groaning and laughing at my size, they slide back out and we sit down at a table under an oil painting of a barn, some black and white cows and a pond with ducks. Without being too obvious, I look around again, but there's nobody here I recognize.

There are two waitresses standing over the ice tea pitchers, talking and laughing. Sue and Jamie. Both women have their hair pulled back in a ponytail. Sue is almost blond and Jamie's hair is a shiny shade of dirt brown.

Every once in a while Jamie waves at her husband, Oswald, who is sitting alone in a booth drinking iced tea. They've been married 23 years. Oswald, drives a gravel truck and is wearing overalls and a t-shirt. Oswald is a nice, quiet guy. He's built like a tanker and still follows Jamie around like a high school boy. Every night he picks her up from work and he always signs his pay check over to her on Friday afternoon so she can put some in the bank and go shopping for groceries. He automatically takes any large bag or package she has to carry. Jamie and Oswald are only in their 40's but they already have a flock of grandchildren who giggle and snatch Oswald's hat and get pennies and nickels out of Jamie's purse for the gumball machine.

Sue, who lives less than a 1/4 mile from us, is pretty, with a fine nose, skinny arched eyebrows, beautiful teeth and a six year old daughter named Whisper. Sue and Jamie arrive at our table at the same time and laugh.

Sue says, "You go on Sweetie, I'll take this table. Oz has been waiting for you for nearly an hour."

Jamie turns to look at Oswald. There is sweetness in her eyes and she unties her apron. She is not a pretty woman. Waitressing for twenty years and raising four children can be hard on a woman. But she has a solid love that grounds her.

Other girls, even young ones, are always asking for Jamies advice and her opinion. And she never hesitates to give them the honest, rock bottom truth with a smile and hug.

The one person Jamie seems unable to help is Sue, who is constantly caught up in a messy world with loser men she naively allows to move into her life and trailer.

Every once in a while, when Oswald takes Jamie to the movies, Sue ends up at our house. She drinks wine coolers and pours her heart out at my kitchen table.

Mike and Felicity study their laminated menus, though they always order the same thing, the fried chicken dinner with mashed potatoes and a salad without any dressing.

Felicity puts her menu down. "Sue, you know what we have in our yard?"

Sue reaches down and fiddles with Felicity's hair, "What, Baby?"

I gently start kicking all the legs on the other side of the table and shake my head just a little. They don't need to tell Sue about my crop circles.

Felicity smiles at me, "We've got bull dozers and graders. They are so huge, it's like having monsters in the yard or something. It's cool. Have you seen them?"

Mike is still looking at his menu, but he isn't really thinking about food. He's thinking about me and what I said and who's going to meet us here. He's trying to figure out what's holding me back.

He and Felicity love Zolton and they are ready for us to get on with our lives.

"I sure have seen them Honey. They wake me up every morning. You ready to order yet?" Sue takes her pad and pen out of her black apron.

"Fried chicken." Felicity says handing over her menu.

"How did I know you were going to say that?" she laughs. "You too, Mike?"

He grins and nods. I think Mike has a crush on Sue. "But I need three pieces of chicken instead of two." He sits up straight so he looks taller. I reach across the table and take his Razorback ball cap off his head.

Sue puts her hand on my stomach and lowers her head in reverence, concentrating with her fingers. We all watch my stomach. Nothing happens.

Felicity looks under the table and says, "Hey, Baby, wake up. It's time to order."

Sue laughs. She always thinks Felicity is hilarious.

"Catfish, hushpuppies and coleslaw." I say, suddenly very sure what I want to eat.

"Fried or broiled?"

"Fried, with tartar sauce, tabasco and extra lemon." I smile at her, proud of my decision making ability.

"I hope we aren't out of catfish," she looks towards the kitchen and yells, "Albert, did you 86 the catfish?"

A deep voice in the kitchen says, "We got fish."

Sue looks at me. "You're lucky, I thought the table full of Baptist Catfish Bitches ate everything in the place."

Mike and Felicity are playing tic tac toe on a paper napkin.

I arch my back, it hurts down low and deep in the muscles. "Catfish Bitches?"

Sue nods toward the big table of older ladies. "They drive me crazy, come in here, all dressed up, eat like pigs, complain about everything, run my butt for more ice tea, talk ugly about everybody they know and discuss tomorrow's sermon, make me give them all separate checks, even though they order the same thing, and hardly tip me a damn nickel. Cheapest bunch of women and mean too. And see that one with sort of red hair at the end of the table? She's my aunt." Sue takes a deep breath. "Alright, I feel better now." She grins at me again and I feel better. I like the little gap between her front teeth. Her face is pretty but the gap makes her sexy.

She points her pen at each of us as she speaks. "Ok, we got fried chicken and fried chicken and catfish with tabasco, tartar and lemon. Girl, you can eat that fried stuff? When I was pregnant I had heartburn something terrible. Couldn't eat nothing fried or spicy. Thought I was gonna die from boredom every time I sat down to dinner."

The baby kicks and when I look up, I see her.

My mother is sitting at the table with the Catfish Bitches. Blood drains from my brain and a sweet humming begins. My fingers go numb. I'll be damned. There she is, waiting for me. She's sitting right next to Sue's aunt. My mom, she's smoking a cigarette, her face is still as tanned and wrinkled, as it was when she shot herself. She stares back at me, nods and smiles professionally, then looks at the unlit cigarette in her hand. Now she's not even looking at me, she speaks to someone else, waves her hand with the cigarette as she explains something. What the hell is going on? Why isn't she looking at me? She's got nothing to say to the Catfish Bitches.

I look at the children and get ready to stand up but when I look back at mom, I can see it's not her at all. It's a woman I've never seen before. She doesn't really look anything like my mother. I'm loosing it, right here in Ed's Chicken City.

Sue turns in our order then says good-bye to Jamie and Oswald again. She takes their empty tea glass away. Jamie and Oswald stand up to leave. Then the door opens and a man wearing blue jeans, a well ironed button down checked shirt and camouflage hunting cap walks in. It's Sue's new boyfriend. He shakes hands with Oswald, but there is a tight anger in his movements. Jamie nudges Oswald and they turn around and sit back down.

I think the new boyfriend is named Jay. He swaggers to the cash register and waits. Jingling the keys in his pocket, he looks as though he's in a hurry. When Sue comes out of the kitchen she smiles until she sees him. As they speak, his agitation mounts. He shifts his weight back and forth and rolls his fingers as though warming up his hand. He touches Sue's shoulder but she turns away and that makes him even angrier. I want to go over and help her.

Finally, Jamie approaches. Oswald watches from their booth and that makes me feel much better. He is a man who watches quietly but he's always watching..

Jay and Sue are getting louder and louder. He's mad because she's not ready to leave or won't give him some keys.

We all hear Sue say, "At least I know how to keep a job, that's more than you can say." Sue looks at Jamie, "He's been fired from three jobs in the last six months."

"Listen," Jay says stepping closer to Sue and points a heavy finger at her fine nose. "I don't have to take this shit. Now give me the God damn keys." Oswald stands up slowly and begins to walk.

Sue is crying, but she's not backing down. Jamie says, "Listen Jay, let us finish working. This ain't the place to make a fuss, then me and Oswald will go over with you and Sue to get your belongings."

He nearly yells at Jamie "I want in my God damn trailer right now and I don't need you baby-sitting me."

Sue is strong now, she steps up to the plate." It's not our trailer, it's my trailer, you lazy son of a bitch. It took me five years, but it's my damn trailer and I'll lock anybody I want out." She turns to Jamie, "He got so drunk last night, he ran over his own damn dog in the driveway. I don't need that in my life." She steps even closer to Jay. Daring him. "You're not settin' a foot in my door. Besides I already took all your crap to your brother's house."

Jay looks at the cash register as though he wants to push it off the counter. "You bitch, what did you go and do that for?"

Oswald is there, next to Jamie.

Jay looks at Oswald for a long moment then says, "Fuck this shit. I don't need it," and stalks out the door. We all listen as he starts his truck and peels out of the parking lot.

Oswald sits back down while Jamie and Sue talk for a moment then a bell rings in the kitchen. Our order is ready.

Felicity looks at me with raised eyebrows. "You think he killed the dog when he ran over it?" Her eyes are the color of the ocean on a cloudy day.

The restaurant is too quiet again. Sue puts our plates on the table with an embarrassed smile.

Felicity whispers to Mike, "I wish Jamie's husband had kicked his ass across the parking lot."

Mike looks at me with his mouth full of chicken. I shake my head. I'm not up to yelling at Felicity right now. I'll pretend I didn't hear it for the sake of our dinner and deal with her mouth later.

We eat, but it's obvious the kids are waiting for me to comment on Sue's situation.

Finally I say, "There are a lot of idiots in the world and there are some horrible mean people too, men and women. If you ever find yourself stuck with one of those people, just remember, you can always leave. Always. And I'll always come help. Don't every put up with crap like that. If somebody makes you feel bad, get away from them."

Mike leans in close to me. "That guy was a jerk Mom, why do you think Sue was even going out with him?"

"Yeah, he ran over his own dog." Felicity adds as she stabs a piece of lettuce with a little too much aggression.

"I don't know. Sometimes you meet people and they seem pretty nice for a while. People tend to be on their best behavior for the first month or so then you find out the truth. Some people have hidden sides."

"Not Zolton, he's only got one side, right?" Felicity says, chewing.

They need reassurance, they want me to say nice things about Z. "Well maybe he started burping a little more in front of me after a month, but he's still the same person he was a few years ago."

"And that's why you love him?" Felicity stares right into my eyes. She loves talking about relationships.

"There are a lot of reasons I love him."

"You're lucky, Mom. You could have fallen in love with some guy like Sue did." Felicity leans back. She's finished eating.

"No kidding. I am lucky." Sitting with my children, talking about Z, I do feel lucky, blessed to have so much love in my world. My life is a good place to be right now, except for Hurlie and Mom, Helen and my yard.

Mike has been silent. Working on his chicken and listening to our conversation. Finally, he says exactly what I've been waiting for him to say, "And that's why you should marry him, Mom."

I'm tired of Mike hounding me but I am glad he feels strongly enough to take me on, to challenge the decisions I make which effect everyone's world.

Looking at his dark and serious face, I am glad Granny wants to go to church tomorrow. If God is responsible for giving me these children, then I should worship and praise him for all of eternity. My love for them is nearly pure, that is how I know there is a heaven. My love is holy.

I look at the Catfish Bitches again. B. Wallace isn't with them. Why would she be. I'm her family, if she's gonna come back from the dead, she should sit with me. I'll always make room at the table, Mom.

When Mike and Felicity grow up and leave me, I will travel. I won't hold still and miss them. I'll keep moving and doing, so I can call them on the phone and tell them stories and they will smile when they hear my voice. I will travel far from them, then when I come to visit, when I ring their doorbell, they will hug me and let me come into my church again.

Mom couldn't have loved me this way or she wouldn't have killed herself. She told me she was going to do it. She said she had to leave me so she wouldn't destroy me with her illness. She said she knew I would stop living my life to take care of her and she couldn't let that happen. But none of her words make what she's done to my heart acceptable. She left me, just like everybody else.

I look at Mike and Felicity. I could easily kill myself if it meant they would be happy. But I know that's not what Mom was thinking.

Felicity offers me a chicken leg. I shake my head. "You guys have been eating chicken for two days now, aren't you sick of it?"

Mike wipes his mouth and shakes his head, "Never."

Pushing my plate to the side, I fold my paper place mat into a triangle foot ball. Felicity makes a goal post with her greasy fingers.

Balancing the triangle on one tip, I flick it through Felicity's fingers and onto the table behind us.

Mike says, "Nice shot for a pregnant woman."

I wish my mom was still sitting over there so I could ask her something. So I could hear her deep, smoke-filled voice once more.

The baby flutters in my body, filling my torso with beautiful movement.

When I was pregnant with Mike and Felicity, I didn't loose my sanity. I was normal and fat and tired. I'm crazy now, that seems pretty obvious, even to me. Everything, even conversations, whirl, lights zoom and ping. Why are my senses buzzing and humming? I smell everything, see every extraordinary and tiny detail in life.

When I touch a smooth sweating glass, I can feel the sand it used to be.

Mike keeps on eating. He gnaws on the chicken bones and happily swallows mouthfuls of mashed potatoes. I'm not hungry any more, just sleepy. I want to make decisions now just to get them over with.

I need to see Zoltan. If he rubs my exploding skin with his callused fingers, I'll be better.

I take two more bites because Z has convinced me I need more protein. Live cell. The catfish falls apart, flaky and white, when I prod it with my fork.

Sue messes with Mike's long hair as she apologizes for the scene. "I hope you won't let that affect my tip," she jokes and puts the ticket on the table.

Sue starts to turn away then touches my hand. "That was something about Hurlie, huh?"

"'Hurlie?"

She looks at the kids, then back to me. "You know, what happened to him today."

"What?," I take hold of her thin wrist, "tell me, I haven't heard anything."

She looks at Mike and Felicity again, then leans over and whispers into my ear, "I don't know how or exactly what happened, I just heard it was God awful. They couldn't hardly find all the piece of him. And there were other dead things there too, you know like animals lyin' around. And the dogs that were still alive were crazy mean like they were rabid. They had to put two of them down, right there."

The lights in Ed's begin to flicker and swirl and my tongue shrivels. Hurlie is dead. And then, over Sue's shoulder I see the woman, who really is my Mom stand up. B. Wallace is wearing the blue linen dress with red trim we bought two months before she died. The gold elephant pendant I gave her for Mother's Day ten years ago glistens. I can even see the elephant's tiny green emerald eye. After she killed herself, I could never find that pendant. At least I know where it is now. Her hair looks pretty good, sort of fluffy and soft.

Mom folds her napkin, places it neatly beside her plate then walks out of the restaurant. The heels of her shoes tap nicely on the black and white tile.

Sue shakes her head and sort of pats me on the back, "Hurlie was a strange one. I guess it'll be in the paper tomorrow."

Something horrible happened to Hurlie after I left him. My brain repeats this to me over and over again as we walk into the night. Mom's perfume lingers just a little. Felicity is looking around and I say, "Do you smell anything Honey?"

She nods as she climbs into the back seat. "Yeah, it's nice, like something is blooming."

My lovely Highway 5 twists and writhes through the night air, taking me further from Sue's voice and closer to my home..

In the back seat, Felicity repeats a word over and over again. I listen to her whispers. "Jupiter jupiter jupiter, ju-pit-er, ju-pit-er."

"'Felicity, why are you saying that?"

"Listen to it Mom, it sounds so weird if you say it enough times, jupiter, jupiter, jupiter. It stops sounding like it means anything, It's just a funny noise. It sounds really happy, like the name of a candy bar, don't you think? Jupiter sounds like a way better candy bar than Mars."

I say, "Maybe so, jupiter, jupiter, jupiter. I like it. It's got a frisky sound."

My back and head ache and I feel gritty, still, I'm smiling. What's wrong with me. My emotions and body are running in opposite directions. Something horrible has happened to a man I've known for years, and I'm giddy.

E'va told me a difficult pregnancy means the baby is a girl because girl baby's suck all the beauty from their mother.

"Can we eat watermelon when we get home?" Mike asks as Felicity looks at me in the rear view mirror.

"Absolutely," Slowing down, I turn on my blinker. It flashes evenly, green left, green left, green left. I'll say yes to anything tonight. I can't breath but I feel nearly euphoric. How horrible. I find out Hurlie is dead and I'm happy, mystified but definitely relieved. Hurlie was a tough son of a bitch, how could anyone have killed him? I always figured he'd live to be a very mean old man. Christ he had so many enemies, I shouldn't be so surprised. And the police are probably ecstatic.

A fat raccoon is in our driveway, holding a wiggling silver minnow in his paws. The raccoon's brown eyes shine in his black mask. He stares into the blazing headlights. What a handsome fellow. It could be God, wanting to feel his world, this lovely little planet, at night, to appreciate his own tiny fingers clutching dinner. Perhaps it's God, wanting to have eyes that can see through the drooping Arkansas underbrush.

I stop and wait.

The raccoon finally walks arrogantly into the bushes.

Zoltan is already home. We all see his truck at the top of the driveway.

Gravel pops under the car tires. My headlights blaze into the dark woods surrounding the house. They light up every black crevice and hidden knot hole, all the spindly pines with bushy green heads. In an instant, I can see the front door. It magically appears in front of us, fully illuminated by the headlights. Our home, in a carved out pocket, surrounded by the entire world.

A light is on in the living room, the globe, the African violet and the red and white Hungarian schnapps glasses Granny bought us in Budapest, are silhouetted in the window. Fred stands next to the front door. He turns his head slowly to look at the car. The headlights shine directly into his bony and befuddled face, but he does not blink.

Felicity throws the passenger door open before I put the car into park. "I'll get the watermelon."

Zolton opens the front door and Felicity lopes past. Fred still hasn't moved. He shakes his little black and white tail.

Using the steering wheel as a handle, I push myself out of the car.

Zolton smiles at me. I feel better. He's wearing his white chef's coat but it's unbuttoned so I can see his dark chest. "Hi there."

"Your family is home," I say as he walks toward me. Obviously he hasn't seen the yard and the grass.

"The house seemed empty. When you're not here, I can't think of anything to do but wait for you. Where'd you go?"

"Ed's." I don't bother telling him about the phone message.

"I brought you food, too."

He holds my hand and helps me across the driveway as though I'm a sacred old woman. "Liz, listen to me for a minute. Hurlie is dead."

"I heard. Tell me what happened."

He shakes his head and grimaces. "It was pretty brutal."

"Just tell me." I glace at the yard. The moon winks at me. "I already heard that whoever killed him made it really messy."

He leads me to the front porch and we sit down on the top step. The concrete is unbearably hard. Z. is still holding my hand. "He wasn't murdered Liz, not really anyway. All those dogs of his attacked him. And nearly every bone in his body was broken, his chest was caved in. The police think maybe the bear sat on him while the dogs went at him. But the police do think somebody intentionally set the animals loose because all the gates had combination padlocks and they were all opened. Hurlie walked out of his trailer and they were on him. And listen to this, half those dogs were dead by the time the police got there, like they'd been poisoned." Z stops and stares into my eyes, obviously trying to read my reaction before continuing. "When the first cop car pulled onto Hurlie's property he swears he saw an older lady sitting on a chair on the porch. She disappeared though."

"What do you mean disappeared." My throat is constricting again because I already know what he's going to say.

"The cop said all he did was look down to pick up his stick and when he looked back, she was gone. Just gone. There wasn't even a chair on the porch. She's the only suspect or at least she might be able to give them some information. The sheriff's department and the police searching the woods all around trailers. There wasn't another car so she must have run into the woods." Absently, he adds, "What I can't figure out is who called 911."

My voice is gone. And if I could speak, what would I say? My skin tingles as Z pulls me close to him. But I remain stiff. I don't know what to do, so I will simply sit here and wait.

A sweet breeze sifts through the black woods. It is filled with my mother's expensive green perfume, and I know she killed Hurlie.

He was everything she hated about the South and he threatened me. She had to keep me safe.

Felicity comes out of the house with half a watermelon. She sits on the front steps, next to our feet.

While Z and I are still holding hands, he and Mike begin pushing at each other like billy goats. Mike jumps, snatches Zolton's Detroit Lions baseball cap and runs to the other side of the car.

They are unaware that anything is wrong.

Zolton looks at me with concern and I surprise him by smiling, just a little.

With paper cut precision, Z flips open his pocket knife and carves the remaining melon into four perfect pieces. He watches me watching him, then, with the very tip of his knife, flicks each black seed from the juicy meat. When he is finished and nothing is left but sweet red flesh, he holds it up for me.

I take a ridiculously large bite. I sort of want to smash my face into the watermelon and rub it around. That would feel good. That would let me know I'm still here on earth.

Every perfect summer, when I was young, my mother was beautiful and our family was whole, is trapped in the heart of this watermelon.

I'm eight years old and B. Wallace holds the green garden hose while I drink, I'm in the country club pool, underwater, swimming like a frog toward the bright and sparkling surface and Mom's distorted figure. I'm ten years old and running, barefoot on hot dry dirt, I'm thirteen and water-skiing with Daniel, on the surface of the lake, while B. Wallace spots us from the back of the boat. She holds her floppy straw hat with one hand and waves at us with the other. The hot summer air dries my skin as water splashes on my ankles and knees.

Summer is right here with us, in the watermelon.

Pausing for a moment, I stare hard at my watermelon to see if anything really is trapped inside.

Mike sits down behind Z.

Between bites, I close my eyes and in the darkness beg God not to take this man and this moment and these children, away from me. 'Please Lord, let me keep them, all of them until we are old. Let me have my family this time. Don't make me watch them die, don't make me bury my heart again and that's all the heaven I'll ever need. Take me before you take them, God. Please don't do to me what you did to B. Wallace'"

Zolton's hand is sticky with juice. He rubs the inside of my wrist with one finger and I want to cry. I want to grab him and hang on, I want to beg him to stay. But he's not going anywhere. I can feel that he is settled here, next to me. Maybe God is answering this time.

Hurlie's blood has soaked into the dirt now and I am overwhelmed with joy because I still have my family. Death brushed past me, bumped up against my shoulder then moved on and took somebody else. I've waited so long for this to happen. It means everything. Maybe I can crawl out of my hiding place and breathe without the fear that death will find me in this ancient, black game of hide and seek.

Did God send Zoltan to replace all the others I've lost? I have my children and this man and the sweet night air, heavy with the smell of the watermelon and perfume.

This is true.

"Are we going with you to church tomorrow?" Mike asks.

"No, not this time. I don't have the strength to iron your clothes."

Zolton nudges me with his shoulder. "God doesn't mind wrinkles."

"I know, but your grandmother does and she has something in mind. I'll deal with it. This is just like her being up on the Mountain Tower." I lean back and look at Mike, "I'll take you to the church supper and Sunday school tomorrow night if you want."

Mike and Felicity spit watermelon seeds across the driveway.

"Mike wants to go tomorrow 'cause that's when Karen and her family go," Felicity explains.

Zolton laughs. "The boy wants the girl not Jesus."

Before Mike responds, the phone rings again.

Mike and Felicity both scream "I got it," and race inside.

As I stand up, Felicity hands me the phone, "For you."

It's Mimi Sunbear. I cover the phone. "Go away so I can talk. I'll be off in a minute." Mike checks his watch, he's going to be a smart ass and time me.

Mimi whispers excitedly, "It's nothing Honey, I just wanted you to know I'm thinking about leaving, I'm really thinking."

"You're thinking! Well come on and do it." I walk into the house.

"No, no, I'm just thinking, but I've never even thought before, so it's a start."

"You deserve better." I don't know where I can sit. The couch is too soft and standing is killing me. Finally, I lower myself to the floor and lie down flat in the middle of the living room. My back bone cracks.

"The truth is Liz, we deserve each other, but I'm thinking about things outside this place, things and days and a life outside Raymond. It's a start. You just can't rush me. I've got to do it myself, getting out of here will be a little like going into labor. Now you run along and let that sweet family take care of you. I love you, Honey."

She hangs up before I can say anything more.

Zolton walks towards me. His long legs cover acres. He straddles me and I stare straight up into his handsome face, miles and miles above me. "You want to get up?"

Smiling, I nod. He takes my hands and tugs me to my feet.

"That was a good phone call," I say to him.

"Good."

"Aren't you going to ask me what it was?"

He shakes his head, "I got enough to think about, but I'm glad it was good."

"You're not curious?"

"Not about that," he says with a sweet sad smile.

Felicity yells. "Mike, come look."

There are still a few fireflies in the woods. They flicker on and off like thrown matches.

"Come on and look at what I brought you." Z says and leads me into the kitchen where he produces two white Styrofoam containers. He could just as well be holding up a 16 point buck.

"Are you hungry?" he asks hopefully.

"I'm going to be starving in about fifteen minutes." This is not exactly true, but I'll fake it.

Proudly, as though showing off his fresh kill, he opens the first box. "Beef Wellington, tenderloin roasted with sherried mushroom duxelle and liver pate, all wrapped up in puff pastry and topped with a superior bordalaise sauce."

"Oh, baby, I love it when you talk food."

"This one fell off the seat at the stop light, so I don't know how it's going to look." He opens the next box, "Strawberry napoleon, puff pastry, strawberries, whipped cream and brandy, gently shaken in styrofoam."

"Ohhh, what is it?" Felicity asks, wedging herself between us.

"Our next dessert," I kiss the top of her head.

Zoltan and I move to the couch. He flicks through television channels and looks at me every few minutes. I think about the yard. It's the first time I've considered the crop circles since hearing of Hurlie's death. Z still doesn't know about them. Maybe I'm over reacting and he won't think it's a big deal.

Finally, I spit it out, "Zoltan, you need to take a look at the yard."

He mutes the television. "Why?"

"There's just something you need to see. Would you take Bear with you? She probably really needs to go out."

"Your telling me to go look at the yard?"

"Please."

He doesn't put Bear on her leash, just opens the door and lets her run. But I don't care about that right now. If there's a dog out that who can make it past Z, he deserves to get laid.

Zolton leaves the front door open and I watch them walk across the yard. Bear is running around, frantically barking at the grass. Zolton stops. He must see the circles now. He squats down on his haunches, rubs the grass, smells his own hand, then rocks back on his heels and looks around. Finally, he stands up. He walks all the way around the circles, Bear follows him, cowering and growling at the same time.

I feel so sad and guilty. I've done something horrible to the man I love, weighted him with more of my family's historic crap. Z. is present tense and I'm always dragging him back.

"Liz," he yells.

I don't want to go out there.

"Liz."

I push myself off the couch and walk to the front door. "I don't know what they are, Zoltan."

"Why didn't you tell me earlier?"

"Cause you were telling me about Hurlie and then I wanted to eat watermelon and they sort of scare me and I was hoping they would go away."

He's striding across the yard toward me. "Where'd they come from?"

"I don't know, I went down to Daisy's and when I came back an hour later they were here. I just don't want to believe what I already know. I think they mean something." I whisper.

Zolton towers over me, dark and ominous, then stomps off without speaking. He walks around the house, inspecting the perimeters, surveying his homestead.

I can hear him in the bushes. There is a huge metal clanking as he pulls the 18 ft. extension ladder away from the tree house. It thunks against the roof. Four shiny silver rungs outside the window.

First Zolton's hands appear, then he goes up. His feet pause on the rung right in front of the window. I need to buy him some new shoe laces, too.

He steps on up and it occurs to me he's just like E'va. When things get confusing he goes up, they both find a better view so they can survey the entire situation.

His foot steps on the roof rumble through the house like a storm.

Mike and Felicity come out of their rooms. Felicity is wearing her flowered long johns and Mike has on a pair of sweat pants.

"What was that?" Mike closes the front door.

"Zolton is up on the roof?"

Felicity opens the door and runs outside to see for herself. Mike looks at me. "Why?"

I shrug and the baby shifts. Taking three deep breaths, I close my eyes and try to imagine something warm and calm. A field full of flowers on a sunny day, a bowl of mushroom soup. My body tightens with the baby's whale like movement. He finally comes to rest directly on my bladder.

The sound of Zolton marching across the roof is frightening, he stands still, then walks again, over my head and onto the kitchen. He is my army above.

"Why is Zolton on the roof?" Mike asks again, his eyebrows

hunching together.

"Just looking around." I say. "Sometimes you gotta get a different perspective to understand what's out there."

All I can do is wait.

10:43 p.m. The house is quiet. The kids are already asleep. Zolton is still on the roof, but it's quiet because he hasn't moved in almost an hour. I want to go outside and call to him but he must need some space.

My toes are cold and my back hurts. Hurlie is dead, eaten by his own pets. I should apologize to my mother, I know now she's been busy bugging me, but she isn't responsible for the flaming mailboxes or dumpster. That was all Hurlie and it's finished.

Finally, I listen as Z starts moving again. He walks slowly to the back of the house, I watch his feet, then knees, then chest and face appear as he climbs down the ladder in front of the window.

Listening, I trace his location as he walks around the house, then appears in the doorway with the night behind him.

He looks better than he did an hour ago, calm, almost cheerful.

"So what do you think?" I ask.

He just shrugs and looks like a man who understands. "I kind of like them."

Chapter 17

Sunday

6:45 a.m. The alarm next to my head goes off. The first thoughts that enter my conscious mind are Hurlie and the crop circles. Maybe it was all a dream.

I'm supposed to pick Nadgymummy up at 7:45. Church is at 8 a.m. I'm so close to turning off the alarm and rolling over, I want to nestle into Zolton's warmth, like a hamster, burrowing down into my cedar chips.

Z is not moved by the alarm; he never is. I slap the clock until the noise stops, then slide out of bed like a hippopotamus with a secret. Once I am gone, the mattress regains it's proper shape and form.

I am too tired and too huge to actually pick up my feet, so I do the pregnant shuffle to the bathroom and then into the kitchen. After turning on the coffee pot, I stare at it, dripping, then drizzling. If I look at it really hard maybe it will make the coffee faster.

Felicity appears in her giant Spice Girls t-shirt.

"Hi honey."

She looks beautiful and sleepy as she glowers at the coffee pot. "Mike got up last night and watched Nick at Nite and VH1."

"Ok," I say checking on my coffee. There's almost a cup.

"He told me to get up with you."

"You're my chaperone? You guys are insane." I sit down like a bull frog at the dining room table, with my legs spread so my huge belly can hang comfortably.

Felicity pours my coffee into a mug from the Atlanta Olympics. She adds milk, then puts the cup in front of me. Just a little sloshes out. Then, without even looking at me, she turns off the coffee maker and dumps the rest of the coffee into the sink. After putting the pot into the sink, Felicity opens a bag of blue berry muffins and hands one to me with the tub of butter and a knife.

"You need to eat something or you'll get weak later on."

I drink the coffee. I butter the muffin and take a bite. I'm really hungry. "Thanks." I smile at her. "Want to go to church with me?"

She shakes her head. "You won't fix any more coffee will you?"

"I promise."

"Ok then, I'm going back to bed. I love you." She gives me a hug that lightens my heart.

7:42 a.m. E'va is standing at the kitchen door with her purse on her arm, keys in hand, waiting for me. I check my watch. I'm three minutes early.

"Servous," I say as she closes the kitchen door, double checks to make sure it's locked, and walks toward me.

She has the glowing expression of a woman who's about to win an argument. Maybe I'm just imagining this. How can wrinkles look smug? It's her eyes though, they are dark, flashing and confident

We do not speak much in the car, but that's alright. E'va studies my stomach, touches my sleeve to see what sort of fabric my dress is made of, and looks out the window. The silence is nice. I have plenty to think about.

It's ok to be quiet with old people. I learned how to be still with WaWa. She never shushed me, but there were times, as we sat on her side porch, that she would look at me and I knew it was time to stop talking.

Sometimes, I would still rattle on because I was young and the silence made me uncomfortable. Then one day, I caught Iolla and WaWa in a private moment, and I suddenly understood the value and beauty of stillness.

I was 16 or 17 years old, lying on a beach towel in the yard, trying to get a tan. Iolla carried a glass of ice tea to WaWa, who was sitting in her white wicker chaise lounge on the side porch.

WaWa was probably 93 or 94 years old. Her always-protected skin was nearly the same color as the wicker. Iolla was close to 90 and still very, very black. I always loved the brilliant contrast between her skin and starched white maid's uniform.

It was an atrociously hot day and WaWa's house was never air-conditioned. But there was always a breeze on the side porch. Iolla stood a moment enjoying the coolness after she gave WaWa her tea.

"Sit down, please." WaWa said, and waved Iolla toward the metal rocker.

Iolla lowered herself into the chair. Her hose, which were much lighter than her skin, sagged around her ankles and she had mashed the back of her shoes down with her heels.

With my chin on my arm, I watched as those two old women, who had been together for fifty years, sat on the side porch in absolute silence for nearly ten minutes. Birds twirped, the wind rustled the trees, the telephone rang on the other side of the house, but Iolla knew she would never make it in time, so she didn't even stand up. No words were spoken and they were content as cats.

They had always seemed so different but in that instant those two women, enjoying a cool moment in their old age, they were identical, old human beings.

Now, as I ride to church with E'va, so close to giving birth, I do not need to speak. My condition says it all. My thoughts are turning inward, as I unconsciously focus on the baby and upcoming labor. I must get ready.

E'va has been pregnant. She's been through a 30 hour labor, she's served as a midwife too. She understands that it is time for me to draw up all my energies.

I park a half block from St. Luke's and we walk together with our arms linked. This time, I think she believes she is supporting me.

St. Luke's Episcopal Church. This has always been my church.

It has always seemed like a mini- cathedral. A traditional stone church, it was built first in the late 1800s. But the building was destroyed by a monster tornado in the early 1920s. Every stained glass window was shattered, every pew splintered, the building was completely leveled. The only thing that survived was the alter and our enormous painting of Jesus, with his out-stretched arms. The linen on the alter, even the candle sticks remained in place, though the walls on all sides were gone.

This St. Luke's was rebuilt two years later, in 1924, around the alter and painting.

My mother and father were married here forty-five years ago. Every time I walk in, I feel my family, my old family.

I know, each pew and hymnal and window, every lofty dedication, worn stone step and creaky hinge. Every breath of polished wood and drop of baptismal water, brings my blood to life with memories.

I remember it all.

When I was little, Daniel would push me on the huge swing set in the playground, I would drag my patent leather Sunday shoes in the gravel. When Daniel pushed too hard and I flew out of the swing, I had to get four stitches on my forehead. I remember looking for Easter eggs while dragging a huge pink bunny by its ears. I remember kissing an acolyte, James Johanson, while we were in the vestry when I was 11 and he was 13. I was wearing a yellow spring dress and he tasted of communion wine. I remember my father's funeral. Trumpets sounded and we stood very straight. We did not cry until they played the Battle Hymn of the the Republic.

My life has unfurled here, like a white flag.

I surrender.

New priests come and go every ten or fifteen years. They are fine smart men with solid handshakes and warm voices. Some have a true light in their eyes. But it is the church building that knows me and remembers my family.

E'va and I are a few minutes late. Bells ring high in the tower and I feel good. I hold the heavy mahogany door and we enter the cool stone foyer. The air is holy and warm. Slowly, Nagymummy and I walk up the eighteen stone steps.

The church is half full. I am surprised there are so many here for the early service. We genuflect, then slide into an empty pew.

After saying a brief prayer, I'm barely able to push up from my knees to a sitting position. But once I do, my body relaxes. My spine is perfectly supported by the rolling dark wood of the bench seat. This wooden pew takes every pain away. The angles and pressure and support are exquisite. Knots of tension disintegrate and for the first time in months my back does not hurt.

Warm colored light pours through the stained glass windows and splays across my skin. Here, I am part of something.

Sitting up straight feels so good. My God, what have I been doing to my body? How have I allowed my spine to be so misshapen and wobbly. I flex and arch again, just a little and fresh blood rolls to my brain.

E'va is still on her knees, her rosary clutched between her lumpy fingers. An old woman's powder and perfume mix with the musty smell of hymnal pages. There will be a neighborhood in heaven that smells just like this, I'm sure.

St. Luke is the patron saint of forgiveness.

Looking around my church, I study the heads in front of me and the deep red carpet that rolls up the center isle to the alter. I know every figure in the glorious stained glass. The greatest hits of the New Testament. There's Mary holding baby Jesus, his fat baby hands are open. Jesus already has his halo. My favorite window, when I was a child, is on my left. It shows Jesus on a tiny burro with one hand open and slightly raised. He is surrounded by children waiving palm fronds. They are singing "Hosanna, Hosanna."

There's Jesus emerging from his burial cave. He has a straight nose, long wavy brown hair, a pointy beard and beautiful-sad eyes. His arms are extended to a woman, who's name I can not remember. And there's the window with Jesus as a young boy, teaching in the temple.

In all the windows his hands are open, his palms exposed and vulnerable.

With my new spine, beautifully erect, my hand resting, like the pregnant Virgins, on my enormous stomach, I fill my lungs with old Episcopal air.

Well here I am, a pregnant unmarried woman in her mid-thirties, mother of two. I have a mother who's haunting me, creepy lawn circles, burned up mail boxes and my boss was recently eaten by his own dogs.

I'm fucked but I feel good.

I cross myself with the congregation. We all say the confession, out loud.

Most merciful god,
We confess that I have sinned against you
in thought, word and deed,
by what we have done, and by what we have left undone.
We have not loved you with our whole heart.
We have not loved our neighbors as ourselves.
We are truly sorry and humbly repent.
For the sake of your Son Jesus Christ,"

I stumble here. The text has been changed. My words are not the same as those everybody else in St. Luke's is saying. But my confessions, my admitting the things I have done to God and my

fellow man seem true enough. He knows.
"We pray you of your mercy.
Forgive what we have been.
Amend what we are,
And direct what I shall be." I love this part. If God will direct me maybe I can sort through this emotional and psychological quagmire.
"That we may delight in your will
and walk in you way.
Through Jesus Christ our Lord.
Amen."
Then, I think of more stuff I should confess.
Silently, I continue. I tell Him all that He already knows. I tell Him all that I have done wrong. I've cursed E'va. Three weeks ago I stole a box of Tic-tacs at the Piggly Wiggly because I had a funny taste in my mouth but didn't have enough money. I've lied to my children. I hide when the Jehovah Witness people come to my door. I've loved Zoltan, but not with my whole heart. If I gave him my whole heart there wouldn't be any fear. I should give him what he gives me. Everything. Still, I hold out on him. If various forms, styles and sexual positions are a sin, then I'm guilty of that too. But maybe I shouldn't make sexual confessions because I know I'll do them all over again. So, I take that part of the confession back. I've lied countless times, to everybody. I make up stories so I don't have to take E'va to the grocery store twice a week. I tell her I feel a little weak and then she worries about me and the baby. The sins roll out of my heart like a waterfall, splashing on the rocks of God's mercy.

I've felt sorry for myself, put my feelings and concerns before others and I've been furious with God for torturing my mother. Some days I've hated him with a bitterness so acidic I felt it bubbling in my stomach. Why, when she was still grieving and broken hearted from Daniel and Daddy's deaths, did she have to face, the IRS and Cancer all at the same time? How could He do that to her?

Finally, I tell him that I've been mad at B. Wallace, I've been filled with fury and pain because she killed herself and left me here, all alone. In my family, the grieving always put on a "show face." We seem strong, that's how we do things, but I've hated her for abandoning me. I haven't been able to stop thinking about her. I tell Him I can't let her go, I can't walk away from her war and so I've dragged her around with me, for years. Loving and cursing her all at the same time. How could a mother leave her child? I tell Him I don't know if I can stop but at least I know I'm doing it and it's wrong.

My head is getting light and fuzzy. The congregation is singing a hymn, but I have to sit down, so I don't pass out.

After a moment, I lower myself onto the kneeler. "I'm not finished yet."

"I know," God says.

"You've come for me, am I going with you now?" I ask him, hopefully. Finally there will be relief. It will be my reward for confessing.

"Not yet Liz, it's not time." I am both hurt and relieved.

"How could you cause us all so much pain? No one deserves the agony you dumped on Mom. For so long you were my enemy, you know. You cursed my family, that's how it's always felt."

"I know," He says again.

"Did you know you were hurting me?"

"You're family was an extraordinary one. I knew moving ahead would be painful, but I did not think I would lose you for so long, Liz. And the further you were from me, the greater the pain. I reached for you, but you would not let me help. "

"Just tell me why? Why would You do those things to my mother, to all of us."

"Betty understood," He says and his voice is warm, it wraps around me like chocolate. "Betty always understood, even in the end."

"But she killed herself to get away from the pain you were causing her. How can you say she understood. Suicide is not understanding."

"Suicide was her choice. But she always understood. It was all part of the construction," God says softly. He is in front of me. The billowing strength and softness of Him touches my cheek.

"Construction?" I pull back just a little. "Hacking up my brother in a boat propeller was construction?"

"There was a purpose. It brought you here." He says.

Now I have to think. He was building, but at our expense. The whole is more important than the individual.

"You are the individual," He interrupts my thought. "Your life is the construction. Betty chose her part."

I look up at E'va, who is standing over me. Behind her there is a flicker of ivory and satin. It's my mother, in her wedding dress. She is beautiful with her smile and tiny waist, holding Doc Blue's arm. Her fingers as light as a butterfly on the dark sleeve of his morning coat. They walk past us and are gone.

The priest is in the pulpit, offering God prayers for the sick, the hungry, the oppressed and those in prison. The congregation prays for justice and peace.

Still on my knees, I twist to look to the back of the church again. My brother, Daniel is sitting with Mom in the last pew. He is adorable with a bow tie and short pants. Mom is wearing those 1950's cat woman glasses. Daniel hops off the pew and runs into the isle, grinning. He's only four or five. His face was so round Mom called him Mr. Moon. B. Wallace is quick, even in heels, and pulls her squirming son into her arms.

Mom is happy and it's nice to see how beautiful she was. Sometimes, because she was so racked in the last ten years of her life, I forget she was a gorgeous woman.

God hears me again and says, "She was always beautiful."

"You know what I mean, at the end she was so eaten up."

"You're looking at Betty's life under a microscope, allowing the last years that you knew her to dominate your understanding and vision. That diminishes her life. She was more than those years. She would tell you not to forget the first two acts of the play. There was depth and texture. Children tend to see only half the picture when thinking about their parents."

"Yes sir. But I know a lot about Mom's life."

"You didn't know she dated Merv Griffith when she was in New York, did you?" I am stunned. He continues. "She was only 23, your father was in Germany, it lasted six months. Betty helped him develop several seed ideas for television. She had four dates with Frank Sinatra too. But she was too much for him, too strong at that moment. Betty changed the lives of those around her and of thousands of children. She saved lives because she fought for that swimming pool. Children who would have drowned, learned to swim. You didn't know she placed 2nd in the Pillsbury Bake off in 1964 with a chocolate and cherry cake. And she was named Arkansas' Woman of the Year by Winthrop Rockafeller in the '70s, you were still so little then. And Liz, she always loved your father, even when they were apart, they knew they were waiting for each other. That sort of love is a precious gift. Her death was inconsequential compared to her life, Liz."

"And now Liz, you're doing exactly what she didn't want you to do. She left you and came to me because she knew you would dedicate yourself to her death. You'd stay with her, right with her until she left. Your caring for her would be a wonderful act of love, but she and I both knew you had more important things to do. And now, look at you, worrying about her still, spending too much time trying to gauge her opinion and needs, and Liz," His hand is on my cheek, tears stream down my face and I rest my forehead on the pew in front of me. "Liz, my child, that I love so so dearly, she is dead to you, but she is here with me."

"She's dead," I say out loud.

"That's right. This is your time, on a beautiful planet. Don't be afraid. Do you remember what Saint Mary said to you?"

Saint Mary? I look at her in the stained glass holding the baby Jesus.

God says, "Saint Mary on Park Avenue. Think back, Liz. What did she say? She said 'Brave,' be brave Liz. Do what needs to be done. Your mother doesn't care what you do with her ashes or name. We just want you to live the life I've given you. Take care of Felicity and Mike and Kristof and Zoltan and yourself. You have things to do, important things that will change the world. Do you understand?"

I nod and sniffle, "Yes sir." The fever of fear and insecurity are cooled by his voice.

"She's been trying to protect you of late, and she wanted to tell you she loved you regardless of your decisions. But that's all over, now. And, those circles in your lawn, they were supposed to make you think of wedding rings, that's all, just wedding rings. You read so much into things. We thought you'd like them. I'm sorry they confused you. The egg shells came from one of the neighbors dogs. It's all gone now."

"No, don't take them, please," I say sniffling again and smiling. "Can you leave them, just for today?" My thoughts now are smooth and true.

"Alright," he says patiently. Then He pauses. His beautiful voice deepens. "I love you so much. I will always adore you, Liz, you must know that." I wait for more but His voice is gone.

They, my mother and God, have moved on and I am still here, in this most wonderful of places.

I follow E'va up to the alter. Walking on the deep red carpet I shuffle my feet. It feels as though I'm sliding on a layer of pudding. All my pregnancy pain and weight and cumbersome gracelessness is gone. I could be floating.

Sun light filters through the blue stained glass in front of me and spills onto the red carpet. I'm standing in a purple puddle.

Jesus looks down at us from the painting behind the alter, almost smiling. He understands. God and Mom told him the story, I can tell by the look in his eyes.

Stone angels look at me, smiling with tears in their smooth eyes.

It's my turn now. Slowly, I lower myself to the plump red kneeler and lean on the alter rail. I love being so close to the alter, studying the details, the embroidery, the intricately carved wood work The musky incense in the air and it is intoxicating. It embeds itself in my brain and I am made sweet and rich.

My outstretched hands form a bowl, just like Jesus in the stained glass. I am vulnerable but strong. The priest places a thin white wafer on my skin. It is warm, like freshly baked bread, and as I raise it to my mouth. As the wafer dissolves on my tongue, I'm filled with a liquid warmth. The priest lowers the huge silver chalice to my lips and I taste the red wine, Christ's blood. I swallow gladly.

Now is the time to begin.

I know and I am not afraid. The clutter is gone. Sticks, rocks, mud and straw have drifted on down stream. The dam has been broken.

I want my family. I want their breath and their thoughts and all their spots and crooked toes, their beautiful eyebrows and belly buttons, the creases in their shell shaped ears, their fibs and promises. Zoltan's voice and smell and touch fill me. I know them all in my heart. They are my neighborhood and home town.

I want to talk to Zoltan for the rest of my life and to feel his hand on my naked back in the middle of the night. I want to eat his food forever.

As we drive to E'va's house, she has a funny little smile. She is satisfied.

Once she is out of the car, I drive home too quickly.

The phone poles turn into fence posts on Highway 5. Houses scoot away from one another. Trees get fatter. Dogs inside yard fences turn into horses, goats and then cows.

I wish I could zap myself home. Driving is taking too long.

On Highway 5 the sun has risen, now it backlights every approaching vehicle. The shotguns and rifles hanging in the rear windows of oncoming pickup trucks are perfectly silhouetted. If it were summer time, I would see all the fishing poles hanging in the same racks.

Kristof, driving across Buck Snort Bridge, I remember God called the baby Kristof. We are having a boy. "Kristof, my boy, my son, my child." I smile and squint into the bright Sunday light. My head hurts I'm so happy.

'Kristof, Kristof, Kristof," I say, then put on my seat belt.

I have to get home before Zoltan leaves. I want to tell him. Let him know I'm going to bury my mother right in the middle of town and put up an enormous and garish monument. And the kids and I will put flowers on it every week and I'll tell them stories about their grandmother, a most remarkable woman.

I'm going so fast, the road construction is just a blur. There are flags stuck in orange cones on the shoulder. The monster road grader is still there, looking like a dinosaur.

I don't slow down enough when I turn into our driveway. The car almost slides off into the ditch. What a great feeling. Fred looks concerned.

I'm going too fast, he knows that. Dry red dust puffs up behind my car. At the last minute, Fred decides I'm going to run over him, so he bolts into the bushes.

Z.'s truck is still parked in front of the house. I lay on the horn and shove the gear shift into park. He comes out wearing blue jeans and his chef's coat. Grinning, with the cigar clutched between his teeth, he looks kind of sexy, like a young Fidel Castro.

"You're here!" I say, struggling out of the car. Thank God he hasn't already left. 'Thank you God,' I say out loud.

"You're right," there is a happy sarcasm in his voice, then he looks at the cigar in his had, as though he's not sure where it came from. "I was smoking in the house. I'm sorry. Felicity griped at me, but I thought 'fuck it.' Why do I work 70 hours a week to pay the mortgage on a house if I can't smoke my big fat smelly cigar in the living room on Sunday morning. I've got an hour before I have to go to work."

"Listen to me," I suck in a big breath, then take his free hand. "I learned something in church today."

"Well, I learned something while smoking my stinky ass cigar, so we're even. I was walking around in the yard and you know what, I don't care if we get married. We are the people we are, right now, " He has one hand on the back of my neck. Warm and hard, his palm melt into my skin. He throws the cigar into the grass.

"Stop," I say, interrupting him.

"No, I'm not going to stop. I really don't care about getting married, I don't care what everybody else wants. I just need for you to be happy. If you and the kids are good, my life is perfect. I think the cigar cleared my head. I wanted to get married, because I used to be an alter boy, because it made Granny happy, anything is easier than arguing with her. But you're the one I should be thinking about. Why would I want to get married if it makes you miserable? I just want us."

"Z, listen to me," I take his hand in both of mine. But I cannot look away from his eyes. I cannot break the brilliant color and light and understanding that connects us. "Will you marry me, please?"

"No," he says, laughing.

"I mean it. I want to marry you. I should be your wife. I already am your wife and I want a ring and I want God to look down and know that we are married, that we are husband and wife. It's the only thing I want. Please marry me."

"You want to get married?" He grins, sounding incredulous. I can feel his hand tightening and loosening on the back of my neck, rubbing my muscles without being aware of it.

I nod.

"You're not just kidding me? This is what you want, you swear?'

I nod.

"No," he says, "you have to say it out loud. Swear to me that you really want to get married; you're not just trying to make me happy."

"I want to marry you, I swear to you, on my mother's grave," I say, smiling and touching my belly because the baby is beating his tiny wings.